'I ha

'I know you
back from her
attended my own
improve a day that sta
your own coffin.'

I know.' My hand tightened arou
myself buried, but I had been…well…murdered.
Sacrificed, in fact. As a virgin.

Cliché? Sure. Painful? Hell yes.

Reversible?

Nope.

Praise for RACHEL VINCENT's

SOUL SCREAMERS series

'Just think *Buffy the Vampire Slayer* meets *Twilight*.'
— *Lovereading*

'A fantastic fun-filled rush of a book'
—*Girls Without a Bookshelf*

'You've got to love it when a series gets better
with each book.' —*YA Book Reads*

'*Twilight* fans will love it.' —*Kirkus Reviews*

'Awesome with a side of awesome' —*Mostly Reading YA*

'I'm so excited about this series.' —*The Eclectic Book Lover*

'A book like this is one of the reasons that I add authors
to my auto-buy list.' —*TeensReadToo.com*

Also available from **Rachel Vincent**

Published by

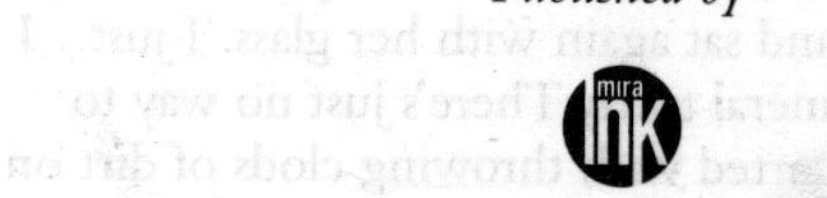

Soul Screamers

MY SOUL TO TAKE
MY SOUL TO SAVE
MY SOUL TO KEEP
MY SOUL TO STEAL
IF I DIE
BEFORE I WAKE

To find out more about Rachel and snag some online exclusive short stories, head to www.miraink.co.uk

RACHEL VINCENT

with all my Soul

Published in Great Britain 2013
MIRA Ink, an imprint of Harlequin (UK) Limited,
Eton House, 18-24 Paradise Road, Richmond, Surrey, TW9 1SR

ISBN 978 1 848 45182 7

47-0413

MIRA Ink's policy is to use papers that are natural, renewable and recyclable products and made from wood grown in sustainable forests. The logging and manufacturing processes conform to the legal environmental regulations of the country of origin.

Printed and bound by
CPI Group (UK) Ltd, Croydon, CR0 4YY

Ending any series is hard. Ending *this* series has been particularly hard for me, both creatively and emotionally. I've been working with Kaylee and her friends and family since January of 2008. We've been through seven novels and several novellas together. Kaylee and the gang have lived in three different houses with me, in three different states. I've spent more time in the Soul Screamers world than in either of my adult series to date.

Saying goodbye has been bittersweet. But Kaylee has grown up and I've grown up a little bit with her, I think.

This book is dedicated to Kaylee, who's suffered through so much for our entertainment. She's been a good sport—a fighter to the end—and it has been my pleasure to finally give her the happy ending she deserves. (Don't peek! I promise, you'll hate yourself for it later…)

And…

This book is dedicated to every reader who's ever written to ask me for a release date, a spoiler or a snippet of the text. My words may have brought Kaylee to life, but your interest kept her going.

Thank you all.

I used to hate the fact that my world is built on half-truths, held together with white lies. My life itself is an illusion requiring constant effort to maintain. I lie better than almost anyone I've ever met. But if I know the truth about anything, it's this: when people say the devil is in the details, they have no idea how right they are....

"It was a nice service, right?" My best friend, Emma, smoothed the front of her simple black dress, both brows furrowed in doubt. She shifted her weight to her right foot and her heel sank half an inch into the soft ground. "I mean, as far as funerals go, it could have been worse. People cried." She shrugged, staring out at the slowly departing crowd. "This would have been awkward if no one had cried."

It was awkward anyway. Funerals are always awkward, especially in my social circle, where the definition of "death" is under constant reevaluation.

"It was a lovely service, Em." I watched as people fled the open grave in slow-motion retreat, eager to be gone but reluctant to let it show. There were teachers, shell-shocked but in control, looking out of place without their desks and whiteboards. Parents, looking helpless and scared. Classmates in dark dresses, black slacks, and uncomfortable shoes, most in the same clothes they'd worn to the past few funerals.

We were all much too familiar with the routine by now. Whispered names and details. A day off for mourning. Excused absences for the viewing. Counselors on call for grieving students during every class period. And finally, the funeral, where we said goodbye to yet another classmate most of us had known for most of our lives.

I was one of those who'd cried, even though I was among the few who knew that the star of the show—the recently deceased herself—was actually still with us. Right next to me, in fact. A guest at her own funeral.

Sabine leaned closer, Nash's hand clasped in her right one, because her left was still encased in a cast. A curtain of thick, dark hair fell over half her face, shielding her from most of the thinning crowd. "So, seeing yourself in a coffin wasn't awkward? 'Cause it was awkward for me, and I'm not the one being buried today."

"Oh, no, the viewing was totally horrible," Em admitted, her brown eyes wide. Those eyes were all that was left of her, other than her soul. Everything else was Lydia's. Thin, angular face. Petite bones and slim build, similar to my own. Limp brown hair. Freckles. Feet that didn't quite fit into Em's favorite pair of shoes, stolen from her own closet while her mother and sisters shopped for her casket. "But the funeral itself—that was nice, don't you think?"

It was, as it damn well should have been. Em had left funeral details—in her own handwriting—in an envelope on her vanity table the day we'd picked up her shoes and a few other essentials. Once Ms. Marshall was thinking clearly, she'd probably wonder why her seventeen-year-old daughter had given so much thought to how she wanted to be buried, but grief had eclipsed her skepticism at least long enough to arrange the funeral of her daughter's—albeit morbid—dreams.

"It was beautiful, Em," Tod whispered, and I glanced up to find him standing next to me, where there'd been only damp grass a second before. It took more self-control than I'd known I had to keep from throwing my arms around him and trying to melt into him, which had recently replaced hoping for world peace as my new favorite impossible task.

I couldn't throw myself at him because most people couldn't see him. Reapers are sneaky that way.

Beyond that, I couldn't indulge in an embrace from my boyfriend—that word felt so inadequate—because today wasn't about comforting me. It was about burying Emma. Being there for her.

And planning vengeance. Justice for Em and for everyone else Avari and his fellow hellions had possessed, tortured, or taken from us. Today was about plotting retribution for Emma's boyfriend. And for Lydia, and for Sabine's foster mother, and for Brant, Nash's baseball teammate.

And for Alec.

My hand twitched at the thought of him, as if I still held the dagger. I could almost smell the blood. I could still see him in my mind, one of my few real friends, his eyes filled with pain and confusion, staring up at me in fear. Until they'd stared at nothing.

I swallowed my anger at Avari and what he'd taken from us, determined to avoid ruining Emma's perfect funeral with the bellow of rage itching to burst free from me.

Today was a new start for Em, and a new start for us all. We could no longer afford to be victims in Avari's quest to walk the human world. Beginning today, we were soldiers. Warriors, battle-weary and not yet focused, but warriors nonetheless.

Warriors, at least for the moment, in black formal funeral attire. All except for Tod, who could wear whatever he wanted because no one other than the five of us could see him.

I started to take his hand, hoping no one would notice such a small motion, but then Emma made a soft, strangling sound and I looked up to see her staring ahead, frozen like a deer in mortal danger.

Her mother was heading straight for us.

"Kaylee, thank you so much for coming." Ms. Marshall sniffled and reached for my hand, and her tears triggered more of my own. "Thank you all." She glanced at everyone but Tod, whom she couldn't see, and when her gaze lingered for a second on her own daughter, hidden behind a stranger's face, Emma burst into fresh sobs.

"We wouldn't have missed it, Ms. Marshall," Nash said, while I wrapped one arm around Emma.

Sabine stared at us both. The funeral hadn't upset her at all, that I could see, and she obviously didn't understand why it had bothered us, beyond the lie we were telling the world, since Emma was still alive and mostly well.

"Thank you." Ms. Marshall sniffled again, and she didn't seem to notice that her own heels were sinking into the soft earth. "I know Emma would be happy if she could see you all here now."

Em sobbed harder.

"I'm sorry, I don't believe we've met." Ms. Marshall dabbed her eyes with a damp tissue and held one hand out to her own daughter.

Emma cleared her throat and shook her mother's hand. Her mouth opened, but nothing came out.

"This is my cousin. Emily," I said. "She's just lost her parents, so she'll be staying with me and my dad." That was the best story we could come up with. It was heavy on coincidence, but just as heavy on necessity—Em had to live somewhere, now that she'd lost everything she'd ever had. Except for us.

Ms. Marshall's expression crumbled beneath a new layer of sympathetic grief, and her voice shook. "I'm so sorry for your loss, Emily."

But if Em heard her, I couldn't tell.

"She loved you so much!" Emma threw her arms around her mother and buried her tear-streaked face in her mom's hair. "She wouldn't want you to forget about her, but she doesn't want you to worry either. Or to..." Em nearly choked on her own tears, and we all stood there looking as helpless as Ms. Marshall looked confused and...devastated. She was crying again, and so was I. "Or to...you know...stop living. She wants you to live," Em said into her mother's ear. "And to hug Traci and Cara a lot. And to make yourself happy. She's sorry she called your boyfriend an idiot. It shouldn't matter that he's kind of stupid, if he makes you happy, so Emma would want you to go for it."

She finally released her mother and stepped back, wiping tears with her bare hands. "So you should go for it."

Ms. Marshall's tissue was soaked and when she blinked, more tears fell. "I didn't realize you knew Emma. Do you go to Eastlake?"

"She will," I said, when I realized Em's flood of words had dried up, leaving her speechless and evidently mortified by her outburst. "But she knew Emma from...before. We were all three really close." I couldn't tell whether or not Ms. Marshall believed me—or whether she was even capable of thinking my hasty explanation through at the moment—but she nodded and wiped at her cheeks again.

"Kaylee, when you feel up to it, I hope you'll come over and take something from Emma's room. To remember her by. I'm sure she'd want you to have whatever you'd like."

"We will," Em said before I could speak.

Ms. Marshall frowned, then nodded again and started backing away from us in heels crusted with mud from the recent rain. "Thank you all for coming." Then her two remaining daughters each put an arm around her and led her to the long black car waiting with its engine running.

"I think I scared her," Emma whispered, clutching my hand.

"Yup." Sabine's nearly black eyes were dilated and her mouth hung open just a little. As a *mara*—a living Nightmare—Sabine fed on fear, but she'd been going hungry a lot lately, since grief and anger had finally overwhelmed the nearly constant state of fear we'd all been living in for the past few months.

"I'm pretty sure it's rude to feed from the dead girl's family at a funeral," Nash said, one arm around her waist, his fingers curled around her narrow hip. He used to hold me like that. I used to like it. But Nash and I were over. We'd been over before we even knew we were over, and I still wasn't sure he'd completely accepted that yet. But it made me feel better to see him touch her in public.

He'd been touching her in private since the very day we broke up.

Sabine lifted both brows at him. "You expect me to believe that if someone threw a pie in your face at a funeral you wouldn't lick your lips?"

"If someone threw a pie in my face at a funeral, I'd..." Nash frowned. "Well, that'd be really weird."

"Weirder than seeing yourself buried?" Tod's hand slid into my grip, his fingers curling around mine, now that there was no one near enough to see me holding hands with empty air. No one except Sophie, my real cousin, and her boyfriend, Luca, who watched us from the other side of the open grave. They knew all about Tod. In fact, my undead reaper boyfriend hardly even registered as "strange" to Sophie anymore, considering that her own boyfriend was a necromancer. And that Luca and Sabine were the only ones among us who'd never died.

Nash's death was classified information, available on a need-to-know basis, and so far, his mom and brother didn't think anyone needed to know. Including Nash.

Emma and I had both died twice, and for me, that second one actually stuck. Now I was a "resurrected American," better known, in colloquial terms, as life-challenged. Or undead. Or the living dead. But I'm not a zombie. I'm just a little less alive than your average high school junior.

"No," Nash said, in that short-tempered voice he seemed to save just for his brother. "Having a pie thrown in my face at a funeral would not be weirder than seeing myself buried."

"Then Em wins this round." He glanced around at the last of the mourners, including my father, who leaned on his crutch, chatting softly with Harmony, Tod and Nash's mom, and his own brother—my uncle Brendon. "Let's get out of here. I've had enough death for one day."

That really means something, coming from a reaper.

"You okay?" I tossed Emma a T-shirt from my dresser, and she pulled it over her head. We were nearly the same size, now that she was Lydia. Which meant that the clothes we'd snuck out of her mom's house no longer fit her.

"Yeah." She kicked one of Styx's rubber dog bones out of

the way and stepped into a pair of my jeans. "I don't know what happened at the cemetery. I mean, it's not like I'm really dead, but as soon as my mom started talking to you, I just lost it."

That was true. She'd been staring at her mother and sisters for two straight days, at the viewing the day before, the funeral today, then the actual burial, and she hadn't lost it once. Not until her mother was within arm's reach.

"Don't worry about it. You've been through hell this year, Em. I'd be worried about you if you weren't upset." Though actually, I *was* worried about her. Very worried.

Emma sat on the edge of her bed to pull on a pair of sneakers, and if I'd reached out from the end of *my* bed, I could have touched her. We'd given up nearly all the floor space in my room for the extra twin bed, and I'd had to get rid of my beanbag chair, which was a real shame, considering we didn't actually need a second bed. Emma could have had mine—I hadn't slept in it once in the nearly two weeks since my birthday/her death-day, in part because I no longer needed sleep, though I'd discovered that I *did* need rest.

But telling my father that I was spending most of my nights at Tod's place, whether or not my reaper boyfriend was actually at home, would have been...

Well, that wouldn't have been a pleasant conversation. Even if my dad had his suspicions about how physical our relationship had become, I was in no hurry to confirm them. I may have been practically grown—and technically dead—but I would always be his little girl. He'd made that more than clear.

And I loved him for it.

More comfortable in our regular clothes, Em and I met everyone else in the front of the house, where Sabine had helped herself to a soda without getting one for anyone else. "All I'm saying is that Emily and Emma are practically the same name. No offense, Em," she added when we walked past my father's chair, where the *mara* was perched on the arm, hopelessly wrinkling the black slacks she only wore to funerals. And, truthfully, she only wore those because Nash had insisted black jeans weren't good enough.

"None taken." Em headed into the kitchen and took a seat at the bar, where she rested her forehead on her folded arms.

"At least she wasn't named after a can of soup," Tod said, and Sabine shot him a scowl. Her last name—Campbell—had come from a hungry worker at the church where she'd been abandoned as a toddler.

"Emma and Emily are pretty similar." Nash sank into my dad's armchair and wrapped one arm around the *mara*'s waist. "Wouldn't you rather pick something different? I mean, you could be anyone you want. It could be fun. None of the rest of us got to pick our names."

Em didn't even look up.

"We called her Cynthia for three days." Tod shoved a pillow over so I could sit with him on the couch. "She couldn't remember to answer. Calling her Emily is just easier."

"Who cares what you call her? Emma is still Emma, and that's all that matters, right? That she survived." Sophie shrugged in her spaghetti strap dress, leaning against the wall by the door like she wanted to stay but needed to be near an exit, just in case.

I could tell she was trying to say the right thing. To be useful and insightful. She'd been doing that a lot since she and Luca got together, which seemed to show her that she had more in common with me and my "freak" friends than she would ever again have in common with her fellow dancers and teen socialites. But when filtered through the lens of narcissism through which my cousin viewed the world "useful and insightful" usually came out sounding more like "pointless and trite."

Sophie had come a long way, but the journey was far from over.

"Yeah, I survived." Em sat up and glared at her over the half wall separating the kitchen from the living room. "Unless you count the part where my neck was snapped by a hellion who wanted to wear me like a perpetual Halloween costume. And the fact that my permanent address is now plot number 436 at the Grandview Cemetery. You think Zappos delivers to burial plots? If so, you must be right! Nothing's changed! So what if I'm now a brunette, and a B-cup, and an *Emily?* At least I *survived,* right?"

"I was just trying to help." Sophie blinked back tears that probably had more to do with her own frustration than with sympathy for Em. "I almost died, too, you know. We all did."

"*Almost* only counts in beauty pageants." Emma slid off her bar stool and pulled a can of soda from the fridge, then took down a tall glass and the bottle of whiskey my dad had confiscated from Nash a couple of weeks earlier. No one said anything when she poured generous helpings of both into the glass.

"We're going to get him," I said through clenched teeth, struggling to hide my anger on her behalf while she drained a quarter of the glass. "We're going to get them *all.*"

She didn't deserve this. It was *my* fault Emma had lost everything she'd ever had, except for a best friend who'd failed to protect her. It was my fault, and it was Avari's, and he was going to pay for what happened to Em and to everyone else he'd hurt.

"Sure we are." Emma rolled her eyes and took another drink. "We're going to sock it to the immortal hellions capable of squashing us like ants on the sidewalk. So what if they can't be killed, or caught, or even hurt, as far as we know. Maybe we can kill them with *kindness.* Or maybe they'll see us wearing our big-boy pants, all ready to take them down, and they'll die laughing. That's the only way we're going to get them. I know nothing about the Netherworld, but I know that."

"I have a plan, Em. A good one."

"I know you do. I'm sorry." She shoved limp brown hair back from her face and sat, still holding her glass. "I just… I attended my own funeral today. There's just no way to improve a day that started with throwing clods of dirt on your own coffin."

"I know." My hand tightened around Tod's. I hadn't seen myself buried, but I had been…well…murdered. Sacrificed, in fact. As a virgin.

Cliché? Sure. Painful? Hell, yes.

Reversible?

Nope.

"Well, at least you're compatible roommates," Sabine said as Luca headed into the kitchen. "Kaylee's dead, but pretending to live in her own body, and Emma's alive in someone else's body, but faking death. Your living situation was meant to be. Unlike mine." The *mara* threw an angry glance at my cousin.

Since her foster mother's death, Sabine had been staying with Sophie and my uncle Brendon, who'd officially applied to be her new foster parent, to keep her within the fold. Because in spite of obvious attitude…*issues,* she'd proved useful.

Also because if we tried to get rid of her, she'd only claw her way back into Nash's life, stepping on everyone in her way. She'd certainly done it before.

Sabine had a unique perspective on boundaries—she refused to recognize them.

Sophie stepped away from the wall she'd been holding up

and adjusted her black silk dress. "Hey, Luca, I told my dad we'd put in an appearance at the reception," she said, but we all saw through that—she looked more comfortable in her three-inch stiletto heels than in my house. "Are you ready?"

"Yeah. Just a sec." Luca looked up from the kitchen peninsula, where he was talking softly to Emma with his back to the rest of us. He said something, and she actually chuckled. When he tucked a strand of hair behind her ear—Lydia's ear—the look Sophie gave them should have boiled the blood in their veins.

Em and I were supposed to go to the reception, too, but when I'd told my dad how she'd reacted to her mother at the funeral, he'd agreed that we should probably forgo any more close contact with Ms. Marshall until they'd both had a little time to adjust to Emma's death.

"Luca?" my cousin repeated.

He stood and gave Emma one more smile before joining Sophie in the living room. "Hey, I was thinking maybe you could give Em a hand with her hair before school tomorrow." He tried to take his girlfriend's hand, but she pulled it firmly from his grasp. His smile faltered, but he barreled forward, and I was impressed by his resolution in the face of imminent temper tantrum. "She's never had to work with thin, fine hair before, so—"

"Are you saying my hair is limp?" Sophie demanded.

"No, your hair is beautiful." He tucked a long blond strand behind her ear and ended the gesture with his palm cupping her jaw. I could practically see Sophie melt. "I was just thinking that Em's a little insecure about her new look, and you're good with stuff like that, and she's your friend, so…?"

"Yeah. Of course." Sophie blinked. "No problem." She almost looked ashamed of herself, and I couldn't resist a smile.

She was nicer when she was with him. She wanted to be better, which made me want to like her.

Luca was the best thing that had ever happened to my cousin, and he'd come at the best possible time—in the middle of the worst year of her life. I think she truly cared about him. I couldn't help hoping that someday she'd actually deserve him.

After Luca and Sophie left to mourn my best friend in public, Emma brought her half-empty glass into the living room and sank onto the couch on my other side. "Okay, let's hear this brilliant plan. How are we going to bring the hurt to everyone's least favorite hellions?"

"We're not." I smiled. I was proud of my plan, even if it still had a few kinks to work out. "You were right—we can't hurt them. But they can hurt one another. A lot, hopefully. Maybe they can even kill each other." Because goodness knows *we* couldn't kill them. We'd never even come close to hurting a hellion, even though a couple of weeks before, I'd been forced to stab Avari over and over every time he took a new form in the human world—stolen from a murder victim—to torture us.

"Okay, that sounds promising." Nash leaned forward in my dad's chair, and Sabine put one hand on his back. "How do we get them to do that?"

"We're going to use their weaknesses against them." Tod's hand tightened around mine again. He already knew the plan. We'd gone over and over it during his breaks at work for nights on end—he was both a reaper at the local hospital and a delivery boy for a nearby pizza place, but the reaper gig came with more free time.

Way more people ordered pizzas than met their death on any given night.

"Weaknesses?" Sabine said. "Hellions have weaknesses?"

"Only one apiece, that we've seen." I scooted forward until I sat on the edge of the couch, excited and relieved to finally tell them what we'd come up with. "Think about it. When Sabine tried to sell me and Emma to—"

"Really? We're on that again?" the *mara* snapped. "You *know* I was under the influence of a hellion of envy. As were *you.* We both did some pretty stupid shit because of Invidia."

"Yeah, but Kaylee didn't try to sell anyone to a demon," Tod pointed out.

"Forgiven and forgotten, remember?" Nash aimed an irritated glance at his brother.

I remembered forgiving Sabine, but I'd never said I could forget…. "Just listen. When we were all with Avari and Invidia in the Netherworld, how did we get away?"

Sabine shrugged. "I crossed over with Nash." Because male *bean sidhes* don't wail, they can't cross to and from the Netherworld on their own. "Tod took Em, then came back for you."

Like his brother, Tod was a male *bean sidhe,* but he could cross freely by virtue of his reaper abilities, most of which didn't work in the Netherworld, much like my own undead skills. Unfortunately.

"Yes, but how did we get that chance?" I waved one hand in a circular motion, encouraging them to follow that thought through to the conclusion.

Nash's brows rose with the realization. "Avari attacked Invidia."

"Why?" Tod said, and his brother—my ex—frowned, trying to remember. He'd been in a lot of pain at the time, and I'm sure the memory was fuzzy.

"Because he wanted what she had," the *mara* said.

"Exactly." Sabine was smart—I had to give her that. "Avari is a hellion of greed. The only weakness I've *ever* seen him display is an obsession with having everything. He wants his toys *and* Invidia's. And Belphegore's. And any others on the playground."

Em set her nearly empty glass on the coffee table. "So we're going to play them against one another? How?"

Tod frowned, and his voice deepened. This was the part he didn't like. "By dangling the same bait in front of all three of them at once."

"What bait?" Em asked, but I could tell by her tone that she was already catching on.

"Us." I glanced around the room. "Some of us, anyway. Including Sophie and Luca, if we need them and they're willing." And we probably would need them. Avari had already gone after them both. "We're the bait."

“We’re the bait? And you’re okay with this?” Nash stared across the room at his brother, challenge swirling in the greens and browns of his eyes—a *bean sidhe*’s emotions could be read in the colors twisting in their irises, at least by fellow *bean sidhes*.

“Hell no, I’m not okay with it. It’s dangerous, and risky, and perilous, and also profoundly unsafe. But I have yet to come up with a better idea, so…” Tod gestured to me, reluctantly yielding the floor, but Em snatched it before I could speak.

“We’re the bait? So we’re going to be dangled? *How* are we going to be dangled?”

“Okay, first of all, no one has to do this.” I stood and Tod scooted over so I could sit on the arm of the couch, from where I could see everyone in the room. “You’re all completely free to just…not participate. But obviously, I can’t promise that staying out of this will keep you safe. We weren’t dangling anything in front of anyone the last time Avari and his hellion posse set their sights on us. Not on purpose, anyway. Which is why I’m pretty sure it’ll be easy to get their attention. The hard part will be keeping them from seeing the setup. So, raise your hand if you want to be a part of this, then I'll—"

"I'm in." Nash didn't bother to raise his hand.

"Just like that?" Em frowned at him.

He nodded. "No one wants to see that bastard pay more than I do."

"I'm fully prepared to debate that statement with you, but there's really no point." I glanced around the room again. "I'm in, obviously, as is Tod." He nodded to confirm, and a single pale curl fell over his forehead. "What about you two?"

"You couldn't keep me out of this if you tried," Sabine said. "This place is dull when there's no evil afoot."

"When is that, exactly?" Tod gave her a sardonic grin, and Sabine returned it.

"Em?" I wasn't yet familiar enough with her new face to tell what she was thinking. "You totally don't have to do this."

"No." She drained the last of her whiskey and soda, made a sour face, then set the glass down a little too hard on the coffee table. "I'm in. Just tell me what to do."

"Yeah. What kind of dangling are we talking about?" Nash said. "Carrot in front of a donkey? Or raw meat over a pit of lions?"

"Probably not the carrot." Sabine shrugged. "Hellions strike me more as carnivores."

I'd rarely heard a truer statement. As far as I could tell, hellions lived only to consume humanity—whichever parts of us they could get. Our emotions. Our blood. Our flesh. And, rumor had it, any other bodily fluids on hand.

"Since they can't cross into the human world, with a few obvious exceptions—" like the recent invasion of hellions wearing the souls and forms of the dead "—we're only going to be dangling our emotions."

"Oh, good. Metaphysical carrots." Emma exhaled in relief and looked like she might want a refill.

"Here's where it gets tricky," Tod said, while I headed into the kitchen for a six-pack of sodas from the fridge. "They're not going to be fooled by anything less than the real thing. Authentic—and very strong—envy and vanity."

"Envy for Invidia and vanity for Belphegore?" Sabine said, and I nodded.

Nash accepted the soda I handed him, then passed it to Sabine. "What about Avari?"

I handed him another can. "We're not going to worry about him. He's harder to get rid of than to trap, and if one of us starts flaunting unusual levels of greed, he'll know something's up. But if he thinks Invidia and Belphegore are closing in on the carrot he's been chasing for months—"

"Or any of us other carrots," Tod added, accepting a can for himself.

"—he'll jump into the game on his own. Which is exactly what we want. So all we really have to do is dangle one carrot in front of each of the other two. And since this involves you all, I'm open to suggestions. Anyone want to dangle?"

Sabine raised her hand. "I nominate Sophie as bait for Invidia."

Tod laughed. He was always able to find humor in even the creepiest situations. I'd thought that was an undead thing, until I became a member of the undead. Then I realized it was a Tod-thing.

"Just because you don't like someone doesn't mean you can feed her to a hellion," Em said. "Haven't we been over this?"

"I don't want to get rid of her, I—" Sabine rolled her eyes and started over. "Okay, I do *kind of* want to get rid of her, but that's not what this is. Think about it. Out of all seven of us, who's currently harboring the most envy?"

The three of them turned to look at Nash, who fired back angry glares. "Screw you all. Just because I don't think my brother should have made out with my girlfriend doesn't mean I'm jealous of him!"

"Forgiven and forgotten..." I reminded him, but his glare only deepened.

"Not Nash," Sabine snapped. "He has everything he could possibly want. Everything. More than he can handle," she added, as if we could possibly have missed her point. "I'm talking about Sophie. Did you all see the look she gave Em when Luca was talking to her in the kitchen?"

I *had* seen that.

"That was nothing. He was trying to make me feel better about my hair. Seriously. He's totally into Sophie."

"I know. I can't figure it out, but I don't doubt it," Sabine said. "But Sophie does. And with a little nudging, I think I can turn your prissy little cousin's shiny new insecurity into a feast of jealousy any hellion of envy would covet." She glanced around for our reactions. "How's that for a carrot?"

"What kind of nudge are you talking about?" I wasn't Sophie's biggest fan either, but that didn't give me the right to put her in any danger she didn't volunteer for.

Sabine shrugged. "A little strategic feeding of her fears. Namely, self-doubt." As a *mara,* she could do that and much more. "And I've been dying to try out my vial of Invidia's hair. That shit is concentrated liquid envy."

"No."

"Oh, come on." The *mara* rolled her eyes at my hesitance. "I figure a drop in her morning diet shake should be enough to do the job. That can't be any worse for her than those pills she pops when she gets upset."

Aunt Val's sedatives.

I made a mental note to sneak into Sophie's room in the middle of the night and flush the whole stash.

"We could at least ask her if she wants to." Em shrugged. "She did look pretty jealous…."

"She can't know about it!" Sabine insisted. "If we tell her, she'll know she has no reason to be jealous, and there goes our carrot."

"We're not going to spike her protein shake and throw her to the wolves!" I insisted.

Tod chuckled. "I thought they were lions. Or donkeys. You're losing control of your metaphors, Kay."

I turned on him, but before I could yell at him to stop lightening the mood, Nash spoke up. "We could watch her. All of us. We could take shifts. That way, if anything goes wrong, we can stomp on the brakes immediately."

"No."

Tod took my hand again. "She's already in danger, Kaylee. You said it yourself. We all are. At least this way, someone will have her back, 24/7. If you think about it, she may actually be safer this way."

So I thought about it, and I had to admit they were right. I'd done everything I could think of to keep Emma safe and only wound up getting her killed. Twice. Maybe the best way to keep Sophie safe was to manipulate her environment.

I thought we should *at least* tell Luca what we were doing, though, so he could watch out for her, too. But he would never go for it. And he was spending almost every waking moment with her anyway, so he'd definitely notice if something went wrong, even if he didn't know she was in any particular danger….

"You all swear you'll help me look out for her?"

Heads nodded all over the living room, but Sabine only shrugged. "I'm in the perfect position for that, unfortunately."

"Fine. But we're not giving her a drop of Invidia's creepy liquid hair until we've tested it."

"Wait." Emma frowned and raised Lydia's thin, pale brown eyebrows. "Isn't that stuff, like, corrosive? It sizzles like acid."

"Yeah, in its concentrated form. It was a challenge to contain. Over time, it'll eat through nearly anything but plastic." Sabine's grin looked almost vindictive, and I started to question her motives. "But it's easily diluted in anything water based, like coffee or tea. Or nondairy diet protein shakes."

Tod set his empty soda can on the coffee table. "You've been experimenting with it?"

"Just a little—I don't want to waste it. But one drop dissolved in eight ounces of water is perfectly safe to touch. I stuck a finger in and felt nothing. Even took a little sip."

"And?" Nash prompted.

"And I dumped the rest of it out. I just wanted to make sure it was safe, not feel the effects myself."

I groaned, "Do we even want to know why you were testing it?"

Sabine shrugged. "Probably not. But I'm willing to take a full dose this time, if that'll convince you that it's safe. Physically, at least."

"No!" Em and I said in unison. She continued, "The last time you were all hopped up on jealousy you tried to sell us in the Netherworld."

"I'll try it," I said. "Otherwise, we're not doing this."

Sabine shrugged again and sank back against Nash's shoulder. "Fine. I'll go get it when we're done here."

"It's not somewhere Sophie could find it, right?" Tod said.

"It's in the toe of my left boot. The dancing queen won't go near shoes without a designer label. She thinks she's allergic to cheap fabric." She twisted to scowl at Nash. "Sophie and I are *not* compatible. I still don't see why your mom won't let me stay with you guys."

Emma actually grinned, for the first time in days. "Because Harmony thinks she's too young to be a grandmother. But she's, like, what? Eighty?"

"Eighty-two," Tod said. From puberty on, *bean sidhes* age much slower than humans. Our average life span is around four hundred years. Not that I'd know from personal experience. Half the *bean sidhes* I knew were already dead or living on borrowed time. But Nash didn't know his brother had traded death dates with him—Tod didn't want him to feel guilty about something that was beyond his control. "Anyway, it's not the grandmother thing that bothers her. It's the thought of you two as parents."

"That thought bothers me, too." Sabine's gaze settled on me and Tod. "Not a risk for you, though, right? You two have all the luck."

"Yeah." Sarcasm dripped from the word as Tod pushed pale curls back from his face, and I could feel my own cheeks flame. "Not having to worry about teen pregnancy *totally* makes up for the fact that we're dead." His eyes flashed in anger, probably on my behalf. "Every time I think you've reached the pinnacle of insensitivity, you exceed your own reach."

"No way. You don't get to be mad about the truth." Sabine turned to Nash, obviously puzzled by social etiquette she didn't understand. "Are they pissed because I mentioned sex or death?"

"New subject!" Nash stood and stomped into the kitchen with his soda.

"I second the motion," I mumbled as he drained his can and dropped it into the recycling bin. I would much rather talk about trekking toward certain death in the Netherworld than ever again discuss sex in front of my boyfriend, his brother/my ex, and his new girlfriend. Who was also his *old* girlfriend/first love, who'd once tried to sell me to a demon to get rid of me.

Some conversations will just never be comfortable.

"Okay. So." I shook my head, trying to mentally strike the previous two minutes from the official record. "Any ideas for how to lure Belphegore into our hellion cage match?"

"Vanity, right?" Nash reappeared in the living room with an open bag of potato chips. "I nominate my venerable brother. He likes to play hero, and one look at him should establish the vanity angle."

"Nash!" I really shouldn't have been surprised by the dig. But I was.

"What?" He raised one brow at me in challenge. "It's okay to call me jealous, but not to call him vain?"

"Awareness of one's obvious advantages doesn't imply vanity," Tod insisted calmly.

Nash turned on him. "Does it imply narcissism?"

Tod huffed. "This coming from the guy who owns more hair products than his girlfriend."

"I don't own *any* hair products," Sabine said. And that was true. Her beauty was natural. Dark, fierce, and kinda scary at times, but completely natural.

Nash glared at his brother. "When you were still alive you spent more time looking at yourself than at girls, and I doubt death changed that."

"Seriously? Are we doing this again?" The overhead light flickered in response to Sabine's irritation—another creepy aspect of hanging out with a *mara*. "*You're* pretty. *He's* pretty." She turned to scowl at Nash. "Your brother's arrogant, and you're confrontational. You're both fed, clothed, sheltered, and sexually satisfied."

"Sabine!" I hissed, while Em stared at the floor, evidently lost in her own thoughts. But the *mara* continued without even glancing at me.

"Now bury the hatchet in this stupid little family feud, or I'm going to bury one in you both!"

For a moment, we all stared at her. I should have been accustomed to her lack of a verbal filter and apparent determination to discuss my private life in front of the entire world, but every now and then she still shocked me.

"Well?" She glanced from one brother to the other, but before either of them decided to make the first move, Emma looked up, her jaw set in a determined line, though she wasn't looking at anyone in particular—in fact, she seemed to be looking inward.

"I'll do it. I'll be Belphegore's carrot."

For a second I could only stare at Emma as what she was saying sank in. Then I shook my head, horrified by the thought. When I'd said we would be the bait, I hadn't meant Emma. More than any of us, she deserved a little peace.

"No, Em, you don't have to do that. You've been through so much already. This is the last thing you need right now."

She twisted on the couch to face me, tucking one leg beneath her, and again I was thrown off by how odd it was to look into Lydia's face and see Emma's eyes. Hear Emma's voice. "Your plan is good, Kaylee," she said. "It's smart, and it's bold, and it could work. But it *won't* work if you're not willing to accept help. To let the rest of us take the risks you've been taking on your own."

"No, Kaylee's right. I'll do it." Tod shrugged. "I prefer to think of myself as a pretty accurate judge of my own gifts, but in the right slant of light, that could be seen as vanity, and—"

"I'm the natural choice," Em insisted.

"You're the least vain person I know—"

"Just listen," my best friend said, and I did, because that was the least I owed her. "I never thought about it until I died and woke up with a stranger's face, but who we are is very much influenced by what we look like. By our own self-images. Think about the crazy things people will do to change the way they look. Dangerous diets. Obsessive workouts. Unnecessary surgeries. And what they're really trying to change is who they are. Or at least how they see themselves. As if changing what they look like can actually do that. It can't. But for the first time, I understand that mind-set. It's like my name."

"Your name?" Nash looked just as confused as I felt.

"Yeah. We went through several baby books and at least a dozen baby-naming websites looking for a new name for me, but no matter what we tried—no matter what names I thought I liked—I couldn't remember to answer to them. Because they weren't *me.* I didn't associate those names with *who I am.* Just like I don't associate this body—this face—with who I am. Every time I look in the mirror, I'm surprised. There's this moment of disorientation when I have to remind myself that I'm seeing my own reflection. And I know I should be grateful. Sophie was right about that. I'm still alive, and that's the most important thing, and I should be grateful to Tod and Kaylee for directing my soul, and to Lydia for giving me her body. Not that she had any choice in the matter."

Em sniffled and a tear fell from each of her eyes to roll slowly down her cheeks. "But I can't help it. Every time I look in the mirror, I'm disappointed."

"Because you're not pretty anymore?" Sabine said, and I'd never wanted worse to smack her.

Okay, except for that time I *did* smack her.

"What?" the *mara* said, like she actually didn't understand her gaffe. "It's true. Lydia's not pretty, and Em's used to being pretty. That can't be easy. I may not go through a lot of trouble in the morning, but that doesn't mean I'd be happy to wake up tomorrow with nothing to fill out my bra, you know?" She gestured toward my nearly flat chest, and that time my palm *itched* to connect with her face.

"She's right." Em frowned and glanced at me apologetically. "Not about your boobs. They're fine."

"*Way* better than fine," Tod leaned over to whisper, and I buried my face in my hands, both embarrassed and relieved to realize that Nash was the only one in the room who'd refrained from commenting on the sad state of my personal assets.

"But Sabine knows what I'm saying," Em said, mercifully diverting attention from me and my subpar endowment. "I *liked* who I was. What I looked like. I liked having curves, and I liked my hair, and loved having clear skin without having to mess with it. I liked seeing my eyes *in my own face.* I'm never going to have that again, and I hate it. So yeah, I'm vain. As it turns out, I'm *really* vain. If Sabine's willing to help manipulate that with a little strategic fear amplification, I *know* I could reel Belphegore in."

She closed her eyes for a second, then met my gaze. "And, frankly, I plan to enjoy the hell out of it. The bitch *broke my neck,* Kaylee. It's *her* fault I died—not yours. And I'm not going to let any of you tell me I can't play a big part in bringing her down. I deserve this. She's going to get what she deserves, too."

"How was the reception?" I set a glass of sweet tea on the end table next to my father, then carefully lifted his leg from the coffee table and slid a pillow beneath it.

"Kaylee, you really don't have to wait on me. I'm fine." He scruffed the fur between Styx's small, pointed ears, and she snuggled closer. The cutest part about their recent bonding was that my dad thought Styx was hungry for attention. I suspected the truth had more to do with her determination to protect him at all costs.

Styx was half-Netherhound. She was fiercely loyal and could snap a human long bone in a single bite.

"You were stabbed in the leg by a psychotic hellion wearing Sabine's foster mother's face." In the kitchen again, I pulled his plate out of the microwave and grabbed a fork from the dish drainer. "What part of that is fine?"

"The part where I lived." My dad sighed, and for a moment his eyes swirled with survivor's guilt. "Some weren't so lucky."

"I heard that!" Em called from the bedroom, where she was obsessing over which of my hopelessly plain T-shirts to wear on her first day of school as Emily Cavanaugh.

"You're a survivor, Em!" I called back. More of a survivor than I was, anyway. At least her heart still beat on its own. Even if it wasn't her original heart.

I shooed Styx off the couch with one hand while I handed my dad's plate to him with the other.

"How's she doing?" My dad pulled back the plastic film covering his dinner as I set the remote control next to him.

"It's going to take a while to adjust, but she'll get there." I shrugged. "She still has all of us." Which was more than most new kids had on the first day. "So? The reception? How's Ms. Marshall? And Em's sisters?"

My father sighed. He no longer looked hungry. "They're hurting, Kay. It kills me that we can't tell them the truth."

We'd thought about it. A lot. After all, we could certainly prove our crazy story. But telling them that Emma was still alive in someone else's body would mean telling them about *bean sidhes,* and reapers, and death dates, and about the Netherworld, and that there were hellions over there just waiting to devour our souls and torture us for all of eternity.

Most humans didn't handle that kind of disclosure well.

"It probably doesn't help that they had to wait nearly two weeks to bury her."

The police had refused to release Emma's body until after a full autopsy. They hadn't bought our claim that she'd broken her neck in a freak fall from the swing set at the lake, where my birthday party had been crashed by hellions.

We didn't tell them about the hellions.

Of course, part of the reason our story was so hard for them to accept was that her boyfriend, Jayson, had died that same day. As had Sabine's foster mother. That was too many deaths related to one high school clique to pass as coincidence.

But in the end, they'd had to release all the bodies for burial when they could find no signs of foul play. Because there *was* no foul play, on our part, anyway.

The hellions were not available for questioning.

"I'm just glad it's over." My dad picked up his fork and poked at a clump of rehydrated mashed potatoes.

"Yeah." Except for the part about us getting rid of the three hellions occupying the Netherworld version of my high school. My dad wasn't ready to hear about that just yet. At least not until his leg had healed.

"Hey," Tod said, and I looked up to find him standing in the middle of the living room, holding a plain manila envelope.

"Is that…?" My dad gestured to the envelope, and Tod nodded.

"Em!" I called when he sat on the couch on my other side and handed me the package.

My bedroom door creaked open, and Emma trudged in from the hall as I dumped the contents of the envelope on the coffee table. She looked more nervous than curious when she saw what Tod had brought.

I picked up a small laminated card from the middle of the pile of papers and held it out to her. "Emily Cavanaugh, you are now officially licensed to drive." Even though Lydia's body was only fifteen years old. It hadn't seemed fair to make Em wait another year and take driver's ed all over again. She'd already lost so much—including her car.

"Where did you get them done?" Em sank into the armchair, staring at her new license.

I wondered what she was thinking. Was she hating her new face again? I couldn't help wishing she'd known Lydia before *becoming* her. Lydia was so kind and selfless. She was so beautiful on the inside that her outside hadn't mattered.

And it's not like she'd had any obvious flaws. She was just…normal.

Obviously normal was hard to get used to, after a lifetime of gorgeous.

"I got yours the same place I got mine." Tod had needed paperwork to get hired as a pizza delivery boy, just like Em needed it to start school. "But I'm sworn to secrecy on that front."

"Like it matters." Emma slid her new license into her back pocket, then leaned forward to study her new birth certificate. "This is bizarre. I'm not sure I've even seen my real one." She frowned and picked up another small paper card. "New social security number. I guess I should memorize this…."

"Thanks for getting these, Tod," my dad said, lifting a forkful of meat loaf toward his mouth.

"No problem."

When my dad turned on the TV and Em sank farther into the chair to study her new social security number, Tod gave his head a subtle nod toward the hall.

"Hey, Dad, we're gonna go…" I hesitated, trying to come up with a quick, reasonable excuse to be alone with Tod, but my father only rolled his eyes.

"Just leave the door open."

I gave him a grateful smile and picked up my glass of water on the way into the hall.

In the middle of my bedroom floor, between the beds, I turned and put one hand over Tod's chest to feel his heartbeat. It was there—faint but very real. The gesture, checking for his heartbeat, had become both habit and a silent communication between us. A reassurance.

A promise too big to be defined by mere words.

He opened his mouth, and I put one finger over my lips in the universal sign for "shhhh."

Tod rolled his eyes. He didn't need to be reminded to make sure the living couldn't hear him—one of the handier perks of our undead state. In fact, he often had to be reminded to *let* others see and hear him. In the two-plus years since his death, most normal human functions had fallen out of habit, and he'd once told me he wasn't sure his heart ever beat when I wasn't there to feel it.

I'd promptly melted into a puddle of Kaylee-goo.

My fingers curled around a handful of his shirt when he kissed me, and I stood on my toes to give him more of me. To taste more of him. "Mmm..." I murmured when his lips trailed from my mouth over my chin, then down my neck. "I missed that."

"It's only been a few hours," he whispered, though no one else could hear us. "Shouldn't eternity make us more patient?"

"It's having the opposite effect. Knowing we should have forever makes me want a little bit of forever *right now*..." I pulled him back up, and my lips met his again. His hands trailed slowly up my sides, and I let the feel of him chase away the anger and sadness I'd been fighting for most of the day. For most of the past two weeks, in fact. Tod felt good. Tod *always* felt good, even when the rest of my world was falling apart.

"Oh!" He pulled away from me and reached into his pocket, then held up a small plastic vial full of a murky greenish liquid. "I almost forgot. I picked this up to save Sabine a trip."

"Is that...?"

"Yeah. She said not to touch it until you dilute it. We're supposed to use this." He dug in his other pocket and came up with a small plastic medicinal dropper. "But for the record, I don't approve of you ingesting Netherworld substances. Especially untested Netherworld substances. So I really have no choice but to hang out until the effects have completely worn off. To make sure you're safe."

I laughed. "My dad and Em are here."

He lifted one pale brow. "And, naturally, you're going to tell your dad what you're up to…?"

I tugged him closer until I could whisper against his cheek. "I thought we agreed there were some things he doesn't need to know about…."

"We did." His hand slid beneath the hem of my shirt, and the dropper grazed my side. "Those are my very favorite things."

"You know, when it's silent in there, I get suspicious!" my dad called from the living room. Em laughed. Tod groaned.

He held me for another second and I breathed in his scent, then let him go and took my water glass from the desk, where I'd set it. I stared down into it, then at the vial. "This is not going to mix well." I pulled out my rolling chair—it wouldn't go far, with Em's bed in the way—and sank into it, then set the glass down again while Tod worked the plug from the vial.

"You sure you want to do this?"

"No. But I can't give it to Sophie if I'm not willing to try it myself."

He stuck the tip of the dropper into the vial and drew up a quarter of an inch of murky green gunk. "My mom calls that the baby food test."

"Baby food?"

"Yeah. When we were little, she wouldn't give us anything to eat until she'd tasted it herself. Which is why she started baking. Evidently baby food is vile."

I watched as he dropped into a squat, so that he was eye level with my glass. "So you really did grow up on cookies and cake. I *knew* it."

"That's why I'm so sweet now. I have no idea what went wrong with Nash." He carefully squeezed the bulb at the top of the dropper, and a single drop of concentrated liquid envy plopped into my glass. For a second, it hung suspended in the water. Then tiny threadlike feelers of dark, dark green stretched out from the drop in all directions, bleeding slowly into the rest of the glass while Tod squirted the rest of what he'd sucked up back into the vial.

In seconds, the drop was gone and my water was an uneven green, paler than the concentrated color. Like an old bruise.

"Yuck." I held the glass up to the light, and the green grew paler. "Maybe we should have mixed it with soda."

Tod opened his mouth, and I took the first sip before he could offer to drink it for me. To test it on himself. The last thing I needed was for him to develop an irrational envy. The only person he could possibly be jealous of was Nash, and it had taken me forever to get the two of them back on speaking terms. Backward momentum was *not* okay.

"Yuck!" I made a face and wished for a cookie to rid my mouth of the foul film. "Envy tastes bitter."

Tod laughed. "I could have told you that without even trying it. You gulp that, and I'll get you something sweet to chase it with."

"Thanks."

I made myself drink the whole glass while he was gone, then made a mental note to warn Sabine to put it in something dark and sweet. Definitely coffee or soda. Or artificially sweetened diet protein shakes.

As I was swallowing the last mouthful, Tod reappeared in my room with a clear plastic cup of pink lemonade from my favorite burger place, a block from school. "Thanks." I set the empty glass down and gulped a quarter of the lemonade through the straw without even taking the cup from him. "Much better."

He set the drink on my nightstand, then sank onto my bed and scooted back until he could lean against the wall. I sat in front of him, my back pressed against his chest, and his arms wrapped around me. "Feel anything yet?"

"Just this." I threaded my fingers between his in my lap. But I was already starting to regret volunteering for our little experiment. The more I thought about it, the easier it was to remember how I'd felt with Invidia spewing envy into the air at my school, poisoning us, amplifying whatever benign envy we felt on a daily basis until it poured from us in bitter, violent waves.

If she hadn't been there—if we hadn't been under the influence of more jealousy than any normal sixteen-year-old could handle—would Sabine and I have fought over Nash? Or would I have seen what was right in front of me sooner?

I didn't have the answer, and thinking about it—about being out of control of my own emotions—made me angry. So I snuggled closer to Tod, determined to distract myself from my fears. "Have you ever been jealous of anyone? Like, really jealous?"

"Is that a serious question?"

Something in his tone made me pull away just enough that I could turn and see his face.

"Nash?"

The blues in his irises twisted for a second before he got his emotions under control.

"Don't," I whispered. "Let me see. Please."

Tod frowned. Then he closed his eyes, and when they opened, the shades of blue they held were churning like a storm at sea, cobalt twisting through thin, fragile shades of glacial ice, then rolling over bold streaks of cerulean.

"That bad, huh?" I couldn't completely hide the satisfaction in my voice. It was nice to be wanted. It was even better to be needed, and I could feel how much Tod needed me every day. He needed me almost as much as I needed him.

"It wasn't just jealousy, Kaylee. I *coveted* you. It was all biblical and forbidden."

"Tell me."

He hesitated just for a second. "I *hated* seeing you with him, but I couldn't stay away because I knew that if I wasn't there, you two would do things you'd never do with me in the room, and then I'd be all alone imagining that—imagining my *brother* touching the girl I was meant to be with for the rest of my afterlife—and then… Well, then things would get worse. But it's not like I could say anything. Not as long as you wanted to be with him."

I smiled. I couldn't help it.

"It's not funny." He frowned, and even his frown was beautiful. "It was torture."

"I'm not laughing. I'm just feeling very, very lucky."

"Is it possible that this liquid envy has some kind of osmosis effect? Like maybe it's leaking out through your pores, and I'm breathing most of it in? Because I'm reliving the worst envy of my entire existence, and you seem just fine."

I shrugged. "I have nothing to be jealous of."

His pale brow rose again, and I realized I'd accidentally laid down a challenge. "I'm perfectly covetable, you know."

"Oh, I know. I'm grateful every single day for the fact that you're invisible to everyone else most of the time, so I'm the only one looking at you." And I looked at him a lot. He was the most beautiful thing I'd ever seen. "So I don't have to beat girls off of you."

"Would you?" He looked intrigued. "Would you fight for me?"

"Would you make me?"

"No. There will never be anyone else for me, Kay." He grinned that evil reaper grin, and I knew what was coming before the words even left his tongue. "But there were a few *before* you…."

"La la la!" I covered my ears and squeezed my eyes shut, pretending I couldn't hear him. But the seed had already taken root in my brain.

He pulled one hand away from my ear. "How are we supposed to evaluate the strength of this essence of envy if you refuse to explore your own jealousy?"

I opened my eyes and dropped my other hand. "Fine. Point taken." But I didn't have to like it. "How many?"

He frowned again. "How many what?"

"How many girls? Before me?"

His frown deepened. "That's not what I was getting at. It's not a competition…."

"I know. It can't be a competition, because I can't compete. Because I've never been with anyone but you. But you can't say that, can you?" He flinched and I felt sorry for him for a second. Just *one* second. "How many, Tod?"

"I think we're losing track of the point, here."

"Addison? Were you with her? Like, *with* her?"

I saw it in his eyes, and my chest ached like I'd been punched. Like someone had tried to rip my heart out through my rib cage. "She was your first." I squeezed my eyes shut and tried to swallow, but my throat didn't want to work right.

"Kaylee." His hands slid down my arms, and my eyes flew open again.

"What is it with you Hudson boys and your first loves? She was a rock star. A TV star. And she would have burst right out of any *one* of my bras. How the hell am I supposed to compete with that?"

"You're not. Addison's dead, Kaylee. Not just dead." Because *I* was dead, and *he* was dead. "She's *gone.*" Her soul had been disintegrated and scattered throughout both worlds two weeks before, and it could take centuries for it to slowly reform.

"I know, and I'm sorry about that, but honestly, I'm a little less sorry than I was a second ago."

His eyes widened, and he looked…surprised.

Crap. What the hell was I saying? Addison had never been anything but kind to me. She'd put herself between me and Avari so I could escape the Netherworld, and she'd suffered horribly for it. *Of course* I was sorry she was gone. But…

"Her memory. Sabine was right. You can never really compete with the memory of a tragically deceased lover."

"You don't need to compete." He lifted my chin so that I had to look into his eyes. "I love you, Kaylee. I love you like I have never loved anyone else. Like I will *never* love anyone else."

I knew that, but… "After her?" I didn't want to know, but suddenly I *had* to ask. "After Addy? How many? Were they pretty? Were they…good?"

His eyes flashed in panic. "Okay, you see that this is the envy talking, right, Kay?"

"I know." But I didn't care. "How many, Tod? When you touch me, how many other girls are you remembering?"

"None. Look at me."

I looked at him, but I could hardly see him through tears. When had that happened?

"When I touch you, I'm not thinking about *anyone* but you. When I look at you, I can't remember what any of the others looked like. When I hear your voice, I can't even remember their names."

"Really?" My tears fell, and he wiped them away with his bare hands.

"Really. Compared to you, they're all nameless. Like... Thing One and Thing Two. And Thing Three. And...okay, that's not helping." His gaze searched mine, and his forehead furrowed. "This sucks. How can I help?"

"I don't..." But I did know. "I think I need you to kiss me."

His features relaxed, and his grin came back slowly, like he expected me to change my mind. When I didn't, he pulled me into his lap, and I tucked my legs around him. "My pleasure."

He kissed me, and my hands slid behind his neck. I wanted to devour him. I really did. And the beauty of being dead and in love is that you don't have to come up for air.

I don't know how long we sat there kissing, tangled up in each other and nearly desperate for more, but I know we didn't stop until Emma came in to get ready for bed. And I only know when that happened because she pretended to gag in the doorway.

"I can't even see you, but I know what you're doing."

"No, you don't," Tod said to her, his lips still pressed against mine. "We're still dressed."

I laughed and concentrated on being visible on the human plane.

Em sank onto the edge of her bed, and I climbed off Tod's lap. "Better?" he said, and I nodded, my face flaming.

"Sorry. That was intense."

"That?" Em waved one hand at the two of us, grinning. "Or the test dose?"

"Both," Tod and I said in unison. He was only partly kidding when he continued, "Tell Sabine to give Sophie a *half* dose."

“So? Do we have any classes together? Let me see. . . .” I pulled Emma’s new schedule from her hands as the office door swung shut behind us. “Crap.” I scanned the schedule again, hoping I’d misread. “There are only a couple hundred juniors in this school. How can we only have one class together?”

French. With Mrs. Brown. The only class “Emily Cavanaugh” and I shared was Em’s least favorite.

She leaned in to whisper, staring out at a sea of faces she’d known most of her life, none of whom recognized her. “If we were going to make up my age anyway, why the hell didn’t we go with eighteen instead of seventeen? Or twenty-one. That would have been nice.”

“You have to finish high school, Em.”

“Why? What’s the point?”

I’m sure there were several dozen good answers to her question, but I couldn’t think of any of them in that moment; I didn’t want to be there, either. So I gave her a little taste of the motivation I was clinging to. “Justice. This is where Avari and the other hellions hang out, remember? Invidia could be exactly where we’re standing right now, on the other side of the world barrier. She could be sniffing us out as we speak. How are you going to draw her into a trap if you're not here?"

"Valid point. But frustratingly ironic. They hang out here to be close to us. To feed from our emotions. And now that I don't have to be here if I don't want to, I'm stuck here *anyway,* to stay close to them."

"Welcome to my afterlife. Where's your first class?"

Emma studied her new schedule as we ambled aimlessly down the hall, and I tried to ignore the stares focused on us—no, focused on *me.* I didn't figure out what the whispers were all about until some idiot underestimated his volume.

"I can't believe she came to school today. Her best friend's been in the ground less than twenty-four hours, and she doesn't even look upset."

Oh. They'd expected me to still be mourning Emma, which had never occurred to me because Emma was standing right next to me. It had been much easier to pretend to grieve during the week and a half before she'd come back to school, when we were still waiting for the police to release her body so we could bury her. Without her next to me, I'd had no trouble remembering that she was supposed to be dead.

"Two-oh-four." Em looked up from her schedule and frowned. "I'm headed upstairs. See you at lunch?"

"Yeah." At least that much hadn't changed.

First period math was weird without Emma. The stares continued all the way through class, and I actually had to do math during the last five minutes of class, when we were supposed to be starting our homework, since I had no one to whisper with.

But there were plenty of people whispering about me.

I was the center of attention when I'd secretly died, yet somehow I was still the center of attention now that Em had secretly lived. I couldn't win for losing.

"Hey, Kaylee." Chelsea Simms sat next to me—uninvited—at my empty lunch table in the quad, and I silently cursed myself for showing up early.

"Hey." I had no third period class, so I usually spent the hour there, knowing that if Tod had a break at work, that's where he'd look for me.

Chelsea pulled a notebook from her bag. "Do you mind if I ask you a few things about Emma? I'm working on a memorial article for the school paper."

Oh, yeah. Journalism was also third period. Just my luck. "Sure."

She frowned, studying my expression. "If this is a bad time, I can…?"

"No, go ahead. I don't mind talking about Em. Feels like I'm keeping her memory alive." *How's that for quotable?*

"Great. Em was a junior, right?" Chelsea said, and I nodded. "And she had two sisters?" Another nod, and I noticed that though her notebook was open, she wasn't taking notes. Whatever she really wanted to ask obviously required courage she hadn't yet worked up.

"And…was she a good student?"

I turned to face her directly, looking right into her eyes. "Chelsea, just ask whatever you really want to know. Otherwise, this sounds like it'll take all day."

She blinked, surprised, then nodded. "Okay." She sat straighter and actually picked up her pen, ready to write. "Do you really think it's a coincidence that Emma Marshall and her boyfriend died on the same day? Just one day after Brant Williams died in his car, here on campus?"

I swallowed, trying to hide my own surprise. Obviously our classmates were just as suspicious as the police had been, but I hadn't expected anyone to actually ask that question.

And I certainly hadn't expected anyone to expect *me* to have an answer.

"Do I think it's a coincidence?" I bought time to think by repeating the question. "I don't know what it is. I don't see how it could be more than that. They died at different times, in different places, in different ways." Sort of. Neither Brant nor Jayson had any obvious cause of death, so the coroner had labeled them both with the generic "heart failure." Which wasn't exactly common in teenagers.

"Were you there when Emma died?" Chelsea asked, her gaze glued to me. Watching closely for my reaction.

"Yeah. A bunch of us were. We took the day off for my birthday." The tears in my eyes were real—I was lying, but the truth was no less traumatic. "We were just goofing off on the swings. At the lake. But Em went too high." I sniffled. "She was showing off. Then she let go and just… She just fell out of the swing. She landed on her back, but she must have hit her head first, and…"

I stopped there, with another sob. A real one. Picturing Em's actual death helped. Seeing Belphegore's hand on her neck. Hearing the gruesome crack. Seeing Emma crumple to the ground.

In my memory, it all happened in some kind of horrible slow motion. That was the only way I'd gotten through the police interview, and I'd seen no sign that they doubted any of my story.

Their suspicion had come later, when they started calculating the death toll.

"It must have been horrible," Chelsea said, and I realized that my tears were like a shield between us. A line of defense she wouldn't cross. At least, not now. Not at sixteen. Though I had no doubt she'd someday dial up the pressure on some poor lying politician, unfazed by tears.

"It was."

"Okay. Thanks." She stood, stuffing her notebook and pen into the front pocket of her scuffed denim backpack. "Kaylee, I just want you to know that…we stopped the presses on the yearbooks. They'd already started printing them, but when we told them about Brant, and Jayson, and Emma, they agreed to reprint at no additional charge. So…the yearbooks will be late, but she'll have a memorial page. They all will."

"Thank you. That means a lot." I hadn't even known Chelsea was on the yearbook staff.

The lunch bell rang as she walked away, looking more frustrated and confused than she had before she sat down. I knew exactly how that felt.

Two minutes later, Sophie appeared in front of me and slapped a newspaper down on the picnic table. "Have you seen the headline? I would have missed it if my dad didn't still read the news in print."

Luca set his tray down and sat across from me, but Sophie was obviously too riled up to relax. She hadn't bought a lunch, either.

"Headline?" I glanced at the paper and had to read it upside down. "'Eastlake High Named Most Dangerous School of Its Size in the Country.'"

Sophie nodded, eyes wide, brows furrowed.

"Wow."

"Look at the picture," Luca said, his burger halfway to his mouth. So I looked.

Beneath the headline was a black-and-white shot of…us. Me, Nash, Sabine, and Emma, in Lydia's body. It was taken at her funeral. The caption read, "Teens Mourn Yet another Lost Classmate."

I mentally crossed my fingers and hoped that Lydia's parents wouldn't see that photo.

"Do you see that?" Sophie demanded, like I was refusing to look. "We're the most dangerous school in the country."

"Of our size," Luca added, looking up at her. "Don't you want something to eat?"

"How could I possibly digest anything with that staring back at me?" She waved one hand at the paper still lying on the table.

"What's wrong?" Nash asked as he and Sabine settled onto the bench next to Luca.

"What's *wrong?* We've just surpassed inner-city alternative schools all over the country as the most dangerous school in the U.S."

"Of our size," Luca added again. "I'm sure there are way more dangerous schools out there with several thousand students."

Nash laughed, and Sophie turned on him. "This isn't funny! All the other schools on this list are plagued by gang violence and organized crime." She lowered her voice and leaned over the table. "We're the only one overrun with demons."

"How do you know?" Sabine plucked a fry from Nash's tray.

"What?" My cousin finally sank onto the bench.

"How do you know those other schools aren't also infested by hellions? I mean, the paper doesn't say that's what's wrong with our school, does it?" she asked, and Sophie shook her head reluctantly. "Then it may not say what's really wrong with those schools, either. For all we know, their 'gang violence' could really be roving bands of gremlins, shaking down students for their lunch money and handheld technology."

"When something's funny, you should let yourself laugh," Nash added. "Otherwise, you'll just stay mad or scared, and those little frown lines in your forehead will become permanent."

Sophie's eyes widened, and Sabine laughed out loud.

"Hey, Sophie!" Someone called from across the quad, and we all looked up to see Jennifer Lamb crossing the grass toward us, holding a chemistry textbook. "Can you give this to your cousin? She left it in class."

"My cousin?" Sophie stood to take the book and glanced at me in confusion, but before I could tell her it wasn't my book, Jennifer elaborated.

"Emily, right? She's my new lab partner. Is she always so… grumpy?"

Sophie's hand clenched around the thick textbook. "She's *Kaylee's* cousin. On a completely different side of the family."

Jennifer frowned. "But her last name is Cavanaugh."

Sophie turned to glare at me. "Great. You made her *my* cousin, too."

I tried to hide a laugh while Jennifer backed away from us in confusion.

Emma finally showed up nearly halfway into the lunch period, about thirty seconds before I would have gone to look for her. "Today sucks!" She dropped her bag on the table, and Luca had to snatch his tray out of the way before his burger got smashed. "My new math teacher made me take some kind of placement test, which made me late for English, so now my English teacher hates me. My new lab partner is an idiot, and I spent half of lunch looking for my damn chemistry book. And I *hate* cafeteria hamburgers." She collapsed onto the bench in a huff and leaned forward to put her forehead on the table.

We stared at her in surprise. I think we all expected her to sit up with a smile and jokingly demand a do-over day. When that didn't happen, I put one hand on her shoulder. "Em."

"What?" She didn't even look up.

Nash took her text from Sophie. "Your idiot lab partner brought your chemistry book."

Em sat up and snatched the book from him. "She probably stole it. Sabotage. I had no idea we went to school with so many stuck-up little bitches."

A sick feeling swelled in the pit of my stomach. Something was wrong. Something beyond the obvious.

Sophie's brows rose. "As one of those stuck-up bitches, I have to say, I'm a little offended."

"Sometimes the truth hurts."

I gaped at Em. She was going through something really difficult—we all knew that—but she was still *Emma.* She was still loyal to her friends and relatively calm, unless she was defending one of them, and generally a pleasant person to be around.

"Em, is something wrong?"

She turned on me, anger flashing in her eyes. "Weren't you paying attention? *Everything* is wrong. I'm too short to see the whiteboard from the back of the class, and no one's even said 'hi' to me all day. And it's *your* fault, Kaylee. *You* stuck me in this stupid twig body, and no one notices twigs. When was the last time you saw a guy hit on a girl shaped like a chopstick?" She frowned, then rolled her eyes. "I guess I'm asking the wrong person, huh? Obviously the Hudsons like girls who look like *little boys.* That androgynous thing might work for you, but for me, it's a definite step *down.*"

I opened my mouth, but nothing came out. I couldn't think past my shock and the sting of her words. I'd never seen her so angry.

And I was *not* androgynous!

"Sabine?" Nash looked as confused as the rest of us. "Are you doing this?" He couldn't be more specific without risking clueing Sophie in on the fact that Sabine was intentionally manipulating fears. Again.

"It's not me." The *mara* looked like she wanted to say more. "I can only mess with fear, and she doesn't have any right now. *None.* This tastes like anger to me."

"*No* fear?" I said, and Sabine shook her head.

No fear of not fitting in? Of standing out for all the wrong reasons? Of having bombed the math placement test? Of being sucked back into the Netherworld by the hellion who'd already killed her once? I'd never met anyone who had *no* fear.

"You bet your ass it's anger." Emma shoved her chemistry text into her bag. "What the hell do I have to be afraid of? I *should* be pissed off to be stuck in a second-rate body, in this stupid-ass school, without my own clothes, and my stuff, and my car. Whose brilliant idea was this, anyway? Yours?" The depth of anger in her gaze stunned me. And scared me a little. "Sounds like something you'd do. Another pathetic attempt to help that only makes shit worse."

"Back off, Em." Sabine stood, both palms planted firmly on the table. "This is the only warning you get. Kaylee may be skinny, and naive, and clueless more often than not, and borderline adulterous, but you're *lucky* to have her as a friend. She saved your life."

"Part of it, anyway," Em mumbled. But she seemed a little calmer.

If I didn't know any better, I'd swear Sabine just came to my defense. Sort of. "I'm not adulterous," I said, for the record.

Sabine shrugged, still frowning at Em like she'd hardly heard me. "I said 'borderline.'"

Nash put a hand on Sabine's arm, and she sat. Reluctantly. Less than mollified by Em's response. "Something's wrong with her."

"Yeah." Emma huffed. "I just rattled off a whole *list* of what's wrong with me."

"Emotionally, she's been kinda all over the place for the past two days," I added, still reeling from her outburst.

"What the hell are you talking about?" Em demanded.

"You cried at the funeral."

"Lots of people cry at funerals," Luca pointed out, and when he said it aloud, it sounded perfectly reasonable. But it *wasn't* reasonable, even if I couldn't explain why.

"She was fine one minute, assessing the funeral she'd planned for herself. Then she was bawling and clinging to her mom."

"Well, yeah. Her mom was crying." Nash stuck a fry upright in a pool of ketchup, but it fell over. "Crying moms are contagious."

But it was more than that… "Then, that afternoon, she got all angry and determined to dish out vengeance to Invidia, and that kind of came out of nowhere, too…."

"That wasn't out of nowhere," Sabine said around a bite of her burger. She swallowed, then continued, "You were feeling the vengeance, too, Kay. We *all* were."

Yeah. And Em caught it from us—like it was contagious.

"Wait, when was that?" Sophie said, and I realized I'd said too much.

"Stop talking about me like I'm not here!" Em stood and people at the next table turned to stare until she noticed and sat again, glowering at them from a distance.

"Sorry," I whispered, leaning toward the center of the table. "This just doesn't make any sense. We've been friends since we were kids, and for more than ten years, I've been the one bouncing from one emotional extreme to the other—"

"That's true," Sophie interjected. "Kaylee's never been incredibly stable."

"Thanks." I scowled at her. "Now stop helping. My point is that Em's always been my rock. Steady. Even. *Nice.*" I turned to her so she'd know I wasn't trying to leave her out of a discussion about her. "You've never blamed me for *anything.* Even things I deserved the blame for. And these are the same cafeteria hamburgers we've been choking down for three years—why are you just now mad about that? And what on earth did Jennifer Lamb do to deserve being called an idiot?"

Em frowned, and her gaze fell. She was thinking. Really thinking. "She… Well, she bumped my elbow and made me spill water all over our lab table. But she did apologize. And clean it up." Her frown deepened. "I do hate those burgers, though. And you…" Her eyes widened. "Oh, Kay, I'm so sorry. I didn't mean any of that. None of this is your fault. You did save my life, and I am lucky to have you as a friend. I don't know what the hell I was thinking. I was just so *mad.*"

But that was only partially true. She'd meant everything she'd said. I could see that in her eyes. She *did* hate living in Lydia's body, and on some level she *did* blame me for that. But the part that made the churning in my stomach ease a little was the fact that Emma—the Em I'd known most of my life—would never admit that. She would go to her grave trying to spare my feelings.

Whatever was wrong with her, it was wearing off.

Luca cleared his throat and pushed his empty tray toward the center of the table. "You know, considering how common it really is, death is actually a strange process. Inhabiting someone else's body is even stranger. Maybe something about her death or her occupation of someone else's body has thrown her emotions out of balance."

Balance.

"Oh, no…" I stared at the table and that sick feeling in my stomach grew to encompass my chest, too.

"What?" Em looked worried now. Everyone else looked curious. "What's wrong?"

"It's about balance." Luca had no idea how right he was. "Lydia was a syphon. And now you're in her body."

"Yeah. What exactly is a syphon?" Sophie said. "I was never very clear on that."

"It's a psychic predator. Like a *mara*," Sabine said, but I shook my head.

"Kinda. But not really. The way Lydia explained it to me was that something inside her is very sensitive to imbalance of any kind. Pain. Stress. *Anger*." I glanced at Em to drive home my point. "And when a syphon feels an imbalance in someone near her, her body has an instinctive need to impose balance, by taking what someone else has too much of, or giving what they have too little of."

"That's how she helped you?" Nash said. "At Lakeside?"

"Yeah." Lydia and I had met as patients in the mental health ward. She'd saved my life. "I needed to wail for one of the patients—for his soul. But I didn't know I was a *bean sidhe,* and I didn't know how to control the need to scream, so trying to bottle it up hurt. A lot. Lydia could feel that, so she took some of my pain. Just enough so that I could manage what was left."

Em frowned. She looked scared now. "And what, this syphon ability comes with the body?"

I shrugged. "Maybe. When Avari possessed Alec and Sabine, their abilities came with their bodies."

Sabine scowled at the reminder that she'd been possessed. She hated knowing that she'd been out of control of her own body, even for a short while.

"Is that what I'm doing?" Em's voice rode the thin edge of panic. "I'm possessing Lydia? Like a hellion? Or like a *ghost?* Because I'm still *dead?*"

"Shhh!" Evidently oblivious to Em's latest trauma, Sophie glanced around to make sure no one else in the quad was listening.

"No!" I sounded surer than I really was. Thank goodness. "You're not a ghost." Fortunately, I didn't have to worry about anyone else hearing me.

"There *are* no ghosts," Luca added.

"Maybe I'm the first." Em's eyes were open so wide I was afraid they'd pop right out of her skull. "Maybe that's all a ghost is—a disembodied soul taking up residence where it doesn't belong. And I don't belong here. I wasn't meant to be a syphon. I don't *want* to be a syphon."

"You belong here." I turned her by both shoulders so that she faced me. So I could look right into her eyes. "You belong here with us, no matter what it takes to make that happen. Even inhabiting someone else's body. And anyway, her body may not be what carries the syphon abilities. It could be that bit of Lydia's soul that got stuck in there with you."

"That bit of her *what?*" Em slapped her own sternum with one hand. "There's part of Lydia's soul still in here?" she hissed. "When were you planning to tell me that?"

"Sorry." I shrugged and tried to look as guilty as I felt. Which was a lot. "I've been kind of preoccupied with the police investigation into your death, and the funeral plans, and figuring out where you were going to live, and how to get you back into school. The soul thing just kind of slipped my mind."

"It's not that bad, Em," Nash said, when nothing I'd said seemed to be helping. "Lydia was syphoning some of your pain when you died, and when Kaylee captured your soul, she got part of Lydia's, too."

"What happened to the rest of it?"

I took a deep breath. There was no good way to say the next part. "It kind of..."

"Got disintegrated," Sabine finished, when I held on to the thought for too long. "Poof. Dissipated throughout all four corners of both the human- and the Netherworld, for as long as it takes to coalesce again."

"Wait. Her soul will coalesce?"

Luca nodded. "From what my aunt's told me—" his aunt Madeline was my boss at the reclamation department "—it will slowly pull itself back together. Until then...it's like being in limbo. Floating. We don't think that it hurts. We don't think they're even aware, when that happens."

"So...Lydia will be back when her soul...congeals, or whatever?" Emma was breathing too fast now, and her face was turning red. "Is it reasonable to assume she's going to want her body back when that happens? Are we going to have to share?" Her hands gripped the picnic table so tightly her fingers looked like they might snap. "Or is she just going to throw me out? Am I going to be a *homeless ghost,* Kaylee?"

"Em, it could be centuries before that happens. That's not on the list of things we need to worry about immediately."

"It *could* be centuries? So it *might not be?*"

"Okay, we need to focus on the positives." Sophie laid both of her palms flat on the table. "That's what we do in dance, when we place second. We don't think about how second place is the first loser. We think about how many other teams we stomped into the dirt and how hard they're probably crying." She shrugged. "That always makes me feel better."

For a moment, there was only silence while we stared at her. Even Luca looked a little...disturbed. But Sabine only shrugged. "Makes sense to me. And the positive side of this, if you ask me, is that now that you know what you are, you can learn how to control your abilities. Trust me, a little control makes all the difference."

"I can control it?" Em looked almost hopeful.

I nodded. "Lydia could." To some degree, anyway. "So, here's what we know. What I think, anyway. At the funeral, you were fine when you were with us, because we knew you weren't dead, so we weren't as upset as the other mourners. But when your mom came over, you lost it because she was devastated by grief, and you took some of that from her. You calmed her down, at the expense of your own composure."

"Okay..." Nash looked fascinated. "So, yesterday when you got all badass and hell-bent on revenge, you were probably taking a little of that from Kaylee. She's been itching to make Avari pay since the day you died."

Since before that. Since the day Avari tricked me into killing Alec. *That's* when I'd started channeling my pain into anger—a much more useful emotion.

Luca frowned. "So then, whose anger was she syphoning today? Somebody must have been really pissed off, if the portion she took was strong enough to make her go off on you like that."

Oh, shit. I hadn't even thought about that. Em's rage had a source, and considering how many hellions were known to frequent the Netherworld version of our school, chances were good that that anger wasn't human in origin. Which meant that someone at Eastlake could be about to lose control.

Again.

"Where are you going?" Nash said when I stood, already pulling my phone from my pocket.

"To find whoever sent Em into anger overdrive before he explodes in someone's face." More violence was the last thing we needed at America's most dangerous high school. Of its size. "You had chemistry before lunch, right?" I said, trying to remember her new schedule, and Em nodded. "Whose class?"

"Mr. Flannery."

"Did anyone look angry in your chem class? Anyone lose his or her temper?"

Em shook her head. "Only me."

"That just means that whoever it was did a good job of hiding his anger." Which meant those around him would be completely unprepared when and if he snapped. "I gotta get a look at Mr. Flannery's roll book before lunch is over. I'll see you guys later."

Before anyone could object, I took off across the quad, headed for the corner of the building, texting Tod on the way. His shift at the hospital had just ended. With any luck, he'd have time to come help me deal with…whatever was about to go horribly wrong.

As soon as I was out of sight of the quad, I let myself fade from human sight, then blinked into Mr. Flannery's first-floor chemistry lab. The room was empty, thank goodness, and his roll book was open on his desk, which was another stroke of luck in itself. Most of the other teachers had long ago switched to an electronic attendance and grade program. Fortunately, Mr. Flannery was nearly sixty and set in his ways. I'd once heard him complain to a colleague about how long it took him to enter the grades into the computer all at once, at the end of each term.

Still invisible, in case anyone came in, I flipped through his roll book to the third period page and scanned the list. Emily Cavanaugh had been penciled in at the bottom. Most of the students were juniors, which meant I knew nearly all of them. All but four had been in the quad with us—underclassmen usually got stuck eating inside on nice days.

All four of the missing kids were members of the baseball team—Nash's former teammates—who'd started eating in the practice field's dugout in the two weeks since Brant Williams's death. They seemed to think that was the best place to remember him. And to avoid adult supervision.

They kind of had a point.

I closed the roll book and blinked onto the baseball practice field, but a quick glance showed me that only three team members were in the dugout. Marco Gutierrez was missing.

After several more minutes of looking—I blinked into every men's room in the building as well as both locker rooms—I finally found him under the bleachers in the gym, just as the bell rang. Lunch was over. In six minutes I'd be late to English.

I faded into the corporeal plane at his back—visible and

audible only to him—then took a deep breath. "Marco? Are you okay?"

He turned, obviously startled, and the moment his gaze found me, it hardened in anger. His eyes narrowed. His nose flared. His fists clenched at his sides. And I knew one thing immediately, though it made no sense.

Marco Gutierrez wasn't just angry. He was angry *at me.*

"Kaylee Cavanaugh. How kind of you to save me the trouble of searching for you."

Chills raced up my spine and tingled at the base of my skull. Marco didn't have such a formal, stilted speech pattern. And he had no reason to be mad at me, that I knew of. "Avari."

Marco was possessed.

"You do not seem surprised to see me…." Marco lifted one brow and clasped his hands at his back in a gesture no high school junior makes, unless he's standing at ease in ROTC.

"Surprised to hear from you? No. The escalating pattern of your intrusions into my life is pretty hard to miss. But I can't say I expected to see you…there." I waved one hand at the body he'd borrowed. The body of another relatively innocent, uninvolved classmate.

Still, seeing him by proxy was much better than seeing Avari in the flesh. And the fact that he hadn't come in a body of his own told me he currently lacked the *ability* to come in a body of his own. Which was a huge relief.

"What do you want? And how did you get *in* there?" Hellions could only possess people who've died—even if they were resuscitated minutes later—people who've been to the Netherworld, and people they have some kind of personal connection to…

That last thought led me to the answer to my own question. "He huffed frost," I concluded, and Avari frowned in confusion. "Demon's Breath. *Your* breath."

"Ah. Yes, Mr. Gutierrez was among those who sampled the product your new lover delivered for me."

"I'm seventeen. Calling Tod my lover makes us sound ancient. Like, forty."

"An accurate term, though, is it not? You seem decidedly less innocent than when we first met."

"That's number one on a huge list of things that are thoroughly none of your business." Unless it made me less interesting to him. Less worthy of being captured and tortured for eternity. If that was the case, I'd happily brand myself a whore, complete with the scarlet letter *A*. Half the school seemed to think I deserved it anyway. "And Tod had no idea what he was ferrying into the human world for you." He'd done it for the chance to help Addison. To keep her sane, even as Avari tortured her damned soul.

But the frost he'd brought into our world had hurt countless people, including Marco Gutierrez. How many more were there like him? How many more of Nash's friends and teammates had huffed Avari's breath, unknowingly nominating themselves for hellion possession?

"What do you want?" I repeated when I realized he was just staring at me. Studying me. Which was somehow even creepier than when he threatened me.

Avari made a *tssk-ing* sound with Marco's tongue—another gesture not native to human adolescence. "That question has been asked and answered so many times surely you are as bored by it as I am. The answer hasn't changed, but the terms have. I want your anguish, both mental and physical. I want to take you apart and see what biological pumps and vessels make you bleed and what psychological gears and levers make you tick. Then I want to put you back together and begin again. I want to hear you scream. I want to see you writhe. I want to taste your flesh, and your blood, and your fears. I want to savor your ill-fated dreams as they burst like berries between my teeth, then melt like sugar on my tongue. I want *you,* Kaylee Cavanaugh."

I swallowed my own fear, so he couldn't have it, and that left me with nothing but anger blazing like a furnace where my heart should have been. "It's always nice to be wanted, but I don't feel like being enslaved and tortured today. Sorry."

"I'm going to make this simple for you, little *bean sidhe.* If you don't cross into the Nether and surrender—today—I will come for those you love most." Because he couldn't just take me. Even if he'd had a way to make me cross over, and at the moment he did not, he couldn't have kept me in the Nether. Not while I was conscious and in my own body, anyway. Female *bean sidhes* can cross between worlds at will, which put us among those least likely to be held captive in the Netherworld.

To keep me in the Nether against my will, Avari would have to keep me unconscious—which would be no fun for him—or dispose of my body and take physical possession of my soul, which was no doubt his intent. The hard part—for him—was getting to my soul. Since my unfortunate demise, he'd decided it would be easier to coerce me into willingly surrendering than to forcibly part my body from my soul.

I rolled my eyes, displaying my disbelief in spite of the fear tightening my chest. "That threat has been posed and ignored so many times surely we're both bored by it." Throwing his words back at him felt good. Seeing the anger rage behind his eyes felt even better.

He moved faster than I'd thought possible for a human body. One second he was three feet away, at proper threatening distance. The next, he had one hand around my throat. He slammed me into a support beam beneath the bleachers, and the blow reverberated down my spine in echoing waves of pain. My mouth fell open and I tried to drag in a shocked breath, but no air came. It couldn't get past his fist squeezing my airway shut.

"You *will* give me what I want," Avari said into my ear with Marco's voice. "Or I will destroy what you treasure most."

My heart pounded almost painfully while my back throbbed, and it took me a second to realize that my fear was *remembered* fear, virtually irrelevant to my current predicament. I didn't need to breathe. Sure, I couldn't talk with his hand around my throat, but I wasn't going to suffocate, either.

Remembering that helped me push fear back again, even farther this time, and anger roared in to take its place.

"And frankly, Miss Cavanaugh, every time we meet like this I am less and less inclined to leave you unbruised. Standing here, touching you with this borrowed—but very real—hand it occurs to me that not all of my corrupt pleasures have to wait for your arrival in the Nether."

And suddenly my fear was back, and *very* relevant to the situation. I could blink out anytime I wanted, but if he was touching me, he'd come with me.

"I've never truly understood the human fondness for nude rutting and the eager exchange of bodily fluids." He stared down into my eyes, studying my panic while I clawed at his hand, but I saw *nothing* of Marco in Avari's expression. I saw only hellion, and the dramatically dilated pupils that told me he was feeding from my fear. He was nearly *drunk* on it. "But this borrowed body seems willing, and you're clearly terrified by the prospect of such an encounter. And naturally, fear makes you taste so much better…." He leaned toward my neck and inhaled, and my stomach churned, though I hadn't eaten much in days.

Avari stepped back without letting go of my neck, and his gaze assessed me with almost clinical detachment. "It's the strangest thing. I don't understand what all the fuss is about, but every time I borrow a human form, my sense of touch is… Well, it's exaggerated. Sensitive. You mortals feel everything so *intensely*. Is it the same for you, or is this a trait exclusive to the human male?"

His free hand—Marco's hand—slid down the side of my arm, and his pupils dilated even farther when my nails broke through the skin on his arm. I made a quick wish for luck, then threw my knee up into his groin, as fast and hard as I could.

Avari yelped, and it was the most satisfying sound I'd ever heard. His hand fell away from my throat, and he hunched over the hopefully paralyzing pain.

"*That* is a trait exclusive to the human male."

Tod laughed out loud, and I looked up just as he appeared behind the demon in stolen flesh. He swung something with both hands, hard enough that the muscles in his arms stood out against his skin, and his weapon slammed into Marco's head with a dull *thunk*. Marco's legs folded, and he collapsed on the gym floor.

Tod stood behind him, holding Emma's three-inch-thick chemistry book. "You know, next time you text to tell me you may need help, I could get here a lot faster if you also tell me *where you are*. I'm a reaper, not a necromancer. Am I going to have to have you fitted with a GPS chip?"

"Sorry. I didn't know where I'd be." I glanced at poor Marco, thoroughly unconscious and probably in a lot of pain, then stepped over him and threw my arms around Tod. "And thank you. How'd you find me?"

"I tried about eight different places, then I found Luca. He said it felt like you were in the gym."

As a necromancer, Luca was like a compass for all things dead but not yet decaying. Including reapers. And me.

Tod let me go and ran one hand through his short curls, and the blue-eyed gaze that met mine was intense. Scared. And kinda…angry. "You have to stop doing this, Kaylee. You're dead, not invincible. Reclaiming souls when Madeline sends backup is one thing. That's your job. I get that. But you can't just go around confronting hellions on your own. Even in a human body they're dangerous. Especially when that human body is bigger than yours, and they're *all* bigger than yours."

The fear in his voice made my chest ache. "I didn't know he was possessed. And anyway, I can handle myself. See?" I made a sweeping gesture toward Marco's unconscious form. "Now he knows that being a teenage guy isn't all getting high and threatening girls."

"Yeah, and that was awesome, even if I can't help but sympathize with the pain he's going to be in when he wakes up. But Avari will be ready for that next time. One of these days you're going to get in too deep, and I'm not going to get there fast enough, and…bad things are going to happen, and *that* will kill me more than my actual death did."

"I think I was *born* 'in too deep,' and bad things happen every day. Sometimes I have to stab hellions. Sometimes I have to frame friends for murder, and stab evil math teachers, and watch my best friend die. Again. We deal with it, then we move on."

"Well, maybe next time you could let the bad things find you, instead of searching them out for yourself. Or take someone with you. I know Nash isn't as much fun to look at, but he'd be decent backup, and even with a broken arm, Sabine's a force to be reckoned with."

"But I'm not?"

"That's not what I'm saying. I think the evidence speaks for itself." He glanced pointedly at Marco, still unconscious on the floor. "But six hands are better than two. Especially when my hands aren't close enough to get to you."

"They're close enough now…" I pulled him toward me, and I could see that he was trying to resist a smile. To stay mad, to emphasize his point.

"That's not gonna work."

I went up on my toes to kiss him, and he groaned. "Do you really think this is appropriate on school grounds?"

"Nope." I wrapped my arms around his neck. "And I happen to know there isn't an appropriate thought running through your head right now."

"Or any other time." Tod pulled me close and held me so tight my ribs almost hurt, but I didn't want him to let go. Ever. "Just promise me you'll be more careful."

"I promise."

"So…" Tod tried on a grin, and I bent to pick up Em's textbook from where he'd dropped it. "What did Tall, Dark, and Evil want?"

"The usual. Devour my soul. Mutilate my corpse. Dissect my psyche. Just another day in the most dangerous high school in the country. Of its size." I nudged Marco's arm with my foot. "Can you help me get him to the nurse? He's going to wake up with several unexplained injuries, and I don't want to be in the room when he starts asking questions."

That night, Tod, my dad, and I made a conscious effort to keep our own emotions in check, so we wouldn't accidentally trigger Emma's as-yet-uncontrollable syphon ability. Which wasn't so much an ability at that point as a constant trial.

I think we did pretty well. Until around ten-thirty, when Em was doing homework on her bed and Tod and I were stretched out on my bed, not doing my homework. After about ten minutes of what I would categorize as PG-rated not-quite-adult content, she threw a balled-up pair of socks at us and said if we didn't go away she would jump my boyfriend herself.

Evidently we weren't very good at keeping *those* emotions in check. And since I did *not* want my best friend syphoning anything quite that intimate, we took the party to Tod's place.

Tuesday morning, Emma was in much better spirits. We picked up coffee on the way to school and met Nash and Sabine in one corner of the cafeteria, as far from the breakfast eaters as we could get.

"Here." I passed out lattes, and Em snatched a napkin dispenser from an empty table.

"What's the occasion?" Sabine looked suspicious. I couldn't blame her. We'd reached an understanding—she could have Nash, and I could never again touch him, for any reason whatsoever, so long as we both shall live. Which isn't as bad as it sounds. Nash and I had made serious strides toward actual friendship, which was more than I could say for him and his brother. Sabine and I would never be like sisters, but we had definitely reached something akin to friendship.

And that was good, considering that the alternative always seemed to involve her trying to kill me, with little regard for the fact that I was already dead.

"I need some information." I took the lid off my cup and blew over the top of my latte. "From Nash."

"What's up?" He dumped a packet of sugar into his open cup, then realized he had nothing to stir with.

"I need you to make a list of everyone you know who tried frost, back when Doug was, um, distributing to your teammates."

Emma flinched at the mention of her ex, and I felt guilty all over again. Both of her most recent boyfriends had died because of me and my otherworldly complications.

"I don't have a list." Nash scowled at the powder that refused to mix with the foam on top of his coffee. "In fact, I don't know a single name for sure. I didn't even know Doug was using, until that party. The night he hit your car."

"You don't have a single name? Seriously? Not even an educated guess?"

He shrugged and put the lid back on his cup. "I can tell you who I saw him with at that last party, when his dealer showed up."

"Was Marco Gutierrez one of them?"

"Yeah."

"Good enough." I pulled a notepad from my bag and pushed it across the table toward him. Em added a pen. "Write down all you can remember. Please."

"Is this about what happened with Marco yesterday?" Sabine sipped from her cup while Nash scribbled on the notepad.

"Yeah. He was just possessed, so it was pretty easy to get rid of Avari, but I'd like to avoid a repetition. Or at least see it coming ahead of time."

"So, where do we stand with Sophie and the liquid envy?" Em cradled her cup in both hands.

Sabine's smile looked almost euphoric. Which kinda scared me. "I gave her the first dose this morning, in her coffee. Had to dump in extra sugar to cover the taste."

"Half a drop?" Em said. "Because Kaylee went bat-shit crazy on a full drop."

"I did not—"

"Yeah. Half a drop, as instructed." Sabine spoke over me. "But I'm telling you, this whole thing would be much more entertaining—and would go a lot faster—if you'd let me really dose her."

"No. I know you enjoy your work, but the object isn't to drive her nuts."

Sabine huffed. "Speak for yourself." Then she shrugged. "At least I'm getting a decent bedtime snack out of this." Because she was feeding from Sophie's relevant fears as part of the process.

Em chuckled, staring into her cup. "I can't believe you put real sugar in her coffee. She'd kill you if she knew it wasn't calorie-free sweetener."

"Here." Nash slid the notepad back to me. "That's all I can remember."

I glanced at the list. "That's only three names."

He shrugged and sipped his coffee. "If I had more, I'd give them to you."

"Thanks." I turned to Em. "What about you? Did you see Doug hang out with anyone in particular?"

"Yeah." She shrugged. "Half the school. But I never even saw him with a balloon." Which is what they'd used to store frost in. Which was kind of…my idea. Though I'd never intended to contribute to the ease of drug trafficking when I'd thought of it.

"Hey, Kaylee, can I talk to you for a minute?" I twisted in my chair to see Chelsea Simms holding a green paper folder.

"Sure." I shoved the notepad into my bag, picked up my coffee, and stood. "I'll see you guys at lunch." Sabine, Nash, and Emma nodded, and I followed Chelsea into the hall.

She opened the folder as we walked in the general direction of our first-period math class, then pulled out a sheet of paper and handed it to me. "I just wanted to show you this." It was a screen print from some kind of layout program. "It's for her memorial page in the yearbook."

In the center was a candid shot of Emma at a football game, from the fall semester. Her cheeks were red from the cold and she wore a green scarf; her thick, golden hair was flying over her shoulder in the wind. She looked happy.

She looked alive.

In that moment, I understood what Emma had lost, beyond her family, her clothes, her car, and the future she'd always assumed she'd have. She'd lost *herself.*

I'd met Emma in the third grade, and in all the time I'd known her, I couldn't remember her ever lacking confidence or self-esteem before I'd exposed her to truths about the world no human should have to deal with. She'd always known who she was and where she fit into the world. She'd known what she wanted to do with her life—even if that changed on a monthly basis—and exactly what she was capable of.

She had none of that now, and even if I spent my entire afterlife trying to make that up to her, I could never give her back what she'd lost. Ever. The best I could do was help her adjust to the life she had now. Show her that she still had her friends, and that this new life could still be a good one.

But I couldn't do that with Avari always two steps behind us. I couldn't honestly tell her that life was still worth living if we were always looking over our shoulders to evade death and eternal torture. I had to get rid of Avari and the rest of the hellions not just to avenge Em's death, and those who'd gone before her, but to make sure that the life she had left was more than just the constant struggle to hold on to it.

"Do you think she'd like it?" Chelsea asked, and I realized we'd stopped walking several doors away from our classroom. And that my hand was clenched around the printout, my knuckles white from the strain.

"Yeah. It's beautiful. I think she'll love it."

Chelsea gave me a confused look, and it took me a second to realize I'd referred to Em in present tense. Again.

"I mean, if she were still here. Which she's not, obviously. Because she died. But if she hadn't, I have no doubt that Emma would *love* this yearbook memorial page."

"I hate it." Em set the memorial page printout on the picnic table and pinned it with her soda can.

"Hate what?" Nash put his tray down, Sabine set hers next to it, and they sank onto the bench across from me and Em.

"My yearbook memorial page."

"That's what Chelsea wanted to show me this morning." I leaned across the table and took an apple wedge from Nash's tray. I wasn't hungry, but if I never ate anything at lunch, people would start to notice, and he rarely bothered with the fruit anyway.

Sabine unscrewed the top on a bottle of flavored water from the vending machine. "What's wrong with it?"

Emma rotated the page beneath her can so they could see it. "The layout is simplistic and too symmetrical, the quote they picked says nothing about me, and I'd complain that the picture's too small, except that it's a horrible shot of me anyway."

"What are you talking about? You look great!" I frowned, studying her. "Are you channeling someone's anger again?"

"Not that I know of. Anyway, I'm not mad. I just hate that picture."

"Oh, that may be my doing," Sabine said around a bite of cheese-slathered corn chip. "Em's afraid she'll never look that good, so I thought this might be a good time to amp up her insecurity and vanity by feeding that fear. Tastes pretty good, too." She washed her bite down with a gulp of water. "Want me to stop?"

"No. It's fine." Em sat with a pout and turned the printout over, so she couldn't see her own face. Her own former face. And suddenly I felt bad for showing it to her. I'd thought it would make her feel better to know how much people cared. How much they missed her. Instead, I'd reminded her of what she'd lost. Again.

"Your dad snuck out of my house at two this morning," Nash said. I glanced up in confusion to find my cousin and her necromancer boyfriend only a few feet away, carrying their lunch. Sophie looked sick.

"Whoa, really?" Luca glanced from Nash to Sophie, who scowled and dropped her tray on the table so hard that her orange bounced into a plastic cup of cottage cheese. "This is the man who threatened to make sure I could never sire children if he ever caught me at your house past nine o'clock?"

"The very same." Sophie sat and started scraping cheese off her orange with a plastic spork. "And that wasn't an idle threat. Turns out I also have three older half brothers—like, *way* older—who would cut off anything you let dangle if they knew half of—"

Luca put a hand over her mouth, and I swear he looked suddenly pale. "Well, then let's not tell them." He frowned and dropped his hand. "Wait, what do you mean, *it turns out* you have older brothers?"

She shrugged. "My dad couldn't tell me about them until I knew he was a *bean sidhe,* because they're in their sixties but they look, like, twenty-five. Like they could be my uncles. But they all have grandkids."

"Wait a minute." Sabine scowled at Nash, and the sun seemed to fade a little. "I can't stay the night at your place, but Sophie's dad can? How is that fair?"

"How's what fair?"

Tod appeared out of nowhere and sat next to me on the bench. He slid one arm around my waist, and it took all the self-control I had not to lean over and kiss him. Which I couldn't do without looking crazy to the hundred or so other students in the quad who couldn't see him.

Em leaned forward to fill him in. "Your mom's sleeping with Sophie's dad, and Sabine thinks—"

"Whoa…" Tod clamped both hands over his ears. "I don't ever need to hear that sentence again. No need to finish it, either."

"At least we agree on something," Nash mumbled, ripping the crust from a slice of cafeteria pizza.

Sabine planted both palms flat on the table. "My point is that it isn't fair that he can come and go as he pleases—no pun intended—"

Everyone at our table groaned in unison, and Nash looked more than a little nauseated.

"—but—and I am not kidding—*I* now have a nine o'clock curfew. Seriously. Nine o'clock! I am a creature of the night! You can't impose a curfew on a living Nightmare! What am I supposed to do for the ten hours after lockdown? *Maras* only need four hours of sleep. Who the hell is he to tell me when I can and can't leave the house?"

"Your legal guardian." Sophie sank her thumbnail through the skin of her orange and began to peel it. "Officially, as of eleven this morning. He called to tell me when he finished

Influencing the juvenile court judge over brunch. I was supposed to tell you, but you know." She shrugged. "I didn't."

Sabine's eyes narrowed and her mouth opened, no doubt ready to spew several inventive and highly entertaining threats aimed at Sophie, but before she could say anything, Luca cleared his throat and smiled at Emma. "Your hair looks nice today. All smooth and shiny."

"Thanks." Em's eyes lit up, and her smile made me want to smile back. It was a very nice change from the previous day's lunch.

Sophie glared daggers at her. "Keratin treatment and some Frizz-Ease. It's not rocket science."

I glanced at Sabine in silent question, and she nodded. She was amplifying Sophie's fears to heighten her envy of…anyone Luca so much as looked at.

"Kaylee Cavanaugh?" a new voice said, and we all turned to see a sophomore whose name I couldn't remember standing at the end of our table, holding a slip of paper out to me. "Are you Kaylee Cavanaugh?"

"Yeah." As if she didn't know. Everyone in school knew who I was. Everyone within a *hundred-mile radius* knew who I was. I was the girl stabbed in her own bed by her evil math teacher. Not that most people knew Mr. Beck was *actually* evil, instead of just your average psychotic pedophile.

"They want you in the counselor's office."

Crap. "Okay. Thanks." I took the slip of paper from her—my official summons—and when the sophomore walked away, I turned back to the rest of the table. "I completely forgot my appointment." Turns out that when you're nearly fatally stabbed, then lose your best friend in a freak park-swing accident less than a month later, the school guidance counselor likes to keep tabs on you.

"Want me to come?" Tod ran his hand up my back, over

my shirt. "If you keep her busy, I could convert the filing system from 'alphabetical' to 'most deserving of psychiatric help.'" He leaned closer, and I knew no one else would hear whatever came out of his mouth next. "I've been meaning to make some special notations in Nash's file anyway. Imagine the level of help he could receive if they knew the root of his recent academic decline was a deep-seated fear of the letter Q."

I laughed. I couldn't help it. And though everyone else at the table looked curious, no one asked what Tod had said. They were finally starting to learn. "Thanks, but it's hard enough to take grief counseling seriously without you singing 'Living Dead Girl' at the top of your lungs behind the counselor's back."

"You mock *one* grief counselor, and you're branded for life," he mumbled. "Er…afterlife. I have a shift at the pizza place this afternoon, but I'll pop in when I get a chance." Tod kissed my cheek—the most we could get away with while only one of us was invisible—then disappeared. I grabbed my bag, said goodbye to my friends, then headed for the counselor's office.

Our school had two counselors, one for the first half of the alphabet and one for the last half. During lunch, the waiting room they shared was nearly empty.

"You can go in," the student aide said when the outer door had closed behind me. "She's been waiting for you."

Because I was eighteen minutes late.

I trudged into Ms. Hirsch's office, trying to summon an expression appropriate for someone who'd just lost her best friend. Nuance was important. My grief had to fall somewhere between "sobbing, devastated heap" and "Emma who?" I knew from experience that either of the extremes would only get me sentenced to more counseling.

"Hey, Ms. Hirsch. Sorry I'm late." I closed the door, then

slouched into one of the chairs in front of her desk. But Ms. Hirsch only watched me from across the desk.

I set my bag on the floor and stared at my feet for a second, riding out the silent treatment—was that supposed to pressure me into talking on my own? But when I looked up, she was still watching me. No, *studying* me. Like she'd never seen me before.

"Ms. Hirsch? You okay?" Was she in shock? Was *I* going to have to counsel *her?*

"You're smaller than I expected," she said. Only she said it with someone else's voice. She said it with a *man's* voice, deep and smooth, and…*rich,* somehow. And totally out of place coming from Ms. Hirsch's slim, delicately curved feminine form.

She was obviously possessed, presumably by a hellion, but I didn't recognize the voice.

My pulse spiked and chill bumps popped up on my arms, but beneath that an angry flush began to build inside me. I knew I should be scared—I was sitting across my guidance counselor's desk from a hellion I couldn't identify—but since my untimely death, I'd discovered that there was a limit to my capacity for fear. I could only be threatened, stalked, intimidated, manipulated, possessed, and actually killed so many times before I began to acclimate to the constant state of fear. Before terror lost its punch, like a scary movie watched too many times.

Anger, though… My capacity for anger at the Netherworld and at the host of Nether-creatures that had turned my afterlife into a living hell…that seemed to know no limits.

Much like hellions themselves.

My hands clenched around the arms of the chair. "Who the hell are you?"

Ms. Hirsch's left brow arched. "You don't know?" At the

sound of his voice, that warmth inside me spread, not comforting, but seditious. Like a fierce flame burning within me, demanding action.

"Should I?" The fact that he couldn't use her voice probably meant he hadn't been in her body often enough to learn how to work all the gears and levers. Hopefully, he'd *never* been in her body before. I hadn't even known she was eligible for possession....

"Not officially, but I'm a big fan of your work."

"My work?" I should have been terrified, but what little fear I felt wasn't because my guidance counselor had been possessed, or because whoever was possessing her had obviously known when and where he could get to me through her. I was scared for Ms. Hirsch. Of what he might do to her—or make her do to herself—if he didn't get whatever he wanted from me.

Ms. Hirsch's head bobbed and a strand of red hair—her bangs were long and trendy—fell across her forehead. "You've managed to thoroughly piss off not one but *three* of my most reviled associates. And to survive their anger." He frowned with my guidance counselor's pink mouth. "Sort of."

Every word he said stoked the fire inside me until the flames of my anger grew hotter, taller, licking the inside of my skin like they wanted to burst free and roast the world.

I knew what he was doing. He was feeding my anger. Nurturing it, like fertilizing a garden until the veggies are ready to harvest. And devour.

The worst part was that whoever this hellion was, he knew exactly who *I* was, and that I wasn't—strictly speaking—alive. And he knew who my enemies were. But I didn't need to be told that when dealing with hellions, the enemy of my enemies was definitely *not* my friend.

"Who are you and what do you want?" The longer I sat

there, the angrier I got. He'd hijacked Ms. Hirsch's body. He'd subpoenaed me from my lunch period like I had nothing better to do than be ordered around by a monster from another world! "Never mind. I don't care who you are or what you want. Get the hell out of my counselor's body, or I'll take you out myself."

I stood and picked up the large, jagged chunk of pink quartz Ms. Hirsch used as a paperweight and hefted it, silently threatening to bash his hellion brains in.

"Nice. Decent buildup from irritation to anger, with a flare of true rage on the end. How long have you been harboring so much hatred, Kaylee? You were only a blip on my radar a few months ago, but now you're a blinking light too bright to ignore."

What the hell? I glared down at him, confused. Was the hellion actually trying to counsel me? Was this some kind of demon identity crisis?

"Oh, and you *do* understand that if you bash me over the head with that rock, your counselor will be the one who wakes up with a headache. Right? If she wakes up at all."

Crap. I *did* know that. Blazing anger did nothing to help my logic.

The twitch at one corner of her mouth looked suspiciously like amusement. "If we're going to be any use to each other, you'll have to learn to think through your anger."

I desperately wanted to know what he was talking about, but I knew better than to ask. I needed to cruise *below* hellion-radar, not actively engage it.

"My name is Ira, incidentally." He leaned back in Ms. Hirsch's chair and crossed her slim legs, and the ease with which he moved told me that even if he wasn't familiar with her particular body, this wasn't his first time in human form. "In case you haven't figured it out, I'm a hellion of wrath.

And I've been *itching* to make your acquaintance of late. I think we can help each other out."

"Not gonna happen." I remained standing, but I put the rock down. I couldn't hurt Ms. Hirsch, which Ira obviously knew.

"Oh, I think it might, if you knew what I had to offer."

"No." *Never make a deal with a hellion.* That's the first thing they tell you in "Surviving the Netherworld 101." Or it would be, if such a class existed. Hellions love to bargain, but they never agree to a deal if they're not getting the better end of it. The *vastly* better end.

That *other* end tends to leave humans dead, or dying, or injured, or addicted. Or worse.

"There's nothing I want from the evil incarnation of anger." Nothing I was willing to pay for, anyway.

"Belittling my existence with understatement doesn't change the facts. I am much more than an 'incarnation of anger.'" Ms. Hirsch sat straighter and pinned me with a gaze too steady and merciless to come from anything other than a hellion. "I am in the clench of every fist. I am the hot thrum of blood rushing through your veins. Every thud of knuckles against flesh is the cry of my true name. I am the glint of rage in your ex's eyes, the livid grinding of his teeth. My pulse is the wave of anger washing over the crowd. The swing of a corpse from the noose. The final twitch of a man murdered in revenge. I know you, Kaylee Cavanaugh. I know you very, very well, and I can give you what you want most in the world. What no one else can give you."

"I don't want anything from you," I insisted, with less certainty this time, but repeating that didn't make it true.

"Really? Not even justice for everything they've taken from you? For everyone they've killed? For everything they've cost your friends and family?"

Oh, crap.

The hellion smiled slowly with Ms. Hirsch's perfectly glossed lips. "You want Avari, Invidia, and Belphegore to pay for what they've done."

My chill bumps were back, and this time they felt like small mountains. I sucked in a breath I didn't truly need and tried to swallow my fear and unease. I tried to bury that traitorous spark of interest piqued within me by his words—that soft voice whispering that it wouldn't hurt to hear him out. Just to see what he was offering…

Because that *would* hurt. I *knew* better. Hellions don't hand out free samples. But I couldn't help wondering….

"And you're going to do that for me?" Surely sarcasm disguised my curiosity. "Why would you conspire against your own kind?"

"My kind?" He actually laughed, and laughter looked nothing on him like it looked on the real Ms. Hirsch. "Avari is no more my kind than a garden spider is your kind. We inhabit the same world, but he would stomp on me with no more thought than you'd give to stomping on that spider." He leaned forward, pinning me with a familiar brown-eyed gaze. "I would stomp on him, too. Then I would grind him into the dirt beneath my heel, just like you would, if you were capable of exacting justice on your own."

"Hellions don't deal in justice." That was too noble a concept. "You're talking about revenge."

Ira shrugged. "That's just as well, because justice isn't really what you want." He leaned forward again, and his gaze intensified, as if he were looking for more than he could possibly find in my face. Behind my eyes. "Your wrath is graceful. Has anyone ever told you that? Your anger has the bold, sweet overtones of blind rage, but the delicate tang of self-righteousness, because you actually think you're after justice. But that's not true, is it?

You know there is no justice to be had. Hurting those who've hurt you and yours cannot undo what's been done. Nothing can bring the dead back to life or unscar the wounded. But you still want to hurt them, don't you? You still want to kill Avari in cold blood for what he's done to you. That, my sweet, vengeful little flame, is revenge, not justice."

I blinked, mentally denying everything he'd said. "So, I'm getting ethics lectures from demons now?" That was new.

"You misunderstand." His smile was back. "I stand in full support of your thirst for vengeance. I would gladly feed it to you drop by decadent drop. I would see you nourished and strengthened by the taste of blood spilled in anger. Of course, that offer comes with a price...."

"We're done here."

He rolled Ms. Hirsch's eyes. "And sanctimony rears its ugly head again. You are in denial, child. You won't be satisfied until you get what you crave, and that can't happen until you admit to yourself what it is you truly want."

"You're wrong." Hellions couldn't lie, but they could be wrong. *Way* wrong. "I'm not looking for revenge. I want *justice* for Emma and Alec, and everyone else Avari has hurt or killed."

"And for yourself? Don't you want this 'justice' for what he's done to you? For commandeering your body? For putting possessed hands on you? For making you the instrument of your friend's death? For abducting your loved ones? You *seethe* with anger, little flame. You practically glow with it. And some of that ire feels very, very personal."

"You don't know what you're talking about." My pulse whooshed in my ears, which rarely happened now that I was dead. He was wrong. He had to be. "Get out of Ms. Hirsch. Now."

"Don't you at least want to know the price for your vengeance? It may be less than you think. I'm feeling generous."

"No. Get out." I turned and headed for the door.

"You'll be back, little flame, and I'll be waiting. When you're ready to deal, you may summon me. You have my word that I will answer. You need only bleed and use my name."

I fled the office as fast as I could go without running. I left Ms. Hirsch in the hands of a hellion, not because I didn't know how to evict him without being expelled for attacking a staff member—though that was true—but because I was scared to listen to him anymore. I couldn't hear one more loaded word from the hellion of wrath, because deep down, part of me wondered if he might be right.

And that wasn't a question I was prepared to answer. Not yet, anyway.

On my way back from the counselor's office, I was texting Tod to fill him in when I looked up and realized I'd wandered down the wrong hall. I was standing in front of the nurse's office, which reminded me of Marco. Because that's where we'd left him the day before—unconscious in one of the two empty patient rooms.

I should check on him. And I would check on Ms. Hirsch, too. But I just couldn't bring myself to hit my guidance counselor in the head, even to expel a demon.

I ducked into the bathroom, glanced around to make sure it was empty, then let myself fade from all human sight. Then I blinked into nearly two dozen different classrooms until I finally found Marco Gutierrez in a fourth period senior AP English class. Another jock with a brain. Which meant he was too smart to inhale unfamiliar substances from balloons just because some idiot like Doug Fuller handed it to him.

Marco looked okay. He was wide-awake and taking notes on *Heart of Darkness,* which—based on the title alone—

sounded like a good reason to dread senior English. I had plenty of darkness already without reading about someone else's.

A glance at the clock over the whiteboard told me most of the period was over, and I now had an unexcused absence for English. So I decided to wait and talk to him after the bell. One minute before class ended, I blinked into the hall, checked for onlookers, then willed myself back into human sight. When the bell rang, I stood outside his class, and when Marco appeared, I fell into step beside him.

"Hey, Marco, can I talk to you for a second?"

He glanced at me in surprise. I couldn't blame him. We'd never said more than three consecutive words to each other, and none of those had been since Nash and I had broken up, officially severing any connection I had to the baseball team.

Finally he shrugged. "If you can walk and talk at the same time. I can't be late for statistics."

"So, I kinda just wanted to check on you. I heard you were sick yesterday? Or hurt?"

Marco frowned and stopped in the middle of the hall, and the steady flow of traffic parted around us. "Look, I don't care what you're into, or how many starting players you have left on your list, but I'm not into that kind of thing. I have a girlfriend, and I like her, and I'm not gonna..."

My horrified expression must have made an impression. If not that, my sudden inability to form a coherent reply obviously did the trick.

"Wait, that's just some stupid rumor, isn't it? That you're working your way through the baseball starting lineup?"

"*Yes,* it's a rumor! I guess." I hadn't actually heard that one. "A totally fallacious and false rumor, that's completely unfounded in truth!"

"Sorry. I would never have believed it, except I know you

were with Nash. And there was that thing with Scott. And there was talk about Doug. And someone saw you dancing with Brant Williams. And that guy you made out with in the hall after school." That was Tod. And the only part of what he'd heard that was true. "So it did kind of look like you were…interested."

"Well, I'm not! There was never a thing with Scott or Doug. And I was never *with* Nash. Like that. Why, did he say we…?"

"No. Not to me, anyway. But we all just assumed, because you were with him for so long."

"Well, *un*assume!"

"Done." He smiled, and he looked friendly. Like he might not be such a bad guy. Which meant he definitely didn't deserve to be possessed by a hellion or knocked out by my undead boyfriend. "So, you're really just checking on me?" He started walking again, and I kept up.

"Yeah. I saw you in the nurse's office, and you didn't look so good."

"That's what I hear. I don't know what happened. I dozed off in third period, and the next thing I know I'm lying on a table in the nurse's office with a cold pack on my head and another one on my…lower. The nurse said she found me there, and no one even saw me go in."

"So…you're okay?"

"Except for the part where my dad wants me to see a shrink. He says blackouts are a sign of a more serious underlying problem."

I gave him as confident and reassuring a smile as I could muster. "You're not crazy. Just…don't fall asleep in school anymore."

"No shit. That all you wanted?" He stopped walking outside his next class, and I was dimly aware that mine was all the way across the building and up a floor.

"Yeah. Oh, wait." I stepped closer and lowered my voice, uncomfortably aware that anyone who saw us would assume the rumors about me were true. One of the rumors, anyway. "I also wanted to ask you a question." He nodded, so I continued, "I heard that back before he died, Doug gave you a sample of this stuff he had. The stuff in the balloon."

"Frost?" he asked. When I nodded, his expression darkened and he motioned for me to follow him closer to the lockers, out of the main stream of traffic. "Stay away from that shit, Kaylee. They say it can't be detected in a drug test, but everyone else I know who's tried it is dead now. That can't be a coincidence."

"Everyone?" So, he didn't know Nash had used, too?

"Yeah. There were some other guys who wanted to try it at Doug's last party." Right before he'd died. "But then Nash threatened to kick the shit out of the guy with the balloon bouquet if he didn't get lost, and that night Doug died. I haven't seen any balloons since. And the more time that passes, the happier I am about that. You shouldn't—"

"I'm not," I assured him. "I was just…curious. Thanks, Marco."

I sped off into the thinning crowd before he could say anything else, and the one time I looked back, he was still staring after me, looking thoroughly confused.

7

"Are you girls ready?" Long blond curls fell over Harmony's shoulder as she twisted in the driver's seat to glance at Emma, then met my gaze in the rearview mirror.

"I will *never* be ready for this." Em stared through the windshield at her house. Her former house. Which held her former room and all her former stuff. Even her former dog, Toto, who was still a dog but no longer hers. "Let's get it over with."

Harmony laid one hand on her arm. "We're sure your mom's still at work?"

"Yeah." I leaned forward between the front seats. "I called to verify, and she said Traci would be here to let us in."

"That's her car." Em pointed to the dusty Chevy parked in front of us in the driveway.

"Okay. I just need one of you to ask for a drink." Harmony pulled the keys from the ignition and leaned to one side so she could slide them into her pocket, and again I was struck by how young she looked—thirty years old, at the most. You'd never know from looking at her that her sons were eighteen and twenty. Well, Tod *would* have been twenty, if he'd lived. "I'll take care of the rest," she continued. "If you're sure you're up to this."

"No choice." Em unbuckled her seat belt, and her hand trembled with the motion. "We can't afford to put it off any longer."

I unbuckled my own belt, one hand on the door handle. "If it's too much for you—if she gets upset and you can't control the syphoning—just let me know, and we'll get you out of there." She had been through so much already, and my heart ached at the thought of what lay ahead for her and for Traci. A decision no woman should ever have to make. A choice no human could ever anticipate.

Another devastating decision neither of them would be facing if they'd never met me.

I was a disease, infecting everyone I came into contact with, and the rot spread too fast to be contained. I went around with my scalpel, excising the infected bits of tissue—operating on lives and memories I didn't have the right to slice up—but the only way to truly stop the infection was to cut off the source.

To excise *me.*

I'd been struggling to clean up my own mess for so long that I could no longer tell if continuing to fight made me brave or selfish.

"Thanks. I'll be fine, though." Em opened her door and got out of the car, and when I stood, still trying to gather my thoughts, I was surprised for the dozenth time by the fact that I could almost see over her head. In her own body, Emma had been taller than I was.

Traci answered the door on the second knock, and the first thing I noticed when she let us in were the bags beneath her eyes. She'd looked tired at Emma's funeral, but I'd attributed that to the stress of losing, then burying, her sister. But now, I couldn't deny that it was more than that.

It was the pregnancy.

Traci, Emma's middle sister, was pregnant with my murderer's child. And, like nearly everything else that had gone wrong over the past few months, that was my fault. Mr. Beck had been looking for me when he'd found her.

"Hey, Kaylee. It's good to see you." Traci pulled me into a hug with too-thin arms, and I had to stop myself from blurting out how sorry I was for what she was going through, and how I'd do anything for a cosmic do-over. For the chance to take it all back.

Instead I swallowed apologies she wouldn't understand and returned her hug. "Thanks." I was careful not to squeeze her too hard. She hardly had any belly yet, and she looked like she'd blow over in a light breeze. "This is Harmony Hudson, Nash's mom. And this is my cousin Emily. They came to… help. Moral support."

"Nice to meet you." Traci shook Harmony's hand, then motioned for us to come in. Then she turned to shake her sister's hand without a single sign of recognition. "Kaylee can show you Emma's room. Take whatever you want to remember Emma by. Mom, Cara, and I have already been through it all and taken what we wanted. What means the most to us."

Em's eyes watered. Traci didn't notice.

"How are you?" I said, instead of leading everyone to Em's room. Traci was leaning against the doorframe. I was afraid she might fall.

"Um…I'm having a rough first trimester." She let go of the doorframe and sank onto the arm of the couch. "Emma told you about…the baby?"

Actually, *I'd* told *Em* about the baby, weeks before Traci had even known she was pregnant.

When Mr. Beck had come to Emma's house looking for me and my best friend, he'd found Traci instead. What he'd done to Em's sister might not have been rape by any human legal definition, but I couldn't think of it any other way. Mr. Beck was an incubus. He'd *made* Traci want to sleep with him. She didn't know it, but she'd had no choice.

If her baby was a boy—an incubus—the pregnancy would probably kill her. All signs were pointing toward that already. And if the pregnancy didn't kill her, the child's birth almost certainly would.

We hadn't really come so I could take something to remember Em by. We'd come to help Traci.

"Is there anything I can do?" I asked. Harmony looked like she had plenty of suggestions, but I knew she wanted to wait until Traci'd had something to drink.

"No, thanks, hon. I'm fine. Just tired."

"Do you want something to drink?" Emma asked a second before I would have. "I could use a soda, if you have any." She knew they had some. All her mother ever drank was Dr. Pepper. Pretending to be unfamiliar with her own house must have been killing her.

"Sure." Traci stood. "Just give me a minute."

"You don't look like you feel good," Harmony said, right on cue. "If you don't mind, I can get everyone a drink while the girls go through Emma's things."

Traci only hesitated for a second. Then she sighed and sank onto the couch again. "That'd be great. Thanks."

Harmony disappeared into the kitchen while Em and I headed to her room and Traci stayed on the couch.

"She looks sick," Em whispered to me in the hall.

I nodded. "We're going to help her." But Traci's health would come with a price only she could pay.

Emma's room was a mess. There were open cardboard

boxes on the floor, photos missing from the walls, and clothes draped over the back of Em's desk chair. Her bed was unmade, too, but that had nothing to do with her death. The bed probably looked just like it had when she'd woken up after her last night in it.

I was halfway across Emma's room when I realized she'd stopped in the doorway. "You okay?" I called over my shoulder.

"This is weird. They've already started packing stuff up," she whispered. "Like they can't wait to get rid of me."

"That's not it." I pulled her inside and mostly closed the door, to keep Traci from overhearing. "Nash said his mom did the same thing after their dad died, then after Tod died, not because she wanted to forget about them, but because it hurt too much to look at everything that reminded them of what they'd lost."

Her chin quivered. She didn't look like she believed me.

"They're packing this stuff up because they miss you, Em. Not because they're glad to be rid of you. Besides—" I glanced into several of the open boxes "—most of these are still empty. Grab one and pack up what you want."

For a couple of minutes, I went through the clothes in her closet, looking for anything that might still fit, while she went through what little remained on her shelves. Her mom and sisters had claimed everything but some elementary school soccer medals, a participation trophy from the one year she'd tried middle school cheerleading, and the first-place ribbon from fourth-grade field day, when we'd won the egg toss.

"Is that all you want?" I set the shirts I thought Em could still wear in the box she was using, on top of the medals and several pictures of the two of us, dating all the way back to third grade.

Emma shrugged. "They took most of the good stuff. And

I think I'm happy about that. I don't need stuff to remember myself by, right? I'm still here. And I *want* them to remember me."

She had a valid point. And she seemed to be in good spirits, considering.

"Any luck with my jeans? Or some shorts? It's already getting warm outside."

"The pants are a total loss. Sorry. You just don't have the hips for them anymore. Maybe a couple of skirts, though…."

We were going through the last of her clothes when Harmony called us from the living room. "Girls? I think she's ready."

My heartbeat was a hollow thump my chest suddenly felt too small to contain.

Em looked as nervous as I felt. We put down the clothes and filed into the living room, where Harmony now sat next to Traci on the couch. Em and I took the two armchairs facing the couch at opposite angles.

"Traci? You okay?" She frowned at her sister in concern. Traci looked…confused.

"I feel weird. Tired." She looked like she could fall asleep where she sat.

I scooted to the edge of my chair to take the can of soda Harmony offered me. Traci had a cup of what looked like hot tea. I peered into it, but saw no trace of whatever Harmony had spiked it with. "So…how does this stuff work?"

"'This stuff' is just water from a natural source in the Netherworld. Water there has various properties, and this one—" she held up a plastic vial, very much like the one Sabine kept her liquid envy in "—works like an amnesic. Traci is sleepy, but her cognition is not impaired, so she can talk to us just like she normally would. But she won't remember anything that happens in the next hour or so."

"What about after that?" Em asked.

"She'll probably fall asleep, then wake up here and only remember that she took a nap."

I glanced at Traci, who was watching us in mounting confusion. "So we can tell her everything?"

Harmony nodded.

"*Everything,* everything?" Em clenched the arms of her chair. "Like, about me?"

"If that's what you want to do."

Emma didn't look sure, and I was hyperaware that the clock was ticking. So I started. "Traci, we have some things to tell you, and most of them are going to be hard for you to believe. But don't worry about that, because you're not going to remember this anyway." We only needed her to understand long enough to make a very difficult decision.

Traci focused on me sluggishly. "This feels like a dream."

"Are you sure that stuff won't hurt the baby?" Em asked.

Harmony smiled and leaned back on the couch, still facing Emma. "I'm sure. It's really just water. And the baby's way too young to worry about memory loss."

"What does this have to do with my baby?" Traci laid one hand across her mostly flat stomach.

"Okay. Here goes...." I closed my eyes and took a deep breath, then swallowed my own nerves and uncertainties and met her gaze. "Traci, there's a better than average chance that your baby isn't human."

Traci blinked. Then she laughed kinda sluggishly. "Have you two been drinking? It's, like, three in the afternoon." She seemed to have forgotten Harmony was even there.

"No." Em gripped the arms of her chair. "Your baby's not human, but that's okay, 'cause Kaylee's not, either. In fact, she's dead."

"Who are you again?" Traci frowned at her.

"We'll get to that in a minute." I stood. "Traci." She turned to see me and suddenly seemed more drunk than tired. "I'm a *bean sidhe.* Most people call us banshees, but whatever you know about banshees is probably wrong. Incomplete, at the least. Also, like she said, I'm dead."

There were probably a million better ways to tell her what she needed to know and a million people better prepared than I was to deliver the news—like Harmony—but we were short on time and on volunteers Traci knew well enough to trust.

"You're dead." It wasn't a question. Yet she obviously didn't understand. "And you're a banshee."

"I know it sounds weird. I didn't believe it at first either. But I can prove it. At least, I can prove the part about being dead. Are you ready?"

"Sure." She shrugged listlessly, then crossed her arms beneath a well-endowed chest, obviously humoring us. "Knock yourself out. Be as dead as you want to be. 'Cause we haven't had enough of *that* around here."

Valid point.

I caught Traci's skeptical gaze and held it. Then I let myself fade from sight. I didn't actually go anywhere, but they couldn't see me.

As soon as I started to fade, Traci sat up straight. She didn't look sleepy anymore.

"What the *hell* just happened?" She turned to Em and Harmony. "Did you see that? Did she just disappear?"

Em nodded solemnly. "She does that now. A lot. Because she's dead."

"How did…? When did she…?" Traci closed her eyes and shook her head, then opened her eyes to stare at the spot where I stood, though she still couldn't see me. *"What?"*

"Remember the night I got stabbed?"

Traci actually jumped. Her gaze flitted over the room

but couldn't find me until I let myself reappear. "You got stabbed, and now you can do that?" She waved a hand in my general direction. "So you're saying...you died? When you got stabbed by...?"

She couldn't say the name of the man who'd fathered her child and stolen my life.

I couldn't blame her. And for the first time, I thought about what that whole thing must have been like for her. What it must *still* be like. I was all over the news for weeks—the girl who'd survived being stabbed by her teacher. What most people didn't know was that I hadn't really survived.

What even fewer people knew was that before Mr. Beck had gotten to me, he'd gotten to Traci Marshall, who'd had no choice about what they did together, though she didn't know her will was being subverted.

Now she was carrying the inhuman child of a serial rapist and murderer. The daily reminder of even what little of that she understood must have been hell.

"Yeah. I died." I stared at the floor for a moment, pushing back remembered terror, blazing pain, and the overwhelming memory-scent of my own blood. "I've been faking life ever since. There was a whole cover-up and everything."

"I don't... How is that possible? If you're really dead, why are you still here? *How* are you here?"

"The how part is a little complicated. The short version is this—there are lots of things out there you don't know about. Things you'll *never* know about, if you're lucky. Most of those things are dangerous and scary. I'm neither, I hope. But I am dead. I can make my heart beat, but it doesn't do that on its own, and when it doesn't pump blood, I get cold. Not refrigerator-cold, but cooler than the natural body temperature. I don't have to eat, but I can if I want to. I can get hurt, and if I do, I heal really slowly, because my body isn't as alive as it used to be."

Though in some ways, I was more alive than I'd ever been. Thanks to Tod.

"And you can…disappear?"

"Yeah. That's one of the convenient aspects. The downside is that I'll never age, which means I'll never get to live in one spot for very long." At least, not visibly. "And I'll never grow up or have children."

Traci looked so sad that I wished I'd left that last part off.

"But there's more." I sat in my chair again, and Emma scooted hers closer. "The night I died was the night you got pregnant. Do you remember that?"

Traci flushed with the memory. "But I never told anyone…?"

"I know because the father of your baby is the man who killed me."

"How the hell did you know that?" She leaned forward so far I was afraid she'd fall off the couch. "I never told anyone who he is. Not even my mom. I couldn't, after I found out what he did to you."

"He told me." Beck had wanted me to know exactly what he'd done to Traci, and that it was all my fault, and that he would do the same to Sophie and Emma if I put up a fight while he killed me and stole my soul for his unborn son.

Traci's gaze lost focus. "It was so weird. I'd never even met him, but the moment I saw him on the front porch, I wanted him. I didn't *want* to want him—he was a total stranger—but I couldn't help it. Then I saw him on the news and heard what he'd done, and after that, I couldn't tell anyone…." Her eyes filled with tears, and her hand spread over her stomach.

"Traci, Mr. Beck wasn't human," Harmony said, and I envied the control she had over her voice. How she was able to sound calm and soothing, when surely she was as affected by Traci's trauma as Em and I were. "He was a predator and a parasite. What he did to you wasn't your fault. In fact, it had nothing to do with you—you were just in the wrong place at the wrong time."

Her tears fell. "I was at *home!*"

"I know." My heart ached for her, but the terrifying truth was that sometimes home *is* the wrong place. It certainly was for me the night I'd died. "Unfortunately, it gets worse. Traci, if your child is what his father was, there's a really good chance you won't survive this pregnancy. So...you have to make a decision. We'll give you all the information we have, but the choice is yours."

Thank goodness. I'd had to make several impossible decisions recently, but nothing like the one Traci was facing. I'd never had to decide the fate of a child.

"Wait..." She scrubbed her face with both hands, like she was trying to wake herself up, and Harmony handed Traci her teacup. Traci pushed hair back from her face, then drained the rest of her tea, though it must have been cold by then. "What was Mr. Beck? What is my *baby?*"

The cool thing about disappearing before someone's eyes is that they tend to believe anything you say afterward, which cuts down on a lot of the time I would normally have spent trying to convince someone that humans are not alone in the world. *Either* world. Traci had taken the expressway to all things supernatural. For me, that was kinda nice.

For her, it was understandably traumatic, and the more of the truth she heard, the worse that would get.

"Beck was an incubus," Emma said. "That's basically a sex demon."

"A *sex demon?*" Traci stared at the coffee table like it might contain a translation of that phrase that was easier to stomach. "I had…" She swallowed thickly. "With a demon?"

"Actually, an incubus is just one of several kinds of psychic parasites. This kind happens to feed on…desire."

"Lust," Emma corrected, her voice sharp enough to sting. "Don't sugarcoat it. She needs to know what really happened." Em turned to her sister. "He came here that night looking for us, and he found you instead."

"Why would he be looking for you here?" Traci's frown deepened. "Who *are* you?"

Emma groaned, frustrated by the reminder that her own sister still didn't recognize her. "Who I am doesn't matter. The point is that he was mad that we stood him up, and he took that out on you, and I'm so sorry. He raped you, Traci."

"No…" She shook her head, confusion momentarily overridden by denial that bruised me all the way to my soul. "I wanted to…."

"You didn't have any choice," Harmony said softly, and I could have hugged her for stepping in. Em and I…we were in over our heads. I didn't know how to explain the truth to Traci without further upsetting her. "He made you want to. It's as much a violation of your will as of your body. There's nothing you could have done any differently."

"No." She shook her head again and swiped tears from her cheeks in one determined motion. "That's not how it happened. I—"

"Traci." Emma reached for her hand, but her sister pulled away from the touch she didn't recognize, and my heart ached for Em. "Under what other circumstance would you have opened the door for a perfect stranger, then invited him straight to your bed?" Fresh tears swelled in Traci's eyes, and her sister continued, "The only difference between Mr. Beck and half the men in prison for assault right now is that he violated you on multiple levels. Which makes me wish Kaylee could kill him all over again. And that I could help this time."

Traci stared at the floor, her gaze unfocused, one hand still spread over her stomach. I wasn't sure how much more of this she could take. Or how well she was handling what she'd already heard.

Hell, I wasn't sure how well *I* was handling it.

"So the baby…?"

"Your baby is almost certainly an incubus," Harmony said. "So we need to discuss the best way for you to…survive."

Traci blinked, then frowned, and my heart ached as I watched her struggle to bring Harmony into focus through pain, confusion, and the Netherworld contaminate in her system. "Why wouldn't I survive?"

"Because incubus babies are notoriously hard for human women to carry. They…" Harmony only hesitated for a moment, but I could see how much she dreaded speaking the necessary truth. "Well, they drain their mothers, from the inside out."

Em set her soda on the coffee table and ran one hand through her hair. She seemed surprised when there was less hair than she remembered. "Then, when they're born—*if* they're born—they have no soul of their own, and if there isn't one ready for the baby, it'll take the mother's soul. Unless she's human."

"Even if she's human," Harmony clarified, to my horror and confusion. "A human soul can't support an incubus baby for long, but that's no help to a mother who's already passed away for want of a soul by the time her baby dies. Usually the father spends most of the gestational period hunting for a non-human soul for his child, but in this case, there's no father."

"May he rot in hell for all of eternity," Em added.

"I don't…" Traci shook her head, like she was trying to

clear cobwebs from her mind. "That's a lot of information about something I'm not sure I understand." She glanced from one to the other of us in mounting fear. "What does all that mean?"

Harmony exhaled slowly. "It means that if you manage to carry the baby to term and deliver it, at birth he will take your soul, which will kill you. Then, when your soul fails to support him long-term, the baby will die anyway."

Em met her sister's gaze with a wide-eyed, urgent one of her own. "So, basically, the only way for you to survive an incubus pregnancy is for your baby...not to."

Traci nodded. Then she stared at her hands, sitting idly in her lap, obviously thinking. Hard. When she finally looked up, I was impressed by how calm she seemed, and I wondered how much of that was because of what Harmony had put in her drink. "So, what are the chances that the baby is actually an incubus? I mean, I'm human, so the baby could be human, too, right?"

I nodded, but Harmony shook her head. "Traci, hon, your baby is an incubus. I can tell that from looking at you. At how sick you are. You're sick because your baby is sharing your soul at the moment, just like it's sharing your blood and everything you eat. All of that puts a huge strain on you, and, frankly, you're older than anyone I've heard of who's successfully delivered an incubus."

"But I'm only twenty-two."

"The younger, the better. Evidently," I said. Which was why Beck had posed as a high school math teacher—for virtually limitless access to underage girls. The bastard.

"Okay." Traci took a deep breath and stared at her hands. Then she took another deep breath and looked up, her mouth set in a firm line. "I'm not ending my pregnancy—I don't care what kind of baby I'm carrying. I don't care who or what his father was. I care that this baby is *mine* and I want him. So…what do we do?"

Harmony frowned, and I recognized the worry lines in the center of her forehead—the only sign that she might be older than the thirty-year-old she looked like. She got those same lines every time she saw Nash and Sabine together.

Emma exhaled heavily. "Trace, you're not thinking this through. If you try to have this baby, you're going to die. That's, like, ninety-nine percent certain. You can't do that to Mom and Cara. Not after the funeral."

"Who are you?" Traci's eyes flashed with anger, and in that moment she looked so much like Emma—the old Emma—that I caught my breath. "I don't even *know* you!"

Em's eyes filled with tears again. "Traci. It's me." She waited, searching her sister's face for some sign of recognition, and when she found none, she turned to me, heartbreak drawn in every feature on her face. "I thought she'd be able to see it, at least in my eyes."

I got up to sit on the arm of Emma's chair so I could put one arm around her, hating how helpless I felt in the face of her pain. "Traci, this is Emma. Your sister. She didn't really die. Well, she did. But…it's complicated, and now she has a new body."

Somehow, even as the words fell out of my mouth, that part sounded much less believable than, "Hey, Traci, you've inadvertently taken on the role of human incubator for a demon's spawn."

Traci blinked at me. Then her gaze hardened. "What is *wrong* with you? My sister—your best friend—*just died,* and I don't care whether you can make yourself disappear, or run at the speed of light, or fly to China with no airplane, it is *never* going to be okay for you to joke about that."

"It's true," Harmony said. "There was an…accident. I'd

appreciate it if you don't make us explain every little detail, because it's complicated, and we don't have all night. What you really need to know is that this is Emma. Your sister. Her death has been just as hard on her as it has been on you and your mom and sister."

"I can prove it," Em said before Traci could start arguing or get more upset. She leaned forward in her chair, obviously desperate to have her say before her sister kicked us out. "I know things no one else but you and I know. Like…I know what flavor bubble gum you stuck in Cara's hair the night before picture day when she was nine. It was that horrible watermelon flavor. The kind that's green on the outside and red in the middle. Only when you chew it, it turns brown and looks as gross as it tastes. And I know about the time you accidentally took nighttime cold medicine instead of daytime cold medicine and you fell asleep in first period, and some jackass wrote all over your face with permanent marker. I guess there's probably a whole class full of people who remember that, and Mom and Cara know, but why would any of them tell me? I know because I was there while Mom tried to scrub four-letter words off your forehead with rubbing alcohol, and I was with Cara when she went out to buy stage makeup to cover up the ghost of the F-word on your cheek, when the alcohol didn't work. I saw you cry into the mirror every day for a week, waiting for the ink to wear off."

"Oh my…" Traci's eyes were huge and her cheeks were pink, but I saw no sign of doubt on her face now. "Emma?"

"Yeah. It's me." Em smiled bigger than I'd seen her smile since the day she woke up in Lydia's body. "Death sucks. I mean, I'm still alive, but everything's different, and I hate my new hair, and my old clothes don't fit now, and the world looks different when you're only five foot two, and I don't have a car anymore, and… But I'm taking Toto with me. He's all I have left now."

Traci stood so fast I got dizzy just watching. She launched herself over the coffee table and threw her arms around Emma, squeezing her harder than I would have thought possible, considering how frail the expectant mother's frame looked. "I can't believe it. I don't really understand what's happening here, but this is real?" She sounded half-choked, like she was speaking through tears, and we all nodded. "I thought you were dead." Traci pushed Em away and held her at arm's length, suddenly as furious as she'd been relieved a moment earlier. "*I thought you were dead!* How could you do that? How could you let us think you *died?*"

"I didn't have any choice. Don't be mad. What was I supposed to say, 'Hey, guys, I died, but then Kaylee got me a new body, but you're still gonna have to bury me, and pretend you don't know I'm still here'?"

"I guess not." Traci sank into her seat again, but she couldn't stop staring at Emma. "You look so different. Except your eyes…"

Emma glanced at me with her brows arched. "Oh, *now* she notices my eyes."

"Girls, I truly wish we had time for the reunion this moment deserves. But we're running out of time on this dose." She gestured to Traci's empty teacup. "And I'd rather not risk Traci still being under the influence of a second dose when her mother comes home. I'd hate for her to forget something she needs to remember."

"So, I'm really not going to remember any of this? I won't remember about Emma?"

"I'm afraid not. However, you may subconsciously remember that she's alive, and that could make it easier for you to move on, even if you still believe on the surface that your sister is dead."

Traci nodded, and I privately wondered how many good uses I could find for a vial of Netherworld forget-me water if I had one.

"But as sorry as I am for everything you've been through," Harmony continued, "we really need to get back to the matter at hand. Do you understand what we've been telling you?"

"I think so." Traci's eyes narrowed in thought. "My sister's still alive, but my baby's going to die. Or else I will."

"No. You're not going to die." Harmony looked…heartbroken. She leaned toward Traci on the couch to emphasize the importance of what she was saying. "We came here to tell you the truth, so you can do what needs to be done. To save your life."

"Well, I won't do it." Traci leaned back against the cushion, one hand on her small belly, as if the matter was already decided. "I'm not going to kill my baby."

"Traci…" Em said, but her sister shook her head firmly.

"No. He's sharing my soul. My *soul,* Emma. That means he's part of me. How am I supposed to kill part of myself? I can't live with myself, knowing his death was the price for my life."

A storm of horror and empathy collided within me, trapping me between that figurative rock and hard place. The decision was Traci's to make—but I wasn't sure she fully understood the choice she was making. Or the consequences of letting an incubus baby live.

"But, Trace, he's probably going to die anyway!" Emma insisted. "You can't carry him, and if you try, you'll both die. You're already sick, and it's still your first trimester!"

"There's another problem, Traci," I said quietly, and Harmony's attention settled on me like a comforting hand on my back, silently encouraging me to say what had to be said, even as waves of nausea rolled over me at the very thought. I took a deep breath. When I was sure I had Traci's full attention, I continued, "Your son isn't human. The male offspring of an incubus is always an incubus, so…you need to understand that even if you could carry and deliver this baby, and even if you both survived, you wouldn't be raising a normal little boy. You'd be raising a predator."

Her uncertain frown deepened. "What does that mean, exactly?"

"When your son reaches puberty, he'll develop an appetite—a *need*—to feed on lust, in any form. If he doesn't, he'll starve to death, just like he would without food." I scooted forward in my chair. I could practically *feel* her taking in every word I said, studying them for truth and, beyond that, for meaning. "Your son will grow up to do to other girls what Beck did to you. He will bowl them over with a desire he exudes—and won't be able to control without practice—then he'll take what he needs, when he needs it, from whoever is convenient at the time. Like you were convenient for Beck. At best, he'll try and fail to control his appetite, unintentionally victimizing girls who don't even know they're victims. Girls who won't understand why they slept with a strange boy and might think of themselves as sluts because of something they had no control over. I can only imagine how damaging that kind of self-image will be for the rest of their lives. At worst, your son will be a flat-out rapist and murderer, like his father."

I could see her horror growing with every word I said, but I continued because she needed to know all of it. She needed to understand.

"Either way, he will be the most dangerous thing on the middle school playground, and that will only get worse the older he gets. He'll be a sexual predator, Traci. There's nothing any of us can do to change that. That's what incubi *are.* It's how they survive, and their survival is in direct opposition to the free will of every woman in their path. You know that even better than we do."

Traci's hands started to shake in her lap, and her gaze lost focus beneath the tears now standing in her eyes.

"And it'll be even worse than that when he feels the need to...reproduce, about once a century," Harmony added. "During each of those spawning periods—for lack of a better term—up to a dozen young girls could die trying to carry his child. Which is the same risk you're facing now. Do you understand?"

Please, please let her understand. Somehow, telling Traci that her child would grow up to be a monster was even harder than telling her that the conception was a crime of convenience committed against both her mind and her body. I hated myself for having to tell her either of those things, and suddenly I understood why some people might be inclined to shoot the messenger.

"You're telling me that my son will be a psychological rapist, right?" Harmony nodded, and for the first time since we'd arrived at Emma's house she looked uncomfortable to be there. "Well, I don't accept that," Traci continued. "You may know *what* this baby will be, but you don't know *who* he'll be. You can't possibly know how much nurture can affect his nature, and you don't have any right to judge him now for crimes he *may* commit sixteen years from now. And you don't have the right to judge the kind of mother I'm going to be. The kind who would *never* let her child turn into the monster you're describing. He deserves a chance. *I* deserve a chance. And he's *mine.*" Tears filled her eyes again, and she sniffled, trying to hold herself together.

"Trace—" Emma started, but her sister interrupted.

"No! You can't just come in here and tell me that this thing happened to me. This thing I couldn't stop and didn't even understand. You can't tell me that this murdering bastard came into my house and got into my head and scrambled everything up, and made me think I wanted him to do what he did, and that none of what I felt about that was real. That the whole thing was…corrupt." She gestured angrily at the front door and at her own head as she spoke, and my heart beat so hard my chest ached from the pounding. "You can't come in here and tell me all that, then tell me I can't keep the one good thing to come out of the most horrible thing that's ever happened to me. He might have taken a decision away from me, but *you're* not going to. This is *my* choice. This is *my* baby." Traci stood, staring boldly down at the sister she'd just rediscovered. "I'm not going to end my pregnancy. If that's what you expect me to do, then…get out. Thanks for coming and telling me all these horrible things, but now you need to go. All of you. Now."

"Wait." Emma stood. Unspent tears trembled in her eyes. "Wait." She turned to me. "We have to help her."

"Em, there's nothing I could do." I'd rarely felt more helpless. More useless. But we were *way* out of my league.

"She just needs a soul. You can get her a soul. I know you can. You're a *bean sidhe,* and you're a reclamationist. Or whatever. Right?"

Traci looked so suddenly hopeful that my heart broke for her all over again. "Can you?"

"No! I'm sorry, but it doesn't work like that. I don't get to keep the souls I reclaim! I have to turn them in. And it's not like I have extras lying around." But as soon as I'd said it, I realized that might not be true.

"What?" Em's gaze narrowed on me. "What are you thinking?"

"Nothing. Just…maybe. It might be possible. But I can't promise anything."

Harmony stood, her hands opening and closing at her sides like she was nervous. Like we were making her nervous. "Girls, this won't work. It's not our place to…give people souls that don't belong to them. That's beyond what a *bean sidhe* can do. It's beyond what we're *supposed* to do."

"But Kaylee did it! She put my soul here in Lydia's body, so I know she could do that for Traci's baby. If we had a soul for him."

Harmony blinked. She opened her mouth like she'd make another objection or tell us how dangerous that idea was. But nothing came out.

"But finding a soul for your baby will be a moot point if you don't survive the pregnancy," I said, and Traci's expression fell so far I thought her jaw might actually drop off her face.

Emma turned to Harmony. "You have another vial in your purse, don't you?" Her voice was quiet. Sad. Thoughtful. "What does the other vial do?"

"It's a mixture of some plants and roots from the Netherworld. For Traci. For if she decides to end her pregnancy." She reached into her purse and pulled out a second plastic vial a quarter of the way full with a pale yellow liquid. "This is the safest way."

"If you can do that…" Em's voice broke, and I realized she was crying. "If you can help her lose the baby safely…can't you help her keep it safely? Isn't there some plant or root in the Netherworld that can…I don't know. Boost her immune system, or give her a superdose of vitamins, or somehow make her healthy enough to carry the baby to term?"

"Emma, Traci, I know this is hard, but the chances of this ending well are so small," Harmony said.

Em swiped one arm across her eyes angrily. "No. This

is my nephew we're talking about. And my sister. She's lost enough already. She can't lose the baby, too. If you can help her, you *have* to."

Harmony sighed. She closed her eyes, and her lips moved without making any sound. Like she was praying. When she finally looked at us again, her blue eyes were swirling with… sadness. Or maybe regret. I couldn't tell for sure. I'd never seen her unable to control the swirling before.

"I can't promise anything. I can help, but…there are no guarantees. The chances are still slim—"

"I'll take them." Traci wiped tears from her cheeks. "I'll take those chances. Please. I'll do whatever you want. I'll pay you. Just please do whatever you can for my baby."

"Oh, honey…" Harmony took Traci's hand and pulled her closer. "I would never charge you. I just need you to understand that I have no idea whether or not this will work. We'll have to take it day by day. And your baby may come early. We may have to *make* him come early, if your body starts to fail you."

"Fine. Whatever it takes."

"Okay." Harmony sat, and Traci sat next to her. Em and I sank into our seats, fascinated and a little scared. "First, let's put this away." She slid the yellow vial back into her purse. "Second, you'll need to eat healthily. Exercise, but don't overdo it. Get plenty of rest. And…I'll be back tomorrow with something for you to take every day. With tea or water. No coffee."

Emma frowned. "Harmony, is she going to remember this?"

"No." Harmony glanced at the ground for a second, thinking. "You'll have to introduce me to her again, Kaylee, and I'll give her the mixture as a prenatal supplement." She turned back to Traci. "Are you sure you want to do this? You won't remember what we've told you. You won't remember the risks. You won't remember…so much of this."

"Doesn't matter," Traci insisted. "I would never give him up, no matter what I know or don't know about this pregnancy. If you tell me tomorrow that I need whatever you're bringing, I'll believe you. I'll take it."

"If she doesn't, Nash can help, right?" Emma leaned closer to whisper.

I nodded. "Nash, or Tod, or my dad." Any one of them could Influence Traci into wanting to take what she needed to take to help her keep the baby. And I was only willing to let them do that—to play with her mind—because we'd all seen how badly she wanted to keep her baby.

But… "Traci, there's one more thing." I'd never hated myself as badly as I did for what I was about to say. She nodded for me to go on, and I could see in her eyes that though she might not have anticipated the wording, she knew at least some of what I was going to say. "If you can't do this…" I took a deep breath, then started over.

"If it turns out that nurture can't trump nature and your son becomes dangerous, I'll have to…stop him." That wasn't in my job description, strictly speaking, but I already felt responsible for whatever this theoretic incubus might do later in life, because I'd agreed to help bring him into the world. Against my better judgment. "I can't let him hurt people, Traci. I'll be watching him. And I won't be alone. Your son will get a chance, but he'll only get *this one chance.* And the next tough decision on his behalf won't be yours to make."

It would be mine.

And I would damn well make the right one.

“You know, there were times when we were little when I would have done almost anything to be an only child, but now all I want in the world is to be her sister again.”

“You’ll always be her sister, Em,” I said as we backed out of the drive, wishing I could see her face from the backseat. “Even if she doesn’t remember that.”

I’d never had a sister. I’d had Sophie for thirteen years, but she never let anyone labor long under the impression that we were anything more than cousins. Emma was the closest thing I’d ever had to a sister, and I knew exactly how Traci felt having lost her, because I’d lost Emma twice before, and both times I’d found a way to bring her back from the dead.

And even if she died a dozen more times, I would move heaven, earth, and the Netherworld as many times as it took to bring her back.

But it would be much easier if I could figure out how to keep her from dying again in the first place.

“Girls.” The tone of Harmony’s voice told me I wasn’t going to like whatever she had to say next. “I can’t explain how badly I hate to have to say this, but I think we need to consider the hard truth here.”

"No." Em crossed her arms over her chest and stared out the passenger's-side window. "We're not killing her baby."

"Of course not!" Harmony stomped on the brake and the tires squealed as she pulled to a stop two full feet from the curb. She shifted into Park, then twisted in the driver's seat to face us both. "I would never suggest anything like that. Whether or not to end her pregnancy is your sister's choice. But you both need to understand that even with my help, there's every chance in the world that Traci will still lose this baby and maybe her own life in the process. In fact, whatever help I'm able to give her may make that more likely."

"What? Why?" Em looked almost as confused as she was clearly terrified.

"Because if left alone, her body will almost certainly reject the pregnancy when it starts to threaten her life. That's the case in a full two-thirds of incubus pregnancies. But if I help her keep the baby into her second or third trimester and her body still rejects it, the miscarriage could kill her, too. You'd be losing not just your nephew, but your sister. Is that something you're willing to risk?" She was talking to Emma now. I had no say in this.

Emma shouldn't have either. She shouldn't have had to wrestle with a decision like that. But she was the only one of Traci's relatives who knew the truth.

"Me? No." Em shook her head firmly. "But Traci knows the risks. She made her own decision, and I don't think that would change, even if she remembered making it."

"So you're sure you want me to help her, rather than letting nature run its course?"

Em turned on her, and the spark of anger in her eyes surprised me for a second. "There's nothing natural about this. *Nothing.*" She swiped unshed tears from her eyes in one angry motion. "My sister was raped by a monster, and now she's carrying one. I was killed by another monster. Nothing will ever be the same for either of us." She glanced at me and seemed to reconsider. "For *any* of us. But Traci's made her choice, and we are damn well going to respect it."

Harmony nodded. And that was the last of that.

"Where were you today?" I dropped onto the end of Tod's bed and crossed my legs beneath me, then set my shoes on the floor. They landed on a pile of laundry he wouldn't get around to washing until he had nothing left to wear. At all.

Laundry day was my favorite day to visit for that very reason.

"Work. I didn't get your text till this afternoon." He came out of the teeny bathroom—the only other room in his tiny suite in the reaper headquarters building—holding two plastic cups of water. "I'm all yours now, though. What *will* you do with me?"

"What are my options?"

"Anything you want, Kaylee." The heat in his gaze set me on fire in all the right places. "Time is on our side, youth is our immortal legacy, and you are all I've ever wanted. This could be the best night of our afterlives."

"Then what would we do tomorrow night?"

"Tomorrow, we top our personal best." He set the cups on the minifridge serving as his bedside table, and the dim overhead light cast highlights and shadows on every plane and ridge of his bare chest. "I like a challenge."

"I like *you*." I pulled him onto the twin mattress with me. Tod landed on his side, propped up on one elbow. I leaned down to kiss him, and when I started to pull away, his hand slid behind the back of my head, his fingers in my hair, holding me in place gently so our kiss would last. And last. And last…

When Tod finally let me go, my head was spinning, and that had nothing to do with the fact that I hadn't taken a breath in several minutes and everything to do with the fact that he made me feel alive. He was the closest thing to a drug that I'd ever experienced, and I had yet to find a limit to what I'd be willing to do to protect him. To keep us together.

I'd spent most of my life setting boundaries. Lines I wouldn't cross. Lines I wouldn't let others cross. But with Tod, there were no boundaries. No limits. Time was not an issue. I loved him without reservation. I'd given him everything I had and everything I was, and he'd done the same. He'd given up his life for Nash, but he'd been willing to give up eternity for me. Not just willing—he'd actually done it.

I'd seen Levi, his boss, confiscate his soul and end his afterlife because he'd refused to kill me and reap my soul.

We had eternity to love each other, but after the way our relationship had begun—with loss and death and sacrifice—every single moment felt like a gift neither of us was willing to take for granted.

"Oh! I almost forgot." Tod rolled away from me and reached past the edge of the mattress to pull open the top door of the minifridge, which exposed the even more mini freezer. When he rolled toward me again, he held a small container of Phish Food, my favorite ice cream, and two plastic spoons. "I know it's small. This is the only size that would fit in the freezer."

"What's the occasion?" I took the spoon he handed me while he opened the carton and peeled off the plastic seal.

"Tuesday." He frowned and twisted to glance at the alarm clock on top of the freezer. "For another forty minutes, anyway." He handed me the plastic seal and I licked ice cream from it, then leaned over to drop it into the trash can at the foot of his bed. Which was wedged into a scant foot of space between the mattress and the only chair in the room. His place was so small we could practically reach everything in the room from one end of the bed or another.

But it was all his. Ours, he insisted, on nearly a daily basis. We were the only two people in either world who knew exactly where his place was. Nash had been in the room, but Tod had blinked him there, so on his own, Nash couldn't find reaper headquarters again even if he wanted to. And he did not.

The rest of the reapers and my dad knew where the headquarters building was but not which room was Tod's.

And the best part about Tod's place was that there was no exit. Literally. The only door was the one separating the tiny bathroom from the small main room. There was no exit because reapers didn't need doors, and now I didn't either, and that was *beyond* convenient, because this way neither of us could lose the key. The absence of windows made things feel a little claustrophobic sometimes, but the fact that no one could burst in on us made up for that completely.

"Do you have any idea how hot it is when you lick that plastic ice cream thing?" Tod's eyes were swirling when I scooted across the mattress toward him, rumpling the already chaotic mess of sheets and blankets. It never ceased to amaze me how disheveled his bed always was, considering that he rarely slept at all. If ever. I'd never seen him sleep, anyway.

"No. But you're welcome to tell me…."

"It's so hot I'm considering opening another carton, just to watch the replay."

I smiled. "Sounds like you need to cool off."

"That's not what I need. In fact, that's the opposite of what I need. But I might accept a short delay in the form of one of those little chocolate fishes."

Laughing, I dug a fish-shaped bite of fudge out with my spoon and fed it to him.

"Mmm… This is the best part of being dead."

"No, *this* is the best part of being dead." I kissed him, and his tongue was cold and he tasted like fudge. So I kissed him again.

"We did that when you were alive, you know."

Yeah, but only for a day. Because I'd died on the second day of our relationship. And… "But never here. Never in absolute privacy. Never after my father went to sleep, in a totally separate building, with no idea where we are or what we're doing." If I were still alive, my dad would be enforcing my curfew much more strictly.

I took a bite of ice cream and let it melt slowly in my mouth. We'd suffered a criminal lack of perfect moments since the day I'd kissed him in the hall at school. There always seemed to be something or someone standing in the way of perfection, however brief, and that something was a hellion more often than not. But *this* moment was perfect. This moment was chocolate, and privacy, and bare skin, and cold mouths, and warm hands, and cell phones set on Silent.

I didn't want to ruin the moment, but Tod seemed to realize at about the same point I did that we could eat ice cream and hold hands, but if we didn't also do something constructive, we would look back on this moment plagued with guilt, when our lack of preparation got someone killed.

Someone who wasn't already supposed to die, that is.

"Anything new with Sophie?" he said, but his tone and the eye contact he was making with my mouth told me he was less interested in the answer than he was in…me.

"Sabine says half a drop of liquid envy is more than enough. We were right about that. Turns out my cousin is a possessive little monster, though, so Sabine's going to skip the morning dose tomorrow, because no one has any pre-lunch classes with Sophie, and we don't want her to...well...go psycho when no one's there to help."

"Really? I think that might be kind of entertaining. What's the worst that could happen?"

"You know how Laura Bell has this horrible Pat Benatar-from-the-eighties haircut?"

"I don't even know who Laura Bell is, and I can't honestly say I care about her hair. Your hair is the only hair I care about." He ran a strand of it through his fingers. "And I love how it looks kinda red in the light, and how it feels when it trails over my skin when we're—"

I could feel my cheeks burn. "Well, Laura has tragically short hair, courtesy of Sophie, from back when Invidia was polluting the entire school with a monster dose of jealousy. We're trying to avoid as many civilian casualties as possible this time. Especially since the point of this whole thing is to keep the hellions from doing any more damage at Eastlake."

"Great. Good plan. I approve. Now can we do that thing where your hair trails over...?" He made a vague gesture encompassing his chest and my hair.

I laughed. "In a minute. Business first." I slid another spoonful of ice cream into his mouth when he started to object.

"Fine," Tod said when his mouth was empty again. "So, how's Emma holding up? Any more accidental syphoning?"

"Yeah," I said around a bite of chocolate-laced marshmallow cream. "I think she was taking a bit of her sister's... pregnancy emotion this afternoon."

"What emotion would that be?"

"Several at once, as near as I can tell. Fear. Grief. This fierce love for her unborn child, which was kind of amazing to watch. I mean, she's never even seen the baby. And she can't have felt it kick yet. I looked it up, and it's too early for that, unless things are different for an incubus pregnancy. But she loves that baby like it's the only thing she has in the whole world." Which wasn't true. But that didn't make the intense love I'd seen in her eyes any less real.

"I guess sometimes the parental bond begins in utero."

"I guess." I sat up and put the lid on the ice cream carton, then handed it to him. "Tod, do you ever wind up with any...*extras?*"

"Extra what?" He swiveled on the edge of the mattress to put up the ice cream, and when he turned again, he handed me one of the cups of water, then took a sip from his own.

"Extra souls."

Tod choked on his drink, then coughed while I pounded on his back. Dead people can't choke to death, but you'd never know that from the way it still feels when you inhale water.

"You okay?" I said, when he finally stopped coughing and met my gaze.

He set his cup on the fridge without even glancing away from me. "Kaylee, I know what you're thinking, and you need to stop thinking it. Seriously. It won't work."

"He's a *baby*. We can't just let Traci's baby die."

"Yes, we can. We have to."

"What is wrong with you?" Angry and disappointed, I stood and stomped across the floor and into the bathroom—a four-step trip—and dumped my water into the sink.

Tod followed but hovered in the doorway. Giving me space but not giving in. "Kay, listen to me. Please. I'm not just being randomly cruel. I have nothing against Traci Marshall, and you know I'd never intentionally hurt Emma."

Unless it was to save me. He'd hurt Em to save me. He'd hurt *anyone* to save me, and I didn't quite know how to deal with that knowledge.

"Traci's baby is an incubus. She wouldn't be so sick otherwise, right?"

I nodded. But I didn't look up. I couldn't look at him, because I wasn't sure what I'd see swirling in his eyes this time.

"That baby will never be on my list. Just like his father never would have. Just like Avari never will be. Because they're… they're monsters, Kaylee. Predators."

"Sabine's a predator. She can't live without hurting others." That sucked, but it was true. "If she can control it, so can Traci's baby."

"No." Tod stepped into the bathroom and stood at my back, close enough that I could feel the warmth of his skin through my shirt but not close enough to actually touch me. "Sabine's the exception, Kaylee. She's native to our world. She's the product of two human parents. She's a predator, but not a monster. Beck was different. His son will be different. You know what Beck did to Traci. You know that he would have done the same thing to Emma. And to Sophie. And to you, if you weren't immune to his abilities." Because I was a *bean sidhe.* "He feeds to survive, just like everyone else in both worlds. The difference for incubi is…what he did to Traci. To your friend Danica. They had no choice." He stopped talking, waiting for a response from me, but I had none. I didn't know what to say.

"Kaylee, look at me, please. I need to know that you know I'm not just being cruel." He closed what little distance stood between us and pressed his chest against my back. He ran his hands slowly down my arms, and finally I met his gaze in the mirror and saw the truth swirling in his eyes.

Regret. Disappointment. Fear.

He didn't like telling me what he was telling me, but he felt it had to be done.

"If we help Traci bring another incubus into the world,

he's going to do what his father did, to hundreds of girls your age or younger. Maybe thousands over his lifetime. But I can't live with the knowledge that he did it even once, and we helped make that possible."

Finally, I turned, and he was so close I had to crane my neck to look into his eyes. "But you don't know that. Incubi don't have to feed during sex. They can feed from lust. Without…touching. Traci could raise him to do that. Surely nurture has as much as nature to do with how any kid turns out. Even incubi."

Tod shook his head slowly. Sadly. "Kaylee, that won't happen. Yes, it *could* happen, but it won't. That'd be the incubi version of living on nothing but cabbage. He'd slowly starve until he got so desperate for sustenance that he gave in to hunger. And maybe that's not entirely his fault. I'm in no position to judge a creature for doing what's in his nature. But would you seriously want your teenage daughter anywhere near Traci's son when he hits puberty and his appetite kicks in?"

"I'm not going to have a daughter." Ever. Nor a son.

Tod exhaled slowly. "I know. Me, neither. But you get my point, right? What if it were you? What if you weren't a *bean sidhe* and Beck had made you…do things?" The swirling in his eyes grew angrier and more intense at the thought. "But what if you didn't *know* he'd made you do it? What if you thought you were just the kind of person who'd cheat on her boyfriend, or sleep with a teacher, or give away something that should mean something? What if *that* had been your first time?"

My stomach churned. What if I'd lost my virginity to my evil math teacher with no idea I'd been under the influence of incubus pheromones at the time? What would that have done to my relationship with Tod? What would that have done to the rest of my life?

"Do you really want some other girl to go through that because we helped bring an incubus into the world?"

I shook my head. "But I promised Emma I'd try." And I wasn't going to let those horrible things happen. If her son grew up to be dangerous, I was both prepared and willing to do what had to be done. At least, I would be by then. Surely.

"You did try. And it's a moot point anyway, because I don't have any extras. Reapers never have extras, unless they've gone rogue."

I'd only met two rogue reapers, and that was two more than most people would ever meet. But one of them was dead, and the other—Thane—I had no way to find. And I wouldn't go looking for him even if I knew how, because there's a big difference between risky and dangerous. Between determined and stupid.

And anyway, I wasn't that desperate just yet. There was still one more possibility....

But I clamped a lid on that thought before it could show in my eyes. I rarely disagreed with Tod, and I wasn't sure this was actually one of those times. I needed more time to think, and there was no use worrying him before I knew there was anything for him to worry *about.*

9

I stayed with Tod, and we made the most of the last half hour of the day, then, when he had to go to work, I blinked into my room at home to check on everyone.

My dad was asleep in his recliner in the living room with the TV on, his crutches on the floor next to the chair. "Dad." I shook him awake, and he blinked at me slowly. Groggily. "You fell asleep in your chair again."

He pulled the lever to retract the attached ottoman and I helped him stand, then handed him his crutches. He glanced at his watch. "Tod went to work?"

"Yeah." No sense denying where I'd been until midnight.

He adjusted the crutches beneath his arms. "I know you don't sleep here anymore, Kaylee. But I'm not mad. You're as grown as you're going to get."

"I don't sleep anywhere, Dad. Try not to read too much into that."

He wouldn't have said that if he were fully awake. If he weren't on pain pills, because the stab wound in his thigh still hurt like hell. It bothered him that curfews, healthy meals, and a good night's sleep were wasted on me. It bothered him that I spent so much time at Tod's, where there wasn't a door to leave open. It bothered him that there was little he could do to protect me now, and it bothered me that he seemed to think that meant I no longer needed a dad.

Nothing could have been further from the truth. I still needed him. I loved him more than ever. And there were days when I wanted nothing more than to be a normal seventeen-year-old, worried about her dad watching the clock on prom night, which was coming up in…four days.

How the hell had that snuck up on me?

Em and I had picked out our dresses together. She'd sworn that prom was exactly the motivation she needed to return to school after her own murder and that dress shopping would help her get to know her new body, but I saw her face in the mirror every time a slinky, sparkly gown fit too loose in the bust and hips and fell too long over her legs. She didn't want to go to prom as Lydia.

I wasn't sure I wanted to go at all, but I'd promised her months ago that we'd go together, with or without dates, and she'd been planning our first junior/senior prom since we were freshmen.

Her dress was red and sleek and dramatic, and it looked great with her darker Lydia hair.

My dress was gold. It was long and full, and it sparkled in every little bit of available light. My dad had spent money we probably couldn't afford on that dress because he'd said that in it, I shined brighter than the sun. Just like my mother.

Tod said my dress glittered like sunlight on the ocean. He found a gold vest and tie to match, but he refused to show off his tux in advance for fear of forever tainting the other guys' prom experience with feelings of inadequacy.

So I would have to wait to see him in it, but I had no doubt the wait would be worth it.

With my father in his room for the night, snoring two minutes after I'd closed the door, I opened my own bedroom door to find Styx sitting on the end of the bed staring at me, like she'd just been waiting for me to appear.

She probably had. Something about the fact that she was a Netherworld half-breed meant that she could see and hear me even when normal people couldn't. She'd probably known I was home before I'd even woken up my dad.

As soon as I stepped into my room, she jumped down from the bed and ran at me expectantly, tiny pink tongue hanging from her mouth by half an inch. I picked her up and scruffed her fur, amazed for the millionth time how small and fluffy and normal-looking she was in that moment, considering that if there was danger lurking anywhere near me, on either plane of existence, she'd be baring small teeth sharp enough to shred human flesh all the way to the bone.

Em was asleep on her bed with her bedside table lamp on, and I noticed that while Styx curled up with me anytime I sat in one place for more than five minutes, she never curled up with my best friend, even though they saw each other much more often now that Em lived here and I was dead. Styx tolerated her. She even seemed to like her. But Styx and I had bonded in her infancy, and she would forever be loyal to me above all others.

Sometimes I wondered what would happen to her if and when I died...permanently.

Before her death, Emma and Toto were just as close as Styx and I, but she'd decided to leave Toto—Styx's littermate—with Traci, to protect her and the baby. Just in case.

I set Styx down and carefully untangled the knot of earbud wires from Emma's hand, wrapped them around her iPod, then set it on the nightstand. Then I pulled her covers up to her waist—her feet looked cold—and turned off the lamp.

After I fed Styx and checked to make sure all the doors were locked—not that anything I truly feared needed an open door to get to me—I blinked out of my house and into the middle of Madeline's office. She stood with her back to me, a stack of papers in her hand, like she'd just picked them up from the credenza behind her desk.

She turned and saw me and gave an uncharacteristically undignified little *yip* of surprise. And dropped the entire stack of papers to clutch her heart. As if she could possibly have a heart attack when she was already dead. I wasn't sure how long she'd been dead, but we had a pool going, with a bonus included for whoever was able to actually obtain the answer.

"Kaylee! You've certainly gotten stealthier in the past few weeks." She didn't look entirely impressed by that fact.

"Thanks, I guess."

"What can I do for you?" Madeline sat in the chair behind her large dark wood desk and waved a hand at the pair of leather-padded armchairs on my side. When her boss had found out exactly how dire our situation was, when Avari was stealing souls pell-mell from the human plane, he'd increased our department's budget and tossed a little more manpower our way.

Too bad all of that came after all the death and chaos and after Thane stole the hellions' collection of souls, which prevented them from appearing on the human plane again, at least until they could renew their supply.

I was assuming they hadn't yet managed that, based on the fact that I'd only seen them in borrowed—possessed—bodies since then.

"I...um..." I sank into the chair on the right and clasped my hands in my lap to keep from fidgeting. Looking nervous wouldn't do me any favors. "Well, Tod's at work, and everyone else I know is asleep, and I..."

Her smile got a little kinder. "You're bored."

"Yeah." That wasn't entirely a lie. My boredom usually peaked in the middle of the night, and at first the shortage of company and the complete lack of anything to keep me busy had led to a dangerous melancholy period, during which I'd lost the desire to do…well, anything. I hadn't snapped out of it until Avari started parading the ghosts of my past—everyone I'd failed to save—before me and making me "kill" them all over again.

The melancholy hadn't returned. It had been replaced with a relentless thirst for justice.

Though Ira would call that rage.

"Well, fortunately, things have slowed down around here, and you know we have two new reclamation agents now."

Yes, I knew. My dad called it the "hurry up and wait" phenomenon. They raised me from the dead to help them with a very *bean sidhe*–specific emergency job, and now that that job was over—at least, as long as Avari was stuck in the Netherworld—they had much less immediate need of me. And since I was the rookie among more experienced employees again, I got the smallest, simplest, least complicated jobs. Which I was fine with. I was still in high school, after all. But…

"I was thinking. Thane got away with several stolen souls. Shouldn't we be…reclaiming them? I mean, if the others are too busy, I guess I could look into it." That sounded casual. Right?

Madeline folded her hands on her desk. "Kaylee, Thane is a rogue reaper. He's completely beyond our authority. The reapers police their own."

"But he stole souls. Lots of them." I hadn't been able to rescue them from him at the time, because Em had just died and Lydia's body was on the verge of death. I'd had to act quickly to save one of them. Or, a piece of each of them. "Besides, we deal with hellions who've stolen souls, and they're way more dangerous than rogue reapers."

Madeline nodded. "It's not about the danger. It's about the jurisdiction. There's no other agency in place to deal with hellions when they steal souls, but the reapers have their own authority. Around here, that's Levi, and I'm not going to step on his toes, especially after everything he's done to help us recently."

"But—"

"No." She leaned closer to me over her desk. "Thane's a reaper. Let the reapers deal with him."

"They're the ones who lost him in the first place!" When he'd killed my mother, then come back to kill me when I was three.

Madeline's frown deepened. "Was there something else I can help you with, Kaylee?"

That was a dismissal if I'd ever heard one.

"No. Thanks." I stood and headed toward the door, because using it seemed more polite than just disappearing right in front of her, and I'd obviously already pissed her off. I paused in the doorway with my hand wrapped around the doorframe. "Hey, Madeline?"

"Yes?" She sounded annoyed now.

"Whatever happened to Mr. Beck's soul?"

"Mr. Beck?"

"The incubus. The one who killed me. His soul was in my dagger when I turned it in that first time. Did it get recycled along with the others?"

Madeline's brows rose in sudden interest, and she put down the pen she'd picked up. "No. As it turns out, an incubus soul is a relative rarity, and it carries quite a bit of power. And since no one was expecting it at the recycling facility—your incubus wasn't on the list, of course—Levi decided to keep it as a sort of…souvenir. A conversation piece."

"Is he allowed to do that?"

"Well, no. Not technically. But he wasn't allowed to bring back your young reaper suitor either. He did that as a favor to me—" because I'd refused to work for her if she couldn't bring Tod back to me "—so I will, of course, be overlooking his small indiscretion. As will you, naturally."

"Naturally…" I hardly heard the word as I spoke it, because my head was spinning with other thoughts. Other possibilities.

Levi still had Beck's soul. If it would work for the father, it would work for the son. No one else would have to die to give Traci's baby life—a pattern that would hopefully continue throughout the little parasite's existence.

"What exactly is a conversation piece, anyway?" That wasn't really a lie either, because I hadn't actually said I didn't know the definition. I'd just implied it.

"It's a piece of art or decor intended to start conversations. Thus the name. In this case, it's a highly stylized letter opener. It's obviously just for show. Something interesting to set on his desk. And now when people ask about it, he can tell them not only the history of the letter opener itself—it's hellion-forged steel he won in some kind of gambling game—but that it contains the soul of the only incubus ever known to have died at the hands of one of his victims."

I started to argue with that statement. I wasn't an incubus's victim in the traditional sense. He hadn't wanted my body; he'd wanted my soul. However, he had killed me, so Levi's story wasn't really inaccurate….

But I had just as much right to Beck's soul as he did. More really. And I wanted Traci to have it.

"Thanks, Madeline. Just let me know when you need me. I'll be…around."

"Thank you, Kaylee." I'd been dismissed again, and this time I was eager to go.

I blinked from Madeline's office back into my bedroom, where I silently lifted the broken dagger from my dresser. I'd taken it from Beck—it was the weapon that had killed us both—and he'd bought it from Avari, who'd evidently ripped the metal from the Netherworld ground and forged the dagger himself.

That thought made me pause, stunned to realize that Avari, Beck, and I were tangled up in as intimate and distressing a knot as Nash, Sabine, Tod, and I. Hundreds of years before my birth Avari had made the blade that would kill me, but I'd survived its use—and my own death—to retain ownership of my own murder weapon. Which he no doubt wanted back.

On second thought, the Avari/Beck/me tangle was much more disturbing than anything forged in adolescent hormones and rooted in love.

I stared at the dagger in my hand for a moment, tracing the jagged, broken edges with my gaze. Invidia, the hellion of envy, had broken off both of the points on the night Emma had died. Afterward, Tod had gone back to the Netherworld to retrieve it for me, but he wasn't able to find the severed points.

Fortunately, the jagged blades were just as scary—and almost as sharp—as the original weapon had been.

I slid the double-bladed dagger beneath the waistband of my jeans, at the base of my spine, uncomfortably aware that if I made the wrong move, I'd knick my own backside with both broken points. But I couldn't exactly walk into reaper headquarters wielding a weapon.

In fact, I couldn't just walk into reaper headquarters at all.

I wasn't even supposed to know where it was, and if Levi found out Tod had told me, he'd get in trouble. Which meant I couldn't afford to wander around looking for his office. I'd need to know exactly where I was going. Or as exactly as possible, to cut down on the walking I'd have to do. I couldn't make myself invisible to reapers.

And I only knew one person who might know where Levi's office was *and* be willing to tell me.

I blinked into Madeline's apartment and spared a moment for relief over the fact that I already knew she was still at work. Luca's room was easy to find—there were only two bedrooms, and Madeline's didn't even have a bed. Did the woman truly never sleep?

Luca was out cold in a twin bed, covered only in a thin sheet, which I could see easily in the red glow of his alarm clock numbers and the light from the bathroom across the hall.

Was Luca afraid of the dark?

I tiptoed silently to the side of his bed, but when I bent over to shake him awake, the broken dagger blades scratched the inside of my jeans. I pulled the blade out before I could accidentally slice open the seat of my own pants, then shook Luca awake with my other hand.

His eyes opened groggily, and that surprised me. For some reason, I'd expected a boy with such an intimate connection to death to be a lighter sleeper. It took him several seconds to focus on my face, and another one to recognize it.

"Kaylee?"

"Yeah. It's me."

And suddenly he was wide-awake. "What are you…?" His gaze fell on the broken dagger, which must have looked threatening from his perspective—flat on his back in the middle of the night with a dead girl standing over him—because he screamed like a little kid.

"Relax. I just need some help."

"What happened? Was I possessed?"

It took me a second to figure out what he was talking about, and why my reassurance had failed to reassure him.

Alec.

Like the rest of my friends and family, Luca knew that I'd killed Alec when I'd mistaken him for Avari. I'd killed him in the middle of the night, with the very dagger I now held inches from Luca's stomach. By total coincidence.

"No!" I reached back and slid the dagger into my waistband again, to get it out of sight. "I just need you to find something for me."

Luca exhaled, then glanced at his alarm clock. "It's two in the morning."

"I know. Sorry."

He leaned over and turned on his bedside lamp, then tossed off the sheet, and I had to admit that Sophie had good taste. The necromancer was hot. Which I could tell, because he slept in nothing but boxer briefs.

"You may as well sit down and let me put on some pants." Luca knelt to pick up a pair of flannel pj bottoms from the floor at the foot of his bed. I pulled the dagger from my waistband again, then set it in my lap as I sank into his desk chair and glanced around his room, which was easier to see in the light.

He had a beanbag chair, which made me miss mine. His held three different soccer balls. There was a small TV on top of a chest of drawers, but no gaming system that I could see. Four different pictures of Sophie were wedged into the space between his mirror and its frame.

I suspected she'd stuck them there herself, but the fact that he'd left them said a lot.

"You sleep here alone?" I swiveled in his chair, one foot on the ground for stability.

He sat on the end of his bed, facing me, his bare feet dangling an inch from the floor. "I practically live here alone. Aunt Madeline doesn't need to eat or sleep. I suspect she only rented this place for me."

"That must get lonely." I was lucky enough to have my dad, my dog, and now Emma to keep me company, even in the afterlife.

Luca shrugged. "I really only sleep here. Sophie and I..." He shrugged, and I could fill in for myself the part he'd left out. He spent as much time at my cousin's house as Tod spent at mine. The only difference was that they didn't bring the party to his place after my uncle Brendon went to sleep. Though they might, if they could do it on the sly. "So, what's up, Kay? Though something tells me I don't really want to know."

"Have you ever been to reaper headquarters?"

"Nope."

"You know where it is, though, right?"

He shrugged. "I could make an educated guess. A very educated guess. The PhD of guesses, really. There's only one spot in the city where more than a dozen dead people hang out 24/7. And those are only the ones off-shift."

"Great. Do you happen to know where Levi's office is in that building?"

"Again, I can only guess. I know where he spends most of his time...."

"And that would be?"

Luca frowned, like he was just now awake enough to have questions of his own. "Why? What are you doing?"

"Just a favor for a friend."

"Without Tod? You wouldn't need my help if he knew what you were up to."

"He's my boyfriend, not my dad." Besides, Tod had warned me early in our relationship that he was no role model. I was starting to realize I might not be, either. "Anyway, I'm not doing anything wrong. I'm not even breaking any rules." Taking back what should still belong to me wasn't really stealing, right? "I just need to get something from Levi."

"Something he doesn't know about? Something that requires a scary-looking knife?"

Irritation flared in my chest. "Why do you care? I'm not doing anything wrong, and no one will get hurt. Haven't you figured that out about me yet?"

But I could see the answer in his eyes, and it stung. He knew I wouldn't intentionally hurt anyone. But he also knew that my friends and acquaintances had a shorter-than-normal life expectancy.

"Just help me. Please. I'll owe you."

Luca looked intrigued at that. "Fine. Levi's usually in a room on the third floor. Northwest corner of the building. I'm pretty sure that's his office."

"Is he there now?"

Luca closed his eyes for a second, and his forehead wrinkled, like he was thinking. Or seeing something I'd never be able to see. "No. He's down the hall with another reaper. And Tod."

Crap. What was Tod doing in the reaper building, in the middle of his shift?

"Thanks." I stood and replaced the dagger beneath my waistband. "I gotta go."

"Okay, so when you say you'll owe—"

I blinked out of his room before he could finish his sentence. We could work out the details at school.

10

Blinking into the reaper headquarters building was like playing hide-and-seek in pitch-dark—I had no idea where I'd wind up. Fortunately, I remembered to take the common-sense precaution Tod had taught me. I blinked out of Luca's room and into the reaper building in incorporeal form. That wouldn't keep reapers from seeing me, if there were any in the room when I appeared, but it would keep me from becoming a permanent piece of whatever furniture my arrival collided with. Which was good, because I landed in the middle of a table.

Fortunately, the room—some kind of break room, with a coffee bar and a couple of vending machines—was empty.

I stayed incorporeal, so that if I saw anyone coming before I was spotted, I could step through a door and into another room. Where I had an equal chance of being seen, come to think of it.

Reaper headquarters was *not* a good place for a dead girl to hang out.

The hall outside the break room was empty, but I could hear voices coming from several of the rooms that opened into the hall. The plaques outside the doors read things like "The West End" and "Downtown" and "DFW." As near as I could tell, those were zones of the Dallas/Fort Worth metroplex, each of which had obviously been assigned an office and probably a crew of reapers.

Would a rookie like Tod have an office?

The door at the end of the hall—at the northwest corner, unless my navigation was off—was a door marked "Administration."

Bingo.

I tiptoed down the hall, my heart pounding from nerves, like it had when I was still alive, until I realized that the more suspicious I looked, the greater my chance of being identified as a trespasser. But if I walked through the hall like I belonged there, maybe anyone who saw me would assume I was a reaper.

After all, who'd be stupid enough to break into reaper headquarters?

Well, me, obviously. But I tried the confidence approach anyway, and I stuck with it even when my pulse began to race like it hadn't since the day I'd died. I walked past two open doors, through which I caught glimpses of reapers at work. Or on break. I couldn't really tell the difference, since no one was swinging a scythe or donning a long black cape.

The other rooms were empty, and when I got to the end of the hall, I walked right through Levi's door, trusting that Luca was right. That the boss wasn't home.

When I saw the empty room, I actually exhaled with relief. Then I jogged across the good-size room and snatched the letter opener from its obviously custom-made wooden stand.

The moment my hand touched the metal, I knew Madeline had been right. It hummed against my flesh, more a feeling than a sound—the soul trapped inside calling out to me.

With the letter opener in my left hand, I held the broken dagger in my right, ready to make the switch. Until I realized I had no idea how to do that. Calling the soul from its current home should be easy, but leading it into the dagger? I wasn't sure how to do that. Normally, the soul would be attracted to the dagger on its own, because hellion-forged steel seems to call to displaced souls. But both the letter opener and my dagger were made of the same material, and I had no male *bean sidhe* around to help guide the soul.

Nor did I have time to stand around and think for very long. So, with my mouth closed, to keep most of the volume in, I let just a thin ribbon of my *bean sidhe* wail leak from my throat, calling to the displaced soul. That used to be a very difficult task for me. I'd only known my true species for eight months, and since then I'd learned what I could do mostly through trial and error. And a little trial by fire. And a lot of help from Harmony, the only other female *bean sidhe* I knew.

She's the one who'd taught me to call for a soul without letting loose the full power of my scream, which humans found painful, at the very least.

After less than a second, the soul within the letter opener began to leak out in a thin stream of foglike substance, attracted to the muffled version of my soul song. But I still had no idea how to get it into the dagger. I tried waving the severed blades through the ethereal stream of…soul, but nothing happened. My rough chopping motions sliced through the disembodied soul, which flowed right back together afterward.

Finally, when I heard footsteps outside Levi's office, and my pulse began to race in panic, I set the letter opener back on its stand and backed away from it, still singing softly for the soul. It followed me, trailing out from Levi's "conversation piece" until it hung in the air. When the soul, the dagger, and I were all as far from the desk as we could get without walking through the door, I let my wail fade into silence.

The soul hung in the air for just a second, and when I held the dagger up near it, the soul soaked into the hellion-forged steel on its own. To my immense relief.

I was about to blink out of reaper headquarters and into my room to wake Emma up and tell her the good news, when I heard voices headed my way through the door. Very familiar voices…

"Any leads?" Levi asked, and my heart nearly ruptured my sternum in an attempt to flee my body. If I didn't leave immediately, I would get caught. But before I could go, Tod answered his boss's question.

"No, but I still have a few more people to talk to. Have any of the souls turned up yet?"

"No. He's either selling them outside our district, or he's holding on to them. I've alerted the managers of all the closest districts, but no one's seen or heard from him so far."

They were talking about Thane. They *had* to be. Tod was tracking him. Was that why he'd been out of reach so much recently? Why hadn't he told me he was hunting down my mother's murderer? *My* murderer. I would have helped!

But then, that's probably exactly why he hadn't told me. To keep me from putting myself in danger. Tod never stood in my way, but he didn't go out of his way to show me new risks I could take, either. And I couldn't really blame him for that.

When the footsteps got too close to Levi's office, I blinked out reluctantly, wishing I could have heard the rest of the conversation.

In my room, I set the broken dagger on top of my dresser, then turned on my bedside lamp and shook my best friend's shoulder.

"Em. Wake up."

"Mmmm?" Her eyes fluttered open, then closed, then opened again. She pushed thin brown hair back from her face and sat up slowly. "What's wrong?"

"Nothing." I sank onto the edge of my own bed, facing her. "Nothing new, anyway. I got it." I couldn't help smiling from ear to ear. "I got a soul for Traci's baby."

"You did? How?" Em was wide-awake now. She tossed back her covers and crossed her legs beneath her on the mattress. "Where is it?"

I pointed at my dresser. "It's in the dagger. I kind of...took it from Levi's office. He doesn't know yet." I was hoping he wouldn't figure out the incubus soul was missing for a very long time, and that when he did, I wouldn't be the first suspect to come to mind. Hopefully lots of people were envious of his "conversation piece."

Em stared at the dagger, which was thin in profile from across the room. "How? Whose soul is it?"

"That's the best part. It's Beck's. Traci's baby can inherit his father's soul! No one else has to die so he can live!"

But Em's expression fell suddenly, and I knew what she was thinking, because I'd had a very similar thought. "Until he needs to feed." She suddenly seemed much less sure of what we'd agreed to without Traci's emotions there to syphon. "How many will die then?"

"None." I kicked off my shoes and folded my feet beneath me. "I can't let that happen. I'm hoping Traci's baby will be like Sabine, in a way." In several ways, actually. More ways than I really cared to think about. "He'll have to learn to eat without killing, but first he'll have to learn to control his charm long enough to find girls who actually, legitimately *want* to be with him. Maybe if we help Traci raise him—teach him—he'll be able to control his appetite like Sabine does. Maybe even *better* than Sabine does."

Maybe he wouldn't have to actually *touch* anyone to feed....

Tod didn't think that was much of a possibility, but he hadn't called it an impossibility, either. And I was personally acquainted with more living, breathing impossibilities than I could count at the moment. My very existence was one of them. As was Tod's. And it was worth a shot, if we were willing to make sure the teen incubus didn't accidentally hurt anyone while he was learning his limits.

"So...how do we...make it happen? How do we get the soul from your dagger into the baby?"

"I'm not sure, but I don't think we can do that until he's actually born. *Very shortly* after he's born. And I'm really hoping that Tod and I—" or my dad or Nash or my uncle "—can just install the soul in him, like we did for you."

Maybe it would be that easy.

Please let it be that easy...

"So, can I tell Traci?"

"No! She doesn't remember any of what we told her, remember? We'll have to make another disclosure, without Harmony's forget-me water, later on. Closer to the birth. For now, no one else needs to know about this. But I had to tell you. I couldn't let you worry about your nephew's soul for the next six months or so." Especially considering that she was still going to be worrying about her sister's health that whole time.

Wednesday at school was blissfully uneventful—for the first time all week, no hellions showed up at Eastlake. Sabine seemed to be playing nice for once, only feeding Sophie's and Emma's fears as necessary, careful not to take things too far, at least that I could tell.

Tod showed up early for lunch, so we had some alone time in the quad, visible to no one, while we waited for the rest of the group to show up. And I realized as we ate that it had been nearly twenty-four hours since the Hudson brothers had been intentionally snippy with one another.

Maybe their relationship was starting to heal.

With that thought on my mind and a relatively peaceful day behind me, I went home right after school, feeling additionally fortunate that the theater where I worked most afternoons had given me a couple of weeks off to mourn Emma, who'd worked there, too.

Maybe I could get Emily hired.... That would be at least one part of Em's life that I could give back to her.

Emma had stayed after school to meet with the guidance counselor—something to do with being a new student—and Sabine and Nash had promised to give her a ride home, so I had the house to myself for the first time in weeks.

I was reaching for the remote control, intending to scroll through the menu for an action movie, when my gaze caught on the blinking red light on our answering machine.

Weird. We hardly ever used the home phone, because both my dad and I had cell phones. Even Em had a new one, on our family plan.

I dropped the remote on the coffee table and crossed the room. That's the problem with answering machines and home phones—you have to actually get up to go use them. I pressed the button, and my dad's boss started speaking, asking if he was okay and why he hadn't called in sick. Or answered his cell.

I tried not to panic. It wasn't beyond the realm of possibility that my dad might skip work, considering everything he'd been through recently. Everything *I'd* put him through. It wasn't much like him not to at least call in sick, though.

"Dad?" I pressed the button to save his boss's message, then glanced into the kitchen to confirm that it was empty.

That he wasn't lying on the floor having a heart attack or convulsion. He was still relatively young for a *bean sidhe,* but you never know.…

"Hey, Dad? Are you here?" I checked the garage, the bathroom, and even my bedroom before heading into his room at the end of the hall. The last room in the house.

My father's bed was made. His curtains were closed. His clothes were folded and still sitting on the chair in the corner, where I'd left them that morning—I felt bad about him getting stabbed by a demon, so I was doing more chores than usual, but I drew the line at putting his clothes in his dresser.

I was about to leave the room when I noticed my dad's cell phone lying on his pillow. I picked it up and pressed a button to wake up the screen, then froze. Staring. I couldn't think past the horror of what I saw on the screen. My father's cell phone background had been changed to a picture of him, bound and evidently unconscious, sitting on the floor of a room I didn't recognize. Propped up on his lap was a sign written in unidentifiable and strangely gloppy ink—*please* let it be ink—in handwriting I didn't recognize.

The sign read, "Come and find me."

On the edge of the photo, less than a foot from his shoe, was a familiar green vine. I zoomed in on the photo to be sure. To confirm my worst fear.

Sure enough, the serrated edges of the leaves on that vine were bloodred. The thorns between the leaves were very thin and at least an inch long. Crimson creeper only grows in one place.

The Netherworld.

My shock lasted for about a minute and a half. Then there was another fraction of a moment when I wondered how on earth Avari had gotten to my father in the human world. But then I realized that "how" didn't matter. There would probably always be some minion with crossover potential willing to do the hellion's bidding for a price.

Avari's return to active-threat status was inevitable, and it always would be until we managed to turn the other hellions against him. But my plan obviously wasn't working fast enough.

Fear chased away my shock, and hot on its tail was a blinding fury unlike anything I'd ever felt. Avari and his hellion colleagues had already taken so much from me and from my friends and family. They weren't going to get my father, too.

Well, they weren't going to get to *keep* him, anyway.

Uncle Brendon was the first person I called. His phone rang in my ear three times, then Sabine answered. "Hey, Kaylee, what's up?"

"Why the hell are you answering my uncle's phone?" I could hear the anger in my voice. It echoed back at me over the line and from every corner of my own house. I regretted it—for once, Sabine wasn't the problem—but I couldn't control it.

"Whoa, rein it in. Just 'cause we're friends now doesn't mean you get to raise your voice at me."

"Sorry. I just… Where's Uncle Brendon?"

"He's kinda tied up with Sophie right now."

"Well, untie him. It's an emergency."

"Those must be going around. We're at the police station."

"Why? What did you do?"

"Why do you assume *I* did something?"

"Because you have an arrest record and two convictions? Because no one knows how or *if* you paid for your car? Because you tried to sell me and Emma into eternal torture in the Netherworld?"

"You know, eventually you're going to have to get over that. But you make a valid point."

"I made several valid points."

"Whatever. Sophie slashed some chick's tires in the parking lot, and the school cop caught her walking away from the scene with a pair of scissors in her hand. Rookie mistake."

"Why on earth would Sophie slash someone's tires?"

"Because the girl who owns the car hit on her boyfriend. And she mighta…kinda…been overwrought with jealousy."

"Any chance you had something to do with that?"

"I *might* have told the car owner in question that Luca was looking to…expand his social circle. And there's a *slight* chance I might have been a bit overzealous in my amplification of your cousin's worst fear—which, at the moment, is losing everyone she loves. Including Luca."

"Sabine! I swear, every time I think you're turning into a decent person, you do something to prove me wrong."

"I was trying to expedite the process. I had no idea she was capable of vandalism. But I have to say, I'm a little impressed. Which is why I let her dad and the cops think I slashed the tires, then made her carry the weapon. He's in there right now trying to influence us out of here."

"You took the blame because you're impressed that my cousin committed a crime?"

"Yeah. And I *might* be feeling a tiny bit of something similar to but definitely not the same as…guilt. Kind of."

I groaned into the phone and sank onto the couch again, with my elbows on my knees, my forehead resting in my free hand.

"Is Luca there, too?"

"Yeah. It's kind of a public spectacle. Sophie's totally humiliated, and Luca can't convince her that it'll be all right. And she's refusing to tell him why she did it." Sabine made a wet chomping noise in my ear, and I realized she was chewing gum. At the police station. Like being there was no big deal. "So, what's the emergency? What'd you need?"

"Backup. When you guys get out of there, come straight here. And bring my uncle." I hung up before she could ask why, and I had to admit, hanging up on Sabine felt kinda good.

Next I called Harmony. She didn't answer her phone either, which was really weird. Harmony always answered her cell except when she was working, and her shift at the hospital didn't start until eleven. It was only four in the afternoon.

I dialed Tod next. When he didn't answer, either, I got so frustrated I nearly threw my phone at the wall. Where the hell *was* everyone? Well, Em was still at school, but she wouldn't be able to help me locate my father anyway. Neither would Nash, but…there was no one left to call.

He answered on the first ring.

"Hey."

"I am so glad you answered your phone." I pushed hair away from my face and leaned back on the couch, suddenly hating the empty house I'd been thrilled with ten minutes earlier.

"You…are?" I could hear the confusion in his voice and the road noise in the background. He was in a car.

"Yeah. I can't get a hold of anyone else. Where are you going?"

"I'm picking up Emma in Sabine's car. Bina's at the police station with—"

"I know. I just talked to her."

"Didn't you just say people aren't answering their phones?"

"She answered my uncle's. Hey, have you talked to Tod today?"

His silence stretched over the wireless line between us, and

I realized I'd said the wrong thing. I was getting really good at that. "Is that all you want? You called me looking for Tod?"

"No, that's not all I want. But, yes, I called looking for him. It's important, Nash."

"I haven't talked to him since lunch. Why?"

"I need help, and I can't find him. Or your mom."

"She crossed over."

Harmony was in the Netherworld? "Why?"

"She's looking for some kind of herb, or root, or leaf, or something to help Traci keep her baby. Which is a really dumbass idea, you know. Why on earth would you want to bring another incubus into the world when the last one killed you?"

"It's more complicated than that. And it's not my decision." I exhaled, trying to decide exactly how close we'd gotten to true friendship. "Nash, I need help. Not that you owe me anything, so it's totally okay if you don't want to help me, but I'm asking. In fact, I'm kind of begging."

"I'm in." He didn't even hesitate. "What's wrong?"

"Avari took my dad."

"Seriously?" I heard the squeal of his tires on pavement as he stomped on the brake. "How? Is he okay?"

"I don't know. I don't have any of the answers, but I have to get him back."

"It's a trap. You know this is a trap, right?"

"I know. Which is why I need help." If I went after him alone, I was as good as dead. Well, dead*er,* anyway.

"Okay, I'm coming. Let me turn around…"

"No, get Em first, then meet me at my house. Please. I have to find him before we can go after him, anyway. Maybe by the time I manage that, we'll have more people willing to follow us into the breach."

"Oh." I could hear the disappointment in his voice. "Okay.

Yeah. I'll get Em, and we'll meet at your place in half an hour."

"Thanks, Nash. Just…thank you."

"Anytime, Kaylee. That much hasn't changed."

11

I stood alone in my high school cafeteria, feeling like a fool. The room was empty, but I was incorporeal anyway, just in case. Nash and Emma were probably pulling out of the parking lot at that very moment, but they had no idea I was there. I couldn't tell them, because they'd never let me do what I was planning. What, under normal circumstances, I would never even have considered.

You need only bleed and use my name.

I understood the words but not their meaning. I'd had no idea hellions could even *be* summoned until Ira had told me. In fact, I wasn't sure exactly *what* he'd told me. But I knew how to bleed.

It took a minute of searching through commercial-grade stainless steel drawers in the kitchen, but I finally found a drawer full of knives. I selected the shortest—a paring knife—and slid the drawer closed with the clang of metal. Then I sat on the floor, my legs crossed in front of me, and silently hoped I was doing the right thing. And that whatever summoning involved, it wouldn't put me in danger of being killed or captured in the next few minutes.

Then I sliced open my palm.

It was a small cut. In the movies, they always make a huge gash whenever they need blood to summon the forces of evil, but that had always felt like overkill to me. Surely evil doesn't care how dramatic your blood loss is, right?

In the movies, it never really looks like those gruesome self-inflicted cuts hurt, but in real life—even for the undead—it hurt. A lot.

I set the knife down and let blood well up into my palm until there was a pool the width of a dime. It was slow going, until I realized my heart wasn't beating, which meant my blood wasn't flowing. Not very quickly, anyway. So I concentrated on making my heart function, and blood collected faster.

Then I made a fist and let it drip onto the tile floor in front of me, because I wasn't sure what else to do with the blood. Or what exactly Ira meant when he told me to "use" his name.

"Ira."

My voice didn't echo, because I was inaudible to human ears and thus most of the physical plane. So I wasn't really surprised when nothing happened.

"Ira." I tried it again, audible to the whole world, had anyone been there to hear me. That time there was a slight echo of my voice in the empty room. But no hellion appeared.

"Come on! You promised you'd…be summonable!" And hellions couldn't lie.

My frustration and anger built as I stared at the blood still dripping slowly from my hand onto the floor. There were a couple of little red squiggles, because my hand had jiggled. They almost looked like…

Letters.

And suddenly I understood. He hadn't told me to *say* his name. He'd told me to *use* his name.

I unclenched my fist and dipped my forefinger into the blood. Then I wrote his name in capital letters, several inches above the small pool of my own blood.

"Ira." I wasn't sure if saying it again would really help, but I wasn't taking any chances.

For a moment, nothing happened. Then, out of nowhere, the hellion appeared in front of me, his denim-clad knees level with my eyes.

I looked up. And up. And up. Ira was *tall.* He was also the youngest-looking hellion I'd ever seen, and it bothered me more than I could even comprehend that I actually had a basis for that comparison.

"I knew you would call." The hellion dropped effortlessly into a squat in front of me, and I lurched backward when he was suddenly staring into my eyes. "Blue. Nice, but they'd look better in red. If you're ever mine, your eyes will be red. It's a painful procedure, of course—not that it has to be, but it will be—yet utterly worth the effort. You would look brilliant in red."

While I gaped at him in shock, the hellion sank onto the floor in front of me, leaving his name and the small pool of my blood between us. He crossed his legs, and I was almost certain he was mirroring my position on purpose.

"Ira?"

"Of course. No one else can come when I'm summoned by name. That's how it works." He must have seen the confusion in my face. Or else he was reading my thoughts—a possibility that terrified me, but that I couldn't safely rule out. "This is your first summoning?"

I nodded, nearly mesmerized by the dark red veins in his

solid-black eyes. By his shoulder-length hair, so deeply red it was almost black. He looked like an evil rock star. In jeans.

I'd never seen a hellion in jeans.

"That's because none of the other hellions you've dealt with are strong enough to appear when called. They don't like admitting that—it makes them look weak—so they simply refrain from mentioning the possibility."

"Avari is too weak for…summoning?" My fear was back, and it was rapidly bleeding into true terror. Avari could snap me in half with two fingers. He could breathe in my general direction and freeze me solid. If he was too weak for this, then just how powerful was Ira?

The hellion frowned, but no lines appeared on his broad, clear forehead. "Oh, no, my little fury, don't be scared. I enjoy your fear, true, but I'd much rather have your anger."

"I don't give a shit what you want."

"Ah, that's better." Somehow, his smile made him look even scarier. And…oddly satisfied, for a hellion of rage. "And true, no doubt. Because this is about what *you* want, isn't it?"

"How does this work?" I wasn't going to say another word until I understood just how much danger I'd put myself in. Had I just unleashed a hellion into the human world, with no restrictions? "What exactly does 'summoning' mean?"

"Think of this like a phone call, only we're talking face-to-face. Convenient, huh?"

"So, you're not really here?"

"Of course I'm here. But because you summoned me, and I accepted your invitation, I can't touch you without your permission. And I can't interact with anyone else while I'm here."

"How do I send you back?"

"Tired of me already?"

I nodded. "Before you even got here."

Ira chuckled, and I saw that his tongue was as dark red as

his hair. Nearly black. "All you have to do is swipe my name from the floor." He leaned toward me, over the mess between us. Like he'd whisper a secret. "But you should know that I can end this appointment as well, so you may not want to truly anger me until you've gotten what you want from me."

I had no intention of truly angering him. Ever. At all. Under any circumstances.

"So, what can I do for you today, Kaylee Cavanaugh?"

"Take me to my father."

"Of course. The price is your immortal soul."

"No."

Ira didn't look surprised in the slightest by my refusal. "This is not a negotiation, little fury. That's the price for what you've asked for."

"Well, I can't pay it."

"You can. But you won't." He frowned, staring down into my eyes, as if to confirm the statement he'd just made. "Fine. If the price is too high, ask for something less expensive."

"I don't suppose you'd bring my father back to the human world for me, alive and as unharmed as he is now, for anything less than my soul. Right?"

"That is correct. You're taking this negotiation in the wrong direction."

"I thought we weren't negotiating."

"We're not negotiating a new price for your original request. But each task comes with its own price. Think smaller, unless you're ready to pay a big bill."

"Can you tell me where my father is right now? Do you know where Avari's keeping him?"

"I do know, and I can tell you."

"How much."

"A taste of your anger."

"A taste? What does that involve?"

"Just a kiss, little fury."

"A kiss?" *Eww! Seriously?* "Does that mean the same thing in the Netherworld as it does here?"

What little I knew about kissing on the other side of the world barrier, I'd learned from Addison and Nash, who'd both kissed hellions as part of a business arrangement—an exchange of service for payment.

But for me, kissing meant Tod, and private moments, and delicious tingles deep down in my stomach and sometimes lower. Kissing meant sharing something vital and intimate with someone I loved with all my soul, and I had no intention of sharing that with anyone else, much less with a hellion.

"As far as I know," he said. "But we're not in the Nether, are we? Might that fact broaden our options a little?"

"No." No way in *hell.* Chill bumps rose on my arms, and nausea churned in my stomach.

"I have a boyfriend."

"I fail to see the relevance."

I frowned. "He's relevant because I love him. He's the only one I kiss. I'm not going to hurt him."

Ira's eyes narrowed with impatience. "Human adolescent drama doesn't appeal to me until it involves homicidal rage. Does your boyfriend have that kind of destructive potential?"

My frown deepened. "Are you asking if he'd kill you for kissing me?"

The hellion laughed out loud, a deep, creepy sound of malevolent amusement. "Killing me isn't an option, though I suspect I would find the attempt highly entertaining. I'm asking if he would kill *you.*"

Over a kiss? "Skimming right over the fact that I'm already dead…no." Nothing in the world—in either world—could make Tod want to kill me. He'd already proved that.

But losing him because I'd kissed a demon might make my afterlife not worth living....

"Then this conversation is already starting to bore me. Make a choice. Your father's location or your boyfriend's 'feelings.'"

"I'm not going to kiss you. There must be some other way."

His dark brows rose. "It has to be a physical exchange, little fury. Perhaps you'd like to suggest an alternative method of connection?"

That nausea swelled into an all-out roil of disgust twisting inside me. "About this kiss..." Definitely the lesser of two evils—I hoped with all my heart that Tod would understand that, even as I hated myself for thinking it. "I need specifics. What kind of kiss?"

"My mouth and your mouth. And my tongue, of course. For that taste of your anger." He leaned forward again and winked at me with one of his creepy red-veined black eyes. "I promise you'll enjoy it."

"I highly doubt that."

"What's your answer, little fury?"

"One kiss? Mouth-to-mouth? No biting or taking of any liberties whatsoever?"

"You're a smart little thing, aren't you?"

Only smart enough to know that everything has a price. A horrible, unthinkable, irreversible price. "I've learned to take nothing for granted."

That time his frown looked truly irritated. "Remind me to thank Avari for that."

"Take your taste. Then back the hell off."

"As you like, little fury."

My pulse raced in fear. My skin crawled at the thought of him touching me, and my heart ached at the sudden brutal understanding of what I'd agreed to. It took every drop of courage left in my veins to keep me from swiping my hand over the blood on the floor and running faster and farther than I'd ever gone in my life.

I concentrated on my dad. On the thought of bringing him home. Of keeping him safe. And I kept my eyes wide open, even though Ira seemed to be enjoying whatever he saw in them.

Instead of leaning toward me, he dipped one finger into the pool of blood between us, careful not to smudge his name. Then he reached for me, and before I realized what he intended, he ran his finger over my lower lip, coating it in my blood.

The moment he touched me, anger swelled inside me, hot and bright. Raging almost out of control. I was drowning in it. Choking on it. He traced my upper lip with what remained of the blood on his finger, and that anger inside me tried to burst through my chest.

When he could clearly see the rage churning in my irises, he leaned forward and slid one hand behind my neck. He pulled me closer, and we met in the middle over the blood on the floor.

His mouth touched mine, and every grievance I'd ever harbored was suddenly there in the front of my mind. All of them at once. Everything from the boy who'd pushed me off the swings on my first day of kindergarten to the hatred I'd felt for Sabine the day I met her.

His lips opened, and his tongue slid into my mouth. I tasted my own blood, but beneath that, I tasted him. I expected him to taste like anger. Like rage. But Ira tasted like calm. Like peace, perfect and still. And as we kissed, he pulled the anger from me. He sucked it *out* of me. Yet the fury burning within me never abated.

My cup ran over, and though he drank and drank, kissing me deeper and deeper, the fount of rage inside me only seemed to swell, and I couldn't pull away because I needed him to take it. All of it. I couldn't exist with that much bitter fury storming inside me, so I gave it to him, and I kept giving.

And Ira kept taking.

I didn't come back to myself until he made a noise. A deep moan of satisfaction against my lips. Somehow inside my mouth. That's when I realized what was happening. What I'd done. And what it damn well better buy me.

I shoved him away and his hand trailed around my neck and over my chin as he let me go. "Enough!" I swiped the back of my uncut hand across my lips, and it came away bloody.

"Oh, that will *never* be enough for me, little fury. But it's enough to make your hellion of avarice *green* with envy. Which will then produce hate, maybe for you, certainly for me. And the only thing more powerful than righteous anger is the rage of a hellion."

"You got what you wanted. Now pay up."

"I'd say there's no need to get angry, but we both know I like it." He chuckled again, then licked my blood from his dark, dark lips. "Your father is being held in the basement of the local insane asylum. Are they still called that? But you won't be able to retrieve him. And when you return for my help again, the price will be higher...." Ira winked one black eye at me and swiped his palm across the floor between us, smudging his name into a smear of my blood.

Then he faded from the human world, right in front of me.

I shuddered with revulsion and wished desperately for something to wash the taste of my own blood from my mouth. I closed my eyes, and silent tears slid down my cheeks. Then I sucked in a deep breath and made myself still. Completely motionless, as only the dead can do. No heartbeat. No pulse.

No breathing. A moment of self-imposed, absolute calm while I tried to control the anger Ira had left coursing through me.

It didn't work. In the end, I could only ride the wave while the pressure built inside me, pushing me toward an edge I didn't know how to come back from.

When I realized I couldn't just bury that much anger, I opened my eyes, swiped my hand over the blood finally starting to dry on the tile floor, just in case, then blinked into my own bathroom.

My house still felt empty when I arrived—there were no voices, and Styx was there to greet me almost instantly, which she wouldn't have done if she was standing watch over guests or intruders. So I rinsed my bloody hand in the bathroom sink, blotted it dry around the cut, then dug beneath the counter for a large bandage.

I didn't even glance in the mirror, because I was afraid of what I'd find. Afraid that I'd see the rage that had drawn Ira to me. The rage he'd *fed,* damn it, and that if I saw that in myself, I'd know he was right about me. That I was changing. That I was fighting for revenge, rather than justice.

Instead, I turned and stomped into the hallway—and ran smack into Tod, who was scowling at his phone. "Hey, Kaylee, I have a missed call from you and five nasty voice mails from Nash. What's going—" He looked up from his phone and his eyes widened. "What happened?" His gaze dropped to my chin, and he shoved his phone into his pocket, then turned my face to the right for a better look. "Is that blood? Are you okay?"

"Where the hell were you?" Tears filled my eyes, and I spoke through teeth clenched to stop the flow of more angry words I knew I had no right to speak. Tod wasn't the problem. I was angry. I wasn't thinking straight.

"I was in the Netherworld. They don't have cell towers. What happened?"

With one glance at the concern in his eyes, my anger fled and guilt washed over me.

"Avari took my dad. Again." I let him lead me into the bathroom. "I have to go after him, but I don't think I can get to him on my own without going through Avari, so I called everyone, but Nash was the only one who answered. Well, Sabine answered my uncle's phone, but they can't come because Sophie committed her first criminal act, and the police aren't a forgive-and-forget kind of operation."

When I stopped talking I realized I stood in front of the mirror, where Tod was wetting a rag at the sink. Which is when I noticed that blood streaked the lower right side of my face, from where Ira's hand had trailed down my chin. And that more of it was smeared around my mouth, like a clown's lipstick, in spite of my attempt to wipe it off.

I didn't just look angry. I looked *scary.*

"Kaylee, I'm so sorry." Tod wrung out the rag and started wiping blood from the back of my jaw. "Whose is this? What happened?"

"I summoned Ira."

His hand went still, and his irises churned with tight, twisting streaks of cobalt fear. "You *what?* How? Why?"

"I summoned him with my blood—this is all mine—and his name. Because I couldn't get a hold of anyone else who could help me."

"Please tell me you did *not* make a deal with a hellion of wrath."

"I'm not going to lie to you."

"Oh, Kaylee." He sank onto the edge of the tub, the rag in his hand forgotten as he stared up at me in true fear. "What did you *do?*"

"I asked him to get my dad back safely, but the price was too high. He wanted my soul. I said no."

Tod slumped with relief for a second, then sat straighter and pushed pale curls back from his forehead. "So what's with the blood?"

"He said he'd tell me where my dad was being held for a smaller fee."

"What fee?" There was no end to the depth of his voice in those two words. They were a bottomless chasm of fear and dismay and dread, and I stood on the brink, poised to fall in. Balancing on the edge. "What did you do?"

"He just wanted a kiss." My tears finally fell, and they burned all the way down my cheeks. "He wanted a taste of my anger, so he wiped my own blood on my mouth and kissed me. And I let him."

Tod blinked at me. His arms rested against his legs, his hands hanging between his knees, and his eyes were *so still.* Still like true death. And for the first time since I'd met him, he looked like I might have expected a reaper to look. Like death itself, he was both the object that could not be moved and the force that could not be resisted, and the longer he stared at me without reacting—without showing a single ripple of emotion beneath his frozen-lake eyes—the deeper my heart ached, until I thought it would split open and fall apart.

"Please say something." I sank onto the closed toilet seat, my knees inches from his. "I'm so sorry. I didn't know what else to do. I would take it back if I could, but I'm not going to lie about it, and… Are you mad?"

"You kissed a hellion."

My heart pumped once, painfully, then stopped. "Yes, but it wasn't like that. It wasn't like kissing you—"

"I sure as hell hope not!" A single thread of ice-blue anger twisted through his irises, then they burst into a dizzying range of shades from cornflower to cobalt, displaying a storm of emotion like I'd never seen. Anger. Fear. Jealousy. Confusion. Frustration. They were all there, but the scariest of all was grief, as if he'd lost something he couldn't get back.

As if *we'd* lost something…

He stood, and I stood in front of him, as if I could possibly block a reaper's path if he wanted to leave. "No. Tod, wait." I put one hand on his chest, feeling for his heartbeat, but it wasn't there. "It wasn't like that. I swear on my afterlife. I swear on my *soul.* It wasn't a kiss like people kiss. I don't think hellions even truly understand why people kiss. This was an exchange of information."

"It was an exchange of saliva." That churning continued in his eyes, and my heart shattered when I saw a midnight twist of disappointment.

"No!" I grabbed his hand—if he tried to blink out, he'd have to take me with him. "Well, yes, but it wasn't about saliva. It was about blood. My blood, and the anger it carried. That's what he wanted."

"That's *part* of what he wanted." Instead of pulling his hand away, Tod squeezed mine, like everything important he wanted to say could be read in his grip, when I couldn't make any sense of what I saw in his eyes. "He wanted to taste your anger, but he also wanted to cause more of it. And he did, right? Making you kiss him pissed you off, didn't it? It's sure as hell pissing *me* off, and he probably wanted that, too. Nothing hellions want is simple, Kaylee. Nothing they take is simple, either, and they always take more than you realize you're giving."

Suddenly the maelstrom churning in his eyes collapsed into a single sapphire coil of pain. "I can't stand the thought of him touching you." His free hand rose, and his thumb brushed the fullest part of my lower lip, still crusted with dried blood.

"Kissing you… I don't even know what he looks like, but I can't stop seeing it."

I tried to breathe and realized I couldn't. "I'm sorry." More tears trailed down my cheeks, and I took the rag from the sink where he'd dropped it. The cloth was cold now, but I swiped at my face furiously, scrubbing the blood off without the benefit of the mirror, trying to erase what I'd done. "I'm *so* sorry. I wish I could take it back, but I can't, and I had to do *something.* I can't just leave my dad there, but I'm *so sorry* for how I paid, and if I lose you—"

"Kaylee. Stop." Tod took the rag and stared at it for a second. Then he used one clean corner to gently wipe the blood I'd missed from around my lips. "You're not going to lose me. I'm not happy about what happened, but losing you would make that worse, not better. You're *never* going to lose me, and *certainly* not because one of hell's ambassadors bullied you into kissing him."

My heart started beating again, and the sudden rush of my pulse made me light-headed. Tod wiped the last of the blood from my mouth, then leaned forward and kissed me, and I let the feel of him and the taste of him—of all things good and safe and strong—drive the memory of that other kiss from my head.

"Just…in the future, save all the good stuff for me, okay?" he whispered into my hair, holding me so tight I couldn't have breathed if I'd needed to.

"It's yours. All of it. All of *me.*" I put my head on his shoulder and clutched handfuls of his shirt. "I'm all yours."

That was the only thing I could see clearly, when I tried to picture forever.

When Tod finally pulled away, it was only so that he could see my eyes. "We're going to get your dad back. I'm sorry I was out of reach when this happened. I was looking for Thane."

"Oh, yeah." *That's* why he'd been in the Netherworld.

"What does that mean?" He frowned, studying my face. "You knew?"

"I went to reaper headquarters last night and I overheard. I didn't mean to, but once I figured out Levi had given you a special assignment, I was kind of glad. We *need* to catch Thane. And I figured you didn't tell me because Levi wouldn't let you, right? This is a secret assignment?"

Tod exhaled and held my gaze. "Kay, this was my idea. Levi thought he'd be too far away by now, and we'd have to wait on a sighting from one of the other districts, but I asked him to let me look into it. At first, I didn't find anything, but then early this morning I found one of the souls he took off with after Emma died."

"Where?" I wasn't sure I'd processed everything he'd said yet, but that question couldn't wait. "Where is he?"

"I haven't found Thane yet, but he sold one of the souls in

the Netherworld, one district over. I'm not sure what he got for it, but that's proof that he didn't leave the area immediately. He may still be close." Tod smiled, and his whole face lit up with the possibility shining in his eyes. "We're going to catch him, Kaylee, and he's going to pay for his part in… everything."

"Why didn't you tell me you requested this?"

"I wanted it to be a surprise. I wanted to catch him as a sort of late birthday present. Because your party…well, it kinda sucked, and you deserve to get something you really want for your birthday. Something other than death, horror, and mayhem."

"I *have* what I really want." I grabbed a handful of his tee and pulled him closer for another kiss. "And I don't like secrets."

"Not a secret. A *surprise.* Similar meaning—completely different tone and intent." He grinned. "I wanted to *surprise* you. What were you doing at headquarters, anyway?"

Well, crap. Tod would have been the first—possibly only—person I told after Emma, but timing was definitely not on my side lately. "I…um…may have taken Beck's soul back from Levi to give to Traci's baby."

"You *what?*" Tod sat on the edge of the tub and ran one hand through his curls, and when he met my gaze again, his irises were twisting slowly in frustration. "For someone who doesn't like secrets, you sure keep a lot of them. Does my boss know you stole his letter opener?"

"If he hasn't said anything to you, I'm guessing he doesn't know. But I didn't take the letter opener, I just took the soul. And I wasn't stealing it, I was taking it back. The way I see it, several people have a legitimate claim to that soul, including me. But Levi's not one of them. It should go to Beck's son. Traci and her baby deserve a chance, and that soul is the very *least* that bastard owes them."

"Kaylee, I sympathize with Traci. I really do. But you can't get involved with another incubus. It's not safe."

"I can't *not* get involved with this incubus. His mother may not even be alive when he reaches his first fertile period, but I will. Traci deserves a chance to raise her son, but the rest of the world deserves not to be preyed on by him. So, like it or not, I'm involved." I shrugged. "And honestly, I can't swear that I'm not going to get involved in other crazy Netherworld chaos between now and forever. Eternity's a long time." I hesitated, searching his eyes while I took a deep, nervous breath. "Are you still with me?"

He took my hand, and that tension inside me eased, just a little bit. "I meant it when I said forever, Kay. You've been mixed up in crazy Netherworld chaos since the day we met, and I kind of like knowing that even if we live another thousand years, we'll never be bored, in any sense of the word." The heat in his eyes hinted at double entendre, and I couldn't resist a smile. "But I wouldn't mind a heads-up next time you decide to jump into the crazy end of the pool."

"Fair enough. Though you should probably know there isn't really a not-crazy end of the—"

The front door flew open and smashed into the wall, and Tod and I both turned toward the sound as Styx began growling furiously. "Kaylee!" Nash called.

Tod groaned. "You left the front door unlocked?"

"That was probably Emma. I don't use doors much anymore. Besides, everyone who wants to kill me is on another plane of existence." I shrugged. "The front door doesn't seem like a particularly meaningful barrier."

"Well, I hope you've learned your lesson." He said it loud

enough that I knew no one else could hear him. As they couldn't yet hear me.

"Kaylee?" It took me a second to recognize Emma's voice, even though I'd had two weeks to get used to it. Because it wasn't Emma's voice. It was Lydia's.

"Back here, guys," I called, and both sets of footsteps hurried our way. "I'm fine."

Nash stepped into the bathroom doorway, nearly tripping over Styx, who came to growl at him, and I saw Em over his shoulder. His attention narrowed on the rag his brother still held, then rose to meet my gaze. "Then what's with the blood?"

"When you cross the bridge, you have to pay the toll…."

I squeezed past him into the hall, and Emma fell into step beside me. "What bridge?"

"She made a deal with Ira to find out where Avari's holding her dad," Tod explained, and I looked up to find him waiting for us in the living room, one hand on the dead bolt on the front door. "His price was her blood."

"Blood? How much? Are you okay?" Em looked terrified.

I showed her the bandage on my hand. "Just a little. He only wanted a…taste."

"And he told you where your dad is?"

"Yeah. Avari's holding him in the Netherworld version of Lakeside. In the basement. I'm assuming he considers that some kind of irony."

"Or a joke," Nash said. "Please tell me you didn't go into the Netherworld by yourself to make this deal."

"Nope. I summoned Ira. He came to me." I held my hand up again, showing off the bandage. "Thus the blood."

"You *summoned* him?" Nash said. "What does that even mean?"

"He came here?" Emma asked before I could answer Nash. "They can cross over again?"

"No." I frowned. "Well, yes, but only because I summoned him with my blood and his name. While he's summoned, he can only interact with me, and I can get rid of him just by wiping his name off whatever I wrote it on. He can send himself back the same way."

"So you think that makes it safe?" Nash demanded. "Please tell me you don't think what you just did was safe!"

"Of course not. Dealing with a hellion is never safe, but I didn't have much of a choice. Avari's latest game appears to be evil hide-and-seek. That way I don't just suffer once I get to the Netherworld—I also suffer while I track my father down."

"I didn't know hellions could be summoned," Em said, and I could only shrug. I hadn't known, either.

"Most of them can't." Tod sank onto the arm of the couch. "Only the most powerful can cross over when called, and then only for very short periods. Once the blood used to summon them dries completely, they get sucked back into the Netherworld. And Kaylee's right. There's very little a summoned hellion can do in the human world. It's mostly used for face-to-face communication and…exchanges."

"Exchanges?" Nash looked suspicious, so I ignored his question.

"So, that means Ira really is more powerful than Avari?"

"My guess would be way more powerful. He's a hellion of wrath, and wrath is one of the oldest, most primal emotions."

"Weird." I frowned. "He looked pretty young."

"So does Levi," Tod pointed out. "But then, compared to Ira, Levi's practically still in utero."

"So, how much trouble are we in with this new hellion?" Emma asked. "If he's that powerful, maybe we should try drawing him out, as well. I mean, is he strong enough to just…squish Avari for us?"

"I don't know. What I do know is that he wouldn't do that for free, and I'm not willing to pay the price he'd ask. And I'm not eager to spend any more time with him, because just hearing his voice makes me angry. Touching him is even worse—that makes me truly furious, about things I haven't even thought about in years."

Nash scowled. "You touched him?"

"He touched *me.* That was part of the price. And when he touched me, I couldn't think about anything except how furious I was about every time anyone has ever been…wronged. And I think he could see those times. All of them. I think he tasted them in my blood. Or maybe sucked them right out of my head when we kissed."

"You kissed him?" The horror clear in Emma's wide-eyed expression echoed in her voice as well.

"Not by choice. It was weird, though, because he didn't taste like wrath. He tasted like peace. Like calm. But he was *hungry* for wrath, like he devours every drop he ever tastes immediately and is then starving for more."

Tod scowled. "Feel free to stop telling me what hellions taste like."

"She kissed someone else." Nash wasn't exactly smiling at his brother, but he didn't look entire unhappy, either. "Wow. I wonder what *that* felt like?"

"That felt like Kaylee sacrificing a part of herself to help her father. And if memory serves, she's not the only one in this room who's ever kissed a hellion. Were *your* motives so pure?"

"Is that always going to be your default insult?"

"Okay, both of you calm down, please." I was worried enough about the anger I couldn't seem to purge. I couldn't deal with more brother drama on top of everything else.

Someone knocked on the door, and Nash headed into the kitchen—hopefully to collect his temper—while I peeked through the curtains to see my uncle's car parked in the driveway. I unlocked the front door, and Sabine walked in without being invited, followed by my cousin and Luca. My uncle brought up the rear.

"So, what'd we miss?" Sabine dropped onto the couch.

Nash returned from the kitchen with a bottle of water and took the cushion next to her. "Avari has Kaylee's dad, and she kissed a hellion to find out where he's being held."

"What?" Uncle Brendon demanded, and I couldn't tell which part he was more upset about. "Why didn't you call me?"

"I did. You were bailing Sophie out of jail. Or something like that."

"Sabine was the perpetrator. Sophie was just an accomplice after the fact." My uncle sank into my father's recliner and ran one hand through his thick brown hair.

I glanced at Sophie to see if she'd correct him or let Sabine's lie by implication stand. She stared at her feet and said nothing. But I couldn't really blame her for not owning up to that one. It was Sabine's fault, at least in part, for playing so loose with her fears and insecurities.

And for letting her carry scissors, my cousin's well-established weapon of choice.

"It's been one hell of a day." Uncle Brendon looked up and glanced around the room. "Where's Harmony? Did you call her?"

"Yeah, but she's in the Netherworld, gathering ingredients for—" I glanced at Em, then decided to keep the details quiet, because I wasn't sure how much everyone else knew about Traci's predicament "—something. Should we go look for her?"

Both Nash and Tod started to nod, but my uncle shook his head. "No. She's careful, and she knows how best to get in and out without being seen. If we go after her, we're just increasing the chance of her—or us—getting caught." Which would be worse for Nash, my uncle, Luca, and Em, who couldn't come back on their own.

Not that I had plans to take Em or Luca into the Netherworld anytime soon. Or even Sophie, though she'd demonstrated the ability to come and go on her own. Once. But once wasn't enough to prove she could stay calm under pressure or cross over without unleashing her full scream—the only trait she seemed to have inherited from her father's side of the family.

She could wail well enough to cross over, with the required intent, but she was not a *bean sidhe.* Her screams would not sing for souls. She could not restore life.

She'd be a sitting duck in the Netherworld. Or an enticing piece of bait…

I shook my head, shaking the thought loose before it could take root. I was not going to use my own cousin for demon bait. Even if she sometimes deserved it.

"Harmony will be back on her own, and the best thing we can do is wait for her."

"But what if Avari has her?" Nash demanded. "He has Kaylee's dad. How do we know he hasn't taken my mom?"

My uncle stood. "If he had your mom, he'd tell us. It does him no good to take her hostage and not tell us how to bargain for her freedom."

"What if she's not a hostage?" Sophie asked, and Emma sank slowly onto the arm of the couch next to Nash in obvious horror. "We weren't hostages when he took us. What if he has Harmony but doesn't intend to give her back?"

Nash stood. "I'm going after her."

Uncle Brendon rolled his eyes. "You can't get there on your own, son."

Nash turned to Sabine. "Take me. Please."

"Nash..." She took his hand, and I realized I'd never seen her look at anyone else the way she looked at him. Like it broke her heart not to be able to give him whatever he wanted. "I can't. It's not safe."

"I know!" He pulled his hand from her grip. "That's why I have to go find her."

"Nash, I want to protect her just as much as you and Tod do," my uncle said. Tod looked skeptical, but Nash looked furious. "But if anyone knows how to get in and out of the Netherworld without getting hurt, it's your mother. She's been gathering stuff for her homemade remedies since she was younger than you are. I'm sure she's fine."

"If she's not, I'm holding *you* responsible." Nash stomped into the kitchen and out into the backyard. The door slammed shut behind him, and Sabine stared at it like she wanted to go after him but knew better.

Tod crossed his arms over his chest. "One hour." His voice was calm and quiet, and betrayed no hint of indecision. "If she's not back in one hour, I'll go after her myself."

No one argued with Tod.

"Okay. Until then, we need to decide on a plan to get Aiden back. How did you find out Avari took him?"

I dug my dad's phone from my pocket, woke up the screen, then handed it to my uncle.

His face paled instantly. "Well, that does seem...certain. Is that crimson creeper near his foot?"

"Yup."

"And you know where he's being held?"

"The basement of the Netherworld version of Lakeside."

"Buried beneath the mental hospital. *That's* not creepy," Emma mumbled.

Sophie flinched. "Did you really kiss a hellion to get that information?"

I met her gaze as boldly as I could, considering that I was still *incredibly* creeped out by what I'd done. "Everything has a price, Sophie. Someone has to pay."

"Okay. Back on topic." My uncle headed into the kitchen, aiming right for the cabinet over the microwave. "We're going to need two teams. A small one, to cause a distraction, and another one, a little larger, to get Aiden out."

"I'm going to turn myself in." I said it softly, but every head in the room swiveled to stare at me. When my uncle turned, he held the bottle of whiskey my father had confiscated from Nash the month before.

"No, you're not," Tod said. "Even if any of us was willing to let that happen, it won't help your dad. We want to get him out, not leave you behind."

"I know. This is a trap. I'm going to pretend to fall for it, while the rest of you get my father the hell out of there. You and Sabine can cross my uncle over." I glanced into the kitchen to find Uncle Brendon pouring whiskey into a short glass of ice. "The two of you should be able to carry him if he can't walk, and Sabine can get you out if anything goes wrong or Tod can't cross with you both. Two who can't cross, two who can." That was the safest ratio.

"No," Tod said, and I glanced at him in surprise. He'd never refused to help. "I'm staying with you. Nash can go with them. He can help lift your dad if necessary."

"But I can cross. My dad, uncle, and Nash can't. They need you more."

"He's right, Kay-bear," Uncle Brendon said. "No one goes in alone."

I stood, my irritation mounting. "That doesn't make any sense. Sabine can't get you, my dad, and Nash out all at once, especially if my dad's still unconscious. You need someone else who can cross over!"

"And we have someone." Luca pulled back the living room curtain to reveal Harmony's car pulling up to the curb in front of my house. As I watched, relieved, she got out and locked her car, then started up the driveway.

The back door opened, and Nash came in, ignoring Styx when she came to growl at him, again. "I heard a car."

Harmony knocked three times, then opened the front door, and, I swear, Nash nearly melted with relief. She stopped in the doorway, sliding her phone into her purse, and glanced around at everyone, surprised to be the center of attention before she was even in the house. "Any news about Aiden? And why are you all staring at me?"

"We thought Avari got to you, too." Nash hugged his mom, then shoved his hands into his pockets, looking both sheepish and relieved at the same time.

Tod ran one hand through his hair, then gave his mother a hug. "Please don't disappear at the same time someone else goes missing. That's very misleading."

She patted his back, then let him go. "I'm fine. I know my way around the Netherworld, sweetie."

Uncle Brendon shook his head, but he was all smiles. "I tried to tell them…." He opened his arms, and she walked into his embrace. Then they kissed, and Nash groaned while the rest of us averted our eyes.

"Dad, gross!" Sophie made a show of covering her eyes, and Luca laughed.

"Okay, so do we have a plan?" Harmony took the glass of whiskey from Brendon, made a face, then dumped it straight down the sink. "And by the way, this is not the time for…

this." She held up the glass for everyone to see—including Brendon, who frowned but didn't argue.

"The plan—" I said, and people gathered around while I filled Harmony in "—if you're up for a return trip to the Netherworld this soon, is for you and Sabine to take Uncle Brendon and Nash to get my dad while I distract Avari. By pretending to turn myself in."

She crossed her arms over her chest. "That doesn't sound even *remotely* safe."

I shrugged. "It's the Netherworld. 'Safe' doesn't really apply."

"And how are you planning to keep Avari from keeping you? What good would it do us to rescue your father but lose you in the process?"

"We're not going to lose her," Tod said. "I'm going with her."

"Yes, and neither of you will have any of your undead abilities once you're there, other than the ability to cross over on your own."

"That's all we need," I insisted. "As soon as we're sure you guys have my dad, we'll just come home."

Harmony's blond brows rose in skepticism, and her resemblance to her elder son was almost uncanny. "And you really think it'll be that easy?"

"No. Nothing's ever easy anymore. Besides, my plan has facets. Components, even."

"Well then, let's hear them," Uncle Brendon said.

"We know better than to expect my dad to be alone, so to buy you time to…kill things, or distract things, or whatever it takes, I'll keep Avari busy by negotiating my surrender."

"Negotiating requires give-and-take," Sabine pointed out. "You really think he'll be willing to give anything? Isn't *taking* everything kind of his thing?"

"He doesn't have to actually give up anything. I just have to keep him talking, even if all he says is no, over and over. I'm not really surrendering, remember, so it doesn't matter whether he gives in to my demands."

"I don't get it." Sophie frowned at me in confusion. "Why would he negotiate with you at all? Why not just…take you?"

"He would if he could," Tod explained. "But Kaylee's even harder to catch now than when she was alive. To take her soul against her will, he'd have to physically remove it from her resurrected body, which will be hard to do, because she's not just going to stand there and let him have it. She's undead *and* she's a *bean sidhe.* She can cross back into the human world whenever she wants."

"But he kept Thane's soul, right?" Em said. "And Thane could cross over, too."

"Yes," I said. "But Thane was unconscious when he was delivered to Avari." By Tod, who'd broken reaper law by turning on one of his own to keep Thane from making my last days miserable. "By the time he woke up, he was already missing his soul. If Avari physically catches me, I have no doubt that the first thing he'll do is knock me out so he could take my soul and replace it with his own breath. Like he did with Thane." Demon's Breath could sustain my body, in absence of my soul, allowing Avari to torture both parts of me separately. And possibly simultaneously.

"But he knows that's not going to happen," Nash said, and Sabine nodded in agreement. "Which is why he's trying to make you hand over your soul voluntarily?"

"Yup." I glanced around at each of them. "And he'll take any and all of your souls, too, if he gets the chance. Which is why I'm going to stall him while you guys look for my dad. I don't want any of you anywhere near Avari."

Uncle Brendon looked unconvinced. "And if he sees through your delay tactic?"

"Then I'll play on his greed and on the envy that will inevitably accompany it when he finds out I kissed Ira."

Harmony glanced at Tod in question, then back at me. "Ira?"

"Hellion of wrath," I explained. "He wanted a taste of my anger in exchange for telling me where my dad's being held."

Sabine smirked. "Kaylee makes friends everywhere she goes."

"Whatever. It was a completely disgusting, totally platonic mistake and I don't want to talk about it. Ever. Are we ready?"

"What about us?" Sophie motioned to Luca and herself. "I can cross over."

"No," her dad said. "You're staying here."

For a second, I thought Sophie might argue. But then she closed her mouth and I realized she was relieved. She would have come with us, if we'd let her, and that actually meant something to me. But she was just as happy to stay in the human world, out of danger.

Relatively speaking.

"Obviously, Emma and Luca will have to stay, too," Harmony added. She got no arguments.

"Okay, let me change into something more appropriate for a descent into hell." Uncle Brendon glanced down at the suit he wore, then up at Tod. "This would go faster if you give me a lift."

Tod nodded, and Brendon leaned over to kiss Harmony one more time. Sophie was still fake gagging when he and Tod disappeared from the kitchen.

Harmony rounded the counter and poured herself a mug of coffee. When she looked up again, she caught me smiling. "What?"

"I just… Don't listen to Sophie and Nash. I think you two are cute together."

"Me and Brendon?" Her sudden flush had nothing to do with the hot coffee.

"Yeah. You obviously make each other happy, and it's good to see someone happy right now, when everything else seems so…dire."

I wondered if Tod and I looked as cute together as she and my uncle looked. My opinion was no doubt biased, but I was pretty sure we were damn near lethally adorable.

"Well…thanks, Kaylee."

"Also, thanks for going out with Sophie's dad instead of mine. It would have been *beyond* weird for my dad to be dating my boyfriend's mother."

Harmony choked on her coffee, and I took the mug while she coughed. Then she gave me a small frown. "Kaylee, your father and I were never serious. Not even before he met your mom." She leaned against the counter, her gaze unfocused with the memory. "Actually, Brendon and I weren't very serious back then, either. We went separate ways *years* before I met my husband and Brendon met Valerie."

"Well, however it happened, I wish it could happen to my dad." He'd had as rough a time the past few months as I had, and he had no one to talk to about everything that had gone wrong. No one but his brother and daughter, anyway, and that wasn't the same at all.

Harmony motioned for me to follow her to the table, where we both sat, and I began to wish I had poured myself a cup of coffee. "Kaylee, I don't think your father's going to be ready for something like that for a very long time."

"Long time by human standards or *bean sidhe* standards?"

She set her mug down. "Has no one explained to you about why your father took your mother's death so hard?"

She blinked, then rephrased. "Well, of course, he took his wife's death hard, and it's no wonder, considering how she died. But has anyone explained to you why he's still taking it hard, more than thirteen years later?"

"I don't..." I hesitated, thinking back about everything my aunt and uncle had ever told me about my parents and about my mother's death. There wasn't much. "You know, people don't exactly line up to explain things to me. So... what have I missed?"

"Kaylee, your parents were soul mates."

I smiled at the thought and wished I could remember more about my mother. "I know he thought so, too."

"No." Harmony smiled, like I'd said something that amused her. "I don't mean that they liked each other a lot, or even that they were destined to be together. Destiny is more of a faerie tale than most people think *bean sidhes* are."

"So then, what does that mean, soul mates? You're saying that's some kind of real thing?"

"Very real." Her smile was back. "Your father and mother were so very much in love that some small part of their souls melded."

"Melded?" That sounded more like metalwork than love.

"Yes. He carried a bit of hers, and she carried a bit of his."

"Seriously?" I said, and she nodded. "What does that have to do with her death?"

Harmony's smile faded, and her eyes went so uncharacteristically still that I hadn't realized I was seeing emotion in them until she hid her thoughts from me entirely. "Your mother's soul wasn't so much reaped as stolen, and because it wasn't turned in to the proper authorities, your father never got that bit of his own soul back. Likewise, he still carries a part of your mother's with him. He is quite literally lovesick, and he won't be able to truly let her go until her soul finds rest and his is made whole again."

The sudden deep ache in my chest caught me by surprise. My father missed my mother so much that he was actually sick from the loss. His soul was incomplete. He might never get over her, and she...

My mother...

That ache deepened until I almost couldn't stand it. "So, we know that for sure, then, that she's not resting in peace?"

Harmony nodded slowly. Sadly. "I'm sorry, Kaylee. I didn't realize you didn't understand that."

I'd had no idea. "So, they're both still suffering. Together."

"Yes. Your father's soul isn't his own, and he won't be able to move on from her death until it's intact again. And, obviously, the same goes for your mother."

I sat there staring at nothing. Stunned. My parents were soul mates. Literally. They carried a part of each other, and neither of them would have peace until their souls were whole again and my mother was finally at rest.

My parents *had* to be the most romantic couple in history, which would have been mind-blowingly cool...if their love story didn't have the most tragic ending ever.

13

We stood in pairs, holding hands in front of Lakeside, the mental health ward attached to the hospital where Tod and Harmony both worked, one to treat people, the other to kill them. Holding hands was the only way Harmony and Sabine could keep my uncle and Nash invisible.

Tod and I just…didn't want to let go.

"I hate this place," I said, and Tod squeezed my hand. "Something tells me it'll only be worse on the other side of the world barrier."

Again, no one argued.

"So, what?" Nash said, staring up at the three-story building. "We cross over first, then head into the basement? Or we blink into the basement, then cross over?"

In truth, there were risks either way. "I vote for blinking in, then crossing over, because once we cross over, there can be no blinking."

"Good point," my uncle said.

I let go of Tod and held my hands out to Nash and Uncle Brendon, while Tod took his mother's hand and Sabine's. A second later, we all six stood in the basement of the mental health building, and I wished I'd thought to bring a flashlight. If the basement had ever been in common use, I couldn't tell from the dripping water, dank smell, and almost total absence of light.

Sabine pulled her cell phone from her pocket and turned on a flashlight app, but I realized quickly that I didn't want to see any of what she was showing me, even in the human world. With some additional light from our cell phones, we found the largest room of the basement—there were only a few of them—and decided that would be the best place to cross over. Even if my dad wasn't actually in that room, if Avari had an audience, or even just a few current victims to play with, he'd probably like room to spread out.

Ira hadn't actually told me that Avari was *with* my dad at Lakeside, but planning for anything less than the worst-case scenario would have been foolish.

We split into our pairs again and agreed that Tod and I would cross over first, to capture Avari's attention. Then the other pairs would cross over in two different areas of the basement, to increase their chances of finding my dad quickly. Instead of walking around in the Netherworld version of the basement, as soon as they'd determined that a room didn't contain my father, they would cross back to the human world, go to another room, then cross over and search again. That would surely decrease the chances of them being caught.

Sabine and Nash had instructions to cross back to the human world immediately if they ran into something they couldn't handle or if either of them got hurt. Tod and I were given the same instructions, but I dismissed them immediately. I had no plans to leave the Netherworld without my father.

My uncle seemed to realize that. He pulled me aside and took both of my hands, staring straight into my eyes, though he couldn't possibly have seen them very well in the dark basement. "Kaylee, please be careful."

"I'm always careful."

Nash laughed out loud.

"Okay, I always *try* to be careful." But the truth was that "careful" doesn't always get the job done. If you're not willing to risk everything you have and everything you are for those you love, what's the point in living? Er, in my case, not living? My afterlife wouldn't be worth having without my friends and my family, and I wasn't going to let Avari take any more of them from me. From the rest of us.

"Just…don't do anything heroic, okay?"

I nodded. I had no plans to take crazy risks. I just wanted my dad back.

My uncle must have seen some of that in my eyes, because he turned to Tod next. "If this goes bad, get her out of there."

Tod nodded. "Count on it."

He and I took up a position near the outermost wall of the large basement, not so close to the cinder blocks that anything growing on them could reach for us, but close enough that we were unlikely to suddenly appear in the middle of a crowd. Or a piece of furniture.

My palms were starting to sweat. Tod took my hand and squeezed it. "It's going to be okay, Kaylee," he whispered. "One way or another."

I let him cross us both over so I wouldn't risk losing touch with him in the process.

When I opened my eyes in the Netherworld, I was nearly blinded. Not that the light was that bright, but after the darkness of the human-world basement, any light shining in my eyes was a shock to my system. I stood as still as possible while my eyes adjusted, clutching Tod's hand, and the first thing I noticed when I could see again was that the light was *dancing.* Shadows jumped and stretched. Light flickered over grimy cinder-block walls, odds-and-ends furniture, and an assortment of bizarre creatures sitting, standing, and lounging all over the large room.

Candles. Avari had lit his creepy basement lair with hundreds of tiny candles, unlike any I'd ever seen. Tiny flames licked the air from shallow, irregularly shaped bowls of thick liquid, but I couldn't see a single wick. The liquid itself was on fire.

Tod squeezed my hand, and I nodded in silent acknowledgment that yes, I saw it. I saw it *all.* I wasn't willing to speak or move, because no one had noticed us yet—an advantage I hadn't expected but intended to use.

The reason no one had noticed us yet was that they were all busy noticing some kind of bloody spectacle at the other end of the room, where one large creature appeared to be systematically devouring another, slightly smaller creature, complete with a disturbing array of *crunchslurpgulp* noises.

I gagged, then slapped my free hand over my mouth to hold back the lunch I now regretted eating.

Tod squeezed my hand again, and I sucked in a deep, silent breath to calm myself, mostly out of habit. I didn't really need to breathe anymore. I made myself scan the large room, my gaze stumbling over misshapen limbs, backward-bending joints, and more kinds of horns, scaly wings, and twitching tails than I could even count. But I saw no sign of my father.

I decided no sign was a good sign.

"Find what you're looking for, little *bean sidhe?*" Avari's voice crawled over me like an army of spiders marching beneath my skin, and as I turned to find him watching us from the nearest corner, a series of soft shuffles, scratches—like claws on concrete—and the whisper of fabrics I couldn't identify told me that everyone else in the room was now watching us, too.

I didn't look at them. I couldn't without losing my composure—just knowing they were there was bad enough. I'd been in a larger Netherworld crowd, once, but I'd hidden my fear and mortality behind a mask. This time I was exposed, no longer mortal, but as vulnerable as ever.

I might have been full of rage earlier, but standing there, surrounded by at least two dozen Nether-creatures, any one of whom would gladly snap off my head and suck out my insides, it was hard to focus on anything more than my own paralyzing fear.

I swallowed, then let go of Tod's hand. That gesture of independence wouldn't hide my fear, but hopefully it would expose my spine. "Where's my dad?"

Avari stalked closer, and it was obvious from his smooth, menacing gait that he was pleased to have me back on his turf, where my options were limited—in the Netherworld, I couldn't become invisible, inaudible, or incorporeal. The hellion looked just like he had the first time I'd seen him. Tall, with dark hair and a dark suit that would have looked normal in any accountant's office in the human world but looked absurdly out of place in the seething pit of bizarrely shaped evil that was the Netherworld.

His featureless black orb eyes seemed to be watching me as he stalked closer, but I couldn't be sure with no irises or pupils to indicate the direction of his focus. "I've put your father away for safekeeping."

"I want him back."

"Of course you do." He stopped and clasped his hands behind his back. "And you know the price. Have you come to discuss the terms of your surrender?"

"Yes."

Avari actually chuckled. "Hellions cannot lie, but we are all fully aware that little dead *bean sidhes* can. So I assume you understand my disinclination to take you at your word."

"Whatever." On the edge of my vision, something slithered closer, and chills crawled over my skin. "Here are my terms." I would ask for the world. It didn't matter whether or not he agreed—what mattered was that I kept him talking. "First, send my father home. Second, swear you'll never attempt to contact any of my friends and family ever again, through any means. Third, swear that you'll stay away from my school and all of its students, past, present, and future. And the staff. When you've done all of that to my satisfaction, I'll hand over my immortal soul. That's what you want, right?"

He needed me to give him my soul of my own free will. With it in his possession, I could not escape. Ever.

"Surrender your soul, and you have my word that your father will be returned to the human world."

"You first." A tentacle slithered past his foot, headed in my direction from the crowd at his back, and I had to concentrate to still my pounding heart before he heard that evidence of my terror. "And that's only my first demand." *Stand strong, Kaylee.* I couldn't afford to let him see anything but confidence. And anger. "You're not getting what you want until I have everything *I* want. Starting with my father's return."

"Immediately," Tod said from my side. "Unharmed."

Avari lifted one dark brow. "Even I cannot undo what has been done to the living. But if you'd like me to kill him, I can then return his undead form to its previous glory. Of course, he would have to remain here…."

"No. Send him back as unharmed as possible, physically, psychologically, mentally, and in any other states of health I may be forgetting." That tentacle still moved in my peripheral vision, but I resisted the urge to actually look at it. "And I want your word that you won't try to hurt him again. Ever."

Odd breathy titters and deep beastly grunts echoed from the crowd at the hellion's back, and another chill ran through me when I realized I was hearing monstrous sounds of amusement.

"You aren't in the position to make so many demands, Ms. Cavanaugh."

"The hell I'm not. I am in possession of my own soul, and we both know you'll do anything to get it. So give me your word, or I'm out of here."

"Little *bean sidhe,* your lies are transparent." Avari was on the move again, pacing in front of his assembled audience, stepping over tails and through trails of sludge I hoped never to identify, and I could no longer ignore the dozens of eyes, ears, and assorted snouts and muzzles aimed my way. "You would never abandon your father to torture and eventual death. To be followed by yet more torture. I don't understand that about you, but I don't doubt it in the slightest."

"I never said I'd abandon him. But if I surrender without your word, you'll torture him anyway, which means I'm better off retreating and regrouping."

Avari scowled. I could practically see him searching for a loophole in what I'd told him to swear. He wanted my soul, most of all, but if he could find a way to keep my father, he would. And if he got Tod in the bargain, too, well...he *was* a hellion of *greed*.

But I'd left no wiggle room.

"It's your turn to talk," Tod said when several seconds had elapsed in pensive, angry silence from the hellion. "Negotiation is like playing tennis with words instead of balls. I thought you'd be better at this, considering your apparent lack of balls."

I didn't know whether to laugh or tell Tod to quit poking the lion with a stick.

Avari's blank gaze narrowed on him, and the hellion gestured to a nearby cluster of those weird candles. "Human fat puts off a nice glow, don't you think?"

I stared at the fiery, viscous substance, fresh horror crawling beneath my skin.

Human fat. Taken from human beings. Dead humans, hopefully, but thanks to Avari's fondness for torture, I couldn't be sure of that.

"Take a nice, long look at your future, reaper. You'll soon be burning as fuel for hundreds of tiny fires."

Tod laughed out loud. "If that's your way of saying I'm hot, rest assured, I already know." He spread his arms, inviting Avari and his monstrous court to look him over. "But I'm going to have to keep lighting up the room with my dazzling personality, because you couldn't scrape enough fat off me to fill even one of your sick-ass human candles. And, based on the crowd behind you, I'm guessing most of your friends look better in the dark anyway."

The hellion's eyes narrowed. His rage-filled voice slid over me like a blade under light pressure, constantly threatening to draw blood. "Someday soon, reaper, your mouth will be the source of your own destruction."

"That does seem likely, doesn't it?" Tod glanced at me and shrugged. "Until then, it remains a source of my own amusement."

"So are you ready to send my father back, or should I pack up my soul and go home?"

Avari's gaze fell on me with malevolent focus, and I remembered every time he'd come after me. Every life he'd destroyed to get to me. He wouldn't stop until he had what he wanted, and when I slipped through his grip again this time, he would only get hungrier. Angrier. More desperate, but no less focused.

His rage made him more dangerous. Mine tended to make me stupid. Ira was right about that.

"Fine. Once we've come to an agreement, your father will suffer no further and I will return him to the human world immediately—after I take possession of your soul."

If this were a real negotiation, I would have argued. "Fine. And you will have no further contact with him, nor attempt to harm him in any way or bring him to the Netherworld, through any means, including but not limited to force, threat, or coercion, personally or through a third party, ever again."

"Wow." Tod whistled. "Where'd you learn all that lawyer-speak?"

"Internet user license agreements. They're almost as hard to navigate as the Netherworld," I said, and Tod chuckled. "Avari? Give me your word, or this discussion is over."

The hellion's jaw tightened, a surprisingly human reaction. "I do so swear. Now hand over your soul."

"I'm not finished."

"You most certainly *are!*" he roared, and I jumped, startled. I couldn't help it. A thin, lacy sheet of ice formed on the floor beneath his feet, flowing out in all directions. Excited murmurs and soft grunts spread throughout the audience. I couldn't understand any of the actual words—if they could be called that—but the gist was clear. They were eager to see him lose his temper with me.

"Careful. You're close to the goal," I taunted, ignoring the fear crawling slowly up my spine. "Do you really want to blow it now?"

"Every word you speak brings your agony closer to hand," Avari warned, and the ice spread until his audience began to step and slither toward the other side of the room, still watching. I wanted to back away from the ice, too—I'd once seen his temper freeze Addison solid—but this was not the time to show weakness or fear. "You will suffer more for the insolence you spew, and I will drink your pain straight from the source, for all of eternity."

"Yeah, I don't think so." I met his black-eyed gaze as boldly as I could. "I think you already intend to hurt me as much as you possibly can, regardless of what I do or say."

Avari scowled, and I think if he'd had normal eyes, I'd have seen realization dawn in them. I was right, and he'd just then realized it. Which meant he had nothing left to threaten me with, except…

"My friends and family." I stood as straight as I could, framing my demand with confidence and determination I didn't really feel. "I want your word that once you have my soul, you will never bother them again in any way, through your own efforts or by enlisting help. And that you won't help anyone else hurt them or even contact them. *Any* of them."

The sheet of ice thickened and spread in a burst of hellion anger, and on my right, one of the nameless Nether-creatures made a strange choking sound. I glanced over to see a small, vaguely humanoid woman—greenish in tone, with gray claws instead of hands—freeze where she stood. Literally. At her back, another monster cackled with echoing laughter, then shoved one huge fist through her frozen torso. The ice-woman cracked into several large chunks, which crashed to the floor amid splinters of ice and tar-colored frozen innards.

"You've outlasted my patience, little *bean sidhe*. Death and the attentions of your dark lover have already eroded your innocence. What makes you think you are worth the demands you've made?"

Eroded innocence? Seriously?

I glanced around the room again, looking for some sign of

Harmony and my uncle or Nash and Sabine. For some indication of how much longer I should keep the hellion talking.

"The fact that we're still having this conversation makes me think I'm worth it. The fact that you haven't actually *said* I'm not worth it. But you know what? You're right. I should go. I need my father back, but I don't necessarily need *you* to give him to me. If I'm going to have to pay for his return either way, I think I'd rather pay someone else. Someone who's already had a taste of me and my 'eroded innocence' and would be happy to have another." My skin crawled at the very thought, but I refused to let that show.

"No one else can get to your father while I have him. You will deal with me, or know that you are responsible for his pain."

"I don't know, Kay," Tod said in a stage whisper. "I think Ira offered you the better deal."

"Ira?" Avari stalked closer, but I held my ground, though fresh thick ice formed beneath his feet with each step. "Another lie. You could never survive an encounter with the hellion of wrath."

"Oh." I frowned, pretending to second-guess my own memory. "Well then, I guess I never summoned him, either, did I? And I have no way of knowing that he's powerful enough to answer a summons, but you're not. And if none of that really happened, then I guess I never let him kiss me, either. Or taste my blood. Or feed my rage. If none of that was real, then you won't mind if I leave you here and go *imagine* another encounter with Ira, who seems more than willing to work with my demands."

"The king of rage gets my vote," Tod said. "Hell, I may make him an offer myself."

Avari threw his arm out, index finger pointed like a weapon, and a thick spear of ice shot across the room to impale a creature in the far corner, who squealed, then collapsed. "The next one goes through your reaper lover. I will not play these games with you, *bean sidhe.* Offer up your soul or go home, and rest assured that your father will suffer in your stead…."

The hellion's words faded and his head turned to the left. He stared at the long south wall of the large room, and unease churned in my stomach. A closed door stood in the middle of that wall. And with sudden cruel insight, I realized he was hearing something we couldn't.

Avari's hand shot out again, and the muscles in his neck bulged above his stiff white collar. The wall to his left exploded in a shower of huge ice daggers and broken cinder blocks. Dust spewed in all directions, and I gasped, choking as Tod pinned me between his body and the other wall. The tension in his entire frame said he was seconds from crossing over, with me in tow. And he might have done that very thing, if not for…

"Oh, no…"

I shoved him back so I could peer through the choking gray haze to see what he'd seen.

As the dust and debris settled, I saw that Avari had blasted through not only the interior wall separating our room from the next, but through part of the ceiling of that other room and part of the floor above it. Through the gaping hole above a pile of still-settling chunks of concrete, I could see the Netherworld sky, a sickly shade of orange at the moment, like pumpkin soup that has started to spoil.

But then my gaze followed the wreckage and I saw what had upset Tod. What everyone was staring at. What Avari had heard through the wall.

In the other room, my uncle Brendon stood with his feet spread, a sledgehammer clenched in a two-handed grip, ready to swing. On the ground in front of him were three bodies, each misshapen and somehow *wrong,* with grayish skin and inverted knee joints.

One had obviously been smashed by the falling debris, when Avari blew the wall in. The other two were the source of the weird grayish blood—or maybe some other bodily fluid—dripping in congealing glops from the hammer my uncle must have found in that room full of old machinery, which had probably never functioned at all in the Netherworld version of the mental hospital.

For a moment, no one moved. My uncle adjusted his grip, eyeing the horde of monsters now twitching, wheezing, and slithering forward slowly in anticipation of some cry of attack by Avari.

I saw no sign of my father. So why was Uncle Brendon still there? Why hadn't he and Harmony crossed over the instant Avari blew out the wall?

Then I saw Harmony's long, pale curls trailing over a large cracked brick on the floor. The rest of her was there, too, surely, but so covered in gray dust and bits of brick that it was hard to see anything other than glimpses of color—blond hair, blue T-shirt, red blood pooling on the bricks downhill from her head.

Harmony wasn't moving.

"Mom!" Tod shouted, and heads turned our way. He pulled me toward the hole in the wall. Hands reached for us. Fingers brushed my arms. Claws caught in my hair. Tails and tentacles tugged at my shirt. My heart beat harder than it ever had, even before my death. But we dodged and slapped and kicked our way through the crowd as it coalesced around us, almost casually slowing our progress, as if they were in no hurry to actually kill us.

As if our fear were enough—for now.

Uncle Brendon heard Tod shout and saw us coming. He turned, looking for Harmony, then let out an anguished cry when he found her. With the huge hammer still clenched in his right fist, he scrambled over the pile of broken cinder blocks to kneel at her side.

We were several feet from the hole in the wall when he swept bloodstained hair from her face and felt for her pulse. We were two feet away when Avari gave another grand sweep of his arm and a thin barrier of ice formed over the hole in the wall like a patch in a pair of jeans. The ice crackled as it thickened, bluish in color but almost perfectly transparent.

Tod pulled me to a stop inches away, and in the second it took us to recover from surprise, the ice thickened layer after layer, trapping tiny cracks and bubbles inside until it was too thick to break. Until it sealed us in and my uncle and his mother out.

Uncle Brendon looked up and hardly seemed to notice the new barrier. He said something, but we couldn't hear him.

"What?" I shouted, my palm an inch from the ice, so close I could feel the cold but was afraid to touch it. For all I knew, making contact with it would freeze me solid, like the green woman, and I would shatter into a million pieces of Kaylee, never to be reassembled.

My uncle shouted again, and that time I heard enough to understand. "She's alive!"

"Go!" I whispered to Tod. "Take them home." He could blink into the human world, then back into the Netherworld on the other side of the ice nearly instantly.

"If Cain so much as twitches, I will have Abel's head torn from his body."

It took me a second to process the reference—an odd one coming from a hellion—but then Avari waved one hand at a door on the other side of the room and one of his monsters threw it open. Nash—Abel—appeared in the doorway, then was shoved through it by Belphegore, the hellion of vanity who'd killed Emma. Belphegore was the personification of beauty, with flawless features that defied ethnic classification but slipped from my memory the moment my gaze left her face.

She had one perfect, graceful hand around Nash's arm, and though his forehead was furrowed in fury, he looked... sober. She hadn't yet forced a dose of her own breath on him.

Behind them, Invidia hauled Sabine into the room. The *mara* took in the seething mob of monsters, and her dark eyes widened. But then her gaze returned to Nash. She could cross into the human world whenever she wanted, but she wouldn't leave him, and with the hellions between them, she couldn't reach Nash to take him with her.

"Your mother or your brother?" Avari watched Tod patiently, savoring his indecision.

Through the ice, we saw my uncle pick Harmony up and carefully begin climbing the huge mound of debris with her broken body limp in his arms. My fists opened and closed uselessly. The ache in my chest rivaled the fevered rush of my pulse, and I felt more helpless—more *human*—than I had since the day I'd died.

"Which will you choose, reaper?"

Nash saw us and exhaled in relief—until he looked past us through the ice. He and Sabine seemed to realize what they were seeing at the same time. "Mom!" He tried to push through the throng of claws, fangs, and horns ready to spill blood and devour flesh at one word from Avari, but Belphegore held him back with no visible effort.

"Go get her!" Nash shouted at his brother. For the first time since we'd met, Tod looked…unsure. Torn. His mother was badly hurt but alive. Yet Nash could lose his head in the blink of an eye.

"Your mortal attachments are like a puppet's strings," Avari said, both hands clasped casually at his back. "One need only pluck the right cord to make the puppet dance." His smile was almost creepier than his threats. "*Dance,* reaper."

Tod's eyes flashed with storms of midnight-blue fury. "You knew."

"That you and the little *bean sidhe* were a distraction? Of course. She might very well have been willing to sacrifice her own soul in exchange for her father's life, but *you* would never go along with that. So now the question is what will you give up for your brother? What is his life worth to you?"

"Just go!" Nash shouted, and Belphegore jerked his head back by a handful of his thick brown hair, stretching his neck at a painful angle. "Tod, go!"

My uncle was shouting again, and when I turned back to the ice, I found him halfway up the pile of rubble, headed for the hole in the building, cradling Harmony to his chest while her arms and head hung limp.

He was shouting for us to go, too, but he couldn't see Nash and Sabine. He wanted us to leave him and Tod's mom and my dad in this Nether-hell and escape with only our own afterlives.

But we couldn't leave without Nash and Sabine, yet we couldn't get to them without abilities that didn't work in the Nether. Sabine could get him out, if she could reach him. But for that, she'd need a distraction. An opportunity.

"My dad's not here, is he?" I demanded, and Avari actually laughed.

"No." And that had to be the truth, because hellions couldn't lie.

"Go get him. This negotiation is over if I don't see him here, alive, in three minutes."

More hellion laughter, and this time it resonated in my spine like a physical blow. "This negotiation was never real."

"I wasn't talking to you. I was talking to her." I looked past Avari to the hellion of vanity, who still clutched one of Nash's arms. "I don't like the way Avari plays, so I'm going to offer you the same deal I offered him. Send my friends and family back to the human world, and my soul is yours. This offer expires in one minute."

"She's lying!" Avari shouted. "She doesn't have to keep her word."

No one listened to him.

"Why would I trade those four souls for your one?" Belphegore called, and Invidia's focus volleyed eagerly between us.

"Because Avari wants mine. Think of what you could get out of him for the trade," I said, and Belphegore's perfectly arched brows rose over the most beautiful eyes I'd ever seen. They seemed to be every color all at once. "You could get anything you want."

"Kaylee…" Tod said, but I ignored him.

"Thirty seconds," I said while Belphegore studied me, trying to assess my sincerity. "If I don't have my dad in thirty seconds, Invidia gets the same offer."

"Done!" the hellion of envy shouted. She turned on Belphegore with an eagerness bordering on mania, and a murmur rolled over the throng of monsters. "*I* want her. Give me the boy…." She let go of the *mara* to reach for Nash, and Belphegore tried to pull him out of reach.

Sabine saw her shot and burst into motion, like I'd hoped she would. She lunged for Nash just as Avari disappeared, right in front of me.

"Go!" I shouted. "Sabine, get him out of here!"

The *mara* grabbed Nash's hand. They both disappeared the very instant Avari appeared behind them, grasping for Sabine. Nash's screams of protest echoed into eternity, eclipsed only by the hellion's shout of rage when he was left with only a thin handful of Sabine's long, dark hair.

Invidia snarled and pounced on Belphegore, cursing her in some language I couldn't identify, which seemed to be made entirely of consonants and birdlike screeches.

Avari bellowed in rage, and I turned to the ice to see my uncle put Harmony on the ground outside the hole in the basement, then climb out with her. The crowd seethed around me, twitching, growling, and panting with impatience, and my nerves buzzed like live wires beneath my skin.

I fumbled for Tod's hand, and it wrapped firmly around mine. Avari's roar echoed in my head even as we materialized in the human-world basement a second later.

Tod dropped my hand as soon as he saw Sabine and Nash, their fear and anger barely visible in the dark as she rubbed a spot on the back of her head. "I'm going back for Mom."

"No!" I reached for him again, but for the first time since I'd met him, Tod pulled away from me. "If he catches you, he'll tear you apart."

"What happened?" Nash demanded, scrubbing angry tears from his face in the deep shadows. "Where's Mom?"

"I'm not just going to appear in the middle of the crowd and ring a dinner bell, Kaylee." Tod's shoes shuffled on the dirty concrete as he stepped closer and kissed me, lingering just for a moment in the dark. A moment we couldn't really afford but that he obviously knew I needed. "I know what I'm doing."

"What happened to Mom?" Nash shouted, and I turned to him, suddenly conscious of the fact that we were in the human world, and that he couldn't make himself inaudible. He was going to bring anyone within hearing range downstairs, and we'd be caught. At least, he and Sabine would.

"Avari blew out the wall, and your mom got hit by the debris. But Uncle Brendon took her out through the hole in the wall." I wasn't sure if he'd seen that part. "He'll protect your mom." Or die trying. I had no doubt of that.

"Bullshit! Avari will catch them," Nash said through clenched teeth, frustrated, angry tears shining in his eyes in the light from Sabine's cell screen. "You *know* he's probably catching them right now. Those monsters probably came pouring out of that building like bees from a hive, and your uncle can't cross over."

"I'll find them," Tod promised his brother. "I'll bring them back."

"I'm going with you."

"No." Tod turned back to me, and his irises were achingly still. I couldn't tell if he was hiding something from me or from Nash. "Take Nash and Sabine back to your house, please, and I'll meet you there. I won't stay long. I just want to cross over and check around the building, in case Brendon's hiding her somewhere where I can get to them quickly. Maybe this isn't as bad as it seems."

But I was pretty sure I wasn't the only one who wished my uncle could have carried both Harmony and the giant hammer.

Nash grabbed his brother's shoulder and pulled him around. "You're not going without me. She's my mother, too."

"And I would take you, if you could get back on your own. But you can't, which means I'd have to look out for *you* while I look for Mom. Stay here. Help Kaylee and Sabine keep an eye on the others. That's the best way you can help."

"That's *bullshit!*" Nash shouted.

"Shhh." Sabine took his hand in her half-casted one. "You have to shut up, or we're going to get caught." He started to argue, but she clamped one hand over his mouth. "If you promise to shut the hell up, I'll go with him and help find your mom."

"No!" He pulled her hand away, and his next words were clearer. "Putting yourself in danger isn't going to help her." About a second after he'd said the words, Nash seemed to realize they applied to him, too. "Fine. Point taken. I'll stay if you stay." When Sabine nodded, Nash turned back to Tod. "You sure you got this?"

The reaper nodded grimly. "And the longer I wait, the harder they'll be to find. Assuming they got away."

Please *let them have gotten away*.... "I'll take Nash and Sabine back, then join you."

"No," Tod said. My temper flared, and I started to argue, but he spoke over me. "*Please* stay here. I may be able to get to my mom and your uncle, but we have no idea where your dad is. And if something happens to you, who's going to find him?"

"He wasn't in that basement," Sabine added. "You got false information."

"That's impossible." I pushed hair back from my face, wishing I had a ponytail holder. "Hellions can't lie."

She shrugged, shining her cell phone screen in my face. "Okay then, your hellion was *wrong*."

"He's not *my* hellion." Ira would devour my soul just as soon as Avari would if he could get it.

"He's as much yours as *I* ever was," Nash said, eyes flashing in anger. "And he got to first base a hell of a lot faster." I gaped at him in shock. Tod's fist was already in motion when Nash backed up, warding off the blow with two open palms. "I'm sorry. That was out of line."

"Sure as hell was," Tod growled.

"I take it back. I'm sorry. I'm just..." He blinked and made a visible effort to push back the fear and frustration obviously sharpening his tongue. "This is messed up. Avari has my *mom*."

"He has my dad, too. And Sophie's," I pointed out. We were all in the same position.

"Shit," Sabine swore. "Who's going to tell her?"

"Isn't scaring the crap out of my cousin kind of your *raison d'être?*" *Look at that. You* can *use French outside of French class!*

Sabine shrugged. "She's not horrible *all* the time. And you gotta respect a girl who travels with a pair of scissors in her purse."

A designer purse, no doubt. Maybe designer scissors.

I exhaled heavily. Until there was no air left in my body. "She's my cousin. I'll tell her." I owed her that much.

"Okay. I'm going back in," Tod said, and I pulled him into another hug before he could blink out.

"If you're not back in half an hour, I'm coming after you," I whispered into his ear, standing on my toes so I could reach. "There's no one left here who can stop me."

He clutched me tighter and nodded. "I'll be back." Then he let me go and disappeared.

I took Sabine's good hand in my left and Nash's in my right, then blinked all three of us into my backyard, where I was pretty sure we wouldn't accidentally land on someone. Or in something.

Styx barked her head off when we came in through the back door, and even after she saw me, she kept barking until I picked her up and scruffed her fur. Tensions were high, and she could feel that. Seeing me was no longer enough to assure her that I was okay.

I heard the plastic clatter of the television remote being dropped on the coffee table—a sound I made on a daily basis—then footsteps pounded through the living room and into the kitchen.

"Well?" Em demanded, while Sophie and Luca fell into place behind her. Their eyes were wide. Sophie clutched Luca's hand. They were all three scared.

"Okay, first of all, when someone walks in through the back door unannounced, don't assume it's someone you know." Sabine marched past me and into the kitchen, where she pulled open the fridge door. "Assume it's someone—or some*thing*—that wants to kill you. And come armed." She turned to me with her good hand wrapped around the door handle. "Where's that baseball bat?"

"I gave it back to Nash." But maybe she was right. Maybe we should be arming ourselves, even on the human plane.

"Did you find your dad?" Luca asked as Nash marched past him into the living room and I locked the back door.

"What's wrong with him?" Em stared after Nash. "What happened?"

"Where's my dad?" Sophie said as I pulled a container of raw meat from the fridge and plopped a chunk of it into Styx's food bowl. She dug in, and Sophie spoke again, quieter this time, as if she already knew the answer. "Kaylee, where's my dad?"

I turned on the kitchen faucet with my elbow and rinsed the deer blood from my hands, then washed with soap. Then I made myself look at her. "He's still there. He's okay, as far as we know."

"As far as you *know?*" Sophie looked stunned, and my heart ached for her.

Luca looked from me to Sabine, then to Nash. "What the hell happened?"

"Avari blew the side out of the building!" Nash sat on the arm of the couch and ran one hand through hair that was once artfully mussed but now just looked messy. Then he swiped both hands over his face, angrily wiping away frustrated tears. "The concrete wall fell on my mom. Sophie's dad carried her out, but he can't cross over, so they're kind of stuck there."

"Shit." Luca put an arm around Sophie, who stared at the floor like she hadn't heard what she'd expected and hadn't quite processed that fact yet. "Is your mom okay?"

"Don't know yet," Sabine said. When I turned, I found her digging through the cabinet over the short kitchen peninsula. She pulled down a bag of Doritos and removed the clip, then shoved a chip into her mouth.

We all stared at her while she chewed.

"What?" She swallowed, then dug out another chip. "Sometimes you have to fix the problem that *can* be fixed. I can't get your parents back, but I can fix the munchies."

"So, he's still there?" Sophie sank into a squat on the kitchen floor and wrapped her arms around her knees. "You *left* him there?"

Luca pulled her up, then guided her to the couch.

"No." I refused the bag of chips when Sabine held it out to me. "Tod went back for them."

"Alone?" Sophie looked up from the couch, and her gaze speared me with the weight of my own guilt. "We only have three good parents left between us." Except for Luca's, who were half a country away and had no idea their son was a necromancer. "You're telling me that they're *all three* trapped in the Netherworld, and only *one* of you went back for them?"

"We all wanted to go, but Tod thought putting more of us in danger would be…well, dangerous. And he was right," I insisted. "If we all go back and get killed, who'll be left to rescue them once we find them?"

"Find them?" Sophie demanded. "You don't even know where they are? You *lost* my dad?"

"He had to run," Sabine said, another orange corn chip held at the ready. "He had to get Harmony out of there before the ice melted and that horde of monsters ate them alive."

Emma sank onto a bar stool, from which she could see both rooms at once. "That sentence is simultaneously unintelligible and terrifying."

Sabine shrugged. "Unintelligible and terrifying is what the Netherworld's all about."

"Screw this." Sophie stood and jerked her hand from Luca's when he tried to take it. "I'll go get him myself. Where did you last see him? At the psych ward?"

"Yup," Sabine said around another mouthful.

"No!" I glared at her, then turned back to my cousin. "He's not there anymore," I insisted. "He would have tried to get as far away from there as he could, as quickly as possible."

Sophie frowned. "Then how the hell is Tod supposed to find them?"

"He's not," Nash said, and I wanted to argue, but I couldn't. Not without lying. "Your dad is *hiding,* and if he does it right, Tod won't be able to find him and neither will you."

"Watch me."

Luca stood and stepped into her path. "Sophie. Wait. On the not-gonna-happen scale, how impossible is it going to be for me to talk you out of this? Pick-up-trash-on-the-side-of-the-highway unlikely or leave-the-house-without-makeup unlikely?"

"Makeup."

"Fine." He nodded decisively. "Then I'm coming with you."

"She's not going," I said. "Sabine, help me out."

Sabine shrugged and stepped into the living room with the bag of chips, her focus set on Sophie. "You're not going. And if you do, I'll drag your ass back here in handcuffs. Chains, if that's what it takes." She folded the top of the cellophane bag. "*Please* give me a reason to go shopping for chains."

"You have a broken arm."

Sabine shrugged. "One of mine's better than two of yours."

Sophie's eyes narrowed. "I *dare* you to stop me."

"Oh, don't dare her," Emma groaned from her bar stool.

"Sophie, think about this," Nash said. "I want to go, too. We all do. But if your dad were here, what would he say? Would he want you to put yourself in that kind of danger?"

My cousin rolled her eyes. "But he's *not* here. That's the point."

Sabine scowled. "No, the point is that if I let you cross over, when your dad gets back—and he *will* get back—he'll kick my ass for letting you out of my sight."

"No, he—" Sophie began, but Sabine spoke over her.

"The hell he won't. Face it, tiny dancer. The only real problem you have is that people actually give a damn about you."

My cousin blinked in surprise. "What the hell are you talking about?"

Sabine stepped closer, her dark eyes flashing in anger, but there was something deeper than that, too. Something more raw peeking through the cracks in the fearless facade she wore like Sophie wore SPF foundation. "I'm talking about this room. This room is full of people who love you. Who don't want you to get yourself killed searching a nightmare dimension for the father who loves you more than life itself." Sabine shoved the chip bag at me, and I took it before I realized what I was doing. "Did you know I had six older sisters?"

"I didn't…" Sophie looked confused. "You have family?"

"Had. I'm a *mara*—the seventh daughter of a seventh daughter—which means I had six older sisters and presumably a set of parents who liked kids enough to have at least seven of them. They must have *loved* kids. But they didn't want me. They left me on a church doorstep, buckled into a car seat, when I was a toddler. So I don't have those sisters anymore. I don't have those parents. What I have is this." She spread her arms to take in all of us. "These same people you have. And like it or not, they have me. And so do you. Your dad just took custody of me, which means you're my sister now. You're the only sister I have left—the only one I'm ever going to have—and I'm *not* gonna screw that up. I'm not going to throw you away, like they threw me away. I'm not going to let you get hurt. And I'm sure as hell not going to let you hurt yourself. So you put your bony little butt back on that couch and start using your head instead of your mouth, because it's your head we need right now."

"My head?" Sophie stared at Sabine in shock. We *all* stared at Sabine in shock.

"You know your dad better than anyone else here," the *mara* said. "You know better than any of us where he's most likely to go. Where he might hide. When we go back in, we'll go together, and *you'll* be the one telling us where to look. Got it?"

Sophie opened her mouth, but nothing came out. She blinked at Sabine. Then, finally, she nodded. And sat back down.

Luca sat with her, and while they talked softly about where her dad might have gone, I headed into the kitchen to start a pot of coffee, partly to give my hands something to do, partly because I like coffee, and partly because I could already tell it was going to be a long night—those who needed sleep would appreciate the offer of caffeine instead.

"So, how bad is this?" Em said from her bar stool, while I ran water into the glass carafe. "I mean, it feels like we've been in a constant state of emergency for the past few months, but is it just me, or do things seem extra dire today?"

I turned off the faucet and poured water from the carafe into the reservoir at the back of the coffeepot. "It's not just you." Avari had been taking things from us for months. People we knew and loved. Opportunities we could never get back. He'd taken Sophie's naivety, Nash's emotions, and Sabine's foster mother and home. He'd been party to the scheme that took Emma's body and Lydia's soul. But throughout all of that, we'd always had a support network to rely on. Parents, older and wiser, who encouraged, overruled, and protected us out of love.

Now, they were gone. We were on our own, and beyond that forced independence, we were missing parts of our families, both blood and extended. Our positions had been reversed—now our parents needed us to find and protect them, without the advantage of their wisdom and guidance.

The game had changed. We now stood to lose much more than our own lives.

"So, what's the plan?" Em asked as I dumped dry coffee grounds into the filter.

"We find them, and we bring them back."

"How?"

"I don't know." That was possibly the scariest sentence I'd ever said aloud. "Footwork? Guesswork? Dumb luck? I don't know how we're going to do it, but it has to be done." And that was the bottom line. "Quickly."

I'd just pressed the brew button when someone gasped from the living room and I looked up to find Tod standing in the middle of the floor, in front of the TV. I only realized I'd reached for a knife from the block by the microwave when my hand closed over the handle.

I let go of the knife as Tod turned toward me, already fielding questions he seemed to have no answers for.

"Did you find them?"

"What about my dad?"

"Are the monsters hunting them? Was there any sign of blood?"

Emma and I stopped in the kitchen doorway while coffee dripped into the carafe.

Tod sat on the end of the coffee table. "I didn't find them, and I really think that's a good sign."

"How on earth is that a good sign?" Sophie demanded. "They're still missing!"

"Not finding them is a hell of a lot better than finding a pile of blood, bones, and shredded flesh," Sabine said.

Sophie sobbed, and Luca glared at the *mara,* who didn't seem to notice.

"I wasn't going to put it like that, but yes," Tod said. "I blinked in and out around the perimeter of the building, because that's safer than actually walking around the Netherworld, and at first it looked pretty bad. There were creatures clustered in groups too tight for me to see what they were looking at. But eventually the groups started breaking up and I got close enough to see that they were gathered around several spots of blood. Just a few drops. They're tracking Mom and Brendon, but they haven't found them yet."

"But they will," Nash said, and Sabine took his hand.

"Yes, eventually, they will." Tod flinched, as if the truth hurt coming out. "Unless we find them first. But the good news is that the blood trail has stopped. The last thing I saw them gathered around was a strip of material. It was part of your dad's shirt." He glanced at Sophie, whose eyes were wide and damp. "It looks like he bandaged my mom's wounds, which has slowed—or maybe even stopped—the bleeding. Which makes them harder to track."

"Okay. Good." I sat next to Tod when he held one hand out to me. "So, we'll keep looking, in shifts. Me, Tod, and Sabine." Because we could cross over safely if we were smart about it.

"I'm coming, too," Sophie said. Before anyone could object, she rushed on, "Not alone. I'm not stupid, and I don't want to die. But I can get there and back, so there's no reason I can't go with one of you. I can help."

The rest of us must have looked skeptical, because she scowled at us all. "Four eyes are better than two, right?"

She'd said the opposite to Chelsea Simms during the two

years she'd been stuck in glasses before her parents let her get contacts. But whatever. I liked Sophie 2.0 better anyway.

"Fine," I said, and my cousin gave me a grim smile of thanks. "You can come with me, but not until you learn how to control that wail of yours. You don't have to unleash it at full volume, you know." Saying that reminded me that Harmony wasn't there to teach Sophie like she'd taught me. I wasn't entirely sure I could do her lessons justice.

"You can come with me, too," Sabine said. "But the first time you do something stupid or put either of us in danger, I'm dragging you back here."

"That won't happen." Sophie looked slightly less thankful for Sabine's concession than she had for mine.

After that, we took up a collection and Emma ordered dinner for those who needed it while Sabine took a shift searching in the Netherworld and I tried to teach Sophie what I knew about the one *bean sidhe* ability she'd inherited.

Turns out my cousin's big mouth was more practical than I'd ever given it credit for.

15

Sabine's shift took longer than it should have, because she couldn't blink from place to place in the human world, nor could she become invisible to humans like Tod and I could. Which meant that she had to actually drive partway to the hospital to pick up the search where Tod had left off, and she had to be away from onlookers when she crossed over, so no one would see her disappear.

She was still gone when the Chinese food delivery arrived, and Sophie and I took a break so she could eat.

I left my cousin at the kitchen table with Luca and Emma scooping rice and chicken from cartons onto paper plates. Then I headed into the back of our small house in search of Tod and Nash.

Halfway down the hall, I heard them, one whispered masculine voice, then the other in answer, coming from my room. I stopped breathing so I could hear them better, torn between the knowledge that I shouldn't be eavesdropping and the relief that for the first time since Nash and I had broken up, the Hudson brothers were alone in the same room and they weren't fighting.

It was a moment I wanted to treasure. Definitely a moment I didn't want to spoil. So I listened, just for a minute.

"The truth, Tod. You think she's still alive?" Nash's voice was low and strained. He was worried.

"Yeah, I do. I think Brendon would do just about anything to protect her."

"He's just one man."

"Yeah, but he's a smart man, and a big man, and a man who's been around for more than a century and a half. He's also a man who has every reason in the world to want to get both himself and our mom back here as soon as possible." Tod paused, and I pictured him shrugging, though all I could see was my mostly closed door. "Anyway, if she were dead—if either of them were—Avari would want us to know. He'd want to feed from our suffering."

"We're suffering just from not knowing where they are. Or *how* they are."

"But not like we would if we knew they were dead. Not knowing allows room for hope, and Avari can't feed from worry and hope like he can feed from true pain."

I snuck closer until I could see Nash through the gap between my door and its frame. He sat on the end of Emma's bed, leaning forward with his elbows on his knees, the toes of his shoes resting on the ground.

"Maybe they're dead and he just doesn't know it." Nash's gaze followed Tod as the reaper paced the rug in front of him, like he had energy to burn. Worried, angry energy. "Maybe one of those man-eating freaks killed them and *ate* them, and Avari hasn't told us because he doesn't know."

Tod stopped pacing and sat on the edge of my desk. "I think it's dangerous to assume there's anything Avari doesn't know."

"He doesn't know what we'd be willing to do to get our mom back."

"Of course he does. Anything. The same thing Kaylee and Sophie would be willing to do to get their dads back. That's what Avari's counting on."

"He'll use our parents against us."

"Yup." Tod nodded. "He'll use us all against one another if he gets the chance."

"Do you think he's found them?"

"No." Tod didn't hesitate. "But he wants to find them almost as badly as we do."

Nash exhaled slowly. "What do you think he'll do with them?"

"There are too many possibilities to even guess at."

Tod was perfectly capable of an educated guess, but listing all the horrible ways our parents could die—or suffer for eternity—wouldn't help anything.

"Think he'll kill them?"

"Maybe."

"Worse?"

"Maybe."

For a moment—a very long moment—Nash was silent. Then he looked up, and his next words sounded fractured with pain. "We're never going to see her again. You know that, right? She's gone. She's dead, or she's wishing she were dead, and she'll never be back."

Wood creaked as Tod lifted his very corporeal weight from my desk, and a second later he sat next to Nash on Em's bed. "I'm not going to let that happen."

Nash laughed, a harsh sound that carried disbelief but no real hostility. "I get that you think you're all badass, with the undead thing you've got going on, but it's been nearly three years. The mystique has worn off, and we all know the truth.

Reapers don't save people—they kill people. Besides, if she dies in the Netherworld, there's nothing you can do." Nash stood, headed for the hall, walking backward, and I scurried away from the door. "I appreciate what you're trying to do, but I'm not the little brother anymore. You don't need to coddle me. The truth is that if Avari wants Mom dead, there's nothing either of us can do to stop that. Especially you. No offense, but you couldn't even save Kaylee, and she was in the human world. Hell, she was in *your* reaping zone."

A lump formed in my throat, and I pushed my bedroom door open. "Food's here." Nash turned, eyes wide with surprise, but Tod looked like he'd known I was there the whole time. He studied me, and I realized he was trying to figure out if I agreed with Nash. If I thought he'd failed me when I'd died. "Sabine's not back yet," I said. "Do you think you could go check on her?"

Tod nodded, almost reluctantly, then stood and slid one hand behind my head and into my hair. The goodbye kiss he gave me lingered, and it tasted like sorrow. "Be back in a few." Then he disappeared.

When he was gone, I closed the door at my back, then leaned against it. Nash's brows rose. "What are you doing?"

"We need to talk."

He frowned. "Is it opposite day? 'Cause I think that's my line."

"I wish you could trust him as much as I trust him." I let go of the doorknob and sat on the edge of my desk, where Tod had been moments earlier. "It would mean the world to him to look at you just once and not see contempt and suspicion."

"Wow, seriously? I kinda thought he was lucky that I'm speaking to him at all, considering…what you two did behind my back. That's not exactly the kind of thing that inspires trust."

Granted. And we were obviously never going to be done paying for that. "But you trust me?"

Nash sat on my bed and thought in silence for a minute. "Yeah, actually, I do."

"Why?"

"I don't know." He shrugged. "We were together for so long…."

"Six months. We were together for six months, about a quarter of which I spent grounded." Since neither of us had to sleep, I'd actually spent more time with Tod in the month and a half we'd been together than I'd spent with Nash during our entire half year as a couple. "But you and Tod have been brothers your whole lives. Why would you trust me but not him? Especially considering that *I'm* responsible for everything you blame him for. I kissed him, Nash. Not the other way around. *I* kissed *him.*"

"I know. But…" He exhaled in frustration. "I understand why you would do that. *I* messed things up between you and me. Looking back, I'm surprised it took as long as it did for you to bail on me—"

"I didn't *bail.* I—"

He held up one hand. "I know. Just let me finish. My point is that I practically pushed you toward him, so I can't really blame you for your part in this. But I never pushed *him* toward *you.* He went after you all on his own."

"But he didn't," I insisted. "And he wasn't going to. If I hadn't kissed him, he'd probably still be watching from the sidelines, holding everything inside because he's your brother. Because he cares about you. Because he wants to protect you, even from himself."

"Oh, that's such *bullshit!*" Anger flashed behind Nash's eyes, and I saw him struggle to control it. Which meant more to me than he could possibly imagine. "I'm sorry, but you're wearing rose-colored glasses, Kay. You think that just because you have a heart of gold everyone else must, too, but that's not—"

"I don't have a heart of gold." Lately it felt more like I had a heart of steel. Like full-body armor was the only way I could protect the muscle that didn't always beat anymore but always felt bruised.

"Yeah, you do. What you don't see is that Tod would do anything for you because he loves you, but he's not like that with everyone else. He's not like that with *anyone* else."

"You're wrong. He's not perfect—none of us are—but he'd do anything for the people he loves, and you're one of them."

"Right. I almost forgot that stealing your brother's girlfriend is the best way to strengthen that fraternal bond," Nash said. I started to object, but he held one hand up again to stop me. "I know. I have to get over that, and I *am* getting over it. I'm getting over *you,* anyway. But he's my brother. We share the same parents. The same blood. He was willing to *die* to keep from reaping your soul, but he wasn't even willing to keep his tongue in his own mouth to keep me from getting dumped. That tells me exactly how much I mean to him."

I exhaled slowly and sank into my desk chair, one foot on the floor to keep it from turning. *Don't say it, Kaylee.* It wasn't my place. I had no *intention* of saying it until the words just fell out of my mouth.

"You died, Nash."

He kind of tilted his head, like he hadn't quite heard me. "What?"

"You died, when you were sixteen. In a car wreck. Hit head-on by a drunk driver who forgot to turn on his headlights. Your heart stopped beating. You stopped breathing. I know you probably don't remember all of that, but I'm assuming you remember at least *part* of it."

"Is this a joke? That's how *Tod* died. I broke a few ribs, but

I was fine. See?" He spread his arms, like that would prove he was right and I was wrong, and I only stared up at him, waiting for him to understand. For him to *let* himself understand what was surely already starting to sink in.

"No." He shook his head a little too hard, and his thick hair looked like a crazy brown halo for a second. "Kay, no, *Tod* died. It nearly killed our mom. It nearly killed *me.* It was my fault, because I went out when I was grounded and my ride got drunk, so I called Tod. If it weren't for me and that stupid party, he wouldn't have been on the road that night, but he still would have died, because it was his time. He was on some reaper's list."

"No, *you* were on the list. And you died, just like you would have died even if your drunk friend had been driving instead of Tod. But lucky for you, Tod *was* driving. He was there when you died, and he was there when Levi showed up for your soul."

"No." Nash stared at his hands, lying limp in his lap. "No, no, no..."

"Do you know what it takes to become a reaper, Nash?" He didn't look at me. He was still trying to see the truth in his own empty palms. "It takes a sacrifice. To even be considered for a position as a reaper, the recruit has to be willing to exchange his death date with someone else's, without knowing about the possibility of being granted an afterlife."

"You're serious?" His irises were a *storm* of browns and greens, twisting too fast for me to interpret. "This is real? You're saying Tod really...?"

"I'm saying that when you died, your brother started shouting for the reaper to show himself. He demanded to be taken in your place. He died way before his time so you could live. So that you could go on and make something of your life."

"My fault..." Nash closed his eyes, and I could no longer

see the tangle of shock and regret swirling in his irises. "All this time I've been telling myself that it wasn't my fault, because he would have died anyway. But it really *is* my fault. I got him killed."

"No, you didn't. It was his choice, and I would bet you the rest of my own afterlife that if he had the chance, he'd do it all over again."

Nash's eyes flew open, and now the emotion in them was clear—heartbreak. "Why didn't he tell me?"

"Because he didn't want you to feel guilty. The same reason he made your mom and me promise not to tell you, either." And I'd just broken that promise. Damn it.

"My mom knows?"

I nodded. "She's known almost from the beginning. I just found out last month."

Nash looked devastated. Confused. Almost…fragile. "Why are you telling me, if he didn't want me to know?"

"I probably shouldn't have. I didn't mean to. I think that's the first promise to him that I've ever broken, and I swear it'll be the last." Tod deserved better than a girlfriend who couldn't keep her word. "But you needed to know what he's given up for you. You need to know that he does care about you, more than you can possibly imagine. We both do. And he would *never* have tried to come between you and me, though goodness knows he had several chances." Sabine had even tried to convince him to work with her to break us up, and he'd refused. "Because he doesn't want to hurt you."

For nearly a minute, Nash sat unmoving on the end of Emma's bed. Staring at the carpet. His heart must have been pounding, because I could see his pulse jump on the side of his neck, even when everything else was so incredibly still.

Then he met my gaze from across the room. "I'm supposed to be dead. Tod's supposed to be alive."

"No. There's no more 'supposed to be,'" I insisted. "It is what it is, for both of you. This is what he wanted. For you."

"But he didn't graduate. He didn't go to college. He didn't even get a senior year of high school. He gave those to me instead, and what did I do with them?"

My heart hurt for him. "Nash, don't—"

"I wasted them. He paid for my future with his own life, and I threw it all away, like it was worth nothing, when the truth is that it was worth everything."

"You didn't waste it. You—"

"I wasted it." Nash shook his head slowly, and his gaze lost focus. "All this time I wanted him to move on. No, I wanted him to *go away.* I thought he took the job as a reaper because he wasn't ready to leave. I thought he was hanging around because he hated me or was jealous of my life. Or wanted to take away the things I care about."

Like me. He didn't say it, but we both heard it.

"But the truth is…" Nash stopped and looked at me again, like he didn't know how to finish his sentence. "I…I don't really know what to do with this information, Kaylee. I don't know how to process it. I'm not supposed to be here. I feel like the past two and a half years of my life have been a lie."

"No, your life isn't a lie, and it never has been. Your life is an opportunity. A gift. Just like mine is. We have that in common, Nash. We got a second chance." Okay, technically I was on my third chance, but then, technically, I was dead.

I took a deep breath I didn't really need, then prepared to say what I'd wanted to say to him for more than a month. I'd imagined this moment a million times, but now that it had come, I was suddenly unsure of the words. And of my right to say them. But someone had to.

"I don't want to put any additional pressure on you or anything, but if you ask me, second chances come with a responsibility." That's what I believed about my own second chance, anyway. "The responsibility to *earn* the extra time you've been given. And to enjoy it. To live with and for everyone you love. To fight harder and longer than anyone else, because you owe it to your brother and I owe it to my mother to make sure that their deaths mean something."

Nash blinked, and when the motion in his irises slowed, I knew he was thinking. He was truly considering what I was saying and its relevance to him. "That's what you're doing? That's why you always jump in headfirst whenever anyone's in trouble, whether they want your help or not? Whether they *deserve* it or not?"

I crossed my arms over my chest and let my rolling chair rotate a little. "I don't do that."

"That's all you *ever* do. It's who you are. And I think I'm starting to understand why." The motion in his irises slowed even more, greens spreading into browns to make that hazel shade I knew so well. "You think you have to earn your place in the world."

"I think we should *all* earn our place in the world. Especially people like me and you, who keep getting our friends and family hurt, whether we mean to or not." I was afraid he would take that the wrong way, but he only nodded, like he might actually eventually agree. "We owe the world something. We owe the world *everything.*"

Nash stared at me like he hadn't in a long time. Studying me, like he might be figuring me out. "You're something else, Kaylee. I'm not sure exactly what that means, but I'm sure it's true."

"Yeah, you, too. You're something special, Nash." And he could be something *great* if he'd stop looking at life as a challenge to be conquered rather than an opportunity to be seized.

"So, now what?" He sat up straight and glanced at the

room around us as if he no longer recognized it. As if what he'd learned had changed the way he saw everything, and a little spark of anticipation shot through me. I hadn't seen him look like that—like he was ready for a challenge—in months.

"Now, you take a few minutes to process all this, then come out and have dinner. No one else knows about any of this, and I need you to keep it quiet until I've had a chance to tell Tod that I told you. But we're going to get your mom back. We're going to get them *all* back, and that's going to be much easier if we're all fighting on the same side. If we all trust one another. If we can all count on one another. Okay?"

Nash nodded, still kind of dazed, and I stood to give him some time to himself.

"When you're ready, there's food in the kitchen."

When I got there, Em, Luca, and Sophie were nearly finished eating, but Tod and Sabine weren't back yet. I scooped some noodles onto a plate for myself, but somehow I had even less appetite than usual. I'd just finished picking all the slivers of carrot from my meal and was about to check on Nash again when Tod suddenly appeared in the living room with Sabine in his arms.

She was unconscious, her head, arms, and legs hanging limp.

"Someone help me with her!" He kicked the coffee table out of the way and laid the *mara* on the couch. Chairs scratched the kitchen floor as we all stood at once. Nash made it into the living room at the same time I did—he must have *flown* down the hall. He shoved the coffee table over even farther and knelt on the floor next to the couch, brushing dark hair back from his girlfriend's forehead.

"What the hell happened?" he demanded as Sophie and Emma sank onto the coffee table where they could see and

Luca stood behind them, watching. Waiting to see how he could help.

"Look at her hand!" Em said, and I glanced at Sabine's right arm—the one without a cast. Her wrist and hand were swollen to the point that the skin should have split, and a bright red web of veins traced the surface of her inflamed flesh, inching up her arm toward her chest. Toward her heart.

But what stood out to me most was a ring of bright red pinpricks encircling her wrist like a bracelet. Or like a tattoo.

"Oh, shit." I knew those marks. I had an identical circle of them around my right ankle—permanent reminders of the day I'd been pricked by a crimson creeper vine. I'd nearly died.

"Avari got her ankles, too." Tod carefully lifted Sabine's leg, where a severed section of creeper vine dangled from the end of her jeans, its thorns still piercing the denim. A thick, viscous fluid dripped slowly from the cut end of the vine to soak into the carpet. "That cast is the only thing that saved her other arm."

"Shit!" Nash carefully unwound the vine from her left ankle. "How did this happen?"

"He must have caught her." Tod lifted the *mara*'s other leg so he could unwind the single loop of vine, and I stepped back to give them room. "I found her alone, unconscious, tied to the ground by all four limbs with creeper vines."

"Live vines?" Sophie's voice flowed thick with horror.

"Yeah. Dead ones wouldn't have held. Fortunately, they were young. Thin, as you can see, and just now sprouting through cracks in the concrete." Tod dropped the severed end of vine on the end table next to the couch, and a single drop of yellow venom leaked onto the wood while the inch-long thorns scratched the already-chipped varnish.

Nash's vine followed a second later, then each brother

rolled up a leg of her jeans and slid her sneakers and socks off so we could get a better look at the damage.

"Not as bad as her arm but not great," Nash said through clenched teeth. His irises swirled with fear, and his voice shook with it. "If we don't do something, this'll kill her."

Em lifted Sabine's right arm and examined it, careful not to touch the puffy flesh. "What *can* we do?" Worry looked much the same on her as it had on Lydia. But Emma's eyes were all her own, and they were so full of sadness I couldn't help wondering whether she was syphoning it all from Nash or had actually started to care about Sabine, as I had.

That damn *mara* was an emotional ninja, sneaking up on your heart when you least expected it.

"Harmony treated me for this once," I said. "She had this stuff—"

"She still has the stuff!" Nash stood so fast *my* head spun. "She has jars of it at home—she started making it in larger batches after you got pricked that time—she even carries some in her purse now, just in case."

"Oh!" Sophie stood and raced into the kitchen. A second later, she was back with Harmony's purse, shoving it at me. "She left it here when you guys crossed over."

"Thanks." I opened the bag and pawed through it, then began laying travel-size plastic bottles on the coffee table. There were three of them, and each was labeled in permanent marker with Harmony's neat, all-caps print.

Water—amnesia. Obviously, that was what she'd put in Traci's tea.

Water—analgesic. A painkiller, made from water native to the Netherworld.

XX.

I could only assume that was the one she would have given

Traci to help safely end her pregnancy, if that had been Traci's decision.

"It's not here." I pawed through the purse again, but there were no more plastic bottles.

"It's glass." Nash took the bag from me and dumped its contents onto the coffee table, and Em stood to get out of the way. "And there should be a syringe. It has to be injected, remember?"

I did remember, but barely. I'd hardly been conscious when Harmony had injected me.

Several of us pawed through the collection of keys, makeup, restaurant ketchup and mayonnaise packets, hand sanitizer, and an assortment of other personal necessities until Em suddenly squealed in triumph.

"Here's the bottle!" She held up a small glass bottle sealed with a rubber stopper.

Nash unzipped a pocket on the inside of his mother's purse and scooped out three tampons and a disposable syringe sealed in plastic, as well as a separate disposable needle in a tiny plastic tube. "Thank goodness." He ripped open the plastic around the syringe, then opened the tube and dumped the needle onto his palm.

"Do you know what you're doing?" Tod watched over his brother's shoulder. "How do you know how much to give her?"

"Mom taught me a few months ago, after...Kaylee brought me back from the Netherworld." When Avari had taken him to get to me. "She figured that the chances of someone getting stuck by creeper thorns got better and better every time we crossed over, and she said someone should know how to treat the venom, in case she couldn't get there in time."

Nash screwed the needle onto the end of the syringe, then held the glass bottle upside down. We all watched, breath held, while he drew liquid into the syringe, then withdrew the needle from the bottle. He held the syringe up to the light to double-check the dose, then turned back to Sabine.

"Here, can you hold her arm?"

I sank to my knees next to Sabine and held her arm out straight while he stared at it for what felt like forever. Then, finally, Nash sucked in a deep breath and held it while he slid the needle into her skin and carefully depressed the plunger.

Once he'd withdrawn the needle and a drop of blood had welled out of her arm, he frowned and sat on the edge of the coffee table. "I was supposed to clean the injection site first. Damn it!"

"Better late than never," Tod said. "What do you need?"

"Cotton swabs and alcohol should do it. And a Band-Aid."

"I'll get them!" Em stood and raced for the bathroom.

"But that won't kill any germs I just injected her with," Nash continued.

Tod put one hand on his shoulder. "Any human doctor can treat an infection. The same cannot be said for crimson creeper venom."

I gathered the used syringe and wrappers and threw them in the trash while Sophie put Harmony's stuff back in her purse. Luca slid the coffee table into place, and Nash cleaned the site of Sabine's injection with a belated dose of alcohol, then covered it with a bandage from the box Emma gave him. Then he sat on the coffee table and stared at her while she slept, periodically checking on her swollen wrist and ankles.

The rest of us gathered around the peninsula in the kitchen, speaking in hushed voices.

"So, how did you find her?" I poured myself a mug of coffee, which had already gone cold. "She was just…lying there?"

Tod nodded. "On the ground, out in the open, about three hundred feet from the hospital. In our world, that would have been the hospital parking lot. Avari must have told everyone not to touch her, because she was all alone, completely unscathed, except for the creeper vines."

"What the hell does that mean?" Sophie demanded in a fierce whisper, with a glance back at Nash, like she didn't want to further upset him. I was impressed. "Why take Sabine, then let us have her back? Why poison her, but not kill her?"

"It's a warning," I said. "It has to be."

"Warning us of what?" Luca said in a whisper of his own. "That he wants to mess with us? That he can kill us anytime he wants? If that's the message, wouldn't actually killing Sabine have said it more clearly?"

I could only shrug. "I don't know."

"And didn't you say he could have killed you and Tod right before you crossed over?" Em said. "But he didn't?"

"Because he doesn't want me dead," I tried to explain. "Well, no deader than I already am. He wants to..." I didn't know how to say the rest of it, and I didn't really want to hear it, even from my own mouth.

"He wants to take his time with her," Tod said, and hearing it in his voice wasn't much better. "He wants to take her apart at his leisure before eventually discarding her body and continuing with just her soul. He has eternity, remember? That's a lot of time to kill, which means he has more patience than we do. And he knows how to make his toys last."

"That may be the creepiest thing I've ever heard," Luca whispered. "And that's coming from someone who sees dead people on a daily basis."

"Agreed," I said, and Tod gave my hand a sympathetic squeeze.

"Hey, you guys, there's something in her pocket," Nash called from the living room. We all turned as he stepped into the kitchen. "I just noticed it sticking out." He unfolded the piece of paper and spread it out on the island in front of us.

It was a note. One line.

Tag. You're it.

"How is she?" I sat on the edge of my desk, and Nash answered without looking up. Without letting go of the fingers sticking out of Sabine's cast.

"About the same. A little less swollen." He'd rolled my desk chair next to her bed—my bed, technically—more than an hour ago and hadn't moved since. "But she's not waking up, and I can't figure that out. When you got pricked, you didn't lose consciousness."

"Yeah, but she got at least three times the venom I got." I shrugged, aiming for casual with the gesture. As if I wasn't almost as worried as he was. "I'm sure she'll be fine. She'll wake up soon." *I hope.* "And you know what? The fact that she's not moving is kind of a blessing. With the dose of venom she got, if she'd been up moving around like I was after I got pricked—" I'd had no idea what creeper venom could do, at the time "—her heart would've beat faster, pumping poison all over her body." Another casual shrug. "Instead, it looks pretty localized, and I'd call that a stroke of good luck."

Unless… I frowned at the thought drawing into focus. *Unless it wasn't the creeper venom, but something Avari did that ren-*

dered Sabine unconscious. In which case, he'd actually saved her life. Or at least prolonged it.

My private frown deepened, but Nash didn't notice. He was watching Sabine again.

Why would Avari do that? Why would he poison her, then make sure she lasted long enough to... To what?

Normally I'd guess that he wanted to extend her suffering, but she was unconscious. How much pain could she possibly feel?

Was he trying to make sure she'd last long enough to be found?

Suddenly Sabine's lack of consciousness scared me almost as much as her swollen skin and the thin puss oozing from every pinprick hole in her arm and legs. What the *hell* was Avari up to?

"Yeah, I'm trying to look at the bright side," Nash said, clearly oblivious to the turn my own thoughts had taken. "She's due for another shot in a couple of hours, and after that, she should get better pretty quickly. If she hasn't woken up by then, though, I claim the right to completely freak out."

"And I fully support that right. Here." I pushed away from my desk and handed him the carton of fried rice I'd brought from the kitchen, with a fork sticking up straight from the center. I didn't know whether or not he could use chopsticks, but I knew Tod could not. At all. "You should eat."

"Thanks." He took the carton and glanced at me, but then turned back to Sabine. I headed for the hall to give him space, but when he spoke, I stopped, one hand on the doorknob. "What if she dies?"

I let go of the door and turned around. "She's not going to die."

"But what if she does? What if she dies without ever waking up, and I don't get the chance to tell her...all the things

I need to say? All the things she needs to hear?" He exhaled slowly, and I could practically see his optimism die. "I've wasted *so* much time. And *so* many words. What if I don't get the chance to make it right?"

He was looking at me now, as if I might have the answer. As if I *had* to have the answer. "Do you love her?"

"Yeah. I'm sorry, but I don't think I ever really stopped. I just didn't realize it until she came back and made me remember…everything we had. But that doesn't mean I didn't love you, too…."

I actually laughed, just a little, over the irony. I couldn't help it. "You don't have to apologize to me for loving your girlfriend, Nash. In fact, don't *ever* apologize for loving someone. Just make sure that when she wakes up—and she *will* wake up—you tell her what you just told me."

The door squeaked open at my back, and Tod stepped into the room. We'd both been making an effort to stay corporeal when we weren't alone, for everyone else's benefit. "Any change?" he asked with a concerned glance in Sabine's direction.

"Nothing yet." Nash cleared his throat nervously, and I realized what he was about to say just a second too late to prevent it. "While you're here, I…um…I just wanted to say I'm sorry."

Tod crossed both arms over his short-sleeved tee. "What did you do now?"

"Nothing. Nothing recent, anyway."

"Then what are you sorry for?"

Crap, crap, crap! I'd wanted to warn Tod that I'd broken my promise….

"Everything. I'm sorry for everything." Nash shoved his hands in his pockets and stared at the ground for a second.

When he looked up, I could see him struggling to hide the conflicting emotions stirring in his irises. "You should have told me what really happened. I could have handled it. But that's not the point." He took another deep breath, and I saw Tod's posture slowly start to relax, though he didn't uncross his arms. "What I'm trying to say is that what you did for me means something. It means *everything.* And I'm so damn sorry for wasting it."

Tod blinked. Then he turned to me, his irises as still as I'd ever seen them. "You told him?"

"I'm sorry. It just kind of…came out. But, Tod, he needed to know. He *deserves* to know."

"Why didn't *you* tell me?" Nash said, and Tod turned back to him, struggling to keep a lid on what he was feeling. Locking us both out.

"Because I didn't want it to be like this. I didn't want you to think you owed me something. I didn't want you to feel like you had to live your life like I would have lived mine. I wanted you to live your own way."

"My way is *stupid,* Tod. Stupid and reckless."

"I know." The reaper finally cracked a small smile. "I knew that going into it. But stupid and reckless can be outgrown—death can't." Tod shoved that single, errant curl back from his forehead, and suddenly he looked serious again. "You're smart enough to be someone important. To do something good. But you weren't going to do any of that from a hole in the ground." He shrugged. "When you died, I realized that the most important thing I could ever do with my life was to make sure you'd keep living yours."

"You are so full of shit," Nash said. Then he threw his arms around his brother, and their long overdue fraternal hug blurred beneath my tears—the first happy ones I'd shed in ages.

★ ★ ★

"Well, *you've* had a busy day." Tod sank onto the couch next to me with two glasses of soda and handed me one of them.

"Thanks." I took a drink, then made myself meet his gaze. "I'm sorry I told your secret. I was going to tell you as soon as you got back, but then Sabine was hurt, and there just hasn't been much of a break since then." I sipped from the glass he gave me, then held it, letting condensation drip down my fingers.

Tod shrugged, and I noticed a mischievous tilt in the corners of his beautiful mouth. "I planned to tell him eventually anyway, but according to the official Big Mouth code of honor, you now owe me a new secret." He took my glass and set it on the coffee table next to his, then took my cold, damp hand in his warm one. "That's the only way to restore the balance of information in this relationship."

"You already know everything worth knowing about me."

His fingers threaded with mine and he leaned so close I could feel his breath on my ear. "You don't have to *tell* me a new secret." His intimate whisper echoed through me in all the best places. "You have to help me *make* one."

My eyes widened. "Here? Now?" I frowned, trying to ignore the cravings that just being so close to him awoke in me. "Just because we *can* be invisible and inaudible doesn't mean—"

Tod laughed, and Emma glanced our way from the kitchen, then turned back to the brainstorming session she, Luca, and Sophie were sharing. "Not now," he whispered. "But soon. You have a *big* secret to replace, so put on your thinking cap. And just FYI, that's the only article of clothing this particular process requires…."

I groaned as his lips grazed my neck and his hand tightened around mine. "This kind of makes me want to tell *all* your secrets."

"Then we'd have even more to make up for." His mouth trailed toward the hollow of my collarbone. "It's a vicious, beautiful cycle."

With another reluctant groan, I took his chin and pulled him back up to eye level. "That vicious, beautiful cycle is going to have to wait. We have nosy friends and missing parents."

"That's kind of my point." The heat in his eyes was suddenly overwhelmed by pale blue twists of a deeper urgency. "Watching Nash watch Sabine makes me think we should all stop waiting."

"Waiting for what?"

"For anything. If we have something to say, we should say it. If we have something to do, we should do it."

I rubbed the sudden chill bumps on my arms. "Because we might not get another chance?"

"Exactly."

"That's depressing."

"Or liberating. If you think about it like that, we have no reason *not* to do whatever we want, right this minute. In fact, we have a *responsibility* to enjoy the time we have together, in case we're about to lose that chance." Tod's brows rose, and that heat was back in his eyes in spite of ominous undertones I couldn't quite dismiss.

"You do realize you're just trying to justify your impulse-control issues, right?"

"I think it's working." His hand slid over my stomach and curled around my hip, and I caught my breath. "Can you guess what kind of impulse I'm not controlling right now?"

"I think we can all guess." Em sank into my dad's recliner across the coffee table from us. "So rein it in before my inner syphon decides your hormonal excess needs to be balanced. I don't think *any* of us want to see that happen."

Sophie dropped into the armchair in the corner. "I've never heard a truer statement."

"I've got a few more true statements for you," Tod mumbled, and I elbowed him, but not as hard as I probably should have. Her dad was missing, too.

"Any change with Sabine?" Luca said on his way in from the kitchen.

"No." I turned to Tod, looking into his eyes for the guilt he no doubt saw in mine. "We shouldn't have let her go. This is our fault."

"Kaylee, Sabine is stronger and more independent than anyone else I know. Other than you and my mom, of course." He squeezed my hand, holding my gaze. "She had as good a chance of walking out of there unhurt as any of us. Better than several of us."

"Except that she didn't. And there's no telling how long we left her like that, tied to the ground, being poisoned, because we expected her to take longer than we would." Because she actually had to drive to and from the crossover site.

"We did the best we could. Now we need to figure out our next move."

I shrugged. "We keep looking. But this time, just the two of us." I wasn't going to put Sophie in danger of what had happened to Sabine. "Agreed?" I glanced around the room and was rewarded with three nodding heads.

"Yeah," Tod said. "And this time I think we should go together."

"Sophie, what do you have for us?"

"Oh. Just a second." She headed into the kitchen and a chair scraped the floor, then she was back a second later with a small spiral notebook.

"Okay, here goes." Sophie sat on the arm of Luca's chair, staring at her notes, and his arm snaked around her. "My dad likes to go camping, remember?" she said, and I nodded. "He's gone every fall as far back as I can remember, and last month he finally told me that those camping trips are usually retreats with my brothers."

My uncle had grown sons from a marriage that had ended with the death of his first wife, nearly a century ago—a fact that continued to blow my mind every time I thought about it.

"And they've been going on these retreats into nature since before most modern camping conveniences were invented," Sophie continued. "So I figure he knows how to live off the land, at least a little. He can find shelter and tie knots and fish without a pole, for sure, though I have no idea how handy those skills will be in the Netherworld. Personally, I think his best bet is to get inside, assuming that most buildings won't be as heavily populated as the Netherworld version of our school is."

"I truly hope they're not." And there was a decent chance of that, because Avari had drawn the current Netherworld populace of our school into the building by living there himself, like some kind of demonic landlord.

"We're kind of assuming he'd forgo the buildings closest to the hospital, because those would be the first place Avari and his monster horde would look," Luca said. "But he wouldn't go too far, because your mom—" he glanced at Tod "—will start to feel heavy after a while."

"And we have a general direction, based on the blood trail and rags Tod found, right?" Em said.

"Yes," I said. "Unless those were intentionally misleading." Which was a good possibility. "If it weren't so close, I'd guess he'd taken her into the actual hospital. That's where he's most likely to find bandages and any other medical supplies that crossed into the Netherworld with the building." And those supplies were likely to be plentiful, considering how highly and consistently populated the hospital was.

But the truth, even after we'd shared our intel and theories, was that we really had no clue where Uncle Brendon and Harmony were. In hiding from Avari and the rest of the Netherworld creatures, they were hiding from us, too.

Tod and I spent most of that night in the Netherworld, searching for his mom and my uncle in and around the buildings we'd decided they were most likely to target. We were looking for my dad, too, of course, but we had much less hope of actually finding him, since he was no doubt both hidden and guarded. And probably unable to call out to us if we got close.

We started at the hospital because as unlikely as I thought my uncle was to actually hide out there, I couldn't help thinking he was *very* likely to have stopped there, at least for a little while, in search of medical supplies. Tod showed me where the easiest-to-access first-floor medical supplies were in the human world, and we crossed over one site at a time, armed with the sledgehammer Tod had dug up from somewhere—he was inspired by the one my uncle had used—and the large meat cleaver he'd taken from the hospital cafeteria for me.

I wasn't surprised to see that all of the closets he showed me had bled through from the human world with at least some of their supplies intact, but I *was* pleasantly surprised to see that the Netherworld version of the hospital was virtually deserted. If Avari's lackeys had looked for Uncle Brendon and Harmony there, they'd obviously long since moved on.

Finally, after checking out three different supply closets, we were rewarded in the fourth, where the doorknob had been beaten off, evidently with the fire extinguisher propped against the wall several feet away.

On the floor of the closet, we found empty bandage wrappers, bloody scraps of gauze and cotton swabs, and an open bottle of rubbing alcohol.

Tod stared at the mess for a minute, and I linked my hand with his, hoping he could feel both my sympathy and empathy in that one touch. I knew how he felt, as few others could—we knew even less about my dad's current state than we knew about his mom's. Tod squeezed my hand, then let it go and knelt to gather the trash my uncle had left behind.

"What are you doing?"

"They obviously haven't found this yet, so I'm taking it. I don't want them to know what my mom tastes like. I don't even want to *think* about the possibility that one of them could develop a taste for her blood specifically, like Avari has for your…you. What if that sparks some kind of similar obsession, and they start hunting her like he hunts you? It's bad enough that I can't protect you. At least I can do this for her."

I wanted to let him think that. I actually considered preserving his well-intentioned fantasy. But eventually he would realize his own mistake, and he'd know that I hadn't told him the truth when I should have.

"Tod, they've already had a taste of her. Didn't you say they were gathered around drops of her blood outside?"

His hands went still, one of them clenched around a handful of empty wrappers. "Fine. But I'm not going to give them any more of it to obsess over. This is part of her, Kaylee, and I'm not just going to leave it here for them to snort and drool and fight over."

"I get it." I would have done the same thing for my dad if I could've.

We traced my uncle's most likely path out of the hospital

from that closet, but we couldn't find footprints or anything else to indicate which way he'd gone from there.

We were about to cross into the human world near the ambulance bay when something scraped concrete behind us. We both tensed and turned toward the sound. In the middle of the hall stood two small grayish creatures whose bulbous heads didn't quite reach my waist. They were bald and wore no clothes, but even without the odd, arrhythmic jerking in their arms, legs, and thin gray tails—not to mention the occasional full-body twitch—I would have recognized them based solely on their double row of needle-sharp, metallic-looking teeth.

Fiends.

I hadn't seen a fiend since the day a creeper vine had nearly ended my life several months ahead of schedule. Or thirteen years late, depending on your perspective. That was the day Nash was first exposed to Demon's Breath, and though I didn't know it at the time, the whole thing was my fault. I'd brought some latex balloons filled with the substance to give to three fiends in exchange for information, accidentally kicking off a series of events that led to Nash's addiction, our eventual breakup, and Avari's inexplicable obsession with owning my soul.

It was not my finest day.

"Victory!" the fiend on the left cried in a voice so high-pitched my ears tried to crawl into my skull. "We found the treasure. We get the prize." He bounced forward, metallic teeth clinking together in excitement—or maybe that was his jaw twitching.

"Stay there!" I brandished the huge knife, suddenly glad we'd come armed.

Tod set the head of his sledgehammer on the ground, resting both palms on the end of the handle, and I had the sudden, irrational thought that he looked like Thor must have as a teenager. Assuming Norse gods were ever teens.

"Treasure!" the other fiend echoed, yellow eyes flashing with eagerness, and mentally I named him Thing Two. "We play the game. We find the treasure. We win the prize. Come! Maybe we will share the prize."

"No!" Thing One turned on his little associate, snarling, and Thing Two sprang backward just in time to avoid losing a chunk of his thin gray arm to Thing One's needle teeth. "No sharing!"

Thing Two snarled back, and they faced off, teeth snapping, thin tails whipping up dust at their feet. Any second, one would pounce.

"Fiends! Focus!" I snapped, my cleaver held ready. I'd had more practice with a blade than I cared to remember, but I'd never chopped anything…off. Which seemed to be what a cleaver was used for. "What prize?"

"The breath of hellions, of course." Thing One cocked his head to one side. "What else would suffice?"

"Avari offered a reward for us," I whispered, and on the edge of my vision, Tod nodded.

"He knew we'd come looking for Mom and Brendon."

"Come!" Thing One shouted. He started to turn, and when we didn't follow, his thin, dark gray brows furrowed at the bottom of his huge, smooth forehead. "Come!"

"Bite me." Tod lifted the hammer and choked up on his grip as Things One and Two gave us scary metallic snarls.

"Maybe not the best choice of words…" I clenched the handle of my cleaver tighter. "They're poisonous, right?" I had just enough time for a moment of thanks that, like Nash, Tod had played both football *and* baseball before the little monsters charged.

Things One and Two took a few running steps on the

floor, then leaped like crazy little monkey-monsters and bounced off opposite walls as if the Sheetrock hid springs. They shrieked as they raced toward us, bounding from floor to wall and back, swapping sides without ever colliding, and I backed up, my heart pounding, my pulse racing. The hallway was wide, but Tod needed room to swing his hammer, and after watching the fiends bound through the hospital hallway like toddlers in a bouncy-house, I was no longer confident that either of us could actually hit them.

We'd backed into the waiting room by the time they got close enough to pounce, and the double doors swung shut between us and them just in time. One fiend slammed into the glass window and slid out of sight, and the thud that followed said his friend had hit too low for us to see.

"Ready to go?" I could hear the tension in my voice.

"In a minute." Tod held the massive hammer like a baseball bat, and I gave him some more room. "We need to find out if they know where—"

The doors flew open, fast and hard, and not two, but a *dozen* or so fiends poured through the opening, evidently drawn by their freaky little brethrens' shrieks. "Treasure!" several of them shouted, limbs twitching, yellow eyes flashing.

Tod groaned. "Never mind. Get back."

I had half a second to process what he'd said, then I backpedaled just as the first fiend pounced, jaw open, metallic teeth shining in the light from overhead.

Tod swung. His hammer thunked into a bulbous skull with a crack like thunder, and the little monster flew across the room to smack into the opposite wall. I flinched at the sound, and the sight, and at the knowledge that what leaked from the massive rupture in the little beast's head was what passed for brains in a fiend.

"You're not going to trade us for a hit of Demon's Breath," Tod said. "But you are going to answer a question."

But before he could ask, a murmur rippled through the small crowd, too soft and squeaky for me to understand until one fiend near the front narrowed his yellow-eyed gaze on me. "Wrong treasure," he said. Then, "Wrong treasure!" He stepped toward me, and Tod tightened his grip on the hammer, ready to swing again. "Too tender. Too young." His focus rose to my head. "No blood. Wrong treasure!"

With that, the murmuring grew in volume, and the crazy little fiends backed out of the lobby almost as one. The door swung shut behind them, and through the window, I caught a glimpse of several small gray bodies springing off the walls as they retreated down the hall without another glance back at us.

"What the hell…?" Tod lowered his hammer.

"They weren't looking for us. They were looking for Harmony and Uncle Brendon." Who weren't so young and tender. And one of whom—Harmony, at least—was bleeding.

Tod turned to me, his hammer propped on the floor. "If they're looking for Mom and Brendon, that means Avari hasn't found them."

And that was the best news we'd had all night.

In the human world, Tod disposed of his mother's medical waste, and after texting Nash with an update, I stayed with Tod at the hospital so that between his few scheduled reapings, we could head back into the Netherworld to keep searching, temporarily bolstered by the knowledge that Avari didn't yet have his mom and my uncle. We tried over and over that night to find them, moving in an ever-widening arc from the hospital and dodging roving bands of fiends searching for their next fix, but after the supply closet, we found no other sign of our missing authority figures.

The only bright spot that entire night was when Emma called around two in the morning to tell us that Sabine had regained consciousness. Tod had to stay at work, but I blinked into my room to find the *mara* sitting up in my bed, surrounded by the rest of my pajama-clad friends. And Sophie.

"Seriously, if you don't get out of my face, I'm going to turn your dreams into a nightmare circus the minute you fall asleep. Creepy clowns and all."

Emma laughed in relief. "Yeah, I think she's back to normal. Well, as normal as she ever was anyway." She turned to head for the hall and saw me about the same time Luca and Sophie did.

"Hey." I gave Emma a relieved hug and noticed again how small she was now in Lydia's body. "Now that she's awake, why don't you guys go get some sleep? We still have school tomorrow."

"That's not gonna happen." Sophie crossed her arms over her chest, and I noticed that her eyes were red-rimmed and bloodshot. "We're in the middle of a supernatural crisis here."

"If we only went to school when life was calm and not plagued by evil forces, I'd have already flunked out for truancy," I said.

"My dad's trapped in a scary alternate dimension, Kaylee. I'm not going to sit through algebra and geography with that on my mind."

I shrugged. "Fair enough. I'm going, though." I wasn't going to let Avari drive me out of my own school, in part because it was *my* school. And in part because if he possessed anyone else, someone would need to be there to exorcize him from the stolen body.

But I was already planning several long bathroom breaks

so I could keep up the search for those still trapped in that scary alternate dimension.

"I'm going, too." Sabine threw back the covers and started to swing her legs out of bed, but Nash put one hand on her knee to stop her.

"You should rest."

"I've been unconscious for, what, five hours?" She glanced at my alarm clock and frowned. "That's more rest than any *mara* needs in one night."

"Being unconscious isn't the same as sleeping," Nash insisted. "And anyway, you were poisoned." He lifted her good arm to show her the ring of tiny red dots now permanently encircling her wrist. Just like the ones around her ankles. Just like the one around *my* ankle. "You need to rest, so your body can fight what's left of the poison."

"Bullshit. Just because it took Kaylee days to recover doesn't mean it'll take me that long. I'm a Nightmare. We're kinda badass."

I laughed, but Nash only crossed his arms over his chest. "If you don't rest, I don't rest. We'll both be exhausted and vulnerable together at school tomorrow."

Sabine rolled her eyes. "Fine. I'll lie here and stare at the ceiling if you'll go to sleep."

"Deal." Nash finally smiled, and I could see exhaustion warring with relief in his eyes.

"You can have my bed." Em followed him into the hall. "I'm fine in the living room, in the recliner."

"Thanks." He ducked into the bathroom. When Em joined Sophie and Luca in the living room, I sat in the chair Nash had vacated next to my bed.

"He was here the entire time, you know," I said softly, and Sabine looked like she didn't know whether or not to believe me. "Seriously. He sat right here the whole time you were out. And he gave you two antivenom injections. And I doubt he ate a bite of his dinner."

I'd rarely seen Sabine speechless. It looked kind of like a fish gasping for air.

"You should have seen him when Tod brought you back, unconscious and poisoned. I haven't seen Nash that focused in a long time. He knew exactly what to do, and he did it well. But he was terrified that you'd die anyway. That he'd lose you."

"Thank you," she said, finally. "I know you didn't have to tell me that."

"Yeah, I did. I just..." I'd been thinking about what she'd said to Sophie, and what Nash had told me about the *mara*. "I want you to know that you're one of us. You're a total pain in the butt, and I may never forget that you tried to sell me to a demon, but I do *forgive* you for that. And you need to know that you belong here. With us. This place wouldn't be the same without you here to throw the truth around like a weapon and call us on our own bullshit. So, try not to get yourself killed, okay?"

I could swear that her black eyes looked a little more damp than usual, but then she blinked, and that was gone. "Look who's talking, living dead girl."

"I know. I'm a total hypocrite." The toilet flushed across the hall, then water ran in the bathroom sink behind the closed door. Nash was getting ready for bed, and my time alone with Sabine was running out. "Can you tell me what happened? What you remember, anyway? How did Avari catch you?"

Sabine's expression darkened from something resembling contentment into anger blazing hot enough to singe my eyebrows. "It wasn't Avari," she said. "It was someone new. A hellion. Tall, with long red hair so dark it almost looked black. His tongue was the same color—like dried blood. His eyes were solid black like a hellion's, but they had red veins running through them. I'm going to be working those details into my next nightmare, FYI. If they scared me, they'll scare anyone."

"That's Ira." My voice sounded sharp. Angry.

"The wrath hellion?" Sabine looked more intrigued than scared now, which worried me.

"Yeah. What did he do? What's the last thing you remember?"

"I don't remember much. I was sneaking around some bushes in front of a building about a mile south of the hospital when I started hearing things. Weird sounds. Wet, heavy breathing, like a giant with a sinus infection. And scratching sounds, like something digging in dry dirt. Then there was this weird hiss.... So I ducked as close to the building as I could and waited to see if I needed to cross over, or if they'd lose my scent and wander off. Then the hellion was just there. Out of nowhere. He was just standing in front of me, backlit by that weird-ass red moon. He had those weird eyes, and they were kind of *glowing,* and for a second, I couldn't look away from him. Then the light from his eyes seemed to kind of flare, and he reached for me."

Spitting sounds came from the bathroom as Nash brushed his teeth, drawing me out of the nightmare she was painting for me, this time with words. "Then what?"

Sabine shrugged. "He grabbed my arm, and I tried to cross back over, but I couldn't concentrate enough to make it happen. All these thoughts kept spinning around in my head. All kinds of stuff. People who've pissed me off. The juvenile court judge who set me up for vandalism. You." She shifted beneath the covers, like she was uncomfortable with whatever she was about to confess. "No offense, but when I first met you, I hated you like I've never hated anything before, and when Ira touched me, I couldn't get you out of my head. You kissing Nash. Him touching you. The two of you dancing at some lame high school party to a song no one with actual ears has ever enjoyed. Stuff like that. Crap I never even saw but used to imagine during the worst days this past winter."

"Yeah." I tucked one leg beneath me in the rolling chair. "Ira's M.O. seems to be fictionalized flashbacks designed to thoroughly piss you off, so he can feed from your anger."

"Well, it musta worked. I couldn't think with all that shit in my head, and then everything went dark." She shrugged again and tugged the covers higher. "The next thing I saw was this." Sabine spread her arms to take in my whole room. "I didn't know how I got here until Nash told me how Tod found me. Crimson creeper? Seriously?"

"Yeah. Tod said you were tied to the ground with four vines of it. Baby vines. And you must not have been there very long, or you couldn't have recovered this fast, even with Harmony's antivenom. Especially with three sets of pinpricks."

"Speaking of which..." Sabine held up her wrist, and I saw that the swelling was almost completely gone. Either *maras* healed faster than *bean sidhes* or Harmony had really perfected that antivenom. "Any way to get rid of the marks?"

"Not that I know of." I propped my foot on the edge of the bed and pulled up the hem of my jeans to show her my own double row of red dots.

She dropped her arm into her lap. "Maybe people will think it's some kind of obscure tattoo. Something tribal."

"Maybe." It was good to see her looking on the bright side.

Across the hall, the bathroom door opened. A second later, Nash stepped into the bedroom. "Did you and Tod have any luck?" he asked, sinking onto Emma's bed as I vacated the desk chair.

"Nothing since the bandages we found at the hospital. But the good news is that Avari has evidently promised a whole horde of fiends that whoever turns them in wins the grand prize—Demon's Breath, of course. Which means—"

"Avari doesn't have them," Nash finished for me.

"Not yet anyway. We haven't found anything since then, but we'll keep looking."

"Be careful," Sabine said. "I don't want to have to go back in after you." But she would if it came to that. That's what she was really saying, and the unspoken promise was not lost on me.

"Don't worry. Tod and I are going in together or not at all. We'll watch out for each other."

Before heading back to the hospital, I went into the living room to check on everyone else. Emma was already asleep in the recliner, stretched out as close to horizontal as the chair would go. Sophie and Luca were curled up on the couch together, even though the twin mattress he'd blown up for himself was only a couple of feet away. He slept on the outside, curled around my cousin with his arm draped over her stomach. Anything that wanted Sophie would have to go through Luca first, and seeing them together made my heart ache.

Seeing Emma alone made my heart ache even more.

Not seeing my dad in his bed—not hearing him snore in the middle of an otherwise quiet night—also made my heart ache so fiercely I let it stop beating altogether, just to spare myself the pain.

"Are you sure you want to go to school? You could just stay here with me." Tod patted the vinyl cushion next to him on the hospital waiting room couch, and I sat sideways to face him, trying to ignore the dozen early morning patients, none of whom could see or hear us.

"I wish I *could* stay here with you. I wish I never had to go anywhere else. But Em, Nash, and Sabine are going. We're still hoping to turn the hellions against one another, and if one of them possesses someone at school, I might be needed."

That was true. But it wasn't the whole truth. I needed to talk to Ira again, and if Tod knew what I was thinking, he'd insist on going with me. I couldn't let that happen for two reasons.

First, I didn't want them to meet. I didn't want Tod manipulated by the hellion of rage like I'd been. I didn't want him touched by evil any more than he already had been.

Second, I didn't want Tod to be upset by—or stand in the way of—any payment made to Ira if I needed to buy more information, and as badly as I hated to think about it, that possibility was looking pretty…um…possible. He understood the lines I would cross—and those I wouldn't—to get my dad back, because he'd do just about anything to protect his mother. But he didn't need to actually see payment rendered. Especially considering that his anger would just make it even easier for Ira to feed from him.

I felt bad about lying to Tod—even a lie of omission—but I'd feel worse if my inaction led to someone else's death. Especially my father's.

"I only have one more reaping this shift, so I'll cross over and keep looking as much as I can."

"Alone?" My heart thumped painfully. "We decided not to go alone." What if Avari caught him? What if something else caught him? What if he disappeared into the Netherworld never to be seen again, and I never found out whether he died, or got lost, or fell victim to eternal torture, or—

"I'll be fine." His blue-eyed gaze cut through the fear spiraling up my spine. "My mom's hurt, and I don't know how bad it is. I need to get her out of there. And while I'm there, I'll be composing a huge list of places your dad isn't." He shrugged. "We've got to narrow it down somehow, right?"

I gave him a halfhearted nod, trying not to think about the possibility that Avari could be moving him around. How, if that were the case, we might never find him. "Just…be careful, and text me once an hour, or I'll assume you've been captured and I'll come after you. I swear I will."

He smiled. "I believe you. And I'll see you at lunch." We'd learned early in our relationship that I couldn't concentrate on school when he came to class with me, even though no one else could see him.

"I'll be there." But lunch felt like an eternity away. Like one of those mirage illusions that got farther away the longer you walked toward it.

Thoughts of what was coming—what I might have to do—

churned in my stomach and weighed heavily in my heart. I wanted to tell him about the idea that had taken root in the back of my brain overnight, and about how I would do almost anything to avoid what was starting to look like the only way out of this, for my friends, my family, and for me. For us.

I wanted to tell Tod everything. Not telling him felt uncomfortable, like I was building a barrier between us. Like I couldn't quite reach him through the wall neither of us could see or touch, but he was surely starting to feel. But I couldn't tell him, because he'd be as determined to stop me as I was determined to go through with it. He'd be more determined, especially if his mother died, because then Nash and I would be all that he had left, and he'd be that much more determined to keep either of us from…

I blinked and buried that thought before he could see it swirling in my eyes. But I wasn't as fast as he was observant.

"You okay?" He turned my face toward his and ran one finger all the way from the back of my jaw to the tip of my chin, and I almost confessed everything with one look at the maelstrom of grief, frustration, and devotion churning in every imaginable shade of blue in his irises.

"No. I'm not okay." I let that one truth resonate in my voice and show in my eyes. "None of us are okay." And we weren't going to be until Avari was no longer a threat. Unfortunately, the longer I thought about the task in front of us, the more impossible it seemed to accomplish. On our own, anyway… "But we will be."

He smiled and pulled me closer. "When you say it like that, with that look in your eyes, I can almost believe it."

Well, that made one of us.

First and second periods dragged like no high school class has ever dragged before or since. I had no idea what I was supposed to learn in chemistry, and if the fate of the world ever came to hinge upon my understanding of time as the fourth dimension—which was only *marginally* relevant to the math lesson—we were all goners.

When the bell rang to end second period, I was the first one out of my chemistry classroom. I waved to Em in the hall and brushed off a question from Chelsea Simms, then ducked into the nearest restroom. As soon as I was sure it was empty—for the moment—I faded from human sight and spared a moment to hope Chelsea wasn't waiting for me to come out of the bathroom.

Then I blinked into the kitchen of a local doughnut shop, which had sat empty since Thane had killed the owner a month earlier. The doughnut shop had both sharp objects and privacy, everything necessary to summon a demon, as far as I could tell. Which was fortunate, because there was no way I'd invite Ira into my home, even if I could be sure of my control over him while he was there under the power of my blood. And I was far from sure of that.

The cut on my left palm hadn't yet healed and I wouldn't be able explain an identical one on my opposite hand, so I made a cut at the top of my forearm instead, near my left elbow. That turned out to be ill-planned, at best. It was much harder to direct the flow of blood from halfway up my arm than from my hand, but after a couple of minutes and several drops spilled on my jeans, I had enough blood on the floor to write with.

I pressed a stack of folded napkins against the new cut and bent my arm at the elbow to hold it in place. Then I made the creepiest finger painting in history.

Ira appeared in front of me the second his name fell from my tongue. He stared down at me with featureless, red-veined black eyes, and though his lips didn't actually curve up on the ends, I could swear he was smiling. "How wonderful to see you again, Ms. Cavanaugh. And you look so blisteringly angry!"

"You lied to me."

Ira sank to the floor in one smooth movement. "That, my little fury, is impossible. In fact, lying is one of very few things I cannot do."

I wanted to know what the other things were—and he obviously *knew* I wanted to know—but I wasn't willing to bargain with a hellion for something I didn't actually need.

"My dad wasn't where you said he'd be, and because of the wild-goose chase you sent us on, more people are hurt." And trapped in the Netherworld. But I wasn't going to mention that, in case he didn't already know about Harmony and my uncle. The last thing we needed was another hellion out there searching for them.

"I wasn't asked where your father *would* be. You asked me where he was, and I told you exactly where he was at the time. Obviously, he was moved before you arrived."

"Obviously." I tried to keep the anger from my voice but failed miserably.

"Look on the bright side—at least you learned something." He actually did smile that time, with lips the color of clotting blood. "You learned to act quickly, before the intelligence you paid for becomes moot, right?"

"Actually, the lesson I learned goes something like, 'Never trust a hellion.'"

Ira laughed, a sound that felt more like an angry dog's growl than a demonstration of joy. "I would have thought you'd learned that one long ago."

I would have thought so, too. Which was part of the problem.

He leaned closer, over the blood on the floor, and it took most of my self-control to keep from backing away from him, which would have felt to both of us like an admission of fear. "But the fact remains—I did not lie to you."

"But you did tie my friend to the ground with crimson creeper vines. Why?"

Somehow, Ira seemed even more amused by my question than by my belated wariness of hellions in general. "Are you surprised when a cat meows? Or when a siren sings her prey to sleep?"

"I'm surprised when someone who agrees to help me turns around and tries to kill one of my friends."

He leaned back again, studying me from a different perspective, and I pretended that didn't creep me out. "Little fury, I'm finding it difficult to express how very mixed-up you seem to be. First of all, I did not, nor will I ever, 'help' you. The information I provided was not a favor. It was a service rendered for payment. And, for the record, I'm only explaining that to you—with great patience, I might add—because I can feel you growing angrier with every word I speak. Which means that so far, I'm profiting from this little encounter without putting forth any effort whatsoever."

"You're...*vile*." I'm not sure where the word came from, but it felt like a good fit.

"Why, thank you. And to continue, I did not try to kill your friend the *mara*. Had I wanted her dead, I would simply have bitten her head off and sucked out the tasty filling. But the fact is that in most cases, death of the victim means an end to its anger, thus an end to my meal. You are the happy exception. Well, the *angry* exception, in this case."

"The exception?" Why am I always the exception?

"Typically, the undead quickly start to lose touch with their human emotions, including anger. At first I thought you were simply too recently dead for that to have happened yet. And that could be the case. But upon subsequent study,

I've discovered that you, little fury, are not the average dead girl. You are a dead girl imitating life, which means that you didn't lose your connections to the human world when you died. You still love, and regret, and hope, and wish, and you still anger. So you still have use to me."

I frowned, trying to untangle his words and rearrange them so that they made sense. "Was that your long-winded way of saying you poisoned Sabine to piss me off?"

He nodded. "Succinctly put. In fact, my original intent was to kill her. However, when I took a taste of her anger, both past and present, I found you prominently displayed among her grievances, in spite of the fact that she was obviously in the Netherworld in an ill-fated attempt to help you and your assorted collection of playmates. Which told me that hurting her would likely anger you."

"So, should I assume that if you catch any of the rest of my 'playmates,' you will hurt them, too, to piss me off?"

Ira's mouth twitched, and I got the impression he was silently laughing at me. "That is a distinct possibility. It is also the last bit of information I will give you without compensation."

"Fine. I don't need anything else from you anyway."

His dark brows rose in a skilled imitation of human surprise. "That tastes like a lie, little fury. And the fact that you haven't yet dismissed me from the human plane seems to support my theory. What could you possibly need?" He crossed both arms over his chest, waiting, but I didn't answer. I couldn't without giving him as much information as I'd be asking him for.

"Information, again?" He was guessing. He was a good guesser. "I think you need more information, but I do look forward to the day you write my name in blood and ask me to take action on your behalf."

"That won't happen." In part because I couldn't afford it. And in part because dealing with Ira was dangerous, and the more I saw him, the more likely I was to forget that. To see him as just another Netherworld resource, like Harmony's herbal remedies.

That kind of casual disrespect would lead to things worse than death.

"Oh, I think it will. Based on the escalation of your rage in the few days since we officially met, I would say our relationship is building toward a sharp crest. You will need something soon. Something beyond information. And when you become angry enough to pay the price…that will be a day to remember, surely."

I stayed silent, well aware that every second I didn't swipe my hand through the bloody letters on the floor was another second confirming his theory that I still needed something from him.

"But just information for now, am I right? You want to know where your father is?" His brows rose again. "Will you pay twice to have the same question answered? Far be it from me to offer unsolicited advice, but if I were you, I'd ask something new. Perhaps you'd like to know the whereabouts of your uncle and your lover's mother? An attractive pair of *bean sidhes*. It would be a shame to see them devoured by the jungle, as it were."

My heart stopped beating for several seconds, and when it kicked into motion again, it overcompensated, pumping blood through my veins so fast my vision started to go dark. "You knew? You've been sitting here toying with me this whole time, when you knew what I wanted?"

"Of course. If I'd told you immediately, we both would have missed out on the titillating climax of your anger."

"You *bastard*."

"Yes, yes..." Ira studied me while I fumed, too angry to form words. "Now, what are you willing to pay for the information I have?"

"Nothing." I'd finally caught on. "You don't know where they are, do you?" He'd never actually said he did. He'd only implied it.

"That's an interesting question. And for another taste of your anger, I will answer it."

"No deal." I stood, and he stared up at me.

"Oh, little fury, do you really want to go away mad?" He laughed at his own joke, and I tried to remember if I'd ever heard a joke from a hellion. "Actually, that works for me, too. I look forward to our next—"

I swiped the sole of my sneaker across the bloody letters on the floor, and Ira disappeared in midsentence. His surprised expression hung there for a second in my mind, but that minor moment of satisfaction wasn't enough to soothe my anger or relieve my fear.

When the echo of his voice faded from my ears, I backed away from the blood on the floor, suddenly horrified by what I'd done. By the fact that I'd summoned a hellion again. That I'd put myself at risk again, and fed him at my own expense again, and that this time, I had nothing to show for it.

I was horrified most of all by the fact that I'd let him leave without telling me where my father was or whether or not he knew where Harmony and Uncle Brendon were. I was furious with myself for having the guts—the rash stupidity—to summon a hellion but not to finish what I'd started. To pay, again, for information that could have saved three lives.

What the hell was wrong with me?

I retreated from the red mess on the floor until my spine hit a stainless steel countertop, then I slid down the cabinet doors to sit with my knees tucked up to my chest, my arms clasped around them. Air slid in and out of my lungs as I stared at the puddle of my blood, trying to get a grip on my racing pulse and pounding heart. On the angry flush burning in my cheeks. Trying to decide how big a mess I'd made of the situation. Trying to figure out how to fix it.

How on earth was I going to find three missing parents when *multiple* hellions were also hunting them?

Then, when my body was finally under control—stupid leftover physiological reactions—and I'd calmed to the point that I could at least sort through my thoughts, I stood and did what had to be done. I found cleaning supplies and wiped up all the blood, then threw my trash into the Dumpster behind the doughnut shop. A glance at my watch showed that third period was almost over. With any luck, no one had noticed me missing during my free period. But my friends would notice if I skipped lunch.

In the doughnut shop's bathroom, I stared at my reflection, looking for any sign of the recent trauma. I ran my fingers through my hair and used a damp brown paper napkin to clean crusted blood from my arm. Which was when I realized my sleeve wasn't long enough to cover the fresh wound.

I blinked into my bedroom and bandaged the cut, then pulled a three-quarter sleeve cardigan from my closet to cover it. I was about to blink back to school when the bloodstains on my jeans caught my eye, reminding me to change them, too.

I arrived in the school bathroom two minutes before lunch, and since the room was empty, I was all clear to become corporeal again.

I'd made it halfway to the cafeteria, headed for my usual table in the quad, when Sabine rounded the corner in front of me. "Kaylee! Where the hell have you been?" She was whispering, but barely. "We've been calling, but you didn't answer your phone!"

Because it never rang. I pulled my phone from my pocket and pressed a button to wake it up, but nothing happened. It was dead. Which made sense, considering that I hadn't been home long enough to charge it the night before.

"We?" I pulled away when Sabine grabbed my arm with her good hand, but she only race-walked toward the quad, assuming I would follow. And I did. "Why? What's wrong?"

"Em had some kind of breakdown. She just freaked the hell out in the middle of third period. We heard her shouting in the hall, yelling for you, and the teachers couldn't calm her down. They called in the nurse, and her guidance counselor, but she just kept shouting for you, so they let me and Nash try to talk to her."

Fear for Emma froze my muscles and muddled my thoughts until I stopped walking and made myself focus. *One thing at a time. First, find Emma.* "Where is she? Is she okay?"

"The nurse sedated her. They took her away in an ambulance, and they wouldn't let us go with her. They tried to call your dad—he's her guardian on record—but of course, they couldn't get a hold of him."

"She's at the hospital? Did you call Tod?"

"Nash did, but he didn't answer."

"He's probably looking for his mom." And after talking to Ira, I had an all-new grasp of just how dangerous the Netherworld had become, for all of us. "I'll find her. Just…you and Nash watch out for each other." I rubbed my forehead with one hand. "Wait, can you just…go home? To my house, with Sophie and Luca? Check yourselves out, or if they won't let you, then just leave. I don't think it's safe for us here."

Or anywhere.

Finally I was grasping what I should have understood much earlier—we brought danger to Eastlake, not the other way around.

Sabine nodded. "You don't have to talk me into skipping school."

I started to blink out of the hall, then turned to her again at the last second. "Oh, how do you feel?" In all the commotion, I almost forgot that she'd been poisoned only twelve hours earlier.

"Tired. But fine other than that," she said, and I spared a moment to wonder if she'd actually admit to a weakness if she had one. Other than an unwavering devotion to Nash.

"Good. And thanks for finding me. I'll see you as soon as I can get Emma out of there."

"Okay." Sabine frowned at my cardigan. "Did you change clothes?"

"Yeah. Long story. Gotta go." I blinked out of school and into the hospital before she could ask any more questions.

The E.R. was nearly deserted, as it was most school days—Tod said the peak hours were always nights and weekends.

Invisible to all human eyes, I ran past rows of empty waiting room chairs, the lady at the check-in desk, and three different triage rooms, where nurses and techs took patients' vital signs and typed their symptoms into computers. I jogged right through the electronic-assist door into the main part of the E.R., past the nurses' station—a large square countertop with several work areas spaced out inside it—and made a quick round of the E.R. patient rooms, looking for Emma.

Four of the rooms were occupied, but Em wasn't in any of them. Had she already been admitted or released? Could they possibly have done the paperwork that quickly?

When I couldn't find her in the bathrooms or at the vending machines, I stopped in the center of the E.R. again, studying the nurses' station. They would have the information I needed, either stored on computers I didn't know how to access or printed in files I couldn't pick up without freaking out people who couldn't see me.

I'd have to look without touching anything. Or wait until no one was looking to go through the charts stacked in a vertical organizer. But someone seemed to be looking in nearly every direction. That's the problem with a room full of people.

I entered the nurses' station and turned in a full circle, watching the doctors and nurses all around me typing, chatting, and jotting things on forms clipped to clipboards. Because I was faking life, I'd only done the invisible-in-a-crowd thing a couple of times before—most of the time, my incorporeity was a precaution, in case someone walked in on me—and watching people talk and act like I wasn't there felt more like a colossal prank perpetrated by the in-crowd than a supernatural ability.

I was visually scanning some random form over a nurse's shoulder when another nurse—Anne, according to her name tag—sat next to her. "You missed all the excitement," the first nurse—Gina—said.

"Another eighty-year-old nudist?"

Gina laughed as I moved to the right, wishing I could open a folder on the desk in front of her. "No. Remember the girl who came in right before you went to lunch? Ambulance brought her from Eastlake?"

I froze. They were talking about Emma.

"The mumbler? Yeah. Dr. Cohen ordered a psych evaluation right before I left. Did she get it?"

"She got more than that. You know Claudia transferred here from Lakeside, right?" Gina said, and Anne nodded. "Well, she recognized the girl from this morning as a psych patient. Get this—the girl was admitted to Lakeside *under another name* nearly two years ago. She hardly said a word the whole time she was there, then, several weeks ago she just *disappeared* from a locked ward. They have no idea how she got out. All the exits were locked and video-monitored, and no one saw her leave. Just *poof,* like Houdini."

"Weird. They take her back?"

"Yeah. The psych ward took her off our hands fifteen minutes ago. Her parents are on the way."

Crap! Em was at Lakeside. Next to the Netherworld, the mental health ward was my least favorite place in either world. Yet somehow, it had become my afterlife's version of Rome.

All roads led to Lakeside.

My skin began to crawl the moment I blinked into the dayroom on the adolescent floor of the Lakeside mental health unit. The psychiatric unit was associated with the hospital but was a separate building. A beast all its own.

I'd been there as a visitor—an invisible, unauthorized visitor—twice and made it out just fine both times, but on this third visit, as on the other two, memories of my involuntary residence at Lakeside overshadowed everything else. I was only a resident for a week, but that was one of the worst weeks of my life.

After a quick glance around to make sure no one could see me, I headed into the nurses' station, an enclosed, locked room with windows set into the top half of the walls—very different from nurses' stations in the main hospital. A room chart hung on the rear wall, the only part that didn't overlook the rest of the floor, but Em's name wasn't on it yet. Neither was Lydia's. She evidently hadn't been there long enough to be penciled in. But the chart showed two empty rooms on the girls' wing—surely she was in one of those.

I headed out of the nurses' station, through the dayroom,

past the dining room, and into the girls' hall, trying my best to ignore the residents. And not to notice the familiar faces of several girls who'd been there when I was a resident almost two years earlier.

I couldn't imagine living at Lakeside for two years. Surely that was enough to drive anyone crazy—even the ones who were supposedly there already.

The first unoccupied room was the third on the right. The door was open, and a quick glance inside revealed that the room was indeed empty.

Four doors down on the left was the other unoccupied room, and I could tell from halfway down the hall that someone was inside—a human-shaped shadow stretched into the corridor, cast by sunlight streaming through a window inside. But that shadow didn't look like Em's new body. It was too tall—though that was hard to judge, since shadows stretch.

Em wasn't alone.

My heart beat in sympathy for her, and my mind raced. Getting her out would be simple. *Keeping* her out would be more complicated. They knew what name she was living under, and what high school she'd been picked up from.

They'd called Lydia's parents.

Balancing our human-world and Netherworld problems had just gotten much more complicated.

When I got closer to the open door, I could hear voices. I recognized Emma/Lydia's, but the other was unfamiliar.

"Do you remember me, Lydia?" The shadow propped hands on broad hips, and triangles of light showed through the loop formed by her arms.

"No." Another shadow crossed in front of the counselor's shadow, moving quickly until it was past the doorway. "I don't remember you because we've never met. I'm not Lydia." The shadow crossed again, in the opposite direction this time.

Emma was pacing.

"You don't remember being here before?" The counselor's shadow turned to track Em as her silhouette paced across the small room again. "You've only been gone a few weeks…."

"No. I don't remember that because it never happened. I've never been here." She paused. "Well, I mean, I've *been* here." When she'd visited me. "But I never *lived* here." Emma's shadow had both hands pressed to her head the next time she crossed the doorway, and I groaned silently. She was making herself sound…unstable. But what else was she supposed to say? A few inaccurately answered questions would make it obvious that she had no memory of Lakeside, even if she gave them the answers they obviously wanted to hear. "And I know I've never met *you*. I'd remember such an unfortunate mole. Have you considered getting that thing checked out?"

I almost laughed out loud.

"Do you want to take a break and calm down?" the nurse asked.

I stepped past the last room before Emma's and caught a glimpse of a large girl in her late teens sitting cross-legged on her bed. As I watched, she pulled her legs up to her chest and covered both ears with her hands, shaking her head slowly. Her lips moved, but no sound came out.

"I am calm!" Em insisted from the next room. "I just don't need to be here!"

"You've been here before, Lydia. Do you remember leaving? Can you tell me how you…left us? The doors were locked, and no one saw you leave your room, much less the ward."

Em's shadow stopped moving and merged with the counselor's to form one dark blur on the floor of the hall. "For the last time, I'm not Lydia! And if you'd just take a closer look at me, I think you could see that for yourself."

The counselor's shadow shifted and stood straighter. "I'm looking. And you look just like Lydia. Exactly like her. How is that possible if you're not her?"

"I don't know!" Shadow Em threw her arms into the air. "Maybe I'm her doppelgänger. No, wait, she's *my* doppelgänger. She has to be, because I'm older, and it's not like I just woke up in this body...." Her voice faded into dismay when she realized what she'd said. But then she pushed on with renewed determination and volume. "Because *that* would be strange and completely impossible to prove. So I've totally looked like this my whole life, and I don't...actually...know how old your Lydia is, but I bet anything she's at least two years younger than I am. Because Lydia sounds like the name a fifteen-year-old would have." Her shadow nodded emphatically. "That's *definitely* the name of someone who can't yet drive. And I bet she didn't have brown eyes. I bet hers were, like, blue, or something. And if her eyes were blue and mine are brown, then I can't be this Lydia, right? Which means I'm right, and you're wrong, and also I think you might actually be the crazy one."

I didn't know whether to laugh or applaud. So I tiptoed closer, sneaking out of habit, though no one could see or hear me. The corner of her room came into sight, but at first all I could see was an open doorway leading to a small bathroom, which I knew from experience would hold nothing at all. Residents had to check out a shower kit every time they wanted to bathe, then return it after each use.

"Oh!" Em shrieked, and I actually jumped, startled. "Also, I probably don't sound like this Lydia either, do I? I mean, my voice might, but not my speech pattern and vocabulary. She probably didn't talk much at all, did she? And obviously I talk all the time. I *love* to talk. Unlike this hypothetical mental patient who stole my face."

One step closer, and I could see the counselor from behind. She was a slim woman with dark hair, wearing a cream-colored blouse and a navy pencil skirt, ending just above her knees. She held something close to her chest, and with one more step I could identify the edge of a file folder, no doubt containing Emma's—Lydia's—file.

"Lydia—"

"Stop calling me that. I'm not Lydia, and I just proved it."

"Okay." The counselor nodded and flipped a page in her file. "It does say here that you—that *Lydia*—has brown eyes, and I remember that y—that *she* rarely spoke. So let's table the issue of your identity until someone with more information at hand can sort that out. For now, let's talk about the issue that brought you here. The report from the emergency room says your school nurse sedated you because you were 'inconsolable and incomprehensible.' Do you remember that?"

"No." Em started pacing again, and I caught just a glimpse of her as she walked away, still wearing the jeans and blouse she'd had on that morning when we'd left for school. Her shoes were the same, too, except that now her sneakers were missing their laces, as per Lakeside policy. That way the residents can't string a bunch of shoelaces together and try to hang themselves. Or one another.

"The last thing I remember is getting sleepy in third period, then there's nothing until I woke up in the E.R. And honestly, I kinda wish I was still asleep, 'cause this shit is the stuff of *nightmares*." Em paused, and though I couldn't see her face, I realized what she must be thinking just a second before she confirmed it. "Sabine, is this you?" Emma shouted, her arms thrown out at her sides. "Are you doing this? Cut it out, or I swear *I will kill you!*"

That time I did groan, but no one heard me. That one

outburst from Em had undone all the progress she'd made in convincing the counselor that she was neither Lydia nor crazy.

"Who's Sabine?" The counselor pulled out the desk chair and sat, and suddenly I had a clear view of Emma. And as soon as I saw her, I realized that the feisty, fast-thinking Em who'd just tried to talk her way out of the mental ward was gone. This Em looked...distracted. Distraught.

"She's a friend, kind of." Em stared at the window, showing me her profile, and her hand slid into her hair and pulled on it, a gesture I'd never seen her use, and that she didn't even seem aware of. "But only because she'd be so much scarier as an enemy. I need to get out of here. You have to let me out of here *now!*"

I was so distracted by how upset she was suddenly that it took me a second to realize what she'd said. She'd gotten sleepy in third period, and she didn't remember anything that had happened after that. Had she fallen asleep? Had she been *possessed* when she'd freaked out at school?

"So, you don't remember the ambulance? Or—"

"I don't remember any of it, okay?" Em's hand tightened around a handful of her hair and pulled so hard I winced. I had to get her out of there, but I couldn't do anything until the counselor left. "I already told you that. I don't know anything except that I'm not supposed to be here, so just shut the hell up!"

A high-pitched whining sound came from the room next door, and I retraced my steps until I could see the girl sitting on her bed, now rocking back and forth, clutching two handfuls of her own hair. Just like Emma.

And that's when I understood. Em was syphoning this girl's...whatever she was feeling too much of. Fear, maybe. Or panic. Or massive discomfort with...everything?

"This report says you didn't know who you are," the counselor continued. "You told your teacher you weren't—" she glanced at the papers again "—Emily Cavanaugh. And now you're telling us that you're not Lydia. Would it be accurate to say that you're still not sure who you are?"

"Do any of us really know who we are?" Em asked as I stepped into her doorway, and this time she was facing me. I didn't realize she could see me—evidently I *wanted* her to—until her gaze focused on me. Her eyes widened, and she gasped out loud.

"Sorry!" I said, my voice audible to only her. "Pretend you don't see me." But, of course, it was too late for that. My interruption had made her look even crazier.

The counselor twisted and looked right through me, then turned back to Emma. "What's wrong?"

"Nothing." Em shrugged, visibly struggling to keep her focus on the counselor. She let go of her hair, obviously surprised to find herself clutching it, and closed her eyes. "I thought I saw something, but it was nothing."

The counselor started to scribble something on her file, and Em's eyes flew open. "Don't write that down! I'm not seeing things. I said I *thought* I saw something, but I was wrong. I'm not *crazy*." She tugged on the hem of her shirt, one of mine, which was a little baggy on her.

"Of course you're not." The counselor laid her hand across the file in her lap, legs crossed in her pencil skirt, her pen tucked beneath one finger. "'Crazy' isn't a diagnosis."

"No, I mean I'm not..." Em exhaled, and her shoulders slumped. I motioned for her to sit on the low, narrow bed, hoping that would make her look calmer, and she did. "Never mind."

The counselor was quiet for a minute, watching Emma. Waiting to see if she'd say anything else. Then, when nothing else came, she tucked a strand of dark, curly hair behind her ear. "Do you feel like seeing your family now? Your parents are eager to see you."

Crap. She still thought Em was Lydia. Perhaps an even crazier version of the Lydia who'd escaped.

"No!" Em's brown eyes flashed, not in anger but in fear. Her hand snaked toward her hair again, but I shook my head and motioned for her to put her hands in her lap, which she did. "I told you, they're not my parents. I don't want to see them. If you make me, I *swear* I'll kill myself."

I shook my head, trying to tell Emma she was taking the wrong approach—threatening suicide in the mental health ward *never* goes well—but I only caught her attention and made her look crazy again.

"Lydia, no one's going to make you do anything you don't want to do."

"I don't want to *be here*." Her voice rose on the end, and the whining from the room next door increased in pitch and volume. One of the two of them was about to lose it, and if Em was that one, we were all screwed.

"Well, that's out of my control, at least for the moment." The counselor clicked the top of her pen repeatedly, retracting and exposing the ballpoint over and over. "But I do have several more questions for you."

Emma scowled with Lydia's face. "I don't want to talk anymore. Go tell my parents to go home. *Please*."

"We're not really finished here…."

"*I'm* finished." Emma stood, staring down at her. "I'm not going to say another word to you until you get rid of Lydia's parents."

"Do you really think that's the best tactic to take? I'm trying to help you, Lydia."

Emma glanced at me, and I motioned for her to sit again. She sank onto the edge of the bed and scooted back to lean against the wall. Then she crossed her arms over her chest and watched the counselor in silence. She wasn't pouting. She wasn't throwing fits. She just...wasn't participating.

That was the best I could hope for, considering the state of the resident next door.

The counselor gave it several more minutes, while we sat there in silence—okay, I stood—and the girl next door whined. Then she sighed and left the room, patient file in hand.

As soon as the counselor was gone, I made myself corporeal enough to close Emma's door. The moment it clicked home, she flew off the bed and hugged me so hard I wouldn't have been able to breathe even if I'd needed to. "Get me out of here. *Please.* I can't stay here. This place makes me feel...*bad.*"

"I know. It did the same thing to Lydia. I think she syphoned every psychosis in the whole damn place." I blinked us both into my living room—with a stop in an empty parking lot on the way, because I couldn't go that far in one shot. The best moment of the day was the moment my feet landed on my own carpet.

Styx perked up from her sleeping spot on my dad's chair and barked in greeting.

"Holy crap, this has been the worst day *ever.*" Emma collapsed on the couch and threw her head back against the cushion. Then she winced and suddenly looked guilty. "Well, for *me,* anyway. I'm sure your dad had a really crappy yesterday."

And his suffering had no doubt continued, which made me feel guilty for being in my own home, out of immediate danger and in no pain.

I went into the kitchen, and Styx followed when she realized I was headed for the fridge. "Are you okay?"

"Traumatized, but yeah." Emma exhaled dramatically.

"Half an hour in that place felt like an eternity. I don't know how you made it a week."

"Me, neither." I opened the fridge and pulled out a plastic container of still-bloody venison.

"They thought I was Lydia." She sat up and frowned at me from the living room. "I *am* Lydia. Except that I'm also Emily Cavanaugh. And Emma Marshall, at least a little. Asking me if I know who I am? Most complicated question in history."

"Yeah. I'm not sure what we're going to do about that." I set the last hunk of meat in Styx's dish, then dropped the bowl into the sink and washed my hands while Styx scarfed down her dinner. "The hospital knows you as Lydia, who just escaped from a locked mental ward. Again. But the school knows you as Emily Cavanaugh, the niece and legal ward of my father. Who can't be contacted at the moment, due to the fact that he's been taken hostage by a demon in another realm."

"Speaking of—any news about your dad, and Harmony and Brendon?"

I dried my hands on the towel hanging from a drawer handle, then grabbed two bottles of water from the fridge. "No. But we'll get them back, and when we do, hopefully a combination of my dad's Influence and your brown eyes will be enough to convince people that you can't possibly be Lydia. I mean, people's eyes don't just change color, right?"

"Blue to green, maybe. Or brown to hazel, depending on the light. But not blue to brown. That just doesn't happen." She looked relieved by her own conclusion.

I handed her a bottle, then sank onto the couch next to her, trying to ignore the visceral chomping sounds coming from the kitchen. "Plus, we have the paperwork Tod...procured. Together, that should be enough to firmly establish your new identity." *I hope.* But I didn't let her see my doubt.

She obviously had plenty of her own. "So, what happened at school? Please tell me you were faking memory loss for the psych ward counselor."

"No, that was real. I don't know what happened, and I think that's the scariest part of this." She collapsed against the back of the couch again and blew hair off of her forehead. "Why don't we ever have normal problems anymore?"

"I've been asking myself that for months." I cracked the top on my water bottle, then scooted over to make room for Styx, who seemed determined to burrow into the few inches between us now that she was finished eating. "So, you fell asleep during third period and…?"

"And…I woke up in a bed in the E.R. My throat hurt like I'd been screaming and I had a headache, but other than that, I felt normal. Well, as normal as I've ever felt in this body. I'd been there for maybe five minutes when the nurse who came in to take my vitals recognized me. Well, she recognized *Lydia*. Then there was a whirlwind transfer to Lakeside—they actually pushed me across the parking lot in a wheelchair—and the next thing I knew, I was a confirmed mental patient."

"We prefer to be called residents. Remember, 'crazy' is not a diagnosis."

"Whatever." She actually smiled, then twisted the lid from her own bottle. "Evidently the fact that Lydia never actually checked out the first time led to me being fast-tracked for admission today. That place is *scary* efficient."

"Yeah. They'll bend over backward to get you in, then they'll move heaven and earth to keep you there."

And for the first time, it occurred to me that Lakeside and the Netherworld weren't so very different—given a chance, either one of them would steal your soul.

19

"That place was hell." Em sipped from her water bottle. "It was like walking around in the opposite of a sensory deprivation chamber. I was in sensory overload. Like being assaulted by everything everyone there was feeling. It was crazy—pardon the expression. Those people are angry, and sad, and frustrated, and confused, and…lost." She stroked Styx's fur absently. "I can't go back there, Kaylee. I can't."

"I know. You won't. I'll make sure of it." Styx climbed into my lap, trying to make herself the center of my attention. My dog was a fascinating contradiction. She was fierce and deadly, with jaws that opened wider than I would have thought possible and could snap a human long bone in a single bite. But in the absence of danger, she was almost…cuddly.

Though I was surprised that she was comfortable enough to nap in a house full of—

I sat up, suddenly startled to realize what should have been obvious the moment we'd blinked into the house. "Where're Sophie and Luca?"

Em frowned. "I don't know. But I'd check your room before you panic. Look for a sequined headband around the doorknob."

"Ew!" Yet I was off the couch in an instant and down the hall two seconds after that. But my room was empty, except for the furniture, including one unmade bed, which told me Nash and Sabine had slept curled up together on my twin mattress.

I pulled my phone from my pocket and started to autodial my cousin, suddenly glad I'd programmed her number into my phone, in spite of my general disinterest in speaking to her. But my battery was still dead.

"Em, I need your phone!" I called, plugging my own into the charger by my bed. Em brought me her cell, and I dialed Sophie's number from memory. She answered on the second ring. "Yes?"

I was so relieved to hear her voice that I didn't even yell at her for the rude greeting. "Where the hell are you? Is Luca with you?"

"I'm at home. And, yes, he's here. Why? What's up?"

"What's up? There are *forces of evil* hunting us, Sophie. They may already have your dad. Do you think it's too much to ask for a warning before you disappear next time?" I sank onto the edge of my bed, fervently hoping Nash and Sabine had only slept there. "You scared the *crap* out of me."

Luca said something in the background, but all I could make out was "Nash."

"Yeah," Sophie said into my ear. "We texted Nash before we left. How is it my fault you two communicate like you both have bananas in your ears?"

"You…?" Nash hadn't told me, which was no surprise, considering that I'd been communing with demons and he and Sabine had been dealing with Em's…breakdown. Not to mention the fact that my phone was dead. "What are you doing there?"

"Not that it's any of your business, but I *live* here. All my clothes are here. My television is big enough to actually see from across the room, and my food isn't full of sugar and carbs. My dad's missing, Kaylee. Is it too much to ask that the rest of my life not be missing right now?"

I exhaled slowly, grasping for control of my temper. Reminding myself that she and I didn't think about things the same way, and that I'd done my fair share of not checking in before I'd realized how badly I'd probably scared my father. Over and over.

"Fine," I said finally. "Just...stay with Luca, and head back this way as soon as you've had your fill of Sophie-land. We really do need to stick together. Em fell asleep this morning and got possessed, then admitted to Lakeside. There's too much going on for us to be spread out and out of reach. Okay?"

Sophie started to object, but I heard Luca in the background, talking sense into her like no one else ever seemed able to.

"Fine. We'll come back as soon as the movie's over."

"Thank you." I ended the call and looked up to find Emma standing in my bedroom doorway, a half-eaten apple in one hand.

"They're okay?"

"Yeah." I gave her back her phone. "Clueless as usual, in Sophie's case, but fine."

Em took another bite from her apple and slid her cell into her pocket. As I followed her into the hall, the front door opened.

"Kaylee? Emma?" Nash called. We stepped into the living room as he slid his key—I'd given him an extra—into his pocket and Sabine pushed the front door closed. "Oh, good, you got her. Is she…okay?"

I deferred to Em, who shrugged. "'Okay' is a relative term at this point."

"Tell me about it." I dropped onto the couch again next to Styx. My head felt like it weighed fifty pounds, and my heart was even heavier. "They mistook her for Lydia and put her in Lakeside."

"Oh, shit." Sabine sat on the arm of my dad's chair. "That complicates things. She just escaped again, I assume?"

I nodded.

"And now they know they can track her through the school," Nash added.

"I'm not going back." Em's hand clenched around her apple. "I'm not crazy. Swear you'll get me out over and over, if that's what it takes."

"I swear. But it won't come to that. My dad can fix this." *Surely* he could, with the whole eye-color defense, plus the forged paperwork. "Sometimes completely unrelated people look a lot alike, and it's not like they have your fingerprints on file." Though they may have blood samples.

I decided not to worry her with the extremely unlikely possibility that the court could order a DNA analysis if Lydia's parents pressed the issue. Which they wouldn't, because my dad would talk them out of it. He was good at talking people out of things.

"So, what the hell happened?" Nash helped himself to a bottle of water from the fridge.

"I think she was possessed."

"No shit." Sabine leaned into Nash when he sat in the chair she'd claimed the arm of. "We could have told you that from what she was shouting."

"What was I saying?" Em looked like she wasn't sure she really wanted to know.

"Mostly you kept yelling that you wanted to talk to Kaylee, and that you weren't Emily." Nash fidgeted with the cap of his bottle but didn't open it. "Then, when they let me try to calm you down, you grabbed my hand and said 'ticktock.'"

"Ticktock?"

"Yeah." He finally cracked the lid. "The creepy thing is that you said that part in Avari's voice."

"That would have been good to know from the beginning," I said, scowling at Sabine.

The *mara* shrugged. "You left before I could tell you. If you want the whole story, stick around until the end."

"I think, 'Hey, Kay, your best friend's been possessed by a hellion' would have been the ideal way to *start* that conversation." I pushed Styx out of my lap and stood. I suddenly needed to move, to combat the feeling of helplessness. The certainty that there was nothing I could do to prevent…whatever else was coming. And something was definitely coming. I could feel it crawling like flies beneath my skin. "So, he spoke in Emma's voice until you got close enough that no one else would hear, then he said 'ticktock' in his own voice?"

Nash nodded. "I assume that's a warning intended to light a fire under us…."

"Warning us about what?" Em said as Styx curled up next to her, following my apparent abandonment.

"That time is running out, obviously." Sabine took Nash's water bottle and drank from it. "But…time for what? To find Brendon and Harmony? To rescue Aiden?"

"No." I leaned against the half wall between the kitchen and living room, rubbing my forehead, thinking how unfair it was that dead girls could still get headaches. "He doesn't expect us to do either of those. He's warning us that time's running out for me to turn myself in. That's why Emma—Avari—was asking for me."

"Wait, why can he use my voice?" Em frowned. "I thought he couldn't do that very much. Didn't you say he could only use Alec's because he knew him so well?"

"That was my theory, yes." Thinking about Alec and how he'd died—how Avari had manipulated me into killing him—made me angry all over again, on Alec's behalf and my own. "But for all we know, he possessed Lydia once a week. We know he was familiar with Lakeside because Scott was there, and he regularly possessed Scott. So he probably knew who and what Lydia was. Or…maybe he's getting better at that in general?" I shrugged. "Who knows?"

"Where were you?" Sabine asked, and everyone turned to look at me. "Where were you during third period, when we were all looking for you?"

I stared at the floor for a second, then made myself look up. "I kind of…summoned Ira in the kitchen of the empty doughnut shop down the street from the school." I held my arm out so they could see the fresh bandage near my elbow, which was visible since I'd taken off the cardigan.

"Again?" Nash said. "Sounds like it's getting serious. Does Tod know about this?"

Sabine elbowed him, and I nearly threw my own water bottle at his head. "Ha ha. It was a total waste of time, though. Except I did confirm that he was the one who tied Sabine to the ground with crimson creeper." Which we were already virtually certain of. "And that he may or may not know where my uncle and your mom are."

Nash's hand clenched around his bottle. "He *may* know where my mom is?"

"He was going to charge me to find out whether or not

he knows, then again, presumably, to find out where they actually are."

"And, what, the price was too high?" Sabine looked confused.

"Well, yeah." I shrugged. "By virtue of the fact that I was dealing with a *hellion*. That's never a good idea."

"But you deal with hellions *all the time!*" Nash insisted. "You were willing to make out with one to help your dad but not to help my mom?"

"No, I…I shouldn't have done that. I shouldn't have let him manipulate me—in the end it was all for nothing anyway." Instead of finding my dad, we'd lost his mom and my uncle. "Besides, I'm pretty sure the price would have gone up this time." I didn't even want to *know* what came after a kiss. A bite? A sip of my blood, straight from the fount? A pound of flesh? Something worse?

"You're *pretty sure?*" Nash demanded, and I realized I'd accidentally led him to an accurate conclusion. "You didn't even ask? You just decided my mom should sit tight in the Netherworld—where she's obviously unconscious and probably still bleeding—because you weren't even willing to listen to the offer on the table?"

"Wait, you think she should have made a deal with a *demon?*" Em demanded, while I stared at him, trying not to get angry. Angri*er,* anyway.

"No, that's not…" Nash scrubbed both hands over his face, and I could practically feel his frustration. "I don't know what to think. I don't want you to put yourself in any more danger, but we *have* to get my mom back. She's hurt, and I have no idea how badly. She'd do anything for me and Tod—and for any of you—and there's nothing we can do to help her without making a deal with a hellion."

"I'll do it. I'll make the deal." Sabine shrugged. "I'm not

giving up my soul, but other than that, I'm flexible. How bad could it be?"

I stared at her in horror. "That's the scariest question I've ever heard."

Em frowned. "Sabine, he already tried to kill you."

"Actually, he wasn't trying to kill her," I admitted, reluctantly aware that they might misinterpret that as my support for her kamikaze mission. "He was trying to piss us all off."

"That's not the point." Nash took Sabine's hand. "I don't want any of you putting yourselves in danger. She's my mom. This is my responsibility. I'll do it." He let go of Sabine and stood, facing me. "Kaylee, how the hell do you summon a hellion?"

"I can't..." I took a deep breath, then started over—he wasn't going to like my answer. "Nash, I can't tell you that. I can't let you summon Ira." He'd get himself killed, and it would be my fault.

His eyes churned with swift currents of brown and green, with flashes of anger like lightning splitting the storm. "Does it give you some kind of perverse pleasure to tell me no? Because that's all I ever hear from you anymore. Actually, that's all I've *ever* heard from you."

"Okay, stop it, Nash." My gaze clashed with his, and I wondered what he saw in my eyes. "I'm trying to protect you."

"Who appointed you defender of mankind? I don't *need* your protection! None of us do!"

"I do, kind of," Em said, but no one was really listening. "Sometimes..."

I stood, facing Nash across the coffee table. "I'm not going to let you summon a hellion, especially when you're so desperate to find your mother that you'd give him whatever he wants."

"That's my call. You have no right to stand in my way."

"I may not have the right, but I have the *responsibility.* You're my friend—you're *more* than a friend—and you have a less-than-stellar record with human-to-hellion interactions. I'm not going to give you what you need to make another mistake, and, frankly, I don't think it's fair of you to ask me to, considering that if something happens to you, we'll all have to put ourselves in even more danger to rescue you. Don't you think we're missing enough loved ones already?"

Yes, I was aware of my own hypocrisy, even as the words left my mouth. But putting myself in danger was different than letting him do the same thing, because Nash was a hellion *addict.* And because he was too emotional to think clearly. And because he'd never even met Ira. And…

And because I was terrified of losing him. Of losing any of them. I wasn't willing to take risks with my friends' lives like I was with my own, because I loved them. All of them. Even the ones I didn't always like. I couldn't give Nash the means to get himself killed via hellion bargain any more than I could hand him a loaded gun and watch him point it at his own head.

But Nash didn't see it that way.

"I can't win with you, can I?" He threw his arms up in frustration. "If I stay safe on the sidelines, I'm not helping, but if I try to do anything, I'm putting myself and everyone else in danger. You're going to be mad at me no matter what I do—or don't do—so I'm *done* worrying about what you think!"

"Guys, calm down," Emma said. On the edge of my vision, I saw Sabine watching me and Nash like we were on opposing sides of a volleyball net.

"This isn't about me being mad at you, Nash. This is about me trying to *protect* you."

"For the last time, I don't need you to protect me! So just

tell me how to contact this Ira asshole and let me decide how much I'm willing to pay to get my mother out of the Netherworld. Let *me* deal with the consequences of my own decisions!"

"That's not how it works!" My cheeks were flushed, and my heart pounded so hard I was almost dizzy—my body was no longer accustomed to such a rapid flow of blood. "This is a team sport, Nash. We're in it together, and we can't afford for you to run off half-cocked playing hero and get yourself killed. You have to think about the group. About what's best for all of us!" I couldn't *believe* how rash he was being. How selfish!

"Kaylee. Nash. It's too tense in here…." Em put both hands over her ears, as if she could physically stop herself from syphoning our anger.

"The *group?*" Nash was shouting now. "Is that what you were thinking about when you summoned Ira all by yourself? How come when you do it, it's noble, but when I want to do it, I'm 'running off half-cocked to play hero'? You didn't even tell anyone what you were doing. You just disappeared. If something had gone wrong, we would never have known what happened to you. How is that acting in the best interest of the group?"

"That's different," I insisted, reeling from the sting of his words. "I've dealt with Ira before. I've dealt with *summoning* before." Only once, but that was one more time than he'd done it. "And I know where my boundaries lie. He can't tempt me with—" I bit off the next words before I could say them and almost bit my tongue in the process.

Why was I so *angry?* Was this because Ira had been feeding from my wrath, or was my wrath what attracted him to me in the first place? Could that much rage have been there all along, buried, just waiting for a chance to burst through my emotional armor, like lava through the crust of the earth?

"With what?" Nash's voice was soft now, but anger roiled beneath the surface of the sound, like water about to break into a boil. "With his breath? Is that what you were going to say? At least he can't tempt you with *drugs?*" He spat the last word at me from across the room, and I flinched.

"I'm sorry. I shouldn't have—"

"Why not?" Nash demanded. "At least that part was the truth. The rest of it is you lying to yourself and to us. I may be an addict, but I didn't exactly choose that path for myself, in case you don't remember. And I'm fighting it every single day. But you're lying and hiding things from the people who care about you the most, and you don't even have addiction as an excuse. How do you justify *that?*"

"Shut up!" Emma shouted, sitting stiff and straight on the center couch cushion, staring from him to me, then back. "Shut the hell up, both of you! Are you *trying* to drive me crazy?"

"Em, I'm sorry." I sat next to her, hoping that my rapidly fading anger would ease her burden. I hadn't meant to trigger abilities she couldn't control yet.

"Me, too." Nash's irises swirled with amber threads of regret, but he didn't sit. He hadn't backed down. "I'm sorry, Emma." He turned to me again. "But I'm going after my mother, and, Kaylee, I swear on my immortal soul that if you stand in my way I will *never* forgive you."

"Whoa, what did I miss?" Tod said from the kitchen, and I looked up to find him staring at all of us.

"More fireworks," Sabine said. "And what we've learned from this little episode is that Kaylee and Nash are like those rocks ancient cave people used to make fire. Bang them together, and you get sparks."

"Let's never again use the phrase 'bang them together' in reference to my brother and my girlfriend," Tod mumbled.

"She means their heads," Emma said. "And *I'd* like to bang them together right now." She scowled at me, then turned her disapproval on Nash. "You two are fighting for no reason. You both want the same thing—to protect people you love. You just don't agree about how to do it."

"She won't tell me how to summon a hellion," Nash explained.

"Good for her." Tod smiled at me, but I couldn't smile back. He hadn't heard the whole thing yet. "I fully support any efforts to keep you and hellions on separate planes of existence."

"So, she can do it, but I can't? That's bullshit! Did she tell you she saw Ira today?" Nash demanded. Tod blinked. The colors in his irises betrayed none of what he was feeling, but I could tell he was hurt, and I felt like the world's biggest jerk. "She said she wanted everyone to go to school for strength in numbers, but when Emma was possessed and Avari was demanding to talk to Kaylee, she was *gone.* She was off summoning a demon, without telling anyone what she was up to or that she might need help. But when I want to contact Ira to find out where our mother is, with full knowledge of the entire group, she won't even tell me how to get in touch with him."

Tod blinked again, and I would have given anything to know what he was thinking. What he was feeling. He leaned against the doorway into the kitchen and crossed both arms over his chest, then met his brother's gaze. "Is that really what you're mad about? That you're not getting quality time with a hellion?"

"No! And yes. But only because she didn't even get the information she went to him for. I'm pissed off that she would put herself in that kind of danger, then walk away with nothing to show for it. That means she could have died or worse—we all could have lost her—for nothing. I'm pissed off that she wasn't willing to do for our mother what she did for her father. I'm pissed off that Mom's gone and there's nothing I can do about it. You can all cross over whenever you want. You can all search and sacrifice and bleed to try to save her, but all I can do is sit here and wait."

"I can't," Em whispered, tears in her brown eyes. "I'm pretty useless, too…."

I took her hand and squeezed it, but Nash didn't seem to hear her.

"I've never felt so worthless in my entire life, and every time I try to do something about that, one of you cuts me off at the kneecaps. I'm pissed at you *all* for standing in my way. For letting my mom suffer in the Netherworld when I could be helping get her back. I'm pissed at her for going to the Netherworld in the first place. I'm pissed at Avari for… relentless existence and nefarious consistency. So I've made a decision."

Tod's pale brow arched high over one blue eye. "I think we're all listening."

Nash ignored him with obvious effort. "You guys have a choice. Either you can include me in all aspects of the planning and execution of any and all rescue efforts or I'm going my own way. I still know people, you know," he added, when Tod looked skeptical. "No one I really want to see again, now that I'm clean, but I *can* find Mom on my own if I have to."

His eye contact with me was steady and determined. He meant it, and the thought that he might actually rekindle old unhealthy relationships because I wouldn't let him take risks alongside me made me…it made me sick to my stomach with fear for him.

"I can get myself to the Netherworld," Nash continued. "And I can get both of us back out again. All *three* of us—I'm not leaving Brendon there, either. So what's it going to be? Are you going to let me contribute to the group effort, or are you going to shut me out again 'for my own protection'?"

Everyone looked at me, not because I was in charge, but because I'd messed up, and she who messes up, cleans up.

"I'm sorry," I said, not just to Nash but to the whole room. "He's right, and I'm so sorry, Nash. I never meant to cut you out of…anything. Everything. And I shouldn't have summoned Ira again without telling anyone what I was up to."

"Or at all…" Em said, and I nodded in acknowledgment, avoiding Tod's gaze because I wasn't ready to see whatever I might find in it.

"Of course we want you to stay." I did meet Nash's gaze, because I owed him that much, at the *very* least. "And of course you're included in everything. I didn't mean to be taking liberties that aren't available to everyone else. I meant to be taking *risks*. So no one else would have to. I couldn't live with myself if any of you got hurt again. You've all been through so much because of me. Our parents are still missing because of their connection to me. I just… I was looking for a way to fix that without getting anyone else hurt. I'm sorry."

"Promise," Nash said, and his voice cracked on that one word. "Promise you won't do it again. That you won't put yourself at risk like that again with no one to back you up."

I looked at him.

I looked hard and deep, and he let me see what he was feeling. He let his eyes swirl so I could understand, and guilt overwhelmed me like heat in the middle of a Texas summer. Relentless. Overpowering. Too much to think through.

He was mad about everything he'd listed. That was all true. But the truest part—the core of an anger that had many heads, like a hydra—was the thought that I could have died in one horrible moment of my own recklessness. I could have died—again—and he'd never know how it happened, or why, or even what happened to my body.

Fear. The root of his anger was fear of losing me, not as his girlfriend—that part of our lives was over, and he loved Sabine; we could all see that—but as his friend. As his more-than-a-friend. As a confidante. As one of the people who'd been with him through life, and death, and addiction, and relapse, and countless moments of imminent threat from untold forms of evil.

And now he wanted to know that I'd never do it again. That I'd never put him through the fear of losing me again.

"Don't make her do it, Nash." Tod's voice was so soft and deep I had to concentrate to understand what I was hearing. "She will if you ask her to, but *I'm* asking you not to make her promise something she can't keep. That's not a promise *any* of us could keep. Like it or not, we're not going to get our parents back without putting ourselves in danger, and Kaylee knows that. She knew it before any of the rest of us came to that conclusion."

But that wasn't true. Tod had known before I'd ever met him. Before I'd met Avari or Invidia or Belphegore. Before I even knew I wasn't human. He'd known what you have to be willing to sacrifice for the people you love long before I'd truly understood the meaning of the words *risk* and *sacrifice.*

He'd known since the moment he'd given up his life so Nash could live.

"What Kaylee doesn't understand is that she's not alone in this." Tod stepped forward and held his hand out to me, and I reached for it like a plant reaches for the sun. Like I couldn't bloom without him there to shine on me. He pulled me up, then he pulled me close, and when he looked into my eyes, I couldn't look away.

"What Kaylee needs to understand is that we all feel just like she does. Like if we make the sacrifice or take the risk, the others won't have to. Ira, Avari, and all the rest of them, they want each of us to believe that because they know we'll make that sacrifice if we think that's the only way to save the people we love. But it's a lie. This is too big for any one of us alone. We can only do this as a team—if we have one another's backs."

His eyes were all for me again then, and I could see how hurt he really was. Beneath that, I could see his fear.

Fear of losing me, just like I'd felt when he'd died. When I'd thought I'd lost him and that my afterlife would be hundreds—maybe thousands—of years spent mourning him.

"What that means is that when we take risks, if they can't be avoided, we let everyone else in on the plan so that if something goes wrong, we can do what we do best. Rescue each other. Got it?"

I nodded. Then I wrapped my arms around him and we held each other until Em started clearing her throat awkwardly.

Sabine was less subtle. "Okay, if you two could form separate people again, we have a fairly serious evil scheme to discuss. Also, I'm hungry."

Tod squeezed me tighter for a second, then let me go. "Are you guys tired of pizza? 'Cause I could have dinner here in about five minutes…."

"Free?" Sabine perked up with interest.

Tod rolled his eyes. "Sure."

"I'm in. Pepperoni, beef, and green bell peppers."

"The free pizza is whatever's ready and not yet claimed," Tod said. Sabine pouted, then shrugged. She finally seemed to be coming to terms with the relationship between beggars and choosers. Which would have been great, if only her *other* appetite were as easy to satisfy.

20

Luca and Sophie showed up while Tod was on his pizza run, and when he got back with two greasy boxes, I set a stack of paper plates on the table and Em dug the last of our cans of soda from the fridge.

If my dad wasn't back soon, I'd have to get a second job just to put food on the table. Er...Coke in the fridge.

I refused to think about the possibility that he might *never* be back. Losing him was not an option.

We got Luca and Sophie all caught up over dinner.

"So, 'ticktock' is, like, the clock running out? So, he's giving us a deadline?" My cousin picked a pepperoni off her slice and dropped it on an extra plate designated as the dumping ground for foods she wouldn't eat, which included pepperoni, sausage, onions, and crust. At first, she'd refused pizza, until Sabine pointed out that "picky little bitches" go hungry.

"Yeah," Nash said around a bite of supreme. "But we don't know when that deadline is."

Luca ate Sophie's pepperoni slice, then followed it with a gulp from the can of diet soda they were sharing. "Why would Avari go to the trouble of possessing Emma with a message for Kaylee, then not deliver the entire message?"

"My theory is that he didn't know how to control Lydia's syphoning abilities any better than Emma does. I'm thinking they overwhelmed him, and that made his message come out all garbled and incomplete."

Em frowned. "But if he hadn't spent enough time in her body to learn to control her abilities, how was he able to use her voice?"

"Crap. I don't know." There was *so* much we still didn't know. So much we might *never* know.

Nash shrugged. "I kinda got the impression that he only wanted to give the message to you, and that's why he was so pissed off. Because you weren't available."

"Because she was summoning the competition?" Sophie said. "Like, his arch nemesis?"

"They're demons, not comic book villains," Emma said.

My cousin dropped her bare crust on the extra plate and frowned at Em. "Excuse me, but I think I can visualize the forces of evil however I like."

Luca stifled a laugh. "As long as you're not expecting them to go 'Oof!' and 'Ka-pow!' when you hit them."

"I'm not planning to hit them," Sophie mumbled, picking a clump of sausage from her second slice.

"Okay, so what's the plan for tonight?"

I shrugged. "Considering that Emma's exhaustion led to her being possessable today, I think you guys should let me and Tod do all the Netherworld searching tonight, so you can get some rest."

"Hell, no," Nash said.

Sabine's brows rose in my direction. "I don't need much sleep. Nash and I will take the first shift. Now, before it gets too late." I started to object, but she spoke again before I could. "Don't bother. I'm not asking for permission. I'm letting you know what we'll be up to, so you won't worry if you can't find us. And so you *can* worry if we're not back in a reasonable amount of time."

Before any of the rest of us could answer, Nash pulled her closer and kissed her fuller and deeper than I'd ever seen him kiss anyone other than me.

Sabine looked surprised for the second it took her to realize what was happening. That Nash was kissing her in front of people.

Then things got awkward. Fast.

"Are you trying to make my pizza come back up?" Em demanded, and Luca laughed.

After dinner, Nash and Sabine went to the Netherworld together, concentrating on the buildings within walking distance of the hospital—the ones Tod and I hadn't already searched.

Luca, Sophie, and Emma curled up on the couch with a movie—no one even suggested doing homework—and Tod and I retreated to my room with a promise not to blink to any more private locations without telling them we were leaving.

My heart started beating on its own when I closed the door and turned to see him sitting in my desk chair. Watching me.

"Okay. So. How mad are you?"

"I'm not mad." He motioned me closer, and I sat in his lap, facing him.

"You're not mad at all?" I frowned. "You understand that when I left the hospital this morning, I already knew I was going to summon Ira and I didn't tell you."

"Yeah. I got that, and it's not like I'm celebrating the omission. But…I went after Thane without telling you, so I figure I don't have much of a leg to stand on in an argument about full disclosures."

"So you're not mad because we're even? I don't want this to be some kind of contest."

"It's not. I'm not mad because I know from personal experience that—like me—you did what you thought you had to do, and you didn't mean to hurt anyone." His gaze seemed to see straight through to my soul. "So, all I need to know is…did you kiss him?"

"No." My eyes filled with tears. "I didn't even ask what his price would be, because I was afraid he would ask for another…taste. Or something worse. I let our parents stay stuck in the Netherworld because I didn't want him to touch me again," I confessed. The tears fell, and I couldn't stop them. I didn't know whether to feel guilty for my own squeamishness or glad that I didn't kiss someone else this time.

He took my hand, and his fingers wound around mine. "Kaylee, you didn't do anything wrong. My mom wouldn't *want* you to pay for her freedom like that, and I know damn well your dad and uncle wouldn't, either." His grip on my hand tightened, and shivers traveled up my arm. "And as selfish as it probably sounds, I can't stand the thought of him touching you for *any* reason."

"I don't think I deserve you," I whispered as those tingles wound their way from my arm down my spine. "I suck as a girlfriend."

"That's not true. The real problem is that hellions suck as nemeses."

"What?"

Tod shrugged. "A proper villain would know when to start overexplaining his dastardly scheme. He'd actually *look* when you point at the sky and shout, 'Look!' When the going gets tough, a real villain would throw one of his minions under the bus and run, or rant against the justice department while he's being shoved into the back of a cop car. Hell, a real villain would at least wear a mask or creepy clown makeup, so we know at a glance who's good and who's bad." Tod grinned and shrugged. "Face it, Kay. The problem here isn't you. It's these subpar villains the universe has thrown at us. Someone should lodge a formal complaint with the bad-guy union."

I laughed, more grateful than ever for his willingness to make me smile even at the worst of times.

I started to kiss Tod, but then Nash pushed the door open and poked his head into the room. "Hey, sorry to interrupt." But he didn't sound *that* sorry—obviously turnabout was fair play. He stepped into the room and closed the door behind him, holding his cell phone, and I realized I'd misinterpreted his expression.

Something was wrong.

"You have a call." He held his cell out to me.

"On your phone?"

"Yeah. It's Marco. Only it's *not* Marco."

"Oh, crap." Tod helped me climb out of his lap without landing on the floor, and I stared at Nash's phone like it might bite me if I touched it. Sure enough, Marco's name was at the top of the screen, but…

"Ms. Cavanaugh, I really don't think you want to keep me waiting." Avari's voice sounded distant coming from a phone not held close to my ear, but it was perfectly audible. He either couldn't work Marco's vocal chords or wasn't bothering.

My hand shook when I took the phone. It shook harder when I held it to my ear. "Hello?" The standard human greeting sounded stupid, considering I was speaking to a hellion, but I didn't know how else to start.

"Ms. Cavanaugh, you've become a difficult *bean sidhe* to get hold of. I've had to resort to…creative means."

I pressed the speaker button and set Nash's phone on my desk, not just so that he and Tod could hear, but so that I could put distance—however worthless—between my ear and the hellion's voice. "What do you want?"

"The real question is what do *you* want? What would you like me to do with your father? Shall I list your options, or would you like to guess?"

"This isn't a game." I leaned against the desk, staring at my feet.

"Of course it's a game. *Life* is a game, little *bean sidhe,* and you are going to lose. The only choice still yours to make is how soon that happens. For instance, if you were to surrender yourself now, or anytime in the next few hours, your father would be returned to the human world, having suffered no permanent damage."

"He's okay?" Was that even possible?

"'Okay' is a relative term, in my world as in yours. He has, as yet, suffered no permanent damage. Physically, at least. It is difficult for me to determine how much and what kind of psychological trauma is recoverable."

Hearing him talk about my father like that made me hate Avari all over again with a loathing rendered raw and fresh, as if the wound were new. But the truth was that he'd cut my heart out months and months ago. Avari kept himself entertained—and fed—by squeezing it whenever he got the chance.

"And if I don't turn myself in?" It hurt to say the words. To vocally betray my father.

"If you haven't surrendered your body and soul by midnight, I will begin amusing myself in earnest with your father's suffering. Physically, at first, and progressing from there. I will push my fingers into his psyche and create excruciating new realities for him. Realities where you are dead and gone, through some negligence on his part, and he drowns in guilt and grief for eternity. Realities where he watches his beloved daughter suffer offenses and indignities beyond human endurance, over and over again while he screams in vain for your freedom and, eventually, for the mercy of your final death."

My skin crawled. "Stop." My eyes closed in horror and my voice carried no sound, which was just as well, because it would have made no difference anyway.

Tod rolled the desk chair closer and took my hand, and Nash sank onto the end of my bed, his eyes swirling with angry, despairing shades of green and brown.

"He will have twelve hours of such agony, while you further consider your choices," Avari continued. "And if you are not in my possession by noon in your human time zone, I will end his life and deliver his soulless corpse—whatever is left of it—into your possession."

My heart went still, and its last beat echoed the hollow length of my body. "You're going to kill him?"

"Yes, of course. Unless you are willing to trade yourself for him. And if you have not surrendered by that next midnight—thirty of your human hours from now, if I understand your maddeningly consistent method of keeping time—I will begin to torture his immortal soul."

"Torture?" I heard the word, but I couldn't process it. Not truly. My mind was a maelstrom of chaos and fear, rapidly sucking me into a pinpoint of darkness from which I was afraid I might never return.

"It's a general term, of course. It reveals nothing of my true intent, or the specific levels of pain I can achieve in one so…attached as your father. You are his weakness, you know. You are the thing he would die for. The thing he would suffer for. The thing he *will* suffer for. And when his sanity starts to slide, he will not be able to differentiate between reality and the mental projection of his worst fears and imaginings.

I believe your cousin saw the result of that particular technique when she met Addison in the Nether."

Sophie met Addison?

"She's a clever little thing, your kin. More like you than you think. And when your father sinks too far into insanity to suffer for me—for *you*—I will move on to your cousin."

"You won't get that chance," I said, and Avari laughed out loud.

"She isn't a pure-blood *bean sidhe,* and her wail is largely pointless, but the pain that sound could carry... She will be my consolation prize while I wait to acquire you. Her screams will whet my appetite for yours. A most appropriate substitute for however long you are willing to let her suffer. Do you have an estimate of how long that might be? It would really help with my planning...."

"Hang up," Tod said. "We've heard more than enough." Avari had officially delivered his horrifying ultimatum.

"Well, if it isn't the knight in tarnished armor. How is that breastplate fitting these days? Has Ms. Cavanaugh discovered how readily you shed the costume of honor when ethical compromise produces faster results—or greater profit?"

Tod glared at the phone, fists clutching the sides of the rolling desk chair like they were the only thing holding him there. "She knows everything I've done."

And I knew that everything he'd done—supernatural drug trafficking and feeding certain criminal elements to the Netherworld—had been done to protect someone else. Tod's methods may have been flawed, but his heart was in the right place. Always.

"How large is my audience?" the hellion said. "Is the other Mr. Hudson listening? The one with the bruised soul and wounded eyes?"

Nash didn't answer. None of us did. We only stared at the

phone, and with each new word my hand inched closer, my finger hovering over the button that would end the call.

"I look forward to resuming our business relationship. I've always found you to be the most pragmatic of your peers," the hellion continued. "The one who best understands business and is least likely to let emotions interfere."

"Not gonna happen," Nash said so softly I wasn't sure Avari could hear him. "We won't be doing any more business."

"Oh, I think we will. I think you and your older, fairer, deader brother will do just about anything to provide for the care and comfort of your lovely mother…."

Nash reached for the phone, but before he could pick it up, the screen flashed black, then the words "call ended" appeared. "Bastard!" Nash shouted, and I grabbed his phone before he could reach it because I could see his intent in his eyes. "He has our mom!" Nash turned on Tod. "How can you just sit there, knowing he has our mother?"

"He doesn't have her." Tod's voice sounded calm, but I could see tension in every line of his body. In the way he sat perfectly still, as if he might lose control of his temper—just like Nash—if he moved at all. "If Avari really had her, he'd come right out and say it, so there could be no doubt. But he didn't say it. He only implied it, because that's as close to lying as a hellion can get. He hasn't found her yet, Nash."

"Are you sure?"

"Yes," I said, and Tod nodded. "That's probably why he hung up so fast—so we couldn't start asking about her."

"So, she's okay?" Nash needed us to say yes. I could see that in the anxious twists of green ringing the edges of his irises. He wouldn't sleep if we said no. In fact, he'd probably stay up all night plotting her rescue from scratch, not that I could blame him. But we owed him the truth.

"Maybe," I finally said. "She's more okay than she'd be if Avari had her, anyway."

"Well, I guess that's probably true." My mattress creaked when he stood. "I'm going to look for her again. Will you guys come with me?"

Tod hesitated, but I nodded, trying to hide the dangerous idea and the grim certainty growing clearer in my mind with every passing second. "Yeah. Of course. But we should give it a little while. Avari's going to be on alert for at least the next few hours, in case I actually lose my mind and decide to turn myself in."

"That's fine. I'm going out with Sabine anyway," Nash said, his hand on the doorknob. Tod shot him a questioning look, which I suspect my expression echoed. "Not *out,* out. Just out to eat. She feeds at night, remember? And I don't want her going alone after what happened last night."

Sabine wasn't going to feed in the Netherworld, which meant she should be safe on her own, but I saw no reason to point that out. Nash feeling protective of his recently poisoned girlfriend was good news for them both.

I was happy for them.

"Don't forget your key," Tod said.

"And this." I held out his phone, and Nash took it, then shoved it in his back pocket. "Be careful."

"We will."

"Hey, baby brother, stay out of trouble," Tod said before Nash could pull open the door.

Nash lifted both brows and grinned. "I'm a year and a half older than you now. I think that makes *you* the baby brother."

"I may be physically younger, but—much like a sweet, golden apricot—I was plucked from life at the peak of perfection." Tod's smile grew and mischief swirled in his irises. "Someday decades from now, when you and Sabine are hobbling around in your old-people pants and orthopedic shoes, yelling at grandchildren and reminiscing about the days when you could still see your feet, unimpeded by the view of your gut, I will still be basking in the glow of eternal youth, forever young, forever golden, forever—"

"In love with the face in the mirror and the sound of your own voice," I finished for him, and Nash laughed.

"I can't take credit for my genetic blessings, but I can't deny them, either." Tod pulled me onto his lap again and his hand settled on my hip, and for a moment my whole world went still beneath the unexpected weight of his intense focus. "But the face and voice I most love to see and hear both belong to you. And they always will, Kaylee."

My heart beat so hard my entire body trembled. I kissed him, and my fingers slid into his hair, and Tod's hands splayed across my back, touching as much of me as possible.

Nash cleared his throat. "I'm going to refrain from acknowledging the awkwardness of this moment, as I quietly retreat…." His shoes whispered against the carpet.

I pulled away from Tod reluctantly and turned to his brother. "Sorry. I didn't mean to make things—"

"Don't be." Nash's smile was small and more than a little melancholy, but he met my gaze and held it a second. Then he gave Tod a small, firm nod, like he'd come to some private decision. "Don't be sorry. Either of you. This is the way it's supposed to be. I've understood that for a few weeks, but I didn't tell you because…well, because I was really mad at you both. But this is…right." He made a gesture encompassing us both. "This is *good.* I hope you both get to stay golden for a long, long time."

Tod was silent for a moment, and I felt his heart go as still as his eyes, which usually meant he was feeling something he didn't know how to express. Then, finally, he grinned. "And I hope you get all those grandkids and that old-man gut."

Nash laughed, and I frowned at Tod.

"What?" He gave me a wide-eyed, innocent look. "I just basically wished him a lifetime of good food and sex. It doesn't get much better than that."

I glanced from one brother to the other, confused. "Food and sex? How do you figure?"

Nash crossed his arms over his chest, still chuckling. "Where do you think the kids and the gut come from?"

On the bright side, the fraternal communication gap had obviously been bridged.

But on that other side…it turned out that nonsense was the official language of testosterone, and I was not a native speaker.

"But we're talking *extreme* future tense, here. Like, hover cars and space colonies." Nash lifted his shirt, showing off one of few physical traits he and his brother actually had in common. "These abs are gonna be around for a long, long time." He disappeared into the hall, still chuckling, and Tod looked at me in astonishment.

"Did that really just happen?"

"I think it did." I exhaled, long and slow, more relieved than I could ever have explained by this breakthrough in their relationship. In the landscape of betrayal and resentment they'd been mired in for months, that relaxed banter was like climbing the Mount Everest of emotions. Together.

When Nash and Sabine had left so she could hunt, Sophie, Luca, and Emma curled up on the couch to try to distract themselves with another movie. Though I could tell during the opening credits just how futile an effort that would be.

When I turned to relinquish the living room to those still actually living, I found Tod watching me from the hall. His eyes swirled with conflicting emotions, in complementing shades of blue, and I watched as rage at Avari and worry for his mother competed with desire for…me.

He smiled when he saw me looking, and I wanted to kiss each of his dimples. I wanted to kiss him until he forgot about everything else. Until all of the fear and anger and horror we'd been living with for so long had faded into the background and—for a few minutes, anyway—there was nothing but us and the comfort we found in each other.

I needed some time alone with Tod, and it had to be soon, because Avari's clock was ticking and what I'd learned from our phone call with the hellion—what I'd finally been forced to admit to myself—was that I was the only one who could stop his macabre countdown.

But first…

I slipped into the hall and tried on a smile of my own. "Hey." I looked up at Tod, and he stared into my eyes like he could see right through me. Into me.

"Hey." His smile faded a little, infused with a more intense, more intimate emotion that couldn't be described with any one word in my vocabulary. "Your irises are spinning like crazy. Whatever could be on your mind, *bean sidhe?*"

I stepped closer and put my hands on his chest for balance while I went up on my toes and whispered, though no one else could hear me anyway. "Well, reaper, I was thinking that we should get out of here for a little while."

The blue spirals in his own eyes tightened in response, and anticipation tingled up my spine. "And where should we go?"

"You know the place."

"Do you think that's safe?" He glanced over my shoulder into the living room. "Leaving them here?"

"Nothing is safe. But we'll be just an autodial away, thanks to the miracle of cell phone technology."

"I'm convinced." But then his gaze narrowed on me, studying me. "You sure you're okay?"

"Considering the circumstances? I'm as okay as I'm ever going to be." I dropped onto the balls of my feet so he couldn't see how very true that was. "Let me tell them we're going, then I'll pick up a snack and meet you there in twenty minutes."

"I can get food. What do you want?"

I shook my head. "My treat this time. I insist."

His brows rose, but he didn't argue. "Okay. I'll see you in a few..." Then he disappeared.

I ducked into the living room and told the three couch potatoes that I'd be at Tod's for a while, and that they should text one of us if anything...happened. Sophie pretended to gag. Luca shut her up with a kiss. And Emma gave me such a wistful look that I almost changed my mind, so I could keep her company. I owed her that.

But I had to talk to Tod in private. And time was running out.

The fact that I hadn't actually lied to Tod didn't ease my guilt as I blinked into his mother's home. The house felt strange and too quiet without Nash and Harmony there. I missed the hum of the dishwasher, the scent of baking chocolate, and the video game sounds usually emanating from Nash's room at the end of the hall.

My shoes squeaked on the linoleum while I searched the kitchen, and I bruised my knees climbing onto the countertop so I could check the upper cabinets, but I didn't find what I was looking for there, or in the bathroom, or the living room.

Walking into Harmony's room while she was suffering in the Netherworld felt like violating a shrine. Her closet was open and her bed was unmade, like she'd just gotten up, but the truth was that she hadn't been home in more than a day, and she wouldn't come home at all if I didn't get what I'd come for, then do what had to be done.

Avari's clock ticked in my head as I searched her drawers and her bedside table, and a countdown of my own added to the pressure when I glanced at her alarm clock and saw that twelve minutes had already slipped away from me. Tod would expect me in eight more. If I was too late, he'd text. Then he'd come looking for me.

I finally found what I needed in a shoe box at the back of Harmony's closet. Eleven vials, neatly labeled in her all-caps print, along with a handful of disposable plastic droppers sealed in cellophane and a small notebook full of notes to herself. Most of the sentences were incomplete, but the dosages were clear.

I wondered how she'd been testing them. Then I decided I didn't really want to know.

I slid the vial I needed into my pocket, along with one of the droppers. Then I took another dropper, just in case. After I'd closed the box, pushed it back into place, and double-checked to make sure I hadn't left anything else out or open, I blinked out of Harmony's house and into Levi's office.

"Kaylee." Tod's boss blinked at me in surprise then hopped down from his rolling chair. His chest barely cleared the surface of his desk. He couldn't have been more than eight years old when he'd died, and I found little else in either world creepier than an undead child. "I'm in the middle of a meeting." He waved one small, freckled hand at something behind me, and I turned to see two reapers I didn't recognize sitting in chairs at my back. I'd appeared out of nowhere between them and Levi's desk.

"I need a favor." *Don't look at his letter opener. Don't look at his letter opener....* If he'd noticed the missing incubus soul, I couldn't tell, and I wasn't about to alert him to the loss.

"If memory serves, you're already in my debt in that regard." He'd restored Tod's afterlife after I'd died. "And did I mention that you don't have an appointment?"

"She's not even a reaper," one of the men at my back said.

Levi crossed tiny arms over his little-boy chest, half covering the Gap Kids logo. "I'm aware, David."

"What *is* she?" the other reaper asked.

"Out of line. That's what she is." Levi planted both palms on his desk and glared up at me. It was like being scolded by a kindergartner. A kindergartner with an old soul and a corpse's eyes. "Kaylee, see my assistant and make an appointment. I think I have an opening around noon tomorrow."

"This can't wait. *Please,* Levi. I need help." I clutched the vial in my pocket and held his gaze, letting desperation show in mine, even though he probably couldn't see the motion in my irises. "Five minutes, max. I swear." That's more than I could afford to spend there anyway.

Finally he exhaled and looked past me to the other reapers. "Wait in the hall."

When they filed out the door without arguing, I realized that Tod was probably the least compliant employee Levi had—much like me in Madeline's service.

The door clicked closed at my back. Levi gestured to one of the chairs in front of his desk, and I sat. "Is this about Tod?"

"No. Not directly, anyway." My feet bounced on the floor, and I couldn't make them stop.

"Good, because he's used all the favors he's going to get—most of them on your behalf—and he's been dead less than three years."

I swallowed a lump of guilt over that. But if this went well, he wouldn't have to worry about me getting Tod in trouble anymore.

"So, what can I do for you, Kaylee?"

I took a deep breath, then exhaled slowly. "I need you to tell a lie."

Levi frowned with pouty child's lips, and his freckled forehead wrinkled below a mop of bright red hair. "Maybe you better start from the beginning."

It took almost five minutes for me to explain what I needed

and why, and another two minutes to persuade him that my lie was necessary, and that he had to be the one to tell it. I then spent one more precious minute convincing him that I hadn't lost my mind and that I would actually go through with my part of the plan.

By the time I shook Levi's hand, unsettled more by the grim respect in his gaze than I was by the reality of what I was planning, I was seven minutes late to meet Tod, and he'd texted twice.

And I still had to pick up the drinks.

While I waited for our cherry limeades, I texted Tod to tell him I was on my way. Then I practiced controlling my pulse and slowing my heartbeat. Letting my true fear show in my eyes while hiding my guilt over what I was about to do.

This is about the war, not the battle, Kaylee. Sacrifices had to be made.

When I blinked into his room, Tod was squatting in front of the minifridge that served as his nightstand. When he saw me, he stood with the small carton of ice cream we'd opened the day before.

"No, thanks." I set the limeades on top of the fridge and held his gaze. "I'm not here for the ice cream."

His eyes widened. "I may not be the sharpest scythe in the shed, but even I can read those signals." He kissed me, and I nearly forgot my own name.

"Mmm..." I said, when his mouth trailed over my chin and down my neck.

"Why do you taste so good?" he mumbled against my skin.

"Cherry limeade." I reached back to hand him his. I'd gotten us each a small, because I needed him to drink as much of his as possible.

Tod took a long drink, then set his cup down. "I love those."

"I know." I slid my hands beneath his shirt, running my fingers over his stomach, then higher.

"I love you more."

"More than processed sugar and fresh-squeezed citrus? You flatter me…."

I leaned into him until he had to take a step back, and then I leaned a little more. He lost his balance and had to sit on the edge of the bed, staring up at me in surprise. I climbed into his lap, then I kissed Tod like I might never see him again. Like the promise of eternity was a cruel joke and the truth was that we might not live to see dawn.

When that kiss finally ended, Tod leaned back a little so he could focus on my face. "Not that I'm complaining—and let me emphasize that I'm *truly* not complaining—but is something wrong, Kaylee? I mean, other than the missing parents/demonic evil thing?" He reached for his cup again, and relief and guilt churned within me, one fading into the other until they were indistinguishable.

"Does something have to be wrong for me to want to spend time alone with my boyfriend?"

His eyes narrowed as he sipped from his straw. "A smarter reaper than I might notice that you're playing the same implication game Avari plays when he doesn't want to admit something."

"I don't want a smarter reaper. I want *you*."

"Ha ha." He took another drink, then set the cup down again. "Kay…?" He knew me too well to fall for my avoidance game, and he loved me too much not to push for the truth when something was obviously wrong.

"I'm just…scared. I'm scared, Tod." I slumped beneath the weight of that admission, and his hands slid up my back, over my shirt. "I'm more scared now than I've ever been in my life. Or my afterlife." That was true. In fact, that was the truest thing I could possibly have told him.

"You're a murder victim. How can you be more scared now than you were the night you died?"

"I don't know. There was no time to be scared then. All I could do was react. Fight. But now there's nothing to do but think about what Avari's doing to my dad and what he'll do to your mom and Brendon when he gets them. Or about how we can't stop it. We've been in and out of the Netherworld a dozen times in the past twenty-four hours, and we haven't seen a single sign of your mom and my uncle since we found those bandages, and what scares me even worse is that Avari hasn't found them yet, either. How is that possible? I mean, if they were still alive, wouldn't he have found them, even if we can't?"

"Maybe not." Tod's eyes went still beneath the burden of a fear I understood very well. As did Sophie and Nash. "They're alive, Kay. And so's your father. We're going to get them back."

"I know. I'll do whatever it takes to make that happen. But..." I sat straighter in his lap and looked right into his eyes. "You know we can't do that without sacrificing something else, right? We can't get them back without casualties."

He shook his head. "No. No one else is going to—"

"Tod. We're both as grown-up as we're going to get, and we have to stop telling each other faerie tales. This isn't a happy-ending kind of world we live in. Nothing comes without a price, and someone has to be willing to pay."

"The bad guys are going to pay. It's their *turn* to pay."

"What part of our recent interaction with the Netherworld leads you to believe that's even possible? If Ira had wanted Sabine dead, she'd be dead, and who knows how many more of us would have died trying in vain to save her. Or even find her. Sometimes I think we're only alive because they haven't decided to kill us yet."

"We're not alive," Tod said, but for once, his grin failed to lighten the mood—because it wasn't a real grin. He was as scared and angry as I was, and there was no way to truly forget that, while those we loved were suffering beyond our reach.

"You know what I mean." I took a sip from my cup and handed him his, careful not to get them confused. Fortunately, I'd depressed the "diet" bubble on the lid of my own, even though there was no such thing as a diet cherry limeade. Thank goodness.

"I also know you're wrong." He took a drink, then set his cup down again. "We're not alive because they haven't decided to kill us yet. We're alive *in spite* of them wanting us dead. Because they *have* tried, and we've come through it okay every single time. Because of you, Kaylee."

"It was a team effort. Besides, not all of us came through it, and that part *was* because of me."

"Don't." Tod took my face in his hands and kissed me before I could argue. Then he pulled me close again and spoke into my ear so softly I wasn't sure if I was hearing words from his mouth or from his heart. "You don't get credit for killing Alec because you would never have hurt him. Never. You've lost everything protecting the people you love. Em and Sophie. Nash. Your dad. And me. I'm here because of you. I'm as close to human as I can be—as I'll *ever* be again—because you're here with me. Every night, I count down the minutes until I can see you. I hate school because it takes you away from me. I wish I could sleep for more than a few minutes at a time, so I could dream about you. My mom and Nash are very important to me. I would do anything for them. But you're the reason I'm still here. You're the reason I'm still me—the reason I still see people instead of potential names on a future list."

He held me tighter, and tears rolled down my cheeks before I even knew they were there. "We're going to get through this. I promise you, Kaylee." He pulled away so he could see my eyes, and I saw sincerity in his. Earnestness. I saw how very much he believed what he was saying. "We're going to get them back. And we're going to be together forever. There's nothing in either world strong or evil enough to come between us."

But he was wrong.

I blinked before he could see the truth in my eyes.

"You want to cross over again?" he asked, and I opened my eyes. "We can go now. I don't have to be at work until midnight, and I won't have a reaping until—"

"No. I mean yes, I do, but not yet. In a couple of hours. For now, I just want...you. Us. This." I kissed him again and ran my hands through his curls, thinking about how soft his hair was. How good his skin felt beneath my hands, smooth and firm, and so very warm.

How this might be the last time...

"Mmm..." he moaned against my skin. He worked his way down my neck while I worked my way up from his stomach, dragging his tee up with my hands, trying to touch all of him at once. When my fingers crawled over his collarbones, he leaned back and lifted his arms so I could pull his shirt off.

I have no idea where it landed.

Tod lifted me and turned, and suddenly I was looking up at him, propped up on my elbows. His eyes churned with an intense blend of pain, and fear, and need, and anger, but at the center, just outside of his pupils, there was a deep spiral of something more powerful than all the others. Something stronger, like it could swallow everything else he was feeling, and with a sudden, startling leap of intuition, I realized that that spiral was *me.* That deep, bright blue that grew and twisted throughout the other colors—that was how he felt about me.

I got lost in his eyes. I got lost in the colors and the emotions, and I stayed lost there as long as I could, because those things he was showing me…those were real. His eyes were truly the windows to his soul, and those colors…they *were* Tod. Seeing them meant knowing him, and I knew that no one else had ever had free access to his soul. Not even Levi, who'd reaped it not once, but twice.

Tod was mine, just as much as I was his. And I *was* his. Completely.

My heart thundered in my chest with a sudden, stunning terror. My hands fell away from him. If Avari ever figured out how much Tod truly meant to me, he would stop at nothing to have him. To hurt him.

Ira would do the same, surely, if he would hurt Sabine just to hurt me.

There were still things I hadn't considered. Things I needed to account for…

"Kay?" Tod sat up, and his fingers trailed down my side. "What's wrong?"

"Nothing. I…" I swallowed thickly, then met his gaze again. "Can you hand me my drink?" My mouth was suddenly so dry I could hardly speak.

While I sipped from my straw, he sipped from his.

"Tod, what's the worst thing you've ever done for the right reason?"

He grinned, and I loved that he could do that—that he could remind me of good times in the middle of the worst times we'd ever experienced. "You may remember that I kissed my brother's girlfriend."

"The way I remember it, she kissed you."

"I kissed her back. A lot. Things escalated from there. Drama. Heartbreak. It was quite the scandal."

I let my fingers trail down his bare arm while he took another drink, then he set both cups on the fridge again. "Do you ever regret it?"

"No. Not even for a second. Kissing you back may have been the wrong thing to do, but I did it for the right reason. I don't ever want you to doubt that. This…" He put one hand over my heart, and I could tell from the sudden swell of color in his eyes that he could feel it beating. "Us… We're *right*. This is the way things are supposed to be, Kaylee. Don't tell me you can't feel that. I can see it in your eyes."

"I know. Do you think…? I mean, it sounds stupid, but your mom said it was true for my parents…." I blinked and could almost feel myself blush. "Do you think we'll ever be soul mates?"

"I think we already are." The blues in his eyes spun so fast they made me dizzy. "I remember the exact moment you took a piece of my soul. I felt it."

I held my breath, which, as it turns out, is completely different than simply ceasing to breathe. "When?" The word carried no sound, yet he heard it.

"When I found you on your bed, bleeding out. I knew you were going to die. I'd been trying to prepare myself for it, but when the moment came, I couldn't let you go. I knew I couldn't stop it, but at the same time I knew that if you died, you'd have to take me with you, because I couldn't be here without you."

My heart beat so hard my entire body shook with each thump.

"That's why Levi was able to get me back, Kaylee. Did Madeline tell you?"

I shook my head. I didn't quite understand what he was trying to say, but I could feel the reality of it slipping into place inside me, like all great, irrefutable truths.

"He turned in my soul after he reaped it, but they couldn't process it because it wasn't whole. I'd given part of it to you. He was on his way to untangle the rest of my soul from yours when Madeline found him and asked for an audience with you. Then, when you told him to bring me back, he knew that might actually be possible, because you still had some of my soul."

Tears filled my eyes and spilled down my cheeks.

"So…I'm yours, Kaylee. Every single part of me, from the hands that itch to touch you to the bit of my soul that you carry. Nothing can *ever* change that."

I held him so tightly my arms ached and I was sure I must have been bruising him, but he didn't complain. "I love you so much, and sometimes that scares the crap out of me."

"Me, too. Have I told you that you're the scariest thing I've ever seen?"

I blinked in surprise. "Well, that's a…nontraditional compliment. Thanks?"

He laughed. "Okay, that was bad phrasing, but it's the truth." He ran his thumb over my lower lip, and the swirling in his irises swelled with the touch and with the thoughts behind it. "This is the most frighteningly beautiful mouth I have ever seen. The most terrifyingly delicious lips I have ever tasted. These lips make me hungry for more every time I kiss them. This mouth, and the tongue inside it…they speak words I hang on to. Words that make me want to be a better man. Words I would gladly build my entire afterlife around. But they also say things that terrify me. Things that send chills all the way to my heart. They speak about dangers I can't prevent. Threats I can't always see. They threaten to do things that could get you hurt, when every single beat of my heart tells me that I need to protect you."

I stared at him, stunned, and he leaned in to kiss me again, softly. Almost chastely.

"This mouth scares the afterlife right out of me, Kaylee, but then every time I see these lips, or feel them, or taste them, I remember exactly why I'm still here. Exactly why I'll still be here a hundred years from now. A thousand, if there are that many years in the cards for us."

"Tod, I—"

He put one finger over my mouth and grinned. "And this nose, by the way, is terrifyingly cute, both head-on and in profile. These cheeks…" He kissed my right cheek. "These cheeks are where smiles were meant to live, and where all my own smiles are born, and if you don't think that's scary, then you obviously haven't noticed how I smile much more often than is expected of the dreaded grim reaper. This forehead…" Another kiss, and my heart nearly exploded. "This forehead hides scary thoughts I wish you didn't have to think, and it crinkles when you're worried."

Tod ran one finger over my left eyebrow, slowly, his gaze holding mine. "These eyes scare me on a daily basis, because they see more of me than I'd even thought possible. They see *all* of me. And they show me things, too." He kissed each of my eyebrows, and tears blurred my vision. "These beautiful blue eyes show me all the things you'd be willing to do for the people you care about. The things you would give up. The pain you would put yourself through for anyone you love—including me—and I can hardly stand to look into these eyes sometimes, because when I do, I know that you're going to do what needs to be done, even if that might take you away from me. From all of us."

He exhaled slowly, and the swirling in his own irises

slowed. "And I know that I have no right to ask you not to do whatever you're thinking about doing right now, but looking into your eyes at this particular moment is scaring me worse than I've ever been scared, Kaylee. Worse than when I died. Worse than when Nash died. Worse than when *you* died, because whatever you're thinking…it's bigger than that, isn't it? This is bigger than one death, because it's bigger than one life. Isn't it?"

"Tod, I can't…." My eyes filled again, and his face blurred beneath my tears.

"Yes, you can." He looked into my eyes, and I blinked. When my tears fell, he got a better look at my irises, and I saw fresh apprehension twist in his. "What are you thinking, Kaylee?" He frowned, looking deeper. "Whatever it is, please tell me you haven't already done it."

"I haven't. But most of the plans are already in place."

"What plans? What did you *do?* Please tell me you didn't make another deal with a hellion."

"I need a drink. My mouth is so dry." I'd never been so nervous or felt so guilty in my life.

Tod handed me my cup, and I took a long sip from mine while he drank from his. When I heard the dry, icy rattle from the bottom of his cup, I knew it was time.

"Thanks."

He set both cups on the fridge one last time. "Better?"

"Yeah." I cleared my throat and crossed my legs beneath me on the mattress, trying to decide how to start the most difficult conversation I'd ever been a part of.

"What's going on, Kaylee?" His voice was low and tense. He watched me in fear, and that was only going to get worse.

"I'm going to tell you some of it. As much as I can. But an hour from now, you're not going to remember what I said. Not consciously, anyway."

"I'm not going to…?" His frown deepened. "Why wouldn't I remember?"

I glanced pointedly at the cups standing on his minifridge, and he followed my gaze. "What the hell did you *do?*" When he turned back to me, irises twisting with a soul-bruising combination of fear, anger, and betrayal, I held the vial out to him, my hand shaking almost uncontrollably.

He took the vial and read his mother's handwriting. Comprehension surfaced in his expression, then bled into anger a split second before he turned and hurled the vial at the wall. It shattered, leaving a wet smear on the paint and shards of glass on the floor.

I flinched but stood my ground. I'd known he'd be mad, but that didn't alter necessity.

"You drugged me?"

"I'm so sorry, Tod." I tried to take his hand, but he pulled away from me, and my heart broke into a thousand splinters of pain and despair. "I had to."

"You had to *drug* me?" He stood and paced the narrow floor space for a second, then turned to me again. "What the hell is wrong with you?"

"This is the only way I could tell you what's going to happen, and you deserve to know that, even if you're not going to remember it."

"That doesn't make any sense! What's the point of telling me if I'm not going to remember?"

"Your mom taught me a little bit about—" I gestured vaguely toward the wet spot on the wall "—when we used it on Traci. You won't remember specifically what I'm about to tell you, but subconsciously you should retain enough to understand that this was my choice. That this is really how I wanted it to happen."

"Kaylee…?" His voice was so thick with fear that it seemed to hang in the air between us. "What did you *do?*"

I wasn't ready to answer that yet, so I continued with my own train of thought. "Also, I wanted to say goodbye. I couldn't just…go."

"No." He sank onto the bed next to me, shaking his head so hard that blond curls bounced on his forehead. "*No.* Whatever you did, we can undo it. You're not going anywhere. I won't let you. None of us will."

I took his hand, and that time he let me keep it. He covered them both with his free hand as if *he* were about to break some tough news to *me.*

I took a long, deep breath. "In a couple of hours, Levi's going to come see you guys at my house."

"Levi?" Tod's hands tightened around mine. "What does he have to do with this?"

"He's going to tell you that I'm gone—"

"No. *No,* Kaylee…" The pain in his eyes echoed deep inside me, and I had to swallow the lump in my throat to continue.

"He's going to tell you that I came to his office tonight—between picking up that vial and going out for cherry limeades—and that I asked him to take my soul and turn it in."

"Kaylee, no. I won't let him. He'll have to go through me to get to you."

My chest ached like someone was prying my ribs open, one at a time, to get at what was left of my poor, shredded heart. "You won't remember this, Tod." I held his gaze. I wouldn't let him look away and deny what I was saying, because this was too important. This part meant everything. "You won't remember that he's coming for me, but later, when he tells you that I'm gone, you'll believe him when he says this was my idea, because subconsciously you'll remember me telling you this. You'll know this is truly what I wanted, and you'll help the others understand."

"No, I won't." Tears stood in his eyes, but he blinked them away, clutching my hand. "I can't help them understand what *I* don't understand. Why are you doing this, Kaylee?"

"This is the only way." I wiped moisture from my own eyes and sniffed back more tears. "We've tried everything else, and nothing worked. Maybe we could have actually turned the hellions against one another if we'd had time, but we *don't* have time. Avari's going to kill my dad in a matter of hours, and he's not going to stop coming after everyone I love until he has me. Or until there's no possibility of him ever getting me." I squeezed his hand and refused to let myself tear up again. "This *has* to stop. I have to *make* this stop before someone else gets hurt."

"There has to be another way. You promised me, Kay." His anguished, accusing gaze ripped through me with every bit as much force and pain as Beck's dagger had. "You said forever."

"I know." I closed my eyes, fighting for composure, then made myself meet his gaze again. "It feels like I've done nothing but break promises to you lately, and I'm so sorry about that, but this one can't be avoided. I'm counting on you, Tod." Another sniffle, and I blinked back more moisture from my eyes. "My dad and Nash and Em...they're not going to understand this. I need you to help them. I need you to make them understand that this was my choice, and that I did it to protect them. Don't let them blame themselves. Make sure they understand that I'm gone and I'm at peace. That the best thing they can possibly do for me is remember me every now and then while they move on with their lives."

"Every now and then..." Tod shook his head. "I can't go five minutes without thinking about you, Kaylee. What makes you think that death—even true death—will change that?"

His words sent a selfish bolt of joy through me and I buried it before he saw, but I couldn't help being relieved by the thought that he would remember me for at least part of forever.

"Besides, your dad's not even here. What makes you think Avari will just pat him on the head and send him home when he finds out you're out of reach? He'll still torture your dad. He doesn't need a reason. He'll do it because he's evil."

"I'm not going to leave him there. I won't leave any of them. That part of my plan is still in progress, but I swear I won't go until my dad, your mom, and Uncle Brendon are back home." That was the hard part. The part I was still figuring out.

"How? Did you develop some superpower I'm not aware of?" His voice was threaded with anger now, and I was almost relieved by that. Anger was much easier to deal with than pain, though there was still plenty of that, too. "They wouldn't want you to do this. None of them would."

"This isn't about what they want for me. This is about what I want for *them*. It's already settled. I just need you to truly understand that this is what I want, so you'll remember that, even after you've forgotten everything I actually said."

"I won't forget." He pulled his hands from mine and stood, feverishly glancing around the room with wide eyes, his forehead furrowed. "I'll write it down. Where the hell are my pens and paper?"

"You don't have any." Which was among the reasons I'd never done homework in his room. "Tod. Please." I stood and pulled him toward me, and he came reluctantly, the anguished blues in his irises pulsing in time with his heartbeat.

"You can't expect me to just accept this, Kaylee. You can't

possibly think I'm just going to sit here for the next half hour and wait for Levi to come and steal your soul and take you away from me forever."

"Fine." I shrugged, hiding my own heartbreak. "Don't wait for it. Don't let it happen. Fight him for me, when he comes." I pulled him even closer and stood on my toes to whisper into his ear while my arms slid around his neck. "But until then, let's pretend this is actually going to happen. Let's pretend that we don't know how much longer we have until you'll fall asleep, and let's pretend I don't want to spend whatever time we have left like this. In anger and denial. Let's pretend we have to say goodbye." My eyes watered, and that time I couldn't stop the tears from falling. "How do you want to say goodbye, Tod?"

His arms wound around me, and he shook with silent sobs. He buried his face in my hair, and his words came out haltingly, stumbling over tears he was obviously fighting. "We're not pretending anymore, are we?"

"We never were. We never have, Tod." My fingers slid into his hair, and I tried to memorize the softness. The curls. "You and I have been real from the start. Don't ever forget that."

"I can't stop you, can I?" His breath was warm on my ear, and his grip almost bruised. "No one ever could stop you once you made up your mind."

I closed my eyes and inhaled his scent. "I want..." I held him as tight as I could. "We don't have much time left. I want to *be* with you. Please. You can't change any of this, so let's just...let's just be together, okay?" My tears fell on his shoulder. "Will you just be with me?"

"You don't even have to ask...." He pulled far enough away that he could see me, and beneath unshed tears, his irises burst into a tight twist of colors that made my head spin and my heart ache.

We sat on the edge of his bed and he leaned in to kiss me, and I buried myself in the feel and taste of him. I pushed everything else from my mind as silent tears trailed down my cheeks and landed in my hair.

We took our time, lingering in touches and kisses that echoed in my heart and haunted my memory. When all our clothes were gone, and most of our time was gone, and my chest ached so badly I could hardly stand it, I pulled him close and whispered into his ear. "I need you to trust me, even after I'm gone. Even after you've forgotten all of this. Do you trust me, Tod?"

"With everything I have and everything I am. With all my soul."

I lost control of a sob. Just one, and Tod kissed the tears from my cheeks.

"And would you wait for me, if it came to that?" I shouldn't have said it, but he wouldn't remember, and I *needed* to know.

I could handle whatever lay ahead if I had that one answer.

"Until the end of time. Love doesn't expire, Kaylee. And love never, ever dies."

With every last beat of my heart and every single bit of my own soul, I hoped that he was right.

Afterward, Tod and I lay side by side, breathing in sync, his arm wrapped around me while he fought sleep and the oblivion it would bring for him. I never wanted that moment to end, but it was doomed from the very beginning. That was a moment stolen from eternity, and those moments were never meant to last.

When I sat up, his arm retreated slowly, and he exhaled so heavily that I almost changed my mind. I almost took the coward's way out. But then I remembered that in the end, the easy way would only be harder. For all of us.

I stood and pulled on my clothes, and I could feel him watching me. In the bathroom doorway, I turned to look at him, gripping the doorframe. "I love you."

He sat up, wearing just his shorts, his feet peeking out beneath the sheet draped over the floor. "I…" He stopped, then started over. "Words don't do it justice, Kaylee." But that was okay, because I could see how he felt. He was showing me, in his eyes. In his soul.

"I know. Words were never enough, were they?"

"None of it was enough." He stood, and a second later I was in his arms, and his hands were in my hair, and he was kissing me, and holding me, and trying to hold *on* to me, and I knew I should push him away. That I should make a clean break. But I needed to feel him. I needed to kiss him. One last time. "I will never, ever have enough of you, Kaylee."

Then, slowly he let me go.

That time I didn't look back, because I knew that if I did, I wouldn't be able to leave. I closed the bathroom door behind me, and silent tears rolled down my cheeks as I pulled my shoes on. I put my hand flat on the closed door for a moment, wondering if he could feel it from the other side. Then I blinked out of Tod's room and out of his life.

I materialized in my father's empty bedroom and fell to my knees on the floor, crying uncontrollably. Sobbing so hard my whole body shook. Tears poured down my face. I clutched my chest, desperate to ease an ache unlike anything I'd ever felt. My sternum hurt like my heart had been ripped from my body, leaving behind an empty, gaping cavity.

I don't know how long I stayed like that, hunched over on the floor, shaking and sniffling and broken in more ways than I'd known a person could be broken. I stayed there until I had no more tears to cry. Until I had no other choice but to stand up, and grow up, and give up the only thing that would finally put my friends and family out of evil's reach.

My soul.

Nash and Sabine were curled up on Emma's twin bed, fully clothed for once. Holding each other.

The living room was quiet, so I peeked in to find Sophie and Luca asleep on the couch, together, and Em passed out in the recliner. Then I went back into my dad's room and closed the door. I sat on his bed and picked up the notepad on his nightstand, then dug through the drawer for a pen, my jaw clenched against any more tears.

The note to my father was the hardest. It took a long time. More time than I could afford. More time than *he* could afford.

The note to my friends wasn't much easier, but the words were flowing by then.

The third note was the most important. The words were critical; they had to be just right.

When I was done, I folded the pages and wrote their names on the outside.

I left the first two notes on my dad's nightstand where—with any luck—they wouldn't be discovered until after Levi had played his part.

The third note, I folded and slid into my back pocket while I watched them sleep, the friends and family I'd put through hell just by virtue of their connection to me.

Then I closed my damp eyes and blinked out of their lives.

The school cafeteria was somehow even creepier than I'd remembered. Maybe because my errand was creepier this time. Or maybe because I was breaking a promise to people I loved. Or maybe because I knew that even if I got what I wanted out of this midnight errand, I wouldn't *really* be getting what I wanted.

There was no way for me to win this game. I'd lost the moment I started playing.

In the massive, stainless steel kitchen, I pulled a small knife from a now-familiar drawer, then sat cross-legged on the floor in a pool of moonlight shining through the window. I peeled the bandage from my left palm. Explaining another cut wouldn't be a problem this time, so I sliced my skin open again. I gasped at the raw pain—still couldn't get used to that—and a line of dark red blood welled parallel to the one scabbed over half an inch away.

This time, I let the blood pool in my cupped palm, and with the knife on the floor at my side, I dipped my right index finger into my own blood and wrote Ira's name on the dingy linoleum tiles. Then I sucked in a deep breath and tried to purge my fear while preserving my anger, which Ira would want to taste.

I had no problem with the anger part. Letting go of my fear was much harder.

I stared at the three letters on the floor, glistening dark, dark red in the moonlight. And for a second, I thought about backing out. Then I closed my eyes and whispered Ira's name into the night.

My eyes opened, and a second later the hellion appeared in front of me, mirroring my cross-legged pose, staring across his own name at me. "Ms. Cavanaugh." On his tongue, my name sounded like the clash of swords, wielded in timeless fury.

"To what do I owe the pleasure?" he continued while I struggled to focus through the anger emanating from him, settling into my bones. Into my hands that wanted to form fists. Or to pick up the knife.

"You owe this pleasure to Avari, but I'd rather reverse the charges so that *he* owes *you*. And I think I know how to make that happen."

His dark brows rose. They were the color of my blood slowly drying on the floor and now dripping from between my fingers. "I'm intrigued…."

"So there's no misunderstanding, I have a proposal. I'm here to make a deal."

He nodded. "Of course you are. State your terms—first, what you need from me, then, how you're willing to pay. But you should know that tonight you reek of fear and sadness, as much as anger, and while I can and will feed from both of those emotions, they do not command as high a price as your rage."

"Acknowledged." It scared me even more to realize that I was picking up the lingo. "But if you agree to my terms, there will be *plenty* of anger for you—and it won't just be mine."

Another arch of a single dark red brow. "Do continue."

"My first demand—" I'd considered calling them requests, but because they were nonnegotiable, "demand" felt more accurate "—is that you deliver my uncle and Harmony Hudson to the human world without inflicting any further harm on them, and that you make no attempt to contact them or to reacquire them for the duration of our agreement."

"You're assuming I know where they are?"

"I am." I nodded firmly and tried not to notice that blood was still pooling in my palm. "I'm further assuming that you have them in your possession. That maybe you've had them since shortly after Tod and I found bloody bandages in the Netherworld version of the local hospital."

"Clever girl…" Ira smiled, clearly delighted, and I had to remind myself that his approval meant less than nothing to me. "How did you know?"

"I know from experience that Avari is powerful and his resources are vast. Yet he doesn't have them. The only reason I can think of for him not to have found them is that you found them first."

"Or they're dead." He watched closely for my reaction.

"If they were dead and Avari knew about it, he would have told me, just to feed from my suffering. You, however, understand that I suffer just as much—if not more—by not knowing where they are or what shape they're in. And you're not shortsighted enough to kill them before you've gotten all possible use out of them as living hostages. Right?"

Please, please let me be right….

"So far, so good," he said, and again I was surprised by his vernacular speech. Was anger that much closer to the general heart of humanity than envy? I didn't want to think about what that said about us as a species.

"My second demand—"

"Can you pay for a second demand?" Ira said. "I'm not sure you truly understand the debt your first request has already accrued."

I might not know what he'd *want* as payment, but I knew what I was willing to give. And that was all that mattered.

"My second demand," I continued, without acknowledging his warning, "is that for the duration of our arrangement, you will protect my friends and family." He started to object, and the first spark of anger I'd seen from him flashed in his dark eyes. *"Specifically,"* I said, talking over him. "Specifically, all of my blood relatives, as well as Emma Marshall, in any body her soul inhabits, Sabine Campbell, Luca Tedesco, and Harmony, Nash, and Tod Hudson." I couldn't risk him deciding on his own that any one of them wasn't a close enough friend to warrant protecting.

"You want me to protect them? You do understand that you're dealing with a hellion, right? Not a guardian angel."

"Don't worry. I'm willing to pay."

His eyes flashed again. "Child, it would take *years* of you existing in a constant state of homicidal fury to pay off a debt like that."

"I know." But I wouldn't be the only one paying.

"Well then…is there anything else on this fantasy list of demands from a child who's obviously grown too big for her mortal britches?"

"Just one more thing…"

As I outlined my last demand—the most selfish of them all—his eyes widened in surprise and delight like I'd never seen before from a hellion. The more excited he grew, the more unnerved I became, in part because a hellion's joy is never pleasant to witness. But also because it was *my* pain, fear, and anger putting that creepy, dried-blood smile on his face, and that was one of the scariest facts I'd ever contemplated.

When I was finished, Ira stared at me in obvious anticipation. "I must admit, I am intrigued by your devious, clever little mind." Then he licked his lips with a dark, dark tongue. "Now, let's discuss payment."

I took another deep breath and clenched my hands into fists to keep them from visibly shaking, though he could probably taste everything I was feeling on the air, whether or not I let it show. Blood dripped between the fingers of my left hand, and the fresh cut throbbed. "You'll get a partial payment up front, and even more over the course of our arrangement. Years of pain, fear, and the resulting homicidal rage, just like you said. Then, the bulk will be paid by a third party, when you've upheld the last part of our deal."

"The bulk?"

I nodded. "Pure, concentrated wrath. *Way* more of it than any mortal body could ever contain. Are you familiar with the term 'mother lode'? Do hellions say that? Because that's what I'm talking about here. The biggest payoff of your immortal existence."

"That's an impressive offer." Ira frowned at me, and I realized he was trying to smell a lie. "How do you intend to produce such a payment?"

"I find your skepticism insulting," I said, and he actually chuckled. "If you come through on your end, I'll come through on mine." In fact, one was contingent on the other. "Okay?"

The hellion nodded slowly. "The delivery schedule is understood and agreed to. Now, for the up-front part of the payment." His eyes glittered with perverse pleasure, and it took all of my self-control to keep from gagging. "What did you have in mind?"

I dipped my right index finger into the blood still pooled in my left palm, then reached out to trace his lower lip. "There will be much, much more, but it starts with another kiss...."

By the time I crossed into the Netherworld, dried blood had crusted on my lips and around my mouth. Ira was not a neat kisser.

That thought—and the fact that I had reason to think it—nearly made me lose what little I'd eaten since lunch the day before. My jaw ached and my tongue throbbed from being bitten, and I wasn't sure I'd ever get the taste of my own blood out of my mouth. Not to mention the taste of hellion.

I scrubbed my mouth with the tail of my shirt as we walked, but since I had no mirror, I couldn't be sure I'd gotten all the blood off.

The hospital rose in front of us, and we veered slowly toward the mental health unit across the parking lot from the main building. I stepped carefully to avoid baby creeper vines reaching for me from cracks in the concrete—they had crossed over from the human world, thanks to the steady human traffic on our side of the barrier. Ira let me set the pace, and I wasn't sure why until he spoke.

"I would tell you not to worry, little fury, except that I've grown to enjoy the taste of your fear."

I had nothing to say to that.

Lakeside looked extra-creepy in the red-tinted Netherworld moonlight, and our stunted shadows, splayed out on the sidewalk in front of us, bore little resemblance to our actual bodies. His even seemed to have an extra limb in my peripheral vision.

Things skittered in the high grass on either side of the walkway, and my instinct was to shy away from sounds I couldn't identify. But Ira had already promised me a safe escort as part of his side of the deal we'd struck. Nothing would mess with me for the next few minutes.

After that, all bets were off.

I wanted to threaten him with the consequences of going back on his word, just to reassure myself, but there *were* no consequences, which was just as well, because he couldn't go back on his word. That was the best thing about a hellion's inability to lie.

However, just because he couldn't back out didn't mean everything would go as I'd planned. If there was something I'd missed—something I'd failed to stipulate or make him agree to—the whole thing would fall apart around me. And I wouldn't be the only one to suffer for it.

"Ready, little fury?" Ira asked, and his words sent waves of anger rolling through me, a fan stoking flames of a rage I'd almost forgotten I'd left burning.

"I will never be ready for this," I whispered, and he stared down into my eyes, as near as I could tell, considering that his had no pupils or irises.

"But you will do it anyway. That's why he wants you. That selflessness is contrary to everything he is and everything he will ever be. He can't understand you, but he will try, and that process will not be pleasant for you."

"But it will be pleasant for *you*." As part of our deal. And it would be pleasant for Avari, because I'd found no way around that.

"Well then, shall we?"

I nodded again, and Ira looked up at the building in front of us. "Avarice!" He didn't shout, but his voice was so loud it rang in my bones, a sensation like the residual ache after a blow from a blunt object. "Come out and claim your prize."

For several seconds, nothing happened, and Ira leaned down—way down—to stage-whisper to me, an intoxicated smile forming on dark lips still smeared with my blood. "He's here, and he's *thoroughly* enraged. How delightful!"

"Ire." Avari appeared several feet in front of Lakeside's main entrance, a double set of glass doors that had both been shattered long ago, judging by the glass already ground into sand on the steps. "I did not realize you were making deliveries."

"Anything, for the right price. Just like you."

Avari's brows furrowed. "You and I have reached no agreement—I acknowledge no debt for this delivery."

"My agreement is with Ms. Cavanaugh. She is here under my escort and protection until she surrenders to your possession or returns to the human world."

"She paid you to deliver her to me?" Avari demanded, and even I could hear the anger and greed dripping from his words. "How? At what price?"

"She is paying for my protection until she surrenders—*if* she surrenders. The price is beyond your concern."

"And none of your damn business," I added, thoroughly enjoying the angry lines that formed around his jaw and the brief moment during which he was obviously too pissed off to speak. "Let's get on with it. You agreed to send my father back if I surrender. I'm here. Go get my dad. Now."

Avari hesitated just long enough to demonstrate that he wasn't taking orders from me; he was merely sticking to the deal *he'd* offered. Then, without looking away from me or raising his voice, he said, "Ladies..."

Belphegore and Invidia appeared behind him on the steps, each gripping one of my father's arms as he sagged, unconscious, between them. Pulverized glass crunched beneath their feet, and the toes of my father's shoes dragged twin paths through it.

"Is he okay?" I didn't bother to screen fear from my voice—Avari already knew I loved my father.

"He yet lives and is not beyond repair."

"Where are the others?" Invidia tossed her hair—an ever-flowing stream of molten envy—over one shoulder. Drops of it splattered around her, burning tiny holes in her dress and sizzling like acid on the steps.

"They will come for her, and when they do, you may each take one of your choosing. As per our arrangement."

I could see how much the words hurt Avari to say. The hellion of greed didn't like to share his toys, but if he'd given Invidia and Belphegore his word, in exchange for their help, he couldn't go back on it.

"You won't even get a shot at them," I said, and Avari laughed.

"I may not understand emotions like love and compassion, but I can anticipate their results, little *bean sidhe.* Human heartstrings function like a marionette's strings if properly manipulated. They will come for you because they value your company. Just like you came for your father."

Leave it to a hellion to define love as "valuing" someone's company.

As for his actual point…

"Ms. Cavanaugh's friends and family are under my sworn protection for the duration of our arrangement." Ira hadn't been pleased with that particular clause when he'd agreed to it, but now pleasure echoed in his voice, as his announcement produced Avari's rage. "Even if they come for her, I cannot let you take them."

That was my fail-safe. If my plan worked, my friends and family would never try to rescue me because—thanks to Levi's lie—they thought I was truly gone. They thought my soul had been recycled and that I was finally resting in peace.

But just in case one of them figured it out—Tod had the best chance because of his subconscious memory and because he worked with Levi—I had Ira. And Ira, as far as I knew, was the only being in existence who could stop Avari from doing what he did best. And Avari obviously knew it.

The sound that burst from the greed hellion's mouth was unlike anything I'd ever heard. It was a roar of outrage. A bellow of fury that crashed over and through me so thoroughly my bones quivered and my teeth clacked together, completely beyond my control.

Ira seemed to swell with the sound. He took it in, sucking it from the very air like a sponge absorbing water, until Avari realized he was feeding his new nemesis and bit the roar off with a painful-sounding gurgle-growl.

But that wasn't the end of his rage. Though he probably had no idea, that was only the very beginning of what he would eventually feed Ira, as payment by proxy for the deal the hellion of rage and I had struck.

"Well played, little fury," Ira said, loud enough for Avari to hear, even if his ears were ringing like mine were. "Hellion rage is not as pure and satisfying as that of a mortal, but what it lacks in quality, it makes up for in quantity. This rage will burn within him for decades."

And that was just the tip of the anger-iceberg.

"You're paying him with my wrath?" the hellion of greed demanded, and yet more fury leaked out with his words, a verbal appetizer for Ira.

"Yes." In part. And I was well aware that Avari's anger would not improve my treatment at his hands. But there was nothing I could do about that, so I tried not to think about it. "Let's talk terms."

"You surrender. Your father goes home. Those are my terms." Avari was more furious than I'd ever seen him. More furious than I could ever have imagined. Ice grew beneath his feet, spreading slowly down the steps and over the sidewalk toward us, and he didn't even seem to see it.

"That's the general idea, but it does me no good to free my father from you if you're just going to go after him or someone else I love later." And he'd do it, after my deal with Ira expired. "With that in mind, I have two demands. If you turn down either one of them, I will walk away from this deal." He didn't look like he believed me. I didn't give a damn. "First, we both agree that in exchange for my immortal soul, you will free my father. Immediately."

"Agreed." If I didn't know any better, I'd swear Avari was rolling featureless eyes at me. "In fact, that is the offer *I* presented to *you*."

Yes. But I needed his offer to me to stand separately—officially—from my real demand.

"Good. Second, I want your word that once I've surrendered, you will never again attempt to contact or hurt any member of my family or any of my established friends, in any way, shape, or form, personally or through any other agency acting on your behalf."

Ira had helped me with the phrasing. Based on Avari's still-escalating expression of fury—he was nearly speechless—the wrath demon didn't regret offering me that little bit of assistance at no additional charge.

Avari growled through clenched teeth, and the familiar—and very human—demonstration of his anger almost pleased me. "For what duration?"

What part of "never again" did he not understand?

I propped both hands on my hips, pretending to think it over. "How long do you plan to keep my soul?"

"As long as I like. The blink of a hellion's eye stretches well beyond a mortal's understanding of the passage of time, and I intend to enjoy the torment of your soul for much longer than that."

"So, forever, at least from a 'mortal's understanding'?" I said. "Is that a reasonable assumption?"

"Depending on your definition of 'reasonable,' yes." He looked hesitant to admit that. Suspicious.

"Well then, I think 'forever' is reasonable in this instance as well. You will have nothing to do with my friends and family, *forever,* beginning the moment I surrender to you."

"No." Avari seemed to take a perverse pleasure in that one word.

"No deal, then." He started to object, and I spoke over him. "Why should I give myself to you to save my father if you're just going to go after my friends and family later? That's not me saving my father—that's me delaying his torture and inevitably painful death. I'm not going to sell my own soul for anything less than the absolute freedom—from *you*—of everyone I love." My heart thundered within my chest. My pulse was the fevered race of fear through my veins as I turned to Ira to say the words that would either pull Avari into our trap or trigger the collapse of everything I'd lied, stolen, and negotiated for. "Let's go."

He nodded triumphantly, virtually glutted on Avari's rage, and we started to turn.

"Wait!" Avari roared at my back, and the sound rolled over me like an arctic gust, raising chill bumps the length of my body even as it threw me forward. I stumbled to keep from falling, grinning the whole time. I could practically feel his greed, at just the *thought* that some other hellion might make off with the prize he'd been chasing for months—which obviously didn't feel like a "blink of the eye" at the moment. "Fine. I agree," he said, and the words sounded like icicles shattering on concrete. "Once I take possession of your soul,

I will have no further contact with your friends or family members, directly or indirectly. From now, until the end of my own existence, should that day ever arrive."

I glanced up at Ira. "Does that about cover it?"

"I believe it does." His black orb eyes shined. "And that means this is goodbye, little fury."

My pulse raced out of control, flushing my system with fear and dread. Panic tripped in my chest, and my heart skipped one beat, then another. My hands tingled, and I could no longer feel my feet. "Don't forget what you promised…."

"Like it or not, I am a hellion of my word. We all are." He shot an amused look at Avari, who seemed to hate the hellion of wrath with an all-new passion. "One more kiss for the road?"

I nodded, and Ira leaned down to kiss me one more time, in front of three other hellions and assorted creepy-crawlies that had gathered to watch, no doubt waiting for the chance to grab a scrap of flesh or a chip of bone should one be tossed their way.

But that kiss wasn't just a goodbye between me and Ira, who was only playing the part of my friend because I was paying him. That kiss was a vital part of my deal with the hellion of wrath.

This time when his lips met mine, he inhaled and warmth seemed to flow from my body, pulled through my throat, then from my mouth into his. A bitter cold remained in its absence, and suddenly I couldn't remember…something.

There was something I'd known a moment earlier, but couldn't…quite…recall. Whatever it was, it was important. So important it had to be removed before Avari could find it in my head, when he took me apart.

And now it was completely gone.

Ira stepped back and licked his lips, and more ice spread

across the ground toward us from beneath Avari's feet. "Your father is waiting," he said, and little crystals of ice seemed to fall from his words.

Greed is a cold emotion; wrath is white-hot. Stuck between them, I felt like an icicle on fire.

"Fine." My head spun, and my stomach cramped. Avari had told me months ago that in the Netherworld, my existence could stretch into eternity, but I'd never imagined that my eternal existence would belong to *him,* much less that I would give it to him of my own free will.

But I had no other option. Nothing else would protect my friends and family, and if I'd learned anything about Avari over the past year, it was that he would not stop hunting us until he got what he wanted.

Until he got me.

"It has to be your choice," he reminded me, and I nodded. I had to agree to stay. I had to give him my soul.

I took in a deep breath, more out of habit than any real need for air. Then I said the words that had been rolling around in my head for the past couple of hours.

"You'll let my dad go if I give you my soul?"

"Yes."

"And beginning from the moment you take possession, you'll never again try to contact anyone I care about, forever and ever, amen?"

"This redundancy is exasperating, Ms. Cavanaugh."

"Just say it."

He growled in frustration, and Ira chuckled. "Yes. Beginning the moment I take possession of your soul, I will never again attempt to contact your friends and family for any reason whatsoever."

I sucked in a deep breath and swallowed the massive lump in my throat to keep from vomiting. "Fine. My soul is yours."

My world changed in that moment. It…darkened. Narrowed. Spiraled toward infinite despair. "Come get it before I change my mind."

Avari's hand closed around my arm. Belphegore and Invidia released my father. The instant they let him go, his eyelids began to flutter. Ira disappeared from my side and appeared at my father's, holding him up.

"Kaylee?" At first, my dad looked as confused as he sounded. Then he blinked, and horror came into focus in his expression as the Netherworld came into focus around him. He looked at me, then at Avari. Then at the demon's hand around my arm. "No! Kaylee, no!"

Tears filled my eyes for the millionth time in the past four days. "This is the only way, Dad." My hands shook. My teeth chattered. My entire body seemed to be *convulsing* with fear and dread. "I'm so sorry I couldn't find some other way."

I wanted to tell him not to worry about me. That I'd be fine. But that wasn't true. I wouldn't be fine. Avari would make sure of that.

"No!" My dad tried to stand, but he was still too weak. Confused. He didn't seem to realize Ira was holding him up.

"You're safe now. Avari can't touch you—any of you." And they were under Ira's protection. That much I remembered, but the rest of my deal with the hellion of wrath was… It was *gone.*

Terror furled through me at that fresh realization. What if I'd gotten something wrong? What if I hadn't covered all the bases? It was too late now. I couldn't even remember the details. I'd have to trust myself. I'd have to trust Ira, as much as any hellion could be trusted, but that was really just trusting myself to have made sure he gave his word.

"Kaylee!" Now my father was crying, and Avari let me

watch. Avari *made* me watch, because my pain was already feeding him.

"Make him forget!" I shouted at Ira, and only once I'd said the words did I remember that he had to. I'd negotiated for that.

Ira put one hand over my father's eyes and whispered something into his ear. Something I couldn't hear and could no longer recall the specifics of, even though I'd made him promise to say it. To…do whatever he was doing.

Then they were gone. Just like that, my father was gone. He was safe.

I was alone in hell.

Avari spun me to face him. The world twisted around me, and pain spread through my flesh at his touch, like his fingers were icicles stabbing into me, spreading through my veins, freezing the blood in them. I would have fallen to my knees if he wasn't holding me up.

"I always knew this day would come, little *bean sidhe.* I knew that someday you would scream just for me. So open your pretty little mouth, and let's have a taste of forever."

His hand clenched around my arm, and pain like a thousand needles shot through every muscle in my body, driving away all thought and all sight. My mouth dropped open, and a scream of agony ripped free from my throat, shredding the soft tissues as it poured out of me.

Avari laughed, and I realized I heard him in my head, because my ears were full of my own screaming. As he dragged me down the cracked sidewalk, my toes scraping concrete, snagging on vines and thorns, his next words seemed to take root in my brain, bypassing my ears entirely.

"Welcome to hell, Ms. Cavanaugh. Please make yourself at home."

The pain begins, and within seconds it consumes me. If I've ever felt anything else, I can't remember it. Maybe I loved, once. Maybe I was loved. Maybe I touched something soft. Maybe I tasted something sweet. Maybe I heard something beautiful.

There is none of that here.

Here is every face that ever taunted me. Here is every heartbreak I've ever felt. Here is every doubt, every lack, and every failure.

In hell, I am the sum of my flaws.

This lasts for eternity, though I have no idea how long eternity really is. There is no time here. A minute, a day, a century, they are all measured by how much agony can be stuffed into a single heartbeat.

I scream as my flesh burns and my organs shrivel. My skin blackens and peels, and flakes of it fall to the floor, like a rain of ashes. This must be hell's version of snow. I'm horrified by my own disintegration, but I never lose consciousness. He won't let me miss a moment of my own torture, and he leaves my throat intact, because my screams are the soundtrack of his triumph, and somehow in hell I never lose my voice.

What he wants most from me is screaming, and I have no choice but to deliver.

Then, when there's so little left of me that I can't recognize the charred, twisted remains of my own body, he puts me back together so he can start from scratch, and there is no end to his imagination or to the pain it inspires. I cannot think. I cannot breathe. I cannot sleep. I can do nothing but suffer and scream, and here it becomes clear that I deserve nothing more. He shows me that I've ruined every life I ever touched, and I will spend eternity paying for every mistake I've ever made. I will pay, and I will pay again, then I will pay some more, and forever will come and go while I am still paying for sins I've long since forgotten I committed.

He wants to know every part of me. Every thought in my head and every cell in my body, and he seems to think that taking me apart one piece at a time—one leg, one finger, one memory, one thought—will show him how I feel things he can't possibly understand. Things like love and pity and compassion, few of which I can even remember, with my own screams carving canyons through my mind.

But dissecting me won't help. He will never understand any human emotion that doesn't feed his appetite for greed or for suffering. Hellions don't have that capacity. And when he figures that out, his anger swells like the ocean tide until I'm afraid we'll both drown in it, and I know his fury should make me happy, for some reason I can't quite remember, but it doesn't, because in this place, his anger only means my pain. In fact, his pleasure means my pain, and his confusion means my pain, and his very presence means my pain.

And then, when my pain finally begins to bore him, hell changes, and I learn all new ways to suffer.

I remember me now. I remember who I was, when I was something other than this. Other than agony given battered shape and shrill voice.

I was a daughter. I was a cousin, a niece, a classmate, a friend, a girlfriend.

I am none of that here, and the pain is infinitely worse now that I know what I've lost.

He shows me what I've missed as I tumble through eternity, banged and bruised and abraded by my own memories. He shows me my friends. My family. He shows me that my attempt to save them has brought them all to ruin.

Hazel eyes, twisting in pain.

Long, thin hair, streaked with blood.

Black eyes flashing in fury, in futility.

Tears trailing down pale cheeks.

Grief and anger lead to violence, and neglect, and relapse, and pain that has no end.

I haven't freed them—I've sentenced them to an existence of guilt and tribulations I've caused but cannot fix from beyond the grave. And I am so *far beyond the grave now that the thought of being buried in a dark, quiet hole in the ground feels like mercy.*

He shows me that Emma is lost. She is drowning in the suffering around her, and it takes over her mind until she can't think. Can't form coherent sentences. This time when they lock her up, I am not there to set her free. She sits in the corner of an empty room and screams my name over and over. I am the only thought she can still express, and the pain in her voice rips through my very center, shattering me into bits too small for the king's horses and his men to ever find, much less put back together. And for no reason he will explain to me, Tod is not there. He does not help her.

Where is Tod?

My captor shows me that Nash has escaped Emma's fate. He's escaped everything, except for a saccharine euphoria and the memories he lives in, convinced they are reality as his body wastes away because he's forgotten about food and rest and life. He pays for his high with bits of himself, and remembered bits of me, and when those are all gone, he pays with bits of Sabine, even as he pushes her away.

Months flow like water beneath the bridge of their lives, and when she cannot wakehimshakehimsavehim, *Nash finally lets it all go, and I cannot see the reaper who comes for his soul, but I know Nash does not resist. He lets the last of his life fade away while he rides on a vaguely pleasant fog, unaware that it is dissolving beneath him until he crashes to the ground, to the floor of his own bedroom, never to rise again. And for no reason I can understand, Tod is not there. He does not help his brother.*

Where is Tod?

Sabine does not go to Nash's funeral. She cannot look at him in his coffin, skin molded to the shape of his bones, cheeks hollow, eyes sunken in dark wells carved out of his skull. But I cannot look away.

I have done this, and I am not allowed to forget that. I have led my first love to his ruin, and with him, so many others fall.

Without Nash, Sabine has no reason for…anything. No reason to care, to be careful, to exercise control. She feeds to numb the pain, and in her wake the bodies pile up, but the police don't catch her until she lets them. Until she decides she has no place in society and no right to freedom.

Then there is broken glass, stolen cash, and handcuffs she doesn't fight. Sabine stares through the bars every day, alone in her private hell while the other prisoners shy away from her. She doesn't feed from them. She doesn't feed from anyone, and I realize she's starving herself, just like Nash did. Soon she will be gone, and there will be no one at her funeral because she is fear itself, and everyone who had the capacity to love in spite of that fear is long gone.

My heart hurts when I realize that they are gone—all three of them. Prisoner, patient, corpse, I have driven them all to their destruction, to ends surely as painful as my own miserable existence.

But even worse than the tragic ends is the conspicuous absence. Where is Tod? Why can't I see him?

When I realize I know what his absence means, I pray for oblivion, but cognizance plays a pivotal role in today's torture. My mind is not allowed to wander….

And when my pain begins to bore him again, hell changes again. And it never ends.

There are infinite variations, and I think they will eventually numb me, because how can anyone hurt for as long as I've been hurting, yet numbness never comes. Each revolution of torture brings its own special brand of hell, and each is more agonizing than the one before, and this goes on forever.

Years have passed, surely. Centuries, maybe. I bruise, I bleed, I fall apart, I die, then I am born again, only to suffer and fall anew, but the pain never becomes routine. It is always fresh and new, welcoming me to an existence I cannot end.

I am hell's phoenix, forever bursting into flames only to be resurrected again in the next heartbeat so we can dance this excruciating dance all over again.

I've forgotten my name. I cannot remember who I am or where I'm from. I think I was born into this. There has never been anything else. I am hell's daughter, and my mind is as fractured as the Netherrealm itself, twisted and torn. There are pieces of me everywhere, and I cannot gather them fast enough. Parts are missing, surely. Memories. Thoughts. Names. Places. They litter the ground and I cannot hold them all together. I cannot hold myself together.

There is little left worth saving anyway.

Light is pain.

Dark is fear.

The scent of burning flesh is seared into my brain—what little remains of it—and I think that flesh is mine. Dinner is served, and I am the main course, and still I scream.

Scars. Screams. Blood. Fire. Ice. These are the pieces of me, crumbling between my fingers, and I can no longer remember how they should fit.

I cower in the corner, in drifts of filth, but I cannot hide. There is nothing left of me. What once intrigued him is gone. Dead. Scorched beyond recognition, and I don't know who or where or why I am, but

I know that my time is almost up. I have nothing left to give him but my screams, and my throat is so, so tired.

His shadow falls over me.

Over the whole room. In the next instant, I scream, and this time I am lost in the sound of my own madness.

"Kaylee."

The voice came from inside my head, because my ears were too full of my own screams to hear anything else.

My eyes opened, and I saw only shadows. A warm, hard hand covered my mouth, and my screaming stopped. The sudden silence was profound. Stunning. Startling.

Disorienting.

Echoes of past screams haunted me, spinning me on edge, hurling me around inside my own head. Reality would not come into focus.

"Wake up, little fury. You're going to miss all the fun." The hand pulled me by my arm, and reality tilted around me as I sat up. The world assaulted me with light and color, sharp edges and cruel angles. Outside of my dirty corner, the room flickered with hundreds of points of light—human fat, crudely rendered, burning in bowls of curved bone.

The stench had made me sick at first—how long ago had that been?—but now I couldn't remember any other scent.

"Kaylee." He stared at me through red-veined, black orb eyes, only inches away.

My hands shook as I pushed myself across the floor, away from him, cowering from those eyes, fleeing from memories I couldn't bring into focus.

He reached for me, and I flinched, then lashed out, swiping with hands that had no claws. Words that had no power. "Don't touch me!"

My voice was raw. My words were slushy. I hadn't played with consonants in…eternity?

"Whether you remember or not, we had a deal, little fury." He hauled me off the floor by one arm and I hung there, bare, filthy toes brushing the dirty floor. "You can come willingly, or I will take you with as much force as I like. Either way, I will be paid."

Was this face different? I blinked, struggling to focus through the pain in my shoulder as I dangled. Did I know this face, the way the flames flickered in his black, black eyes and were shown on his crimson lips? Did it matter? I knew his voice, but couldn't remember how….

"Who are you?" I croaked. For that matter, who was I? *Where* was I? Why had the pain stopped?

He set me on the ground and laughed, exposing a tongue the color of my own dried blood, and the sound rolled through me, drawing anger from me like bubbles floating toward the water's surface. "Today, I find myself in the unlikely role of liberator, but this knight gallant does not work for free. You *will* pay me for my troubles, or I will leave you here to rot for eternity."

"Pay?" *Troubles? Eternity?* Were his words supposed to make sense?

"It's just a kiss, little fury." He slid one hand behind my head and pulled me closer, and I shoved against his granite chest, fighting unburdened by the rational certainty that I'd break my own bruised arms before I could break his hold. "Shhh, it's just a kiss."

His mouth met mine, and my empty stomach churned. Then he sucked my chapped, cracked lower lip into his mouth and his teeth sank into my flesh. I screamed against his lips, and he devoured me whole, blood and outrage as one.

But that wasn't all he took from me. As he sucked at my

mouth, holding me in place in spite of worthless, wordless protest, my pain and fear began to coil up from some unknown depth at my center, swirling through me and into him in a roiling storm of suffering. Fire. Blood. Broken bones. Frozen limbs. Torn flesh. Bruised skin. Skewered hope. Ruined mind. Shredded reality.

I lost the torment infusing each excruciating memory as he sucked them dry, like draining the flavor from a Popsicle of pain, and as he swallowed the madness in each moment, older memories surfaced. Better times. People I loved.

My name.

I am Kaylee. Cavanaugh. I am Kaylee Cavanaugh.

I *was* Kaylee Cavanaugh, anyway, until the bottom fell out of my world and I tumbled into hell.

He drank from my mouth, drawing things from deep inside me, and with each second my pain and fear faded, leaving only thoughts I'd forgotten I ever had. That, and a deep, scorching anger that burned in me unlike anything I'd ever felt.

I put myself here. I'd done this to myself. For one long moment, I couldn't move past that outrageous certainty. *Why* had I done this to myself? Why would I submit to such suffering?

When much of the pain and fear were gone, he got his first taste of the fury and self-loathing raging inside me, and he took it all, bit by bitter bit.

Then I remembered his name.

Ira. Evil, but useful.

Ira licked the cut he'd opened inside my lip, and…

"You want me to play nursemaid and courier?" His black, black eyes mock me. "That is a perverse sort of role-play indeed, my twisted little instigator."

I roll my eyes. "I want you to protect them and deliver a letter." My blood spells out his name on the cafeteria floor. It still pools in my palm, and I hope it will not dry before we are done negotiating. “This *letter.” I pull the folded envelope from my pocket, and blood streaks the front of it.*

His brows rise in obvious curiosity. “What could you possibly offer, little flame, that is worth the performance of such insulting tasks?” He’s interested. I can feel it. I can see *it.*

“Madness. The profit of pain and anger.” I close my eyes, trying not to imagine it. “I guarantee that if you protect them while I’m gone and deliver this letter at the appropriate time, when you come for me, you will find the most dense concentration of agony and rage you’ve ever experienced. I’ll be a human bonbon with a bitter raging center. I’ll be insane *with suffering. Completely out of my mind. And it’s all yours. Every single flame of fury surging through my veins. Every drop of pain I’ve been drowning in. Every mad thought jumping around in my head. They are all yours, if you do this for me.”*

He sucked on my lip, encouraging the flow of my blood, and rage washed through me into him. I didn’t try to fight it. I let it go, because this was what I’d agreed to and because with every bit of anger he took, he gave back one of my memories.

Answers.

The long-forgotten promises that put me there…

“Why would Avari let you go?” Ira’s black, black eyes flash in the pale moonlight shining into the cafeteria.

“He won’t have any choice once he realizes he doesn’t really own my soul. He can’t own it if it wasn’t mine to surrender in the first place, so if the rightful owner comes to claim it, he has to turn it over. Right?”

Ira’s brows rise. “If it wasn’t yours, then you couldn’t rightfully give it to him, and he couldn’t rightfully accept it. So, yes, if the rightful owner demands its return, Avari would have to relinquish your soul.”

"But because he did *take possession of it, his promise to me has to stand, right?"*

"The wording of such a promise is critical, but yes." Ira nods slowly, and his dark, dark lips curl up in a smile. "You are a clever one, little fury. But tell me, why would your soul not be yours to surrender?"

"Because I already gave it to someone else…."

My own blood filled my mouth as fast as it flowed into his, and dimly I was aware that I couldn't have much more to lose. But that probably didn't matter. I was dead, right?

"So then, there's only the matter of duration. How long will you suffer for them? For me?" Ira's blood-smile broadens in anticipation of my answer.

As little as possible, of course. "A week." I say it as firmly as I can, because surely a week in hell is enough for anyone to endure, but he laughs in my face, and the sound is like glass shattering as it's hurled against stone.

"A decade. I won't work without the promise of a hefty profit. By which, of course, I mean your pain and anger. The hellion's fury will be substantial, but you *must suffer to make this creative venture worth my time, little fury."*

But we're arguing about my *time.* My *suffering. And I can't do a decade. There wouldn't be enough of me left to rescue.*

"A year. You'll be paid more than you can possibly *imagine, and you'll continue to collect from Avari for years," I point out. "Decades, maybe." If a hellion's memory is infinite, who knows how long he can hold a grudge?*

"Little flame, I have quite a capable imagination, as does your hellion of avarice. But if I am to protect your loved ones on your behalf, you must suffer on mine. For years. That is how this works."

My heart races in panic. This will fall apart if I can't secure Ira's help. My father will die. He will suffer for eternity because I couldn't save him. My friends will be hunted, one by one.

I have no choice. "Fine. Three years. As measured in the human world." I can already feel the promised years slipping away from me, and I am terrified *of what my time in hell will bring.*

"Five. Not a day less."

"Four, and you can feed from them, too." A last-minute stroke of brilliance on my part. "While you protect my friends and family, you can have their anger. Their grief for me. Take it. Feed from it in my absence." A reciprocal relationship that would surely benefit everyone.

Ira thinks for several minutes, staring at me until my skin begins to crawl in discomfort. Have I messed this up? Have I forgotten something?

Then, finally, he nods. "Shall we seal it with a kiss?"

"If I must. But there's one more thing. I need you to make me forget about this. Take the memory of our bargain, so Avari can't find it."

"That will be my pleasure, my little roaring flame…"

When he pulled away, the world stopped spinning so fast that I almost fell over. I blinked. I licked the inside of my lip and tasted my own blood. Then I looked down at the dingy scrap of linen—maybe white, once—wrapped loosely around me like a towel.

I was dirty and bruised, but not scarred and no thinner than when I'd arrived. Avari must have just put me back together, intending to rip me apart all over again.

I glanced at the filthy room around me, and I almost asked how long I'd been there. Was it four years to the day? The memories felt numerous enough to fill a century, though they were eerily hollow now, without the pain and anger he'd drained from them.

It worked. I hardly dared to believe it. What if this was

part of the torture—what if Avari was letting me believe I was free, only to pull me back into hell, where I would suffer anew? He'd certainly done it before.

My toes curled in the dirt on the floor. "Is it over?" I looked up at Ira and found him smiling the smile of the thoroughly intoxicated. He was drunk on my pain and fury. On the insanity he'd slurped from my soul, leaving me only the bits I could handle.

So far, so good.

"Ira, is it over?" Candlelight flickered over the scrap of my clothing, and he finally looked down at me.

"Almost, little flame. Your knight has arrived."

"You're not my knight." *Please say you're not my knight….*

"No, that was a temporary role, and one that has never fit me well. Knights appear to work for honor, a concept I'm not sure I even fully understand. I work for profit."

Of course he did. He was a hellion, and hellions were evil. He hadn't helped me—he'd performed services in exchange for payment. *Years* worth of payment. Could it really have been only four? It felt like eternity….

"Your knight is fairer than I, and less powerful, but much more determined on his mission. Did I mention that he's here?"

He's here. Tod had come to say the words I'd left for him. Words he'd had no way of understanding until Ira delivered my second letter to him. Until he'd read—in my handwriting—that Levi had lied, and that I wasn't gone.

I stood up straight and buried the memories, ignoring the desperate impatience nipping at the edges of my miserable existence. "Let's go."

The hellion held his hand out, and I took it. A second later, we stood in another room, so fast I had no time to process the change. This room was larger, and populated with dozens of terrifying species I didn't quite recognize, but didn't find unfamiliar, either. Had I seen them during my torture?

My bare feet were silent on the dusty stone floor. Linen whispered against my skin as I moved. Avari's voice was like needles shoved through my ears and into my brain.

"Just because I cannot hurt you does not mean that no one in the Nether will. I cannot decide if you are flaunting courage or idiocy today, reaper."

Reaper!

My heart jolted back to life when I saw him, standing alone among monsters, feet spread, fists clenched. His curls were golden like pure sunlight, which had surely never shone in the Netherworld. He looked the same. Like time had stood still around him while it had stretched monstrously around me.

"Neither. I'm flaunting words." Tod's voice touched places inside me that had not felt kindness in…longer than I could even comprehend. I had to bite my tongue to keep from calling out to him through the crowd. My hands itched to touch him. My mouth *longed* for a taste of him. But I couldn't let Avari see me until the formalities were over. Until he knew he was bound by his own word to let me go. "Specifically, the ones she said to you."

"Which words were those?" Avari demanded, and I could tell that he wasn't yet angry, because he didn't know what was coming. "She's screamed and moaned a great many things to me over the years, though few of them have been coherent of late."

Tod stiffened, *livid* with indignation on my behalf, and I wanted to cry out and tell him I was okay. Because he didn't know. He didn't know what had happened to me, or what state I was in, or whether I would ever again be the girl who'd kissed him in the school hallway, scandalizing everyone around us with what now seemed like such an innocent expression of attraction.

Ira stood in the background with me, practically buzzing with anticipation of the rage destined to glut him.

"My soul is yours," Tod said, and the words burned through me. I remembered saying them, just like that. Just like I'd practiced. Just like I'd written…

"Yes? And?" Avari was losing patience, and surely soon he'd realize I was no longer suffering. That my pain was no longer feeding him.

"Her soul wasn't her own to give, which means she had no right to surrender it to you or to anyone else. You had no right to accept it." He stood straighter, confident and bold in spite of the monsters restlessly milling around him. *"You can't keep her."*

"Nonsense!" Avari roared, and Ira's hand tightened around mine. He practically *swelled,* lapping up the anger Avari had started to exude like sweat from hellion pores. "Who else would own her soul?"

"I would." Tod's voice was strong. Clear. "Her soul is mine, and I have proof, written in her own hand." He pulled a folded envelope from his back pocket, and even from a distance I recognized his name, in my handwriting. It was my first letter to him—the one I'd left for him the night Levi had told his lie. Tod opened the envelope and pulled out a piece of paper that had obviously been folded and unfolded so many times it was nearly falling apart. Then he read from it.

"'I am yours, body, mind, heart, and soul. And I always will be.'" Tod looked up, and Avari's eyes narrowed until they were slits leaking darkness into the Netherworld night. "See? She is mine, body, mind, heart, and *soul.* And if she's *mine,* she can't be *yours. Let. Her. Go.*"

The demand was a formality. Avari had no choice but to

stand by his word. To break it would mean rendering his promise to me a lie, and if I was sure of anything about hellions it was this: they cannot lie.

I knew I was free even before he opened his mouth, but the bellow of rage that he unleashed upon the Netherworld at large was more than confirmation. For a moment, I couldn't move. Couldn't think. Couldn't do anything but cover my ears, trying to protect my brain from the sonic assault.

Ira spread his arms, like a child bathing in sunlight, and began to laugh. The sound of his joy swallowed Avari's rage like a sponge soaking up water.

Avari's mouth closed, and his eyes narrowed. Even without pupils, I could tell when his gaze found us. "You!" he thundered, and Ira laughed some more.

"Kaylee!" Tod shouted. He tried to run to me, but monsters poured into the path between us.

"It has been my *pleasure* to conspire with the young *bean sidhe* to provoke your wrath, an emotion certain to feed me for centuries to come, as you watch her live on, beyond your grasp." Joy dripped from Ira's voice. "Now, return her soul, and let the fun begin!"

Avari roared again, and again I covered my ears. His fists were clenched, and his featureless eyes glowed like black lights, gleaming in fury. He lifted one arm, and for a moment I was afraid his gesture was calling me closer for yet another demon kiss. Instead, he opened his hand and twisted it, curling his fingers in my direction, and something deep within me *unfurled*. It felt like a snake uncoiling in my stomach, a great, frozen serpent, chilling me from the inside out.

Avari jerked his hand back, and that serpentine coldness—his own breath—was ripped up through my core and out my mouth with a metaphysical brutality that made me gasp. For a single second, my insides were a gaping vacuum, sucking at the world—at eternity—in search of something substantial. Something to support my existence and anchor it to the physical reality of my resurrected body.

Then he held up his other hand, but I couldn't clearly see what it held. I could no longer clearly see anything. Sight and sound were already fading as I faded, for the lack of a soul. I collapsed to my knees, but didn't feel the impact.

"Do it!" Tod shouted, and distantly I registered the panic in his voice.

A second later, a blast of something light and warm hit me. It surrounded me like a blanket molded to the shape of my body, then sank into me. Through me.

I didn't realize how cold I'd been on the inside until the warmth of my own returned soul brought me back to myself for the first time in four interminable years. I gasped, sucking in one great breath, and the Netherworld came into focus around me. Creatures eyeing me like Sabine would eye a hamburger. Avari, *simmering* with rage eager to bubble up and over him.

And Tod…

Tod pushed his way through the inhuman crowd toward me, trying to see if it was over. If my soul was indeed restored. If I was *back*.

And I *was* back.

"Little fury, our business is complete," Ira said from my left. "I've already guaranteed your safe passage to the human world, as part of our agreement, and I suggest you leave now, before you find yourself in trouble you cannot bargain your way out of."

He didn't have to tell me twice.

I raced across the room, and what remained of the crowd split for me. Tod's eyes widened and filled with tears. His arms opened. My letter fluttered to the ground. I threw myself at him—arms around his neck, legs around his waist—and the moment we touched, fog rolled up from the floor and over us.

The Netherworld faded, and Avari's bellow of fury faded with it.

The school basement came into focus around us, and I exhaled like I hadn't had a breath to release in years. And in truth, I hadn't.

Tod's arms tightened around me as he lowered us to the floor, my limbs still wrapped around him. Tears poured down my face as I clutched him, feeling the muscles shift beneath his shirt as I ran my hands over his back. He felt so solid. So real. His features didn't shift into monstrous shapes with each change of temperament. His teeth didn't bite. His touch didn't hurt.

I slid my fingers into his hair, and his curls were the softest thing I'd ever felt. He smelled so good—so sweet and clean—and he felt so good, so I kissed my way down his jaw until I found his mouth, then I kissed him. And kissed him. And kissed him some more. And finally I had to make myself stop before I devoured him whole, because I was starving, and he was the first sustenance I'd had in *years,* and he was exactly the *right* sustenance, but I would never feed from him like Avari fed from me, and just that thought sent horror rolling through me and…

I opened my eyes. Tod was shaking. His whole body was trembling beneath mine, and when I pulled away to see his face, I realized he was crying. At first I thought I'd hurt him. Then I realized how ridiculous that was. I couldn't hurt anyone. I was the least threatening thing in the world. In *either* world. I had no claws, or fangs, or tail, or horns, or any abilities strong enough to command respect or fear….

"Are you real?" He pulled me close again and whispered

the halting words into my ear. "Did that really just happen? You're alive?"

My arms slid around him again. "No more now than I was before, but yes." My voice was hoarse and I couldn't stop grinning. I couldn't remember ever seeing a room as glorious as my grungy high school basement, based solely on the fact that it was in the human world. Beyond the reach of hellions.

"You were dead. Gone. For *four years.* We mourned you. We *grieved,*" he said, and I could see the truth of that in his eyes. In the solemn slant of his mouth. "Everyone else moved on."

"They moved on." I blinked, denying fresh tears an exit. That was good. I *wanted* them to move on. That was why they couldn't know. "Did you...move on?"

Tod shook his head. "I tried. I tried so hard. But no matter where I went and what I did, I could still feel you. It was... It felt like I could walk into the next room, and you'd be there smiling. Waiting for me. Like I could turn a corner, and you'd be standing there. I missed you so much. I thought I was losing my mind."

"I'm so sorry."

"It's okay." He put one hand on either side of my face and kissed me. "It makes sense now. I had part of your soul. You gave it to me. That's why I couldn't let you go."

That's why he'd suffered for four years, like my father had been suffering for thirteen, since my mother died.

Nope. Seventeen. The past four years in the Nether had felt like an eternity, yet I could hardly comprehend that same passage of time in the human world. I felt like everything in my native plane should have stood still. Like the world should have stopped revolving in my absence, only to resume when I returned. But that hadn't happened. Tod had lived through those four years without me, suffering a subconscious promise to wait for me. Carrying a bit of my soul with his own.

My eyes closed as I realized the depth of the pain I'd put him through.

But I'd had no choice. If I hadn't done what I'd done, he'd *still* be suffering. We all would. And it would never have ended.

"Are you okay?" he asked, and I opened my eyes to find him staring at me. I started to nod, but he continued before I could. "Of course you're not okay. You've been there for four years. Four years of what?" His features twisted with some form of suffering I couldn't quite wrap my mind around. He wasn't hurt. *I* wasn't hurt. Yet he was clearly in pain.

Empathy. That word came out of nowhere. From deep within the well of things I hadn't needed in the Nether. Things I hadn't seen or used.

But that wasn't it, exactly.

Rage. That one I'd used. That one I'd seen. But that wasn't quite it, either.

Tod was hurting for me. He was angry for me. He felt… powerless. Helpless. Useless. Those I saw in his eyes, in the moment before I became overwhelmed by the fact that I was *staring into his eyes.* In my more rational moments, over the past four years, I'd been convinced I'd never see him again.

"Four years of what, Kaylee?" he whispered, and his voice cracked on my name.

I shook my head slowly. "Doesn't matter. It's over now."

"It matters. I need to know what you…what I let…"

"No." I took his chin in my hand and made him look at me, terrified by what I saw in his eyes now. Guilt. "You didn't do this. You couldn't have stopped it. I went through a lot of trouble to make sure you didn't know about it, because I knew that if you thought I was still here—still *anywhere*—

you would move heaven and the Netherworld to get to me. And I couldn't let that happen."

"What happened to you, Kaylee?"

"Listen to me." I spoke through clenched teeth, desperate to stop the tears standing at the ready. "Forget about that. I plan to."

"Kaylee..."

"No." I shook my head. "I don't have to think about that. Not ever again. And neither do you. Everything's okay now, Tod. Everything is *amazing* now. Perfect." I smiled. I couldn't stop smiling. "We're together." I kissed him again, and when his tears fell, mine followed, but these tears didn't hurt. "And this time, forever is real."

"I love you so much."

"I love you, too. More than anything." I stood and pulled him up with me, swiping tears from my cheek with my free hand. "Now let's go bring me back to life. Again."

24

Bringing me back to life turned out to be a two-step process. The first part involved a very private reunion with the reaper who deserved more gratitude than I even knew how to express for loving me. For waiting for me. For safeguarding my soul from a distance. And for braving the Netherworld one last time to finally bring me home.

Tod still had his room at reaper headquarters. He still had the same bed. The same chair. The same minifridge used as a nightstand. His dirty clothes still littered the floor. His tub was still too short for a proper bath, and he still only owned two towels and five washcloths.

He still had my spare toothbrush.

He still touched me like I was the most precious thing in existence.

I still loved every single second of it.

Based on my first two hours back in the human world, it was tempting to assume very little had changed. I knew that wasn't true, but for those two hours, I let myself pretend.

When we'd finally done enough touching and holding and kissing to be sure I wasn't going to simply melt from reality, like a mirage, we sat cross-legged on his bed, facing each other, eating ice cream with plastic spoons from paper bowls.

"How did you do it?" Tod dumped more caramel syrup on the mound of home-style vanilla in my bowl, then topped it with a scoopful of candied walnuts. "I mean, I know that since your soul wasn't yours in the first place—very clever, by the way—the deal you struck with him was nullified. But doesn't that nullify his promise to leave us all alone forever?"

I took a bite of my victory sundae—which had been preceded by my Welcome Back from the Netherworld pizza—and let the sugar melt in my mouth. If I'd ever tasted anything so sweet before, I couldn't remember it.

But the sugar soured on my tongue with the memory his question triggered.

It's a word game, little fury. You are building a cage made of promises, and Avari must believe that the bars he sees between you are locking you in. Then, later, he will turn and realize he's *the one in the cage, and that you stand on the outside, watching him, a free woman.*

"Ira taught me how to negotiate." But not until *after* he and I had struck our own deal. "The key was phrasing my demands as two separate agreements. The first bargain said that he would let my dad go in exchange for my immortal soul. Since my soul was never mine to give him, that deal is now null and void, and if he still had my dad, Avari wouldn't have to give him up. But he doesn't have my dad. And since the other bargain we struck is still in effect, he never *will* have my dad."

Tod leaned over to set the syrup bottle on top of the mini-fridge, and the mattress creaked beneath his weight. "What was the second part?"

Water dripped from my shower-wet hair and soaked into the T-shirt he'd lent me. I swallowed another bite and licked a smear of caramel from my lower lip. "That one was intentionally simple. Deceptively so. It just said that once he took possession of my soul, he could have no further contact with you guys. Ever again. He *did* take possession of my soul, and since there were no contingencies named in case he ever *lost* possession of it, that deal still stands."

Tod stared at me, a ghost of a smile haunting the corners of his mouth. "You may be the smartest woman I've ever met."

I laughed and plucked a walnut from a peak of ice cream. "The devil is in the details."

"Have I ever told you how sexy your brain is?"

"Finally! A man who wants me for my brain."

"I want you for all of you. Each individual part and the sum of them all. I want you for everything you are and everything you will ever be. I will never have enough of you, because there's no such thing." He stared right into my eyes, and I couldn't have looked away if I'd wanted to. I was trapped, and never in my life had I been so happy to be caught. "I will never let you go again."

"What did you tell them?" I scooped ice into the last of the plastic cups and nearly tripped over Styx for the fourth time in the past quarter hour. She'd been following me everywhere since the moment we'd blinked into my house, and I loved her for it.

I also loved her for the fact that, like Tod, she hadn't changed at all in the four years I'd been gone. That couldn't be said for anyone else, based on the pictures I'd found in Emma's room—my former room. The twin beds had been replaced with a full, and my things were packed into boxes stacked at the back of her closet.

They hadn't gotten rid of me. They'd just packed me up. Seeing those boxes reminded me of the day I'd helped Emma pack up her former life and move into her new one. We'd changed places, sort of. That felt weird.

"I told them I had an announcement," Tod said. "They probably expect me to announce my retirement." Which, for a reaper, meant requesting or accepting his final death. "It's kind of...been coming."

I frowned and dropped the ice scoop into the sink, and he shrugged. "It was hard without you, Kaylee. I couldn't let you go, but I didn't know how to be here without you. If I'd never met you, I probably would have been fine." He shrugged, and that same stubborn curl fell over his forehead. "I mean, creatures who only exist in the dark don't know they're missing the sun, right? But once you've *seen* the sun. Once you've seen it light up the world...once you've felt its heat all around you...inside you..." He clutched his own chest, and my heart cracked open. "It's hard to live in the dark after the sun dies."

"I'm so sorry." I set the last cup on the counter and threw my arms around him again. "I'm so glad you didn't do something...permanent."

"I almost did. I started slipping away again. If not for my mom and Emma, I might have lost most of my humanity by now."

"Em? You and Emma?" I pulled back to look at him, my chest aching, and I had to remind myself that four years was a long time, and they were only human—mostly. And that I'd *left* them, and they'd thought I was *dead,* and they had had every right to move on. To at least *try*...

Tod's eyes widened, then he laughed and pulled me closer. "Not like that. Emma has a boyfriend. A necromancer friend of Luca's. They've been together almost three years now."

"The guy in the picture on her dresser?" They looked happy in the photo. They looked...normal. Emma deserved some normal.

"Yeah. He's a good guy, and he loves her, and he knows how to handle the occasional syphon meltdown. But even if none of that were true…" Tod put a hand on each of my arms and looked right into my eyes. "You have my heart and soul, Kaylee Cavanaugh, and that never changed, even when I thought you were gone. Em and I are just friends. There was never anyone else. Which means that all of this—" he stepped back and spread his arms with a grin I'd missed like I would miss my own heartbeat if I never felt it again "—went to waste for four very long years."

"Well, that's all over now. An ego like that deserves to be stroked." I ran my hands over his chest and stood on my toes to whisper in his ear, "Or at least humored."

"Humored, huh?" He laughed. "I'll take what I can get. For now…"

I pulled his head down for a kiss and didn't let him go until an engine rumbled to a stop out front, and my heart stopped with it. "They're here." One of them, at least. I'd only heard one car.

I raced to the front window and peeked through the gap in the drapes to see an unfamiliar vehicle in the driveway. The driver's door opened, and I hardly recognized the man who stepped out. He had Nash's artfully mussed hair, but I couldn't see his eyes behind a pair of dark sunglasses. And he was…bigger.

My heart ached. Each beat seemed to bruise me from the inside out.

Nash had grown up, like Tod and I never would. Mental math told me he was twenty-two now, and though I could see it, I couldn't truly believe it.

The passenger's-side door opened and a headful of long, straight, dark hair appeared over the roof of the car. A second later, Sabine rounded the front bumper and slid her hand into Nash's, and I'm sure my eyes nearly bugged out of my head.

She'd grown up, too, and she was *gorgeous,* in a mature, collected way the teenage *mara* I'd come to thoroughly tolerate had never been. And she looked…happy. Even with all the eyeliner she still wore and a familiar pair of guys' khakis hanging low on the swell of her hips.

"This is *bizarre,*" I whispered, and Tod's hand settled at my lower back.

"I guess it must be, seeing it all of a sudden like that." He shrugged. "They grew up."

"And they're…okay? They're good?"

"Yeah. Better than I would have expected." His arm slid around my side and pulled me close again, just as the rear door of the car opened, and my breath caught in my throat.

Emma.

Lydia's body had grown up, too, and Em now wore it like it was her own. She'd cut her thin hair, and it looked healthier than I'd ever seen it, bouncing on her shoulders in light brown waves. Her arms were tanned, and she'd finally figured out how to dress a body with no curves to speak of—a dilemma I remembered well.

I was still watching her walk up the sidewalk when Nash knocked on the door, then opened it and came in without waiting for the key Em had dug from her purse. "Hey, Peter Pan? You in here?"

Sabine followed him inside, and I could tell by the way their gazes passed over us, then settled on the cups of ice lined up on the kitchen counter that they couldn't see either of us yet. I hadn't gone spectral on purpose. Evidently—subconsciously, at least—I wasn't ready to be seen.

"Kay?" Tod said, and they didn't hear that, either. "You ready?"

I nodded, and I only realized that was the truth at the very last second.

Tod cleared his throat. Nash and Sabine turned our way just as Em stepped into the house.

For a moment, shocked silence reigned.

Nash took off his sunglasses, and his hazel eyes were as wide and still as I'd ever seen them. Emma dropped her purse, and Styx skittered away from the falling debris. Sabine's mouth widened in a stunning smile. She was the first to believe her eyes, and, somehow, that didn't surprise me.

"Kay?" She crossed the room in an instant and threw strong arms around me, while I tried to ignore the fact that she'd grown at least two inches taller since I'd last seen her. She towered over me now, and was only a couple of inches shorter than Nash. "Are you real?"

Tod laughed. "I've been asking her that for the past three hours. She's real. Solid and thoroughly functional."

"Well then." Sabine let go of me and grinned. "I guess we know how they spent the past three hours, instead of alerting anyone else to the miraculous resurrection." She shrugged. "Not that I blame you. If it were me and Nash, we'd still be sequestered."

Obviously *some* things hadn't changed....

"I—I don't..." Em stuttered, and as soon as Sabine stepped back, Emma was there. She'd grown, too, but that put her at exactly my height, and I hugged her so tight I could almost hear her ribs groan. "How...?"

"She didn't die. Levi lied." Tod still sounded less than pleased by that, and I couldn't blame him.

"I asked him to," I clarified, without letting go of Emma. I couldn't let her go. I wasn't ready. And based on the strength of her hug, neither was Em. "I knew that if you guys knew what I was planning, you'd come after me."

"Come after you *where?*" Sabine frowned, and I could tell by the suspicion dripping from that one question that she'd figured at least part of it out.

"The Netherworld." Tod told them the part I couldn't make myself say out loud. "She turned herself in. Which sounds really *asinine* until you hear about the out clause she built into her deal with Avari. That part's really brilliant."

"You turned yourself in? To *Avari?*" Emma shuddered even as she said his name, and I could see all the questions she obviously wanted to ask hiding just below her surprise and confusion. "You were there the whole time? So you've been…? He's been…?" Horror washed over her face in slow motion as comprehension surfaced. As she realized where and how I'd spent the past four years. And *why* I'd spent them.

"*Damn,* Kay," Sabine whispered.

"Are you sure you're okay?" Tears formed in Emma's eyes. "*How* can you be okay?"

"I made a deal with Ira. I gave him everything I couldn't handle…." Mostly massive amounts of pain and rage. "And that left me with my…um…sanity." I shrugged like it was no big deal, but no one bought that.

"Ira. Damn." Sabine tossed long, dark hair over her shoulder. "I haven't heard that name in years. And you actually talked a hellion of wrath into sucking the crazy right out of you?"

"It was mutually beneficial. And Ira'll be munching on Avari's fury for centuries. That's really why he agreed to the whole thing." I blinked and shook my head, mentally changing the subject. "Enough about the Netherworld. We're done with that now." I'd put myself through hell for four years to make damn sure of that. "I want to talk about you guys! You're all…grown!"

Emma laughed. "Yeah. I guess so. You missed prom. Then… everything else."

"You're in college?" Tod had told me that, but I wanted to hear it from her.

"Yeah. I'm a junior at A&M. But they're about to graduate. Both of them!" She gestured to Sabine and Nash, and when my gaze fell on Nash again, it stuck there. He hadn't moved. He hadn't said a word. He was still staring at me in shock, and his sunglasses lay on his left foot, where he'd dropped them.

"Nash?"

He blinked, and his eyes swirled with confused, surprised twists of brown and green. I took a step toward him, and he studied me. Like he didn't dare believe the signals his eyes were sending him.

So I closed the distance between us on my own, then went up on my toes to hug him.

He felt…different. Bigger. More solid.

Healthy.

Slowly, his arms closed around me. His hug tightened steadily until I couldn't have breathed if I'd needed to. He shook in my arms, and his tears soaked into the shoulder of my shirt.

"It's okay," I said with what little breath remained in my lungs. "It's okay, Nash."

When he finally let me go and wiped tears from his face, I wanted to hug him all over again.

"You know, there are easier ways to make an ex get over you, Kay. You didn't have to fake your own death. Again."

I laughed through my own tears, and I hugged him again. Then I escaped into the kitchen to pull myself together while I poured soda into the cups, hoping they wouldn't see how surreal this was for me. Four hours earlier, I hadn't known my own name. I'd forgotten this world existed. I'd been lost in a hell from which there should have been no mistake.

And now…

I turned and found them all watching me, so I took a long drink from my cup to buy time. To think of what to say.

Tod's hand slid into mine, and he smiled. Without saying a word, he told me that everything was okay. That everything would come back to me, in time. That the world may have moved on without me, but he hadn't.

And that's when I realized what I wanted to talk about. The world had moved on without me, but ignoring that fact wouldn't help me adjust to it. I had to hit it head-on.

"You all look so different!" I couldn't get over it. "So, college and life? How are things?"

"Things are good," Emma said. "I have a boyfriend."

"The necromancer? I heard!"

Her smile was like sunlight emerging from the clouds as she grabbed a cup for herself from the drinks lined up on the counter. "His name's Chad. He knows who I really am and how I…got here." In Lydia's body, obviously. "He knows the truth, and it didn't scare him away."

"It's kinda hard to scare a necromancer." Tod set cups in front of Nash and Sabine when they settled onto bar stools across the counter from us. "They're like reapers, but with less purpose."

"He has purpose!" Em gave Tod a good-natured shoved. "He's an ed major. He wants to teach."

"Not at Eastlake, I hope." I smiled, trying not to feel lost in a conversation about someone I'd never met. "I hear that place is dangerous."

"Not since you…died." Nash frowned at the counter for a moment. "When you left, all that other stuff…it just…stopped."

"Not because you were the cause of it," Tod clarified, squeezing my hand. "You weren't. The hellions left Eastlake because you paid to make them go away." His grin returned. "You didn't just clean up the school, you made a down payment on a miracle—a *mara* with an education!" He made a grand gesture toward Sabine, and she laughed.

"Yeah." The *mara* tossed dark hair over her shoulder. "It turns out that without hellions stalking you constantly, school's not that big of an obstacle. Still boring as hell, though."

"She has a three-point-four GPA." Nash wrapped one arm around her, and I could see the pride in his eyes. "And she'd have a four-point-oh if I could talk her into actually attending most of her classes."

Sabine shrugged. "Waste of time when you already know the material. We're nearly done now, though. Two more finals, then we graduate in two weeks."

My chest ached again, and before I could process how thoroughly they'd all moved on without me, and why that bothered me, despite how happy I was for them all, the front door creaked open again and I turned to find Sophie standing in the doorway, frozen in place. Staring at me like she'd seen a ghost.

Luca nudged her inside, then closed the door at their backs. "Told ya so," he leaned closer to say into her ear. I laughed. Of course he'd known. He'd probably felt me the moment I crossed back into the human world.

"Creepy-ass necromancers," I said with a grin, and he stepped around my cousin to give me a hug.

"*So* glad you're back," he said. "Work sucks without our best reclamationist."

"You're still working for Madeline?"

He nodded, and his grin widened. "As are you. Aunt Madeline says she wants you back on the job by the end of the week. Also, she says, 'Welcome back.'"

Warmth flooded me, and I was surprised to realize how good that made me feel. There was still a place for me, even if that place wasn't at college with Nash, Sabine, and Emma.

Besides, A&M wasn't that far away. Especially with my two-second commute.

"Kaylee?" Sophie's voice sounded strange. Fragile. "I guess I shouldn't be surprised, considering all the weird shit I've seen in the past four years. But I have to admit...I didn't believe Luca when he said you were back."

She hugged me, and I was a little relieved to realize she hadn't changed as much as the others. Of course, she was the youngest, though still older than me, now. "And hey, don't worry about your hair. We can fix that. Three hours at my salon, and no one will ever know your poor head spent four years in that dry Netherworld air."

I laughed out loud.

The next hour was surreal. They asked a dozen questions I didn't want to answer about my time in the Netherworld, and I missed Alec more than ever. He would have understood my silence.

When it became obvious that I'd rather listen than talk, everyone seemed eager to oblige. I heard about classes, and parties, and schoolwork, and new cars, and new jobs, and new friends. I laughed at stories I didn't completely understand and sympathized with disappointments I couldn't really imagine. It seemed impossible that so much could have changed in the human world, when I could still remember my last day there like it was yesterday.

But I'd missed a lot of yesterdays.

We were digging into huge slices of birthday cake—Tod

insisted, since I'd missed four birthdays—when another car pulled into the driveway.

My fork froze inches from my mouth. I dropped it onto my plate and was halfway to the door when it opened on its own. Harmony took one look at me, and her jaw dropped open so fast I was afraid it was going to fall off her face.

"Oh, my..."

I folded her into a long-overdue hug and only then noticed the firm bump between us. The one growing in her belly. I stepped back and glanced at her round stomach in surprise. "Are you...?" The rest of the words got stuck in my throat, and she nodded, beaming at me.

"It's a girl."

"We were going to call her Kaylee," my uncle said, and I looked up to find him in the doorway, watching me through damp, shiny eyes.

Uncle Brendon gave me my millionth hug in the past hour, and only once I'd let him go did I notice that the gold band on his finger matched the one on Harmony's. "Why didn't anyone *tell* me?" I demanded, turning on the rest of my friends and family with a grin that probably spoiled my angry act.

Sophie laughed. "Dad would have killed me if he missed the look on your face. So...I'm going to be a big sister. Weird, huh?"

"Beyond weird." I turned back to Harmony. "Wow! So, when are you due?"

"Three months. We're excited! And your old room at Brendon's will be the nursery."

"Speaking of babies..." Em stepped forward with her phone and showed me a picture of a laughing toddler with her sister's eyes and my old math teacher's wavy brown hair.

I took the phone from her and stared at the picture. "Oh, Em, he's adorable!" Her nephew was so cute, in fact, that though I would have sworn it was impossible, I wasn't creeped out by his resemblance to the man who'd murdered me.

"Yeah. And he never would have survived without you. Without the soul you gave him."

I'd left instructions in my goodbye letter, begging Harmony to help them install the soul in the baby when he was born. "What's his name?"

"I suggested Damien," Tod said while Em showed me how to scroll through the latest pictures on her phone—a leap in technology I'd missed during my sabbatical in hell. "But no one listened."

"Caleb. He's very sweet but quite a handful."

"Have you searched his head for a birthmark in the form of three sixes?"

Emma shoved Tod again, and I got the impression that was a joke he'd told in infinite variations. I didn't get it.

"Most little boys are…challenging," Harmony said. "Including the two of you." She smiled at both her sons.

"Okay, I'm here. What's the big…?"

I froze at the sound of my father's voice, and when it faded in surprise, I turned to find him staring at me.

"Kaylee?" His voice cracked, and disbelief dripped from the fracture. I smiled at him while my heart thundered in my chest. "Is that you? Are you real?"

Tod laughed again. "We've been asking her that all day."

My dad practically floated across the room toward me, and only once his arms were wrapped around me did I realize he was wearing a flannel plaid shirt I'd been trying to get him to throw away for months before he'd disappeared into the Netherworld.

"I'm real." I inhaled his scent, and fresh tears formed in my eyes. "I am so sorry for everything I put you through." I clung to him, crying onto his shirt, burying my face in his shoulder.

My dad held me at arm's length, staring at me through his own tears. "Kaylee, what on earth could you possibly have to be sorry for?"

"I lied to you," I said, between sobbing hiccups. "And I skipped school, and communed with evil forces, and drugged my boyfriend, and went to the Netherworld without permission, and I'm about four years late for my curfew. I totally understand if you want to ground me. With four years' worth of interest."

My father laughed so hard his whole body shook, and tears dripped from his chin. "Is that what it'll take to keep you here?"

I shook my head. When he pulled me into another overdue hug, I laid my head down on his shoulder. "You couldn't get rid of me this time if you tried."

For at least a solid minute, we cried in each other's arms, unleashing four years' worth of grief and pain and guilt.

When he finally let me go, I turned in a slow circle, looking around at everyone I loved. Everyone I'd abandoned in an attempt to protect them. The room blurred beneath my tears. "I can't believe I'm here. I can't believe you're *all* here."

"Um..." Sophie crossed her arms over a designer blouse and arched both manicured brows at me. "Out of all the weird species, out-of-body experiences, resurrections, and octogenarian pregnancies represented by the occupants of this room right now, your presence is the thing most difficult to believe."

"Sophie..." Uncle Brendon said, but my cousin shook her head.

"I have something to say, and I'm going to be heard." She turned to me again, and I braced myself for a well-meaning but offensive critique of my hair, or my face, or the tee I'd borrowed from Tod, which hung nearly to the cuff of my shorts.

But instead, she smiled and glanced around the room. "I think I speak for everyone here when I say…welcome home, Kaylee."

"Are you sure about this?" I called through the closed bathroom door, lifting acres of gold tulle. When I turned in front of the small mirror, light caught the sequins on my bodice and reflected a thousand points of light on the walls of Tod's tiny bathroom.

"I'm sure. Come on out."

"I feel stupid," I moaned, pulling the door open, but my complaint died on my tongue with one look at him. "But *you* look…" I stared at him for a second. Then I had to touch him.

I ran my fingers over his gold tie, feeling the raised thread pattern, then down the right side of the matching vest, half-hidden by his black tux jacket. "You look *gorgeous.*"

"Okay." He nodded hesitantly. "That's a little feminine, as far as compliments go, but I can't argue with the general sentiment. I look great. And so do you. Turns out gold is a good color for us both." He made a spinning motion with one finger, and I turned slowly to show off my dress. To show off me *in* my dress. The prom dress I'd never worn.

I felt simultaneously beautiful and foolish, twirling in what little floor space there was between the unmade twin bed and the pile of unfolded laundry. "Tell me again why we're wearing four-year-old prom clothes, alone in your bedroom?"

"We're making up for lost time." His arms slid around my waist, and mine met behind his neck. "We're going to do everything you missed while you were gone. We'll make up for every single lost moment. All of them."

I looked into his eyes and got lost in them. "That could take a long time."

He started swaying, and I swayed with him, and it didn't matter that we didn't have music, or friends, or punch, or a gym decorated with lights and crepe paper. We had the only two things we needed for our private prom—each other. And pretty clothes.

"I don't care if it takes forever, Kaylee," he said, and warmth trailed down my spine to settle in a dozen pleasant places. "The universe *owes* us forever. And our eternity starts now."

★★★★★

ACKNOWLEDGMENTS

Thanks to Natashya Wilson and the rest of Harlequin Teen for launching the Teen line with Soul Screamers and for supporting Kaylee the whole way.

Thanks to my agent, Merrilee Heifetz, for making things happen.

Thanks to my critique partner, Rinda Elliott, for untold hours plotting, and whining, and planning over the phone. I hope we get to do all that in person very soon.

Thanks to No. 1, who sees the crazy, frazzled writer my official author photos hide well. Thanks for knowing when to offer coffee, when to make fajitas, and when to back quietly away from the office door. You've made this possible.

Thanks most of all to my editor, Mary-Theresa Hussey, for guidance, support, enthusiasm, and—most importantly—for smiley faces in the margins.

Netherworld Survival Guide

A collection of entries salvaged from Alec's personal journal during his twenty-six-year captivity in the Nether…

COMMON HAZARDOUS PLANTS

Note: Flora in the Netherworld is eighty-eight per cent carnivorous, ten per cent omnivorous, and less than two per cent docile. So keep in mind that if you see a plant, it probably wants to eat you.

Razor Wheat

- **Location** – Rural areas with little foot traffic.
- **Description** – Fields full of dense vegetation similar to wheat in structure, ranging in colour from deep red stalks to olive-hued seed clusters. Over six feet tall at mature height.
- **Dangers** – Razor wheat stalks shatters upon contact, raining tiny, sharp shards of plant that can slice through clothing and shred bare flesh.
- **Best Precaution** – Complete avoidance.
- **Second Best Precaution** – Long sleeves, full-length rubber waders and fishing boots, metal trash-can lid wielded like a shield.

Crimson Creeper

- **Location** – Anywhere it can get a foothold. Creeper can take root in as little as a quarter-inch wide crack in concrete and will grow to split the pavement open. It grows quickly and spreads voraciously, climbing walls, towers, trees and anything else that can be made to hold still.
- **Description** – A deep green vine growing up to four inches in diameter, bearing alternating leaves bleeding to crimson or blood red on variegated edges. Vines also sport needle-thin thorns between the leaves.
- **Dangers** – Though anchored by strong, deep roots, which have hallucinogenic properties when consumed, creeper vines slither autonomously and will actually wind around prey, injecting pre-digestive venom through its thorns. The vine will then coil around its meal and wait while the creature is slowly dissolved into liquid fertiliser from the inside out.
- **Best Precaution** – Complete avoidance.

- **Second Best Precaution** – Crimson creeper blooms can be made into a tea which acts as one of two known antidotes to the creeper venom; however, the vine blooms only once every three years. Blooms can be dried and preserved for up to two decades.

COMMON DANGEROUS CREATURES

Note: Whether it intends to consume your mind, body or soul, fauna in the Netherworld is ninety-nine per cent carnivorous, in one form or another. So keep in mind that if you see a creature, it probably wants to eat you.

Hellions
- **Location** – Everywhere. Anywhere. Never close your eyes.
- **Description** – Hellions can look like anything they want.They can be any size, shape or colour. Their only physical limitation is that they cannot exactly duplicate any other creature, living or dead.
- **Dangers** – Hellions feed from chaos in general, and individual emotions in particular. But what they really want is your soul—a never-ending buffet. Since souls cannot be stolen from the living, a hellion will try to bargain for or con you out of it. If you refuse—and even sometimes if you don't—the hellion will either kill you for your soul or torture you, *then* kill you for your soul.
- **Best Precaution** – Complete avoidance.
- **Second Best Precaution** – Pray.

Harpies
- **Location** – Found in large numbers near thin spots in the barrier between worlds, but individual harpies can live anywhere they choose, in either the human world or the Netherworld.
- **Description** – In the human world, harpies can pass for human at a glance, as long as they brush hair over their pointed ears and hide their compact, bat-like wings beneath clothing. In the Netherworld, harpies

appear less human, with mouths full of sharp, thin teeth, claws instead of hands and bird-like, clawed talons instead of feet.

- **Dangers** – Harpies are snatchers. Collectors. They will dive out of the air with no warning to grab whatever catches their eye, which can be anything from broken pots and pans to shiny rings—often still attached to human fingers. Also, they're carnivores and they don't distinguish between human and animal flesh.
- **Best Precaution** – Complete avoidance.
- **Second Best Precaution** – Stay inside or keep one eye trained on the sky and get ready to run.

ESCAPE AND EVASION

Note: The best way to escape a Netherworld threat is to leave the Netherworld, though that won't keep certain species, such as harpies, from crossing into the human world after you. If you are incapable of leaving under your own power, eventually something *will* eat you. But to help put that moment off as long as possible, here is a list of the most effective evasion tactics:

- Find shelter in rural areas. Netherworld creatures are attracted to heavily populated areas, where the overflow of human energy they feed from is most concentrated.
- Fibres from the *dissimulatus* plant can be woven together and worn to disguise your energy signature and keep predators from identifying you as human and thus edible.